dangerous
parking

D0067437

dangerous parking

stuart browne

BLOOMSBURY

First published in Great Britain 2000

Copyright © 2000 by Stuart Browne

The moral right of the author has been asserted

Bloomsbury Publishing Plc,
38 Soho Square, London, W1V 5DF

Extracts from *Krapp's Last Tape* by Samuel Beckett
reprinted by kind permission of the publishers, Faber and Faber.

A CIP catalogue record for this book
is available from the British Library

ISBN 0 7475 4839 0

10 9 8 7 6 5

Typeset by Hewer Text Ltd, Edinburgh
Printed in Great Britain by Clays Ltd, St Ives plc

Heartfelt thanks for their love, encouragement and inspiration –

Daisy and April, Andy Hine, Scott Frank, Bill Mesnik, William Pogson, Sesyle Joslin, David Waterman, Mike Carter, Raad Rawi, Emma Brown, Bill 'W', Doctor Bob, and especially Mic Cheetham and Mike Jones who took me on board.

for Kath

EXPERIENTIA DOCET STULTOS
(EXPERIENCE TEACHES FOOLS)

PROLOGUE
TITLE SEQUENCE

With what strange utterance did the loud dry wind
Blow through my ears! the sky seemed not a sky
Of earth, and with what motion moved the clouds!

The things which I have seen I now can see no more.

William Wordsworth

Heading south on the A595, August 1965

As we round the bend before Calder Bridge, through the drizzle I can just make out the lights of Windscale power station. My arse always puckers up at the sight of it. The fucking place gives me the creeps. So I open the throttle on The Ark and she struggles against the head wind to nudge fifty. Batesy and Baz are about a hundred yards ahead, a bird apiece on their pillions and their parkas fully unfurled, drawn in tight at the calf against the bitter wind. Batesy looks seaward, takes his right hand off the handlebars and shoots the atomic plant the V. I know why. Batesy told me his dad was working there when the big fire broke out ten years ago poisoning all the cows and sheep from Carlisle to Preston. He told Batesy nobody knew the truth of what went on in those few days. He said that him and his mates were pushing the atomic fuel rods back into the reactor

1

core with scaffold poles. Batesy's dad died of leukemia last year.

It takes me less than a minute to catch up with them because they're heavier with two up and The Ark's got twenty-five cc's on them both. The Ark is my pride and joy. She's a one seven five Lambretta which I stripped down and re-bored to two hundred cc. She sports ten chromed wing mirrors, a high-back fur-padded pillion, and a six-foot whippy aerial topped with a fox tail which my Uncle Bart cut from a vixen killed by the Buttermere hounds. He gave it to me for my sixteenth birthday. I'm now eighteen.

My name's Noah. And as if that isn't bad enough, my second name's Arkwright. It's a bugger of a name for anybody, but when you come from Workington, a shithole between the pulp mill and the steel works, where if you can't fuck or fight you're a nancy boy, it makes life a bit more difficult.

When, nearly three years ago, I joined the Working Man's Club, our local Mod gang, and went on my first night with them down to Barrow to hear Junior Walker and the All Stars, some Furness arsehole followed us out into the car park after the show and started chanting my name as all his pinhead cronies joined in with animal sounds. I'd taken about half a dozen French Blues and was in no mood for these shipyard wankers yelling in chorus the insults I'd had yelled at me since I was old enough to remember. So I leaped on the lead chanter and headbutted him to the ground like a bloody woodpecker. The Club piled in behind me and silenced the bastards. There wasn't a moo or an oink to be heard when we fired back up and scooted off.

On the ride home, triumphant but a bit worse for wear, The Workingmen pulled over for a fag and some carry-out India Pale Ales. In the pub car park I jumped on the saddle of my scooter, held my beer up high and christened her The Ark. The next day I painted her name on the engine cowling and added two dozen

2

kid's nursery animal transfers for good measure – and I swore I wouldn't take any shit from anybody again – and that I would get out of Workington. I was totally fucked off with the place.

The time for a breakout was right – 1963 – things were starting to happen. The Beatles were turning music inside out, and all over the country working-class kids were jumping on the rock'n'roll bandwagon. The trouble was, I couldn't play a note, was so completely tone deaf that even Baz and Batesy wouldn't let me into the Sidemen who were so fucking bad that they broke up after their first gig at the fifth form Christmas Party. But there was Mr Oliver. He was our history teacher who was crazy about films. Half his class time we'd sit there watching documentaries about the Russian Revolution, or Mosely's Brownshirts. Everyone knew Oliver was a card-carrying C.P. member, but half the kids he taught came from families whose politics had been fired in the Bessemer Converter and forged on the shop floor, and his job was safe with them. This one week, in the first term of my fifth form, we were studying the Industrial Revolution and the school had a couple of films about it, but Oliver said they were all right-wing rubbish and we could do better. Would any of us be interested in making a short picture with him on the subject down at the local steel works and pulp mill? Mine was the only hand that went up.

So Mr Oliver and me went after school that next Friday and he handed me a camera and a sheet of instructions. As soon as I felt the weight of that Kodak eight millimetre in my hand, turned that chrome winding key, pressed the trigger and heard that whirr by my ear, I knew I was hooked. So did Mr Oliver. He asked me to stay on for A levels. If I did I'd have him for a history teacher, and he'd teach me all he knew about making films. As if that wasn't enough to clinch the deal, he gave me that Kodak after my O level results which really weren't good enough to warrant such a gift from *heaven. Aunty Janet and Uncle Bart were so chuffed that I wanted to stay on in the sixth form, for my birthday they did what they swore they never would and bought me a second-hand scooter. It cost twenty quid and became that scooter within a scooter which is the Noah's Ark I'm riding now.*

So there I was, just sixteen and all set to make my break for freedom. I had wheels, a camera, a third eye, and I had half a brain which if I used it well might just do the trick.

I got rotten A levels, and Janet and Bart were really upset. But I didn't really give a toss. I had six short films which I'd made, and one and a half of them were alright, even good. One was great, Workingmen. *It's a ten-minute piece which rides through a Saturday with the Workington Scooter Boys. The others films showed 'enthusiasm and an ongoing developing skill'. That's what Mr Oliver wrote on my application to art school in London. It hadn't been my idea to apply – I can paint just about as well as I can sing – but Mr Oliver assured me that film was 'in' right now, and Hornsey Art School was just what I needed – they would be sure to 'dig' my stuff which he said was 'hip'. I wasn't so sure, so I ran it by Baz and Batesy. Batesy said he'd heard rock musicians went to art schools and gave me his blessing. Baz said I'd always been a bit of a poofta and gave me a smackeroony kiss on the forehead and a handful of French Blues. I took the blessing and the pills and told Mr Oliver I was going to go for it.*

That was back in February. Hornsey Art School accepted me on the strength of my films, especially Workingmen, *but wanted me to have some new 'footage' – I got the lingo down sharpish – to show them when I started. That's in two weeks' time. So here I am, my trusty Kodak deep in my parka pocket, heading towards the Lakes and hoping to buggery that the rain will clear as my little camera won't handle low light conditions. I've got something specific in mind over at Wast Water, and it has nothing to do with Wordsworth's* daffodils, sheep or dry stone walls – no! – nor lakeland sunsets on lakeland lakes.

Baz's dad's a copper, and when I was round his place yesterday for Sunday tea I heard him saying that the South Lakes police were going to be diving and dragging the lake this afternoon and tomorrow. Some woman swimmer had dived off the western shore and not come back to the surface. As soon as I heard this, my mind started filming. This comes easily – the images just come to life on the inside of my skull, as if they were being projected. It was cinch for me to put myself in that desperate woman's place, strap a camera to my forehead and look out over my water grave. Wast Water is unlike all the other lakes, its spirit is darker, more dangerous, and in a rising morning mist you'd think you were in Iceland not Westmorland. Its eastern scree drops a sheer two hundred feet into black waters and creates a kind of horizontal vertigo that dares you to jump in and try to swim across a mile of treacherous water.

As I took a bite of one of Baz's mum's thin cheese and cress sarnies, I knew for sure that I could really get something gritty and moody if I could get in among the police searchers with my Kodak. So I asked Baz's dad if he thought the cops would let me. He said they would if he gave a mate of his a ring. I asked him if he would. And he did, and his mate did, so I can, as long as I don't make a nuisance of myself.

So that's how I came to be here on this piss-down Monday morning heading for Wast Water and, hopefully, a rendezvous with a corpse. Baz and Batesy aren't coming with me. Any minute now I'm going to turn off at Gosforth and head inland and they're going on down south to a new club called the Ram Jam Inn which they've heard has opened on the A1 somewhere near Peterborough. The word's out that The Wicked Wilson Picket is doing a secret gig there tonight to test the waters before he goes on the first leg of his British tour.

I don't know the names of the two girls with them. All I know is they're sisters who both work in Woolies in Workington, they're good-looking, wear identical clothes – all the latest gear – and they go like a couple of rabbits. They have a cousin who usually knocks around with them who's even better-looking. B&B said they could fix me up with her and I could fuck the project, come with them to the club and fuck her instead. I said no – an artist is supposed to suffer for his art!

Just before my turn off, I open The Ark up full, nip around Baz, Batesy and the girls, beep my horn and scoot off down the Wasdale road, leaving them wobbling, flashing their lights and cursing as they head towards Carnforth and points south.

Half an hour later I'm almost at Wast Water, pushing The Ark up the narrow road under Glad How. All the way from Gosforth I've been praying for the rain to stop, and as I roll the throttle back for the final climb, my prayers are answered, the drizzle stops and the sun starts to peep out. When I crest the hill I look down over Buckbarrow and Greendale to the lake.

I can't believe what I see down below me. Wast Water is covered with mist which rises a good fifty feet up its far-shore scree cliffs. Beyond these, Sca Fell stands, backlit and angry with bruised rain-clouds on three sides. And from behind the mountain's southern flank the sun's rays slice the air all the way down to the lake mist where they make a completely circular rainbow. That's what I'm looking down on now as my hand comes off The Ark's throttle and I glide to a standstill, mouth wide open and head spinning with the mind-boggling beauty of it. I'm sitting here on my scooter, three hundred feet above this miracle, and I swear I can hear voices singing, a chorus of angels. My heart is pounding against my ribs and I'm finding it hard to get my breath. I want to shout out for joy, but I'm afraid to. The rainbow colours get stronger and stronger and as I look at them the

6

ghost circle of an inner rainbow starts to form. My hand moves toward my parka pocket and the Kodak, but is stopped by a soundless voice which whispers in my ear –

'Some things are not for filming, Noah.'

It is at this moment that I know I am being allowed a glimpse of heaven; and I am just beginning to take in how big this fucking thing is, when before my eyes the whole scene appears to expand to fill every rock, every tree, every cubic inch of air in the valley. I almost pass out breathing that magic air deep into my lungs and on into my soul.

I gasp, throw back my head and look up to the sky which is brighter than molten metal. In this instant I understand that everything in this world is one – all part of the same glorious fart. Yes! For a second 'It' all makes sense and I realise that what I am seeing now, even long after I've forgotten it, will be there, deep inside me, behind every action I will ever take for the rest of my life.

Fuck! If Baz and Batesy could hear me now, they'd think I'd totally bloody lost it. Well, I have in a way. I've never felt anything like this before in my life. I've never even read about anything like this. I'm a Mod with two lousy A levels and a knack with a camera for fuck's sake! But I swear to God this is happening!

I take another huge deep breath, steady myself and look back down into the valley.

Oh, Christ! The rainbow has gone! The mist just sits there on the lake like a flat saucer of cream. Above it, Sca Fell looks smaller and almost friendly. Its bruised clouds are now a harmless dove-grey and moving away to the north. It's a scene I've seen many times before – bog-standard beautiful, nothing more. Tears start to well up from deep inside me and I feel a gut-wrenching sadness the likes of which I haven't felt since Dad died. Maybe I have imagined the whole thing. Maybe there was something weird in those Blues Baz gave me last night. No! I saw what I saw, and that circular rainbow was more than a rainbow. I close my eyes and try to bring it all back, but it's useless. It's gone for good and I don't think I'll ever be able get it back again. Again the tears start to rise. This time, even though I clamp my eyes shut even harder, I can't stop them.

I feel the sun hot on my face and the skin of my cheeks tight where the tears have flowed. I open my eyes and blink against the bright light of mid-morning. I must have fallen into a dead sleep. And judging by the ball-shrinking ache in my legs I've been out a hell of a long time with the old Mod balancing instinct holding me and The Ark upright. I struggle to regain focus on the scene.

Down below, the mist has burned off Wast Water and further up towards Wasdale Head I can see the police cars and an ambulance. I can just make out the divers putting on their gear. Out in the lake a police launch buzzes about. Every once in a while voices echo up to me. I take out the Kodak, put it to my eye and zoom in as close as I can. It's not an expensive camera and I can't get in tight. But I get a bead on the launch just as a diver rolls backwards into the water. My finger hovers for a second above the shutter release, then I remember that voice in my ear. I lower the camera, put it back in my parka, fire up The Ark and do a U turn.

I open her up full and nudge seventy as I scoot down the valley where the River Irt glints a very ordinary glint in the sunshine. My short short hair vibrates on my head and my parka billows and buffets out behind me. I open my mouth wide and yell at the top of my voice against the head wind. No words – just a ballsy Mod rebel yell.

A glance at my watch – half twelve. If I keep my head down and the throttle wide open, I might catch up with Baz, Batesy and the Woolies sisters somewhere around Warrington before the pubs shut.

PART ONE

Establishing Shots

And the Lord said, I will destroy man whom I have
created from the face of the earth; both man, and beast,
and the creeping thing, and the fowls of the air; for it
repenteth me that I have made them. But Noah found
grace in the eyes of the Lord.

Genesis 6:7–8

ONE

You can't get there from here.
Punchline to old New England joke

Heading west on the A264, February 1997

The driving rain lashes my kidneys, and a passing truck tries
to suck me back into the road. Through the freezing spray, I
can just make out Clare's silhouette as she waits in the Volvo,
emergency-parked on the hard shoulder. I whisper her name
over and over as I focus on the estate's flashers and take my
breathing rhythm from them as, hardly hidden by a jagged
blackthorn, I try to pee. No joy. Only after a thousand
breaths and a convoy of trucks does something give with that
all-too-familiar pain which shoots back up to my bladder. I
look down to see at my feet a few dark drops in the slush.
The pissing has exhausted me. I stand in this roadside hell,
bent double, gasping and swaying like a drunk as I try to
close my zip, but my fingers are too cold. With open fly, I
summon every ounce of strength and whatever little dignity I
have left, pull myself to full height and head back to the car.
Just as I am about to open the passenger door, another artic
booms by, and I scream a scream which is drowned in the
Doppler effect.

I click the Volvo door shut behind me and sink into the
leather and the sounds of Mozart's *Exsultate, jubilate*. The

windscreen wipers beat in time with the music. I feel Clare's hand on my knee and turn to meet her eye. For a nanosecond we speak the silent truth, then she asks me if I'm OK. I slap my thighs twice in time with the wipers, give her a big grin and peck her on her tired cheek.

'I'm fine.'

She seems to die for a moment, then takes a deep breath and switches on the ignition as I click in my safety belt.

'Your fly's undone.'

'Sorry.'

And with the teenage embarrassment that never leaves a man, I zip up as Clare accelerates along the hard shoulder and on to the northbound M3 slip road. I close my eyes. With a bit of luck I'll manage to make it to Gatwick without another pit-stop. Perhaps I can even catch a few minutes' sleep. I start to drift into the falling zone, then sit bolt upright. No! I'll check my travel documents for the hundredth time instead. That's what any sensible alcoholic would do!

So I take two passports out of my travel wallet. One is British and one American. I open them and place them side by side on my lap. Both identify me as Noah Arkwright, male, born on April Fool's Day 1947. The US passport gives my nationality as American and the UK one British – making me a dual national of dubious legality. The American document expired in May of last year, and the British one was renewed last week and expires on Valentine's Day 2007. If they still listed your occupation in passports, both of mine would read: Film Maker. I stare at the photo on the expired US document. The man looking back at me is a man on the edge of . . . success or failure, who can say? He's certainly in-your-face with a spiky shock of dyed-blond hair. But beneath the hair sits a more traditional face – warm eyes, square jaw, sharp features – it could be that of long-distance runner, except something around the mouth and eyes speaks of inner damage.

Or am I simply looking at him with the insight of hind-sight?

I look over at the recent pic in the British passport and am shocked as I am each time I see it. On first glance, the face is recognisable, unchanged except for the hair. The dyed blond hair is dark again and pulled back into an unseen pony-tail with front-to-back strands trying unsuccessfully to cover up a bald crown. The face, though still square-jawed, is gaunt and sits on the neck of a boiling turkey. If the hair and face are frightening, the eyes are fucking terrifying. Even allowing for the fact that passport photos are always shitty, the eyes in this photo are lifeless. Oh, yes! the Noah in this picture is not long for this wee world. In fact, if I were a bookie, I wouldn't give any odds at all on him reaching the expiration date stamped below his picture.

I snap shut both of the passports, put them back in my travel wallet, close my eyes and try to picture me as I see myself. The image that comes to me is nothing like either of those photos. The image that comes to me is the one that walks beside me with its head held high. He's a celluloid hero.

It's 1984, in a SoHo loft in downtown New York, at the première party for *Wings of Desire*, Wim Wender's master-piece starring pony-tailed, overcoated angels over Berlin. I'm mistaken for Bruno Ganz, the Archangel with his close-set eyes, fleshy nose, full lips and high cheekbones – a Teutonic Cherokee. Bruno's a stone or so heavier and a decade older than me, but our face moulds are off the same rack. And I like the idea of being like him. They say all film directors are jealous of actors – that's why they treat them so badly. Not me – love them – and in my dreams I always act. Waking, I act a lot too. And at this reception I'm acting – I'm acting cool, when in fact I'm feeling like shit and insecure. So there I am, standing in the corner of the loft in my black vicuña overcoat, double Jameson's in hand, not saying a word when a downtown beauty comes over and asks me to sign her film poster. Without saying a word, I do, and from then on I'm signing silently and steadily, basking in the glory of my lie. Bruno never shows up, thank God. And half way through the night, I'm ducking out with that young beauty when she whispers in my ear that she wants to be folded in my wings, or, I should say, Bruno's.

As Clare pulls off the M3 on to the Gatwick approach she pushes a button for the next CD and Mozart's 'Hallelujah' cuts off just before Te Kanawa hits the big top C. It's an act of sacrilege. But Clare is on the nerve edge the same as I am, except that I'm locked in and staring, and she's moving fast, trying to jump ahead of the sadness. For a few seconds there's only the sound of the hissing tyres and the flap-thud of the wipers, then Pergolesi's *Stabat Mater*, his Standing Mary, drifts in, a soaring beauty to fill the speeding car. Beside me I can feel the tension start to drain out of Clare the Mother, as she hears the Angel singing of that other Mother's lament. Without looking at her, I can sense the beginning of a sad smile at the corners of her strong lips. I turn and touch her cheek with my fingertip. With barely perceptible optimism, her neck stretches heavenwards, and for a second the lights of an oncoming car bathe her hair in gold and sweep across the youthful face of the woman I met in New York in 1985.

We pull off the roundabout on to the Gatwick approach road. Pergolesi's music soars even higher, beyond beautiful and into the pain zone. As I enter the airport space, I'm already in another country and ready for the worst. Clare reads my thoughts.

'You're already in Cyprus, aren't you?'

'No', I lie.

'It's not too late, you know. If you're not feeling up to going –'

'I'm fine. I really am.'

I lie again and look out of the aircraft window. In my mind's eye I can see the Tarsus mountains to the north, and far below some Greek island bathed in sunset. I'm thinking in film shots. That always keeps the shit out – for a while.

'Good. Then go, relax and don't worry about us, OK? Dagmar and I'll manage. And Etta arrives with Jara and Maya tomorrow evening. I think between us we girls can handle it, don't you.'

She looks over and winks.

I say 'OK' but I can't disguise my uneasiness. Christ! All that oestrogen! All that Yin energy flooding the house while I'm away! The only Yang will be the trace I've left behind and the dog's, and his is only firing on two cylinders since he had his nuts off. I'll be lucky if they let me back in. As for Etta, well . . .

'Oh, Noah, come on. Don't even start down that track . . . you're bigger than that.'

I wish I could be so sure. I toy with chasing the subject to ground, but feel too much of a fool. She's right. Why should Etta still be a threat? They're in the same quartet for God's sake. She's Second Violin. David the First Violin lives in Farnborough with Isaac the Viola. Sometimes they all come down to Sussex and pile into the Oast for a few days rehearsal. Dagmar takes care of all the kids. They can take woodland walks on breaks. It makes perfect sense. Nothing sinister about it at all. And anyway, all that other stuff was a long time ago.

'That isn't what I'm thinking.' Another lie. 'I'm just gutted that I'll miss your first night.'

She glances hard sideways at me.

'You're a fucking awful liar, Noah.'

Then she stamps down on the accelerator and the Volvo surges forward. My skull whacks back against the headrest. I feel a bloody fool and I need somewhere to run. So, for the second time in less than a week I want a drink, a huge fuck-off triple Jameson's! I want it NOW! And there are no fucking AA meetings where I'm going.

'Well, you chose to go on this trip, Noah!'

'That's right. So pour me that triple and leave me the fuck alone!'

Welcome to the twilight zone of alcoholic logic.

A mile or up the road, I glance at the dash clock – six p.m. Danube Dagmar should be plopping the kids in the tub about now; two-years-and-bit Faith, a cherub with clipped wings, and Coral, seven, a girl Mowgli lookalike. I miss my girls all the time these days – even when I'm with them. Christ! It's bad enough when I have to go on location for weeks on end. But when I start missing them at home, something is very wrong.

This first happened shortly after Christmas, an early morning, when I was sitting watching Coral impatiently trying to show Faith how to play Butthead, a game where you strap on this Velcro skull cap marked with numbered zones and run around like maniacs throwing soft balls at each other's head, trying to score points. I was watching all their moves, hearing every scream and giggle, even refereeing the whole shooting match, but I wasn't in the room with them. I was *in* the room, but not *in* the room with them. When I realised this, I understood that my cancer – there's the C word out of the bag! – that my CANCER was silently doing something in me, greedily but painlessly taking a bigger place at my table. And it wasn't wasting its time either. This Knowing, this Certainty made no medical sense at all – the last look-see into my bladder early that December

16

had shown 'clear' for the first time in six years – but then when you have lived with cancer for a while, you soon come to realise that it creates a world for you where deep feeling can be true knowing, and knowing is often a lie.

It's a world which makes Alice in Wonderland's look normal.

So it was no surprise to me when, about a week after Butthead Day, the pain kicked in and the razor blade cystitis pissing returned with the kind of vengeance it had wreaked immediately after chemotherapy. No bleeding this time round – just sulphuric acid urine and a sense of displacement which got worse by the day.

I could not get enough quiet in the house to even focus on it, never mind understand it. Our perfect pantile Sussex Weald Oast on its perfect pinafore acre belies a very chaotic interior. Clare practises at the house, sometimes solo, sometimes with the full Kairos Quartet at any time of day she can carve out. The girls are a four-plait whirlwind, never still for a moment. Dagmar is given to massive mood switches that alternately fill the perfect rooms with Wagnerian arias and ten-ton silent grumps. Then there's me in my roundel office plotting and planning, or anywhere in the house where there's a phone, trying to sew up this and patch that together. Don't ever make the mistake of thinking films are made with a camera by artistic people on exotic location; they are made with phones by Suits on Wall or Threadneedle streets. On any day the phone is busy, but when I'm trying, as I am now, to get money in place for a new project, the phone lines are so hot they melt all the way back to the exchanges. In fact, right up to the last moment before kissing The Plaits goodbye as I left for the airport, I was on the blower trying to get Mr Sainsbury to give us a chunk of his Christian change for the movie, which is a kind of 'My Dinner with Saint Paul' – a through-the-keyhole look at one night in Antioch when this misogynistic, epileptic first-century spin-doctor answers the door to Mary, Mother of Jesus. Which is probably what he said as he stood there gobsmacked at her arrival.

What all this adds up to is that since the Butthead Revelation Day, the house has been so chaotic, so full of 'stuff' that I haven't been able to hear or feel what is going on with my body, but have been scared enough to be under-functional. It's been a fucking pain-filled nightmare, pushing me to the limit. So much so that two days ago, for the first time in nearly twelve years, I found myself, at dusk, on the edge of taking a drink and/or a line of something speedy. That was terrifying. That was the decider. I had to get away somewhere remote to listen – just to listen to my body. As if on cue, an ex-drunk Fleet Street contact of mine phoned me that same night to see how I was doing (he's an intuitive sensitive journalist – a walking contradiction). He had just come back from Cyprus where he'd been on the Akamas peninsula, the last remote stronghold, holding at bay – only just – the seafront tat that runs from Larnaca to Paphos. Fleet Street said I had to go. I agreed and called BA. They had a seat on an eight p.m. flight to Larnaca on Wednesday – that's today. It'll cost a fortune for the taxi across the Troodhos mountains to the North Shore, but what the Hell, it can come off expenses. I've told all my associates that it's a 'recce' for a possible location for the Paul piece. It's a half-legit excuse. Paul did go to Paphos with Barnabas and they met the Roman governor. It must have been quite a movie moment, because after that Jewish Saul was known as Roman Paul. Anyway, I've already promised myself that I'll drop down to Paphos and toddle around in Saul/Paul's footsteps for a day.

So here I am in the Volvo pulling off the Gatwick North approach road into Short Term Parking, scared to death of death and dying, with Clare beside me as scared as I am. She reaches level three, turns the car into a bay, parks, switches

18

off the ignition, leans back on the headrest and closes her eyes.

'I'm so sorry,' I say.

After a silence, Clare takes my hand and speaks softly with a Texan drawl.

'Could you think about marrying me?'

I let the pause get pregnant, then in matching Dixie I nod my head and reply, 'I reckon I could.'

This is our rerun of a joint favourite scene in *Tender Mercies* when Robert Duval, the drunk country singer, pops the question to motel owner Tess Harper in the cabbage patch. In times of crisis and conflict, this little scenario never fails to ease the heart and bring us together – this time is no exception. Unsnapping my seat-belt, I move over, lay my spinning head on my wife's shoulder, and entwine her cellist fingers in mine. Clare's hands were the first part of her I fell in love with.

Out of the corner of my eye I catch sight of something in the rear-view mirror. I see the flash of the teeth and the red of the eyes a split second before I hear the sound and feel the car shake as seventy pounds of black muscle crashes against the metal guard grille.

'Holy Shit!'

Clare's whole body snaps forward throwing me sideways. The hand-brake goes up my arse, and I scream like a scalded pig, adding to the ear-splitting din of Siddown's high octave barking. The dog! I'd forgotten we'd brought the bloody dog! The black bastard has slept the whole way.

'Shut the fuck up, Siddown!' I shout as Clare starts laughing hard, then harder. The dog won't stop barking and Clare can't stop laughing until she runs out of laugh, looks fleetingly surprised, and collapses on to the steering wheel in floods of tears.

TWO

Be careful what you pray for. You might get it.

Under brilliant moonlight the Mercedes careers down a goat track from mountain-top Kykko where the Tom Conti-in-*Shirley Valentine* lookalike cabbie has slowed down to seventy for a four a.m. drive past the most celebrated monastery in the Orthodox world, where one of history's other great spin-doctors, Archbishop Makarios, was a novice monk.

I wanted Tom to stop so I could get a real shufti at this medieval pile, which could be a great location for *St Paul – The Movie!* But it's already disappearing in a cloud of moonlit dust behind us. As we bump along the 'road' to Panayia, which I'm certain doesn't grace any map, Tom ('my coosin, he lif Wood Green – is nice place?') is trying to tell me a story about a Turkish blasphemer whose arm was turned to brass when he tried to light a fag off a lamp in the monastery sanctuary. That seems to be the gist of it anyway. Concentration is difficult. First there's the problem of the breakneck speed and my rattling brainpan; second there's the problem with the headlights. They are off. Tom refuses to use them. When I ask him every few minutes to turn them on, he laughs and repeats like a mynah bird, 'Iz betta moonlight.' Then there's the problem of the old bladder. Kristos! It was bad enough on the plane doing the pissoire shuffle four times an hour, but on these tracks, in the hands of the Cyprus Night Rider, I want to piss all the time. I try asking Tom to stop, but he won't hear me. And why should I be surprised? If I can't even get him to slow down and to put his headlights on, why should I be able to convince him to stop every ten minutes for me to try and drain the lizard.

So I gulp down the last of 200ml of Volvic water that I've been nursing, and, carefully avoiding Tom's eye in the driver's mirror, shove the bottle inside my pants, squeeze the head of my dick into the neck, squeeze my sphincter, and wait for the pain and the pee. Both come in a pathetic dribble, but it's enough to give me some relief and for me to sit back safe in the knowledge that for the rest of the journey I can dribble willy-nilly, as they say! Exhausted, I listen to Tom drone on. Despite the hellish discomfort, I look out of the window at the passing lemon groves and bumpily fall asleep.

The sun's first rays tickle my face and I wake to find myself still in the Mercedes, parked on the dusty roadside, a coat – not mine – tucked around me and Tom spark out in the front seat. Beyond him the wide-screen sweep of Chrysochou Bay, a deep Prussian blue touched with red. I have the headache from Hell. I groan. Tom turns with a half open eye and a night-filled voice:

'Kali mera. Ti kanis?' He sounds like a sleepy lover. I Greek island-hopped enough in the sixties to understand the greeting and to return his good morning and tell him I'm fine thank you:

'Kali mera. Kala imeh efharisto.'

But it's not and I'm not, so I add:

'Would you mind telling me what the fuck we're doing parked here!'

On the defensive, Tom blurts out a stream of an excuse in Gringlish which, from what I can gather, is that the reception at Elia Lachi Holiday Village – *holiday village – living entertainment every night allowing for season* – whoopee! – was closed when we arrived at four in the morning, and as I was sleeping so nicely and as he was tired himself he'd decided not to wake me, and so on and so on. So he'd covered me with his coat like a long-lost Cypriot father, parked the Merc and crashed out himself.

I am just about to apologise profusely and thank Tom when, as if on an unseen cue, he does a mood U turn. He grabs back his coat, thrusts out his hand and angrily demands his money. Feeling like a shit but too pained to explain my condition, I ask Tom 'Poso kani?' He stares at me, panting, scary as hell. 'How much?' I try again. Tom leans in towards me. 'Fuck you,' he hisses in perfect English. Now I'm scared. I dig into my wallet, grab a handful of Cyprus pounds and hold them out in a gesture of surrender. In silence, he politely takes the correct amount, goes round to the boot, takes out my bag, then opens my door for me. As he gets back in the car, I get out and the forgotten Volvic bottle falls down my leg, out of the bottom of my pants, and pours dark piss on to the litter-strewn hard shoulder. Tom simply looks down, shakes his head, fires up the engine and drives off in a cloud of sunlit dust.

'*Welcome to Cyprus, Noah you dickhead! You came here to take a good look at yourself; so take a look as you stand by another roadside a thousand miles from home with the sun coming up and your spirits sinking fast.*'

'Yes – *fuck my luck!*'

'*No, Noah! Thank your lucky stars that Taxi Tom didn't roll your short-tempered, condescending ass and take you for every penny you have.*'

I nod to myself and head across the dusty road. A truck roars out of nowhere with klaxon blaring and I throw myself to the ground. As it passes within inches of me, it

22

hits a bump, showering me with lemons as hard as cannon-balls.

With my head still reeling, I plop my bag down to check in at the Elia Lachi reception and already wish I was checking out. But I know I have to take this time for myself, a time without the familiar points of reference. I ring the bell, toy with a brochure sporting a sultry Cypriot hotel receptionist, and take in my surroundings. It's a spanking new room built with summer in mind. It has the whitewashed roughcast walls and arches of all new Mediterranean buildings, and it looks as though it's been furnished from an outlet warehouse on the North Circ – probably has been. One of Tom's cousins probably shipped it over. But it's not summer, the sun is now raking the forecourt but with a limp-dick kind of strength, and the whole place feels to be on hold for warmer times.

When somebody friendly appears a hundred years later, it's not the smart, busty Melina of the brochure still in my hand, but a bent old lady, ninety if she's a day, carrying a Keystone Kop bunch of jail keys. She speaks no English and can't understand a word of my Old Hippie Greek. After ten minutes of getting nowhere, she shuffles out of the door and beckons for me to follow.

There's plenty of time to take in my surroundings as I follow her slow climb up the one in four hill to the ridge of snow-white units. Down below on our left Chrysochou Bay makes a pretty impressive sweep of fifteen or so kilometres. The sea is early-morning sparkling blue with whitecaps to order, whipped up by a now *très* chilly February wind which buffets my kidneys so they start to ache and makes me curse for not having packed a heavy sweater.

It also makes me want another piss.

The hamlet of Lachi lies below: a single row of flat-roofed buildings flanking a dusty road. To the east I can see a forbidding cape, and to the west, a still-backlit coastal ridge that is Turkish Cyprus. This place is remote alright, I'll be able to sit by the shore and hear the mermaid sing, and with a bit of luck sing along with her and learn a thing or two about what's what with me and this shooting match called Life and Death.

It's now my third day in the wilderness and I haven't left the Holiday Village. I've been to the restaurant – *cooking cuisine excellent and full choice* – where I've dined alone except for a group of six retired Dutch bulb growers, ardent floraphiles who told me they're here to stalk the wild cyclamen, crown anemones and the purple stars of the eastern sand crocus. I have taken a swim in 'our delighted inside pool' and done the hot tub – which, surprisingly in this spotless complex, sports a ring of scum. And I have made daily dusk raids on the 'profusion of lemon trees' and stolen enough fist-sized fruit to keep me in fresh squeezed lemonade. Each dawn, wearing two jackets, I have breakfasted on my patio – on food nicked from last night's buffet – and watched God painting in the day by numbers. The rest of the time I have defiantly smoked a pack of Marlboro Reds bought on the plane, watched on Satellite the mad bastards in the Extreme Edge Winter Olympics doing snowboard suicide leaps and Grand Slalom runs on mountain bikes. I have wanted to stray further afield but haven't dared because the bladder problem has gone into Warp Factor Two, and since my first piss in this Holiday Village, I haven't been able to go longer than ten minutes without having to empty out. But today it's all much better and I think I might go walkabout. Yes! It's going to be the perfect day. If only the phone would ring.

CUE THE PHONE!

It rings. I grab at it as if it's a lifeline and blurt out: 'Mayday! Mayday! Horny sailor overboard, slither down this phone and let me fuck you!'

The old lady in reception crackles something in Greek and connects me. My face is burning. Fuck her! She's broken the spell.

'Hello, Noah?'

'That's me.' I sound completely flat.

'I thought you might have called.'

'I was going to tonight.' I must do something about these lies.

'Well, it's cheaper on our bill. How are you feeling?'

'Good.' I find a bit of energy. 'Don't worry, sweetie, alright?'

'OK' – ever notice how long-distance phone-calls are all 'alright', 'fine' and 'OK'? – then a massive delay kicks in and our voices become an overlapping mess. I wait for a second to clear a bit of space.

'How's Schoenberg?'

I hate Schoenberg.

'Oh, he's –' The line goes dead. I speak on.

'– just fine. And Etta? How's she?'

I put the phone down. Fuck the walk! I'll go tomorrow instead.

It's twenty-four hours later and I open my shutters to a cerulean blue sky. I take a deep breath. Right, Noah my friend! Let's see if this town's big enough for both of us! I grab my coat and head out of the door. But where to go? I never travel with a guidebook. So I make a detour behind the deserted tennis courts, duck into the deserted reception and scan the rack of leaflets for a destination. There it is! Loutrá tís Afrodhítis – the Baths of Aphrodite – five miles out on the Akamas peninsula. Can I make it? Hell, yes! If St Paul can walk thirty miles across the Cilician tundra after having the shit kicked out of him in some remote garrison town, I can stumble my arse, cancer or no cancer, a few miles up E713. It'll be a walking meditation, a no-nonsense stroll to the heart. I nick a leaflet and head off.

Near the end of the Lachi strip, which in close-up is more than a bit faded, I pass by Yangos and Peter's Seafood Restaurant. I remember my Fleet Street mate telling me that it's a 'must eat' and I promise myself that if I get back from Venus' Toilet alive I'll treat myself to a mountain of calamari, lobster and . . .

'. . . *a chilled bottle of retsina* . . .'

Christ! I'm going to have to watch it – this is real 'I-could-have-just-one-glass-and-nobody-would-know' territory. Maybe I should call AA in Paphos – I had meant to pack my International Directory but somehow it slipped my mind – surprise, surprise, Cilla! Ah, well! Onward and Upward, Noah! I press on.

An hour later, around the next bend, I glimpse a village clinging to the hillside. The walk so far has been peaceful, punctuated by only five pee stops and several others to pick carob pods which I chewed as I once chewed coca leaves on a shoot in the Andes. I spit out sweet brown spit on the dusty verge. Beyond the lemon groves, far below, the sea sparkles, the flowers the Dutch group spoke of bloom everywhere, and high above me a bird soars. I could swear it's an eagle.

The 'village' when I reach it is a mess of old British-made caravans, corrugated lean-tos, and a pair of picture-postcard, blue and white houses opposite an exquisite small church. At its centre is a modern Cyprus Tourist Board restaurant. Yangos and Peter's it isn't! The whole place is thick with goats and the air stinks of shit. I follow the sign to 'Baths of Aphrodite' on to a track which leads beside a huge, empty car park. Since I hit town, the wind has dropped. It's now very hot. Very hot. I look down at the sea far below. If The Goddess of Love had hiked up from the bay on a day like this, she'd have been gasping for a bath.

In the homespun reception leaflet, the Baths are described like this: 'Loutrá tís Afrodhítis is a most beautiful hidden pool where our local Goddess would bathe after times with her lovers. It snuggles [sic!] under a grotto which drips into the four-metre pool below, all surrounded by wild fig trees', etc.

What greets me as I turn the last corner on the litter-edged path is a dismal structure circa nineteen seventy. Modern flagstones surround a semi-stagnant pond, and whatever fig trees are overhanging could do with a spray of heavy-duty fungicide. A used condom and a Diet Coke can float in the water. On the downhill side of the pool, I can see the thirty-millimetre alkathene drainage piping carrying away the Goddess's bath water. Above all this, an in-your-face sign tells you not to bathe in the shallow water, drink it, or climb the trees. Fuck that! I'm overheated and cheated. Using a broken branch, I hook out the dead sheath, strip off, jump in and splash around for a bit. I enjoy the anarchy but not the dip. It doesn't last long. Before I get out, I take a well-earned piss in the Goddess's bath, then grab hold of a forbidden fig branch, haul myself on to the side and put my clothes back on. I'm thirsty, but I decide to leave drinking Venus' water for my next visit.

So much for my consultation with the Oracle – Cyprus style.

It's still only eleven thirty in the morning, so I decide to follow a mountain trail signposted to Smyiés, which, according to my state-of-the-art pamphlet, is a picnic ground on the way to Neokhorio, the hilltop village above the bay, from where I can drop down to my trusty Holiday Village in Lachi. It'll add a mile or two on to the walk, but what the Hell! I'm all refreshed and squeaky clean from my bath. I pick two oranges and some carob from roadside trees and strike out.

The climb is tough and I soon work up a fresh sweat. In about fifteen minutes I reach an outcrop of rocks below a cliff which gives me a stunning view of the whole peninsula. Far below me in the distance there are six flags on poles, tiny and red against the turquoise sea. I'm still puzzling over them when I see the puffs of smoke. A few seconds later the air over my head is filled with deafening screeches one after another. I hit the ground as six huge explosions rock the mountainside. In my dazed state I remember something else Fleet Street had told me. Sometimes the peace of Chrysochou Bay can be shattered by numskull Brit Squaddies playing Bang Bang with Big Gun on the Sovereign Territory of the Akamas Firing Range.

Dazed, I try to stand. A pain shoots through my kidneys. In agony I double up into the foetal position and gasp so loud it echoes from the rock face. For a long minute I kneel there panting like a wounded animal. Finally I struggle to my feet; I look down to see that I've wet my pants like a two-year-old. Oh, shit! If I don't move on immediately, I know I'll start to cry like one. So, summoning military courage to match my surroundings, I stumble off down a path which leads me between a narrow alleyway of sun-drenched rocks, made narrower by an edging of razor-sharp gorse. My socks tear and my ankles bleed. I have a sick feeling that I have turned myself around in the aftershock. I check the position of the sun. It isn't where it should be. I'm lost. And my head is splitting. I emerge from the rock alley and stop dead in my tracks. There, impaled on the split trunk of a mountain pine, is what remains of a mule. Its jaw has been blown away and its purple entrails hang down to the ground. Not two feet from me is a severed leg. Bits of flesh and shards of bone are everywhere. The stench of blood and shit fills the air. And there, feasting on the just dead remains, not giving a toss about my arrival, are four fucking huge vultures! Griffon vultures – they're mentioned in the pamphlet too. One of them stares at me, a piece of something slippery hanging from its beak. Then in one gulp the bird swallows it and tucks back in to the Mulefest.

I can feel my vomit rising and I can't do a damn thing to stop it. It splatters over the severed leg at my feet. I start to sway back and forth in the fetid air.

This is not turning out to be a good day after all.

Dead Man Walking . . . Dead Man Walking . . . Dead Man Walking . . .

This film title marks time in my head as I walk back along the Lachi strip. The Movie Mantra comes only when I'm really tired, and it's recently been *Dead Man Walking*. I am beyond tired now as I shuffle along, bleeding on to my shoes, bruised, dusty and vomit-flecked. Through the window of Yangos and Peter's I see a group of men around a table in front of a roaring fire, drinking, eating and laughing. Two are in police uniform. A waiter with The Greek Moustache glances at me as he puts a large platter of meze in front of the guys.

A hundred yards further on, outside a souvenir shop, there are bags of different-sized sea sponges. I'm looking at them thinking I could get one for each of the women at home, even Etta, when the police car pulls alongside and a brute voice snaps something in Greek at me. Whenever I am approached by the police, my gut tries to jump out of my throat. It's a reflex response to all of those years when I was guaranteed to be in 'possession of illegal substances'. I take a deep breath and, as composed as I can muster, go over to the car.

'Good afternoon, officer.'

His breath stinks of booze. He's one of the policemen from the restaurant. That bloody waiter must've tipped him the wink.

He smiles a nasty smile. 'Pos se leneh?'

I tell him my name and his next words go beyond my simple Greek. As he gets out of the car I catch my reflection in his door window and see myself as he sees me. Christ! I look like a pony-tailed Ratso Rizzo on a very bad day! And I smell like a cess pool. I'm scared now. This cop is a mean-looking bastard and for a moment I see him in civvies, dragging Turkish women out of their houses not ten miles north of here, throwing them to the ground and raping them in front of their screaming children. I brace myself for a blow, but it doesn't come. He simply stands there repeating the word 'Passaporte' like a very pissed-off parrot. I try to tell him, pointing frantically over the road, that my passport is just a few yards away in my room. And for some reason I start pointing at myself and saying 'Film Director' and doing the Charades sign for movie, and then, as if he would know, 'Costa-Gavras?' The cop shakes his head, pats me down *NYPD Blue*-style and pulls two squashed oranges out of my jacket pockets; their juice runs down his arm and on to his crisp white shirt cuffs. He curses some curse and bundles me towards the police car when my knight in shining appears in the guise of one of the retired Dutch bulb growers, trotting across the road shouting at the policemen in perfect Greek.

Dutch – God bless him – takes care of the situation and in less than five minutes I'm delivered back to my cosy Holiday Village home. I take my passport back from the cop, thank my Dutch saviour, close the apartment door and just stand there, my heart and head pounding.

Undressing, I go to the bathroom, turn on the tap and let the water get as hot as I can stand it. Hot day. Hot bath.

'*That old alkie logic again, Noah!*'

'*Yeah, yeah, yeah . . .*'

I zap on the telly. Only golf on the sports channel, so I switch to MTV. The Spice Girls, near naked, are singing some dead song in the desert, doing split beaver kicks and throwing metal boomerangs. Girl Power?

'Who are you kidding?' I mutter to myself as I flop back on

the bed, click off the sound, and make a mental note to 'lose' Coral's 'Wannabe' Spice tape when I get home. Actually the video isn't too bad – it's all formula stuff, but it's tight and gets the job done. If MTV had been around when I was getting started, would I have been seduced?

'Of course you would, Noah . . . come on, admit it! Sex, drugs, rock'n'roll and movies all in one place – young indie director's paradise!'

'You're right – I'd have been there like a shot –'

'And you'd be dead now.'

I switch off the telly and close my eyes for a short kip. I open them again – I can't sleep. I lie there wide awake and stare at the ceiling. I know what's coming.

Sure enough, after a few seconds, I feel a pull, slide off the bed, kneel down beside it and start to pray. Now praying is my dirty secret, by that I mean it is something which I hardly ever talk about and which, on the rare occasions I am caught at it, prompts feelings of shame and embarrassment. I'm always surprised when I utter a little prayer, but every Blue Moon when I go for the Full Monty, on my knees like this, it feels as if I've been ambushed by Faith itself. When I switched off the TV a moment ago, I had genuinely intended to catch a few until the bath was ready. Now here I am, bollock naked, ankles bleeding, eyes cast heavenwards like some desperate saint. Maybe my subconscious guilt is forcing me to justify those dubious expenses and do a little Pauline hands-together research. But I don't think so. I think this is a genuine moment. To tell the truth, I've always been a believer in something bigger than myself: the Higher Power of the recovering alkie. In my youth, I flirted with Buddhism, Taoism, Baba Ram Das, Meher Baba, the Maharishi and the fifty Rolls-Royce Bhagwan. As a film maker I was moved in faith by specific films. When I saw Bergman's *Fanny and Alexander* I became curious about Calvinism. Kurosawa's

31

Ran forced a trip to Japan and a tour of its Shinto temples. After viewing Scorsese's *The Last Temptation of Christ*, I even nipped into a Catholic Church for a quick confession. I was a spiritual gadfly. Then came AA and cancer and I found myself being drawn back to the church of my childhood – good old pew-thumping Methodism.

I don't know why it bothers me so much to admit to it. Perhaps it's not glamorous enough for the jean jacket and black T-shirt image which I hang on to like grim death. But I find calm in those spartan chapels, and a great deal of wisdom in the words preached. Any one of those roaming ministers could direct a film better than most NFT graduates. They can take a single theme, set up a protagonist and drive him through a plot like a hot knife through butter – reversal, subtext, climax and anti-climax – it's all in there. And they apologise for nothing. They fly their banner of faith high and proud. I keep my banner rolled up like an umbrella to be used on rainy days when I don't want to get soaked. Or to hide under when I'm helpless and scared as I am now.

On my knees, I utter a simple prayer.

'Dear God. I'm really scared. Give me a sign. Show me the way forwards out of this chaos and give me the courage to follow it. Amen.'

Then, being a person who can never keep it simple, I add a rambling, self-pitying footnote apologising for not being a good husband of late, for being weak, and asking Him to watch over Clare and the girls.

I don't know how long I've been kneeling in a daze, but now I can hear the sound of a small waterfall.

I reach the bathroom to find the floor an inch deep in water and the hot tap running cold into the steaming tub. I plunge my arm down into the near-scalding water and pull the plug. When the water level and temperature are right, I step in, lie back and close my eyes. This time I drift off nicely.

It's two months after chemotherapy, and I'm back in Bermuda with Clare and Coral – Faith had not yet come along. The morning sky is ultramarine and the water turquoise as we walk along the pink sands of Long Beach toward Jobson's Cove, a small jewel of a bay hidden behind the sand dunes crested with fennel. The cove is deserted; from the top of the path leading down to it, we can see two huge parrot fish swimming lazily, surrounded by black and yellow angels. In a flash we're all in our cossies and into the water. I swim out to the gap which leads to the open sea where I know more exotic fish shoal in the coral. Half way there, I stop, tread water, the sun hot on my back, and take a pee – anyone who says they don't piss in the ocean is a liar or superhuman. In this limpid blue water it is hurting to piss in a way that it hasn't since treatment. In agony, I flail about. I panic and start to sink – I push for the surface and after an eon break through, gasping and—

I'm back in Cyprus sitting in a tub full of blood-red water. Oh, Jesus! What the fuck?! I'm shaking with terror, teeth chattering. I'm bloody freezing. Whining like an animal, I start to beat the surface of the water, but the blood won't go away.

'*You asked for a sign, Noah. Well, here it is, brother! Get your head around it!*'

The phone rings. I struggle to stop my shakes as I get out of the bath and, trailing bloody water, go into the bedroom to answer it. Clare's voice is from another planet.

'Hello, darling. How's it going?'

I drive a double-decker bus through a gap before I answer.

'Great. I did a bit of sightseeing today.'

'Well done. You sound good . . . clear. Look, Faith wants to talk to you.' There's a bustle as Clare hands her the phone, followed by silence punctuated with baby breathing. I can hear Clare coaxing her to talk to me, and I try from my end. It's useless. Clare comes back on the line.

'Cat got her tongue, but she was grinning down the line like a Cheshire.'

I manage a small laugh.

'Look, love. I think I might come home a bit early.'

'Oh?'

'Tomorrow, actually.'

'Why? I thought you said it was going well.'

'It is. That's the point. I've got what I came for.'

'What do you mean?'

'Things are much clearer now.'

'That doesn't tell me a thing, Noah. Are you feeling alright?'

'Yes . . . Look, I'll explain it all when I get home. Don't you worry, OK? Kiss the girls from me. I'll call you from the airport before I fly out.'

'I won't be able to pick you up. It's the recital, remember.'

'Of course I do. I'll take a taxi.'

'This is ridiculous, Noah. If you're feeling fine, then take the time for yourself. Stay the full week and enjoy it.'

'No. I'm ready to leave.'

'Have you been phoning Ray? Is this about work?'

'We'll talk when I get back.'

'Sometimes you can be such an arsehole, Noah!'

'I love you too, sweetie. Break a leg tomorrow.'

I already have the phone half back on to the cradle when Clare's voice crackles out, 'Love you too.'

Shivering, I sit on the edge of the bed and look down at my blood-streaked body, the little pools of water forming at my feet. In a huge gasp, I suck in half the air of the room then I start sobbing like a milk baby.

That night, Yangos or Peter has the fire stoked up so high that the front room of the restaurant is a blast furnace. The whole population of Lachi and half that of the neighbouring villages are eating and drinking, their chatter level nudging at least a hundred decibels. There isn't a single place to sit. I'm about to turn on my heel when the waiter who shopped me to the cops rushes over and greets me like a long-lost lover – maybe it's Yangos or Peter himself. Whoever he is he spews out an apology, 'Sorry, sorry, there is place out by the sea,' as he ushers me into a huge conservatory which is as freezing as the dining room is boiling.

'Soon you will have heat,' he says as he clicks his fingers and sits me down at a red-clothed table for two, whips away the other place setting with one hand and gives me the menu with the other. A swing door slams open and I jump. A young boy wheels in a gas space-heater and places it by my table. With a flourish, Yangos or Peter lights it and asks me:

'You from London, yes?'

'Yes.'

'You know Helena of Wood Green Travel?'

'No – sorry.'

Yangos or Peter seems a bit miffed and snaps back, 'You want to order?'

'I'll have the calamari and lobster, please.'

'Sorry no lobster,' he grins.

'That's OK. Just double the squid.'

For some reason he finds this very funny and guffaws loudly.

'Okey-dokey. You want some wine?'

I hesitate a second too long.

'I'll take a Diet Coke . . .'

He gives me a look which says, 'Oh, you don't drink? That explains why you don't know Helena in Wood Green Travel, you fucking English idiot.' I feel a sweat breaking on the back of my neck.

'. . . if you have some . . . with ice . . . please.'

Suddenly he claps his hand on my shoulder and winks at me. 'Sure we got Diet Coke.' Then Yangos or Peter stabs his finger at my chest. 'I like this T-shirt. It's American?'

I glance down. I'm wearing my Road Kill Café shirt which a Best Boy gave me on a shoot near Sturgis, South Dakota. On the front it sports a twelve-point stag rearing in the headlights of a 4 by 4 which isn't going to take him prisoner, and on the back there's a spoof menu of dishes made out of dead things scraped off the road.

'Yes, it's American.'

'In America they like to hunt. In Chrysochou also we love to hunt.'

He draws a bead on an imaginary animal, squeezes off a round, and actually says, 'Bang Bang!' I smile wanly. He walks off chuckling.

After the bathtub incident, I was feeling like shit, but I thought it would do me good to get out and have that one last meal. Now I'm not so sure it was a great idea. Now I feel like an extra from *Night of the Living Dead*. I look around for any comforting sign of life. Over in the far corner, backlit by a harbour-side light outside the window, another exiled diner sits next to an identical heater. He's smoking a cigarette and looking in my direction. It's a great shot, and I'm filing it in my head when the young heater boy plops a mountain of calamari and chips in front of me, digs deep in his apron and pulls out a can of Diet Coke and a frosted glass. He stares at my T-shirt as he pours my drink.

The chips are wet and greasy, an inedible response to tourist demand. But the squid, which I'm sure is rarely ordered by visitors, is delicious and tender, battered in heaven. I love calamari. I respect calamari. It always makes me think. If ever I'm tempted to take a drink, I remember calamari and Ray.

It's the summer of 1982 or 1983. Ray and I have come with

a second unit to some tiny 'os' of a Greek island. We're picking up some footage for a Mafia Movie of the Week which we don't really need, but we're coming in under budget and we think it's as good a way as any to spend the money we're 'saving' CBS. On the second day we wrap a harbour-side shoot of fishermen unloading a catch, gutting fish, mending nets and pounding the shit out of squid on the quay, then settle into a hard day's night of drinking ouzo at 'os's equivalent of Yangos and Peter's. Ray's two-fisting his drinks, while I'm pacing myself a little because I have my eye on a young PA fresh out of the NYU film programme who I hope I'll make my catch of the day. Around midnight I lead her off to my room, leaving Ray and the crew at the outside tables well on their way to the full moon overhead, being serenaded by the landlord's son on the bouzouki. I guess he will have them up hanky dancing before I can unbutton NYU's blouse.

Early next morning, I pull a white sheet over Frank's perfect arse – that's her name – Frank not Frankie! – and step out into a bright white day to find coffee. It's only eight o'clock and already in the seventies. The harbour-side café is peppered with locals drinking strong espresso at the bar inside, and outside a few clean-cut tourists drinking cappuccino as far away from Ray as possible. Ray, shirtless, wearing a Greek fisherman's cap, is slumped over a table in front of a pyramid of empty bottles which is miraculously still standing. Our fishermen from yesterday's shoot are unloading the morning catch. One of them looks up and waves. 'Kali mera!' I wave back and shout, 'Kali mera!' Ray suddenly sits bolt upright and bellows 'CALAMARI!' The fishermen laugh. The tourists try to ignore Ray. He screams again 'CALAMARI!' and bangs his fist on the table sending the bottle pyramid flying. Then he fixes his hangover gaze on the fishermen, waving like an idiot and chanting 'Calamari!' My fisherman is laughing. He turns to another in the boat and yells something. A large squid comes flying up and he catches it, walks over to Ray's table and plops it down in front of him. 'Calamari,' he says slowly as if to a child, then, 'Kali mera iss Good Morning.' Ray nods and stares at the squid which is still very much alive. Suddenly he picks it up, holds it at arm's length, says, 'Kali mera,' then kisses it. It was love at first sight. The squid responds by wrapping his tentacles around Ray's face. The fisherman laughs. Ray lets out a muffled scream and jumps to his unsteady feet, trying to rip the squid from his face. But the squid holds tight. It's like a scene from *Alien*. Ray is flailing around, unable to breathe. The tourists are recoiling in terror. The locals have come out from the bar to see what's going on. I'm rooted to the quayside, unable to take it all in. Our fisherman stops laughing, grabs Ray by one shoulder and the squid by the other. Using every ounce of strength, he tears the squid off Ray's face. My cinematographer's scream is not muffled now, and the sucker welts on his face are bleeding. I run over to him and he throws his arms around me and starts to sob like I have never heard a man sob before or since . . . except myself.

It was years later before Ray told me that he knew on that morning of the calamari that he either had to kill the booze or it would kill him. I certainly never saw him take another drink after that.

'Hi! You're Noah Arkwright, aren't you?'

What the fuck! I almost knock my plate to the floor as I look up to see Keifer Sutherland standing on the other side of my table. As I pull focus on him, I see it's not Donald's son but a lookalike, the guy from the table by the window.

'I recognise you from this month's spread in *Premiere* magazine. Well, I know your face anyhow. I've been a fan of yours since *Downtown Surf Story*. You mind if I sit down?'

Yes I do mind, but I tell him it's OK and he sits.

'Hey. Don't mind me, Noah. Eat your calamari, man.'

I'm too gobsmacked by his approach, still reeling from my head rerun of Ray's encounter with the squid to do anything but obey his command. I take a mouthful of calamari and he continues talking and doesn't stop. It turns out he's a graduate student at NYU (Frank's younger brother?) and he's taken a semester out to do a 'Light Tour' of the Med. He's got himself a state of the art Bolex to match his state of the art Rolex on his state of the tan forearm and he's doing the 1990s equivalent of Turner's Alpine sketchbooks. He's documenting every possible lighting situation he can find. He wants to be the best cinematographer since Bergman's Sven Nykvist or my Ray Molina a.k.a. Blue Sky who I've known since we met in a parallel universe thirty years ago.

Almost every instinct in me wants to tell this young rich kid to piss off, but there's something in his undisguised passion which I am drawn to. After all, don't I always tell young film students on those God-awful post-screening question and answer sessions that they can't get anywhere without passion? So I let him run on. He tells me the whole plot of his second-year student film project about a wealthy undergrad whose nose gets him involved with the Lower East Side Colombians and finally into a dumpster on the corner of fourth and Avenue D. Then he says, 'Enough about me, why don't you tell me about your next project, Noah?' Christ! The balls on this kid! I never talk about a new project to *anyone* except Ray and Clare.

But there must be something about him, because over the next hour I unwind the whole ball of wax for him. I build a plot right there and then. And I shock myself. It comes out as my *Long Day's Journey into Night* – an autobiographical bungee jump into the gorge of my past, bouncing almost back up to the present.

I even run two working titles by him – Strange Days or A Sense of Tumour – and ask for his opinion.

'*Why the hell are you doing this, Noah? Telling this kid what you haven't even told your own wife.*'

'*I haven't a fucking clue.*'

'*Rubbish! You know why, you're just scared to admit it. Go on. Admit it. Say it. You're scared shitless you won't live to make this next movie.*'

'*That's right, I am. And this youngblood might just might upon news of my death, get it together to make that film.*'

'I like Sense of Tumour – that's crankin', man – fuckin' majeek!'

'Thanks – I'll bear that in mind.'

'Just give me a mention in the credits, eh?'

My next move is to try and stack the odds in favour of his doing it – point him in the right direction – do the set-up for the pay-off after my death. If I can get him together with Ray then perhaps when they've lowered me into the ground and they are strolling away through the sun-dappled churchyard, Ray will ask this young lad what I'd been like at the last, and Richboy will tell him my story and the two of them will . . . Christ! Why don't I just tell this kid that I think I could die very soon and that if I do I want him to tell this story to Ray, tell him that my dying request was that he make the film and bring the kid on board as a thank you. Oh, no! That would be too simple for an alcoholic, even one who's twelve years sober. So instead I say:

'I could do more than that. I was thinking perhaps you'd like to meet Mr Molina. You could come on our next shoot, get a little hands-on experience?' Maybe then he'd think to tell my story to Ray, and the two of them . . .

'Wow! You mean that? Fuck, yeah, man! Thanks, Noah!'

'That's OK, er . . . Keifer?'

I realise I don't know his real name.

'No, Billy – like in Wilder!'

He laughs nervously.

'Or Kid?'

I wink at him. He shifts his weight to the other foot.

'Yeah, right.'

'Well, Billy. I'll be glad to do that for you, but I would appreciate it if you'd keep my plot to yourself . . . you know how it is.'

Saying this will almost guarantee that he'll spill the beans.

Billy makes a gesture to zip his mouth and actually crosses his heart. Then he pulls out a platinum Amex and offers to buy my meal. I let him. And as Yangos or Peter brings the bill, I realise that a minor miracle has taken place. I am in no pain and I haven't taken a piss break throughout the meal.

Billy and I step outside. The night is moonless and a cold north-easterly has sprung up. Simultaneously we pull up our jacket collars, and Billy offers me a lift in his car. Of course he has a car! And what a car! Parked in the sandy lot behind the restaurant is a rented Mercedes which Taxi Tom would kill for! In my head I already have my hand on the door handle when the moon pops out for a look and lights up the beach. I have an immediate need to be alone.

'No thanks, Billy. I could do with a walk.'

'Cool.' And he gives me a complex Harlem handshake which loses me half way through. He heads for his car.

'But I wonder if you wouldn't mind driving me to Limassol tomorrow?'

He stops mid-step and turns with a huge smile.

'I'd be honoured, sir.' – Sir?

He commits my address to memory and actually trots to his car. As I watch the Merc pull away and as Billy the Innocent beeps me goodnight, I realise I haven't even asked him where he's staying and feel like a selfish, jaded bastard for not offering him a sofa for the night.

So I walk for a good twenty minutes east along the beach toward the old Berlin Hippie haunt of Polis, now deserted and, according to Billy – who also managed over dinner to give me the full breakdown on the flora, fauna and geological strata of the whole peninsula – a complete shithole.

As I near the end of the beach, as if to confirm Billy's observations, the moon comes out full, lighting with Hammer Horror blue a pair of gothic pillars with wrought iron gates hanging off their hinges – the entrance to a deserted campsite nestling among tall eucalyptus. Twenty yards inside, the Reception building is a burned-out shell. A few yards further on, two Coke machines stand in the grass like gravestones, and beyond them, nestled under the trees, are two upturned caravans. Beside a clearing, the shower block has a wall missing and inside its tiles hang like bones. Christ! I'm on Cape Fucking Fear. This place looks like a deserted killing field with the smell of brine and rotting vegetation giving it the air of death.

Suddenly from deep in the shadows behind one of the caravans a deer breaks cover, bounds across the clearing and into the three-sided shower block. In blind terror he charges against the walls, once, twice, snapping his antlers until he lurches his way out, leaving streaks of blood on the white tiles. He takes one huge bound and is mid-air on his second when the double blast of a shotgun tears through the night. The deer spins on his axis and drops to the ground. For the second time today I smell cordite in the air.

'In Chrysochou also we love to hunt – Bang Bang!'

I run like hell back down the beach and throw myself to the ground like some stupid extra from *Full Metal Jacket*. There's another shot from the campsite. I let the sound die down then I ease myself up into squatting position, my back against the dunes. I sweat and pant like a dog in the moonlight. I must get my shit together. Come on, Noah. Somebody shot a fucking deer for God's sake! OK? OK I say to myself. I focus on the waves and try to match my breathing to them. I don't know how many crash on to the shore before I start to calm down, to bring the old Chi down below flood level.

I stay there, frozen in my squat, staring at the sea and wishing to God that Venus, in a gesture of forgiveness for my pissing in her pool, would ride in on her half shell with Clare and the girls and drop them off to see me – to comfort me. I wait by the dune all night for them to arrive. My bladder fills. I hold it tight. Then just before first light when it's clear my women won't be coming, I know it's time for me to go home and see them. Half way to my feet, I drop forward on to my knees, pain shooting through every joint. My lower abdomen is on fire. My balls are filled with acid and my dick, filled with slivers of glass, goes semi-hard in its confusion. Take a leak, Noah! Whatever it takes, take a fucking leak! I struggle with my fly and yank out. I bend him down and release my bladder neck. It's so dark now that I can't see a damned thing. But I can feel that the piss is thick. I reach down, put my finger into the stream and then into my mouth.

'Hey, bartender, what the fuck is this!? Blood and Urine with a twist? – I ordered a nice warm milk, you son of bitch!'

I start to laugh in that alkie way which tells me I have to get off this beach now or I could die here. And as dawn bleeds across the sky, I understand that in my fumbling lie, I had actually told Clare the truth on the phone. Things are much clearer now. I have got what I came to Cyprus for. I am now certain of one thing: I am alive. And I want to stay that way.

'You hear that, Death? You may be in my body, but I've got your fucking number now!'

I say these words out loud – loudly – a dawn affirmation as I rise shakily to my feet and start to walk Home. As I clear the dunes and hit the open beach, the sun's first rays hit my back and I feel a hesitant smile beginning and something close to confidence wells up in me as I start to sing to my Lodger from Hell – my cancer:

'Every move you make, every step you take, I'll be watching you.'

As I strain for the high notes on 'Oh, can't you see, you *don't* belong to me?' a bloody great crow breaks cover from the sea grass and flies away cawing a pissed-off caw. Sting I'm not! I stand and watch the bird flapping inland towards the horizon and, the waves pounding at my back, I let out a razor-sharp laugh.

The taxi pulls off Marylebone Road into the High Street. The usual February drizzle and a jack-knifed truck on the M4 have nudged the trip from Heathrow into the two-hour zone. I feel bloody awful. I had to make the cabbie pull over twice so I could piss. He was a real gentleman both times, cursing only lightly under his breath as he let me out in the relative shelter of a motorway bridge. On the second pit-stop, just before the Southall exit, a group of Asian kids in an old Escort slowed right down as they passed, and leaned on the horn.

'MILK IT, BABY! MILK IT!'

I weakly shot them the finger and for a split second thought of joining the National Front. Come to think of it, I could get a membership card from this cab driver. Non-stop from the airport his bullet head has strained over his left shoulder towards me, its twisted, chain-smoking mouth unleashing poisonous invective against fucking queers, lezzies – I wouldn't mind fuckin' one of them though – pakkies, coons and the cuntin' Common Market. At one point he suddenly stopped.

'What you do for a living then?'

'I make films.'

'Yeah? Most films are fuckin' rubbish. You know the best two fuckin' films ever made? *Die Hard* and fuckin' *Terminator* – and p'haps that fuckin' *Alien*. You ever met that Sigourney Weaver?'

'No, I haven't.'

'She's a fuckin' dyke. But I wouldn't mind slippin' her a length of Cockney! I'd soon have her fuckin' screaming to stop!'

I look out of the window as we turn off Thayer Street.

'Yeah . . . full of dykes and fags are films, they should send Bruce and Arnie in to wipe the whole fuckin' lot out.'

I lean forward and breathe in a bit of his fetid air through the sliding panel.

'Could you go up a bit further and turn on to Holly Street, please?'

'But that's past Wigmore Street, guv.'

I *hate* being called Guv. I want to reach through the open partition and whack him in the fucking teeth.

'I know, but I'd like you to go along Holly Street and then back down on to Wigmore Street, *if* that's not too much trouble, guv.'

He turns almost a full turn and looks at me with a sneer; his eyes look like they've been stolen from a corpse. He sucks a venomous suck of his stinking cab air.

'You're the governor.'

And as the cab swings hard into Holly Street I can feel him giving Bruce and Arnie orders to wipe out that poofta film director on their next assault.

I scan the steps of the Methodist church on the corner, home to a million AA meetings, some of which I've been known to attend. I'm looking for Robbie. Robbie can't stay sober. He often dosses against one of the church columns. He asks every recovering alkie for money, but hardly anyone gives him any.

'He'll only spend it on booze, you know. Invite him to come to a meeting instead, tea and a biscuit.'

I often slip him a bit of change, then forget about him. Now tonight I really want Robbie to be there. Tonight I want to give him at least a tenner. And if he goes out and blows the lot on Special Brew, then good luck to the poor bastard! But tonight Robbie's nowhere to be seen. Only a crusty blanket and one old tennis shoe lie at the bottom of the column where he should be. I feel a cold shudder run through me. I try not to see this as a terrible omen, but I can't help it.

The taxi pulls up in front of Wigmore Hall. The metre reads forty-six pounds and eighty pee. Wallet in hand, I step out of the cab and lean back in to pay. Not quite in slo-mo I count out the exact amount and no more into Bullet Head's grubby palm. His nails are bitten to the quick and edged with dried blood. For a century after I finish counting, he stares at his hand as though I've taken a shit in it, then looks up and fixes me with his yellow-flecked eyes. During the Mexican stand-off that follows, I try to place those eyes. It takes a while, but then I remember. That Saatchi and Saatchi 'Demon' poster of Blair! Some out-of-work actor had claimed them to be his, but they weren't. Nope! I'll bet a penny to a pound those eyes belong to this thick-necked Neo-Nazi. Then I shock myself by reaching in, folding the cabbie's fingers back over the fare and holding his clenched fist tight. I force a smile.

'If there's a God in Heaven, your next fare will be Chris Eubank.'

I turn quickly on my heel, duck under the glass and iron awning and into the outer foyer of the concert hall. The brassed and waxed doors shut behind me and silence Bullet Head's stream of obscenities. I stand there panting, looking down at the large W woven into the plush red carpet, separating tuft from tuft, my back turned to the bastard, daring him to follow me in. There's no bravery in it though. In fact it's the act of a coward. You don't come from Workington without learning a thing or two about the British caste system. One thing it does is guarantee the rich places of safety where the underclass, even its ghouls, fear to tread. This esoteric concert hall around the corner from Harley Street is one of those places.

I glance over my shoulder and see the taxi driving away. With a feeling of relief tinged with a bit of class guilt, I open the doors to the inner lobby and am greeted by Schoenberg. I am not a fan of Schoenberg. In fact I fucking hate Schoenberg and any music that sounds like his. If it weren't for the fact that Clare is playing part of what I'm hearing, I would think seriously about going back and risking hailing Hellcab again. I suppose when it comes to music, I'm still a Mod. I've trained myself to like classical stuff, and I like my bit of Mozart and Schubert, even a bit of Liszt. On a good day I can really push the boat out and handle Prokofiev or Mahler. And Pergolesi is guaranteed to bring a lump to my throat. But what my mother used to call 'dying cat' scraping, I've never been able to stand. It amazes me that my visual sense can be pretty sophisticated and I have no trouble handling a movie like Derek Jarman's *Blue*, but the sound equivalent is a kind of torture to me. One glance along my music collection will tell you what I listen to in times of need – soul music – give me Otis Redding over Bach any time.

But right now, I'd settle for anything but what I'm hearing.

I pad along between the alabaster, the marble and the 'head shots' in glass wall cases. I scan for a photograph of Clare. I want to see her in two dimensions before I see and hear her in the flesh and sound. Before I can find one, a voice speaks in a stage whisper.

'Excuse me, sir. May I help you?'

A round-faced young man with gelled hair is leaning out

of the box office. He beckons me with an earnest stage beckon. I stare at him and feel myself swaying slightly. I don't feel well at all. I glance up at the sparkling chandeliers and up to the clock above the doors to the auditorium. The name on the clock face intrigues me – CAMERER CUSS AND CO – and then I see the time – 9.03. Christ! The recital must be almost over. Schoenberg rises to a strident crescendo behind the doors and I feel an arm on my elbow. I turn to find Stage Boy giving me a stage look of concern.

'Are you alright, sir?'

'I'm just fine,' I lie. 'I'm a bit travel-worn, that's all.'

I pressure him slightly and explain that Clare Mathesson is my wife, and that it would mean the world to her and me if I could catch the last few minutes of her gig – I actually use the word 'gig'. I don't expect for a second that he's going to let me in, but to my surprise he produces a programme from nowhere and hands it to me while ushering me toward the Camerer Cuss Clock doors.

'You're in luck, Mr Mathesson. I have a seat that I use just inside these doors, but I didn't take it tonight because, well, because I'm ashamed to say I'm not much of a Schoenberg fan.'

I feel a strong surge of affection for him as he stage-peeks through the crack in between the doors, waits for a tiny lull and pushes me gently into the hall where I take his vacant seat.

As I enter, Clare looks up briefly from her cello. I'm far enough away that I doubt that she'll see that the interrupting Philistine is me. Etta is sawing away intensely at her violin and doesn't register my entrance at all. I breathe out and try to settle into the uncomfortable seat when a wave of nausea breaks over me. I close my eyes and ride it. It retreats leaving behind it a wash of pain in my kidneys. I grip on to the back of the seat in front of me as if I was on the big dipper and force myself to concentrate on the music. It's hard. The music is more painful than my pain.

Wait a minute! This music isn't painful, it *is* pain.

Now I find myself listening like I've never listened to anything before. I can actually hear the gaps in between the notes. High passages cut like scalpels, and harsh phrases burn like chemo. I clutch my lower abdomen. Now I can't tell if the pain is on the inside or the outside. I hold back a scream. Then just as I don't think I can take another second of agony, the music breaks through into a lyrical world, another plane of consciousness beyond the pain, and for an instant I am floating above myself, looking down as I open the recital programme for some further understanding of this man who has just become my palliative care nurse, who is using his sound picture of pain to cancel out mine. I want the music never to end.

The next passage blisters around me as I run my finger down the programme – 'Settled in California 1946 – ill health – asthma, dizziness, blackouts . . .' Then there it is – 'Severe heart attack – Schoenberg clinically dead – revived by an injection directly to the heart – "I have risen from a real death and feel quite well." ' Christ! I can't believe what I'm reading! Schoenberg took the big needle to the heart, came back from the dead and within five weeks wrote this string trio which now fills the air I'm breathing. The programme is shaking in my hand. I want to stand up and shout out loud what I've learned, to let out that scream which I stifled a moment ago and add it to the notes of my newly discovered genius, my partner in pain.

The strings pluck and cut to another peak as I look up from the programme and to Clare at her cello. Her arm swings back and forth, holding the bow as a scythe, and her blonde hair sweeps across her face like the wheat in a field she's harvesting. I fill with love for her. I want to fly across the auditorium, through those black sound holes into her cello, have her hold me and play Schoenberg on me for ever. Suddenly she flings her head back violently. Her hair blazes in the light. It seems to ride on the rising sound up to the mural in the cupola above the stage. My eyes follow . . .

And come to rest on the figure at the centre of the painting. It's a naked man standing against a turquoise sky, holding a ball of fire from which radiate rays of pure light. As if by some preordained force, I find myself being drawn into the fire, riding in on the music as if towards a blinding singularity. I tumble and spin into a pain-free heaven, faster and faster and faster, and I swear to God I'm grinning like the Cheshire Cat.

The air is filled with deafening applause and for a moment I think it's for me. Then I realise that the music has stopped and everyone around me is standing, clapping and shouting 'Bravo!' The Trio of the Kairos Quartet is on its feet, bowing as skillfully as it plays. David holds Clare and Etta by the hand and the three bow. Then they acknowledge each other's virtuosity with sweeping, generous gestures before taking the next bow and curtsy. This time Clare looks at Etta across David and winks at her.

The applause seems never-ending. The trio looks out over the audience, drunk on the response. Clare sweeps a look across the crowd and sees me. Her face lights up. She smiles broadly and starts to applaud directly at me. People beside me look at me. I'm bursting with pride, embarrassment and pain.

Desperately, I look back up into the ball of light in the mural, hoping it will draw me back in. But even before I can focus, it suddenly expands and explodes. Sheets of white hot flame suck the air out of the auditorium. My lungs implode and my innards fry. The cheers around me turn to screams and I am on the floor, rigid, eyes shut tight, almost unable to breathe. I am on the edge of passing out when I hear Clare's voice, clear and strong as she pushes her way through the crowd.

'Let me through. Please. Let me through. He's my husband.'

I force my eyes open and there she is above me, the light blazing around her head like a halo. I am delirious, almost ecstatic. As she bends toward me, I reach out, touch the back of her hand and say her name. Something goes very wrong. Like the stroke victim who tries to say 'I love you' and comes out with 'Fuck off!' I have 'Clare' clear in my brain, but by the time the word has gone over my vocal chords and through my lips, to my horror I hear myself saying:

'Kirstin.'

I see the look of bewildered hurt on Clare's face, but before I can attempt an explanation, I drift into unconsciousness.

THREE

We admitted we were powerless over alcohol – that our
lives had become unmanageable.

First of the Twelve Steps of AA

Ivy League university, north-eastern USA, autumn 1984

I walk the diagonal across the quadrangle and stop a few
yards from Freedom House. Its colonial walls are covered
with Virginia creeper which glows red like a Hell Mouth in
the last rays of this damned-near-perfect New England Fall
evening. For the hundredth time in the twenty minutes since I
stepped off Amtrak into this town built by Quakers and
weaned on Emerson, I check my watch. Five thirty-five!
Twenty-five minutes until I face the Ivy League Elders. Oh,
shit! There goes another of them now, baggy chords and polo
neck, ducking in to add bait to my trap. For two thousand
bucks, I've been shipped in by the faculty of this august
institution to read them extracts from my latest screenplay.
So Baggy and forty or so others like him will be on my every
word like shit on a shingle, making sure they haven't wasted a
penny. After all, I may be young(ish). I may have that Mid-
Atlantic speak. I might even be the hottest 'young' British film
maker. But am I art? Can I cut the academic mustard? Have
they thrown away all that gelt on someone who's turned out

to be an inarticulate flavour of the month, whose main credentials are good Art House box office and critical reviews in obscure European journals. I bet Baggy's sitting down now and thinking perhaps he and his colleagues should have had me up a few days beforehand so they could give me the 'once-over' and put a lid on me if necessary – play the he's-got-the-flu-lost-his-voice-very-very-sorry card. Yes, I'm sure they're all worried. I'm not. I'm fucking terrified. I'm also loaded. I've been hard at the Amtrak bar since I left Grand Central and in my gut there's six double vodkas. In my pocket, a pint of Jameson's. In my head there's two Valium and a quarter of a gram of clinically pure cocaine.

Ah, well! Needs must! So here goes! I try to take a step towards Freedom House. I can't. Terror has me rooted to this perfect herringbone brick path. I can't move a muscle. My leather jacket feels like my coffin. Only my watch wrist moves, right-angled up for viewing, it shakes a mad shake, blurring time in my face. I know this condition well. It is the last few frames of the Set-Up sequence before the Cut to the Alcohol Oblivion scene. But there is a way to avoid this cliché of a climax. If I can unfreeze now, sit down somewhere, and take a few deep breaths, there's a chance I can sober up enough to cut to the chase and do my Monkey Chant for the crowd. Oh, Christ! There's another Tweed scurrying in to the Hell Mouth. Wait a minute! I recognise him. That's Arthur Miller. No, it can't be. Hell, yes it can. Oh, please God make him turn back, then show me a seat where I can park and get into the right gear to do this thing. Miller doesn't change direction, but a voice does cut through the evening air.

'*There's a bench right in front of you, you blind, drunk bastard!*'

I look around – nobody. But sure enough, ten feet from me under a golden ginkgo tree, there's a bench I hadn't noticed before. It beckons me.

'*Come over, Noah. Sit on Me for a little of that Heaven and Salvation.*'

OK, if I can get one good shot of booze inside me, I can bypass blackout, reach the bench, sit down, and live to give this fucking reading. So, focusing every foot pound of energy in my body, I link up across the ether with Yuri Geller and will my right hand to move. I'm on the threshold of passing out with the pain of the effort when I manage to move a little finger. Sweat erupts from my forehead as I put a stranglehold on my bladder neck so I don't piss myself and my hand digs in to my jacket pocket to do what I've trained it to do in these emergencies.

'*Good boy! That's it – there it is on its side.*'

My fingers find the neck then the top and unscrew at the same time as my palm eases the Irish bottle out and on up to my mouth. I suck down a double then another without so much as a dribble down my chinny-chin-chin. I'm still locked on to the bottle neck like a baby to the breast when a beautiful corn-fed student comes towards me. She's wearing sprayed-on jeans and a T-shirt without a jacket. Her breasts bounce on the offbeat and her nipples push into the cool autumn air – Undergraduate Perfection – one of the perks of these college stints. Fighting the paralysing odds, my dick struggles to raise its head. No luck. Flaccid wins. The erection attempt backfires up to my face and comes out as an idiot grimace. Perfection thinks she's looking at a smile and flashes one back at me. Then she gets the Real Picture. For a second there's a Mexican stand-off as we both look at the bottle which I raise to her in a 'Well now you know' salute. She opens her mouth as if to say something, then thinks better of it. As she closes it again, I'd swear I can see love in her eyes, well, deep sympathy at least. But no, she side-steps me like I was dog shit and walks off.

'Cunt,' I mutter as I plunge the bottle back into my jacket, take two stumbling steps, and my arse hits the Salvation Bench.

I lean back, spread my arms along the back-rest, take a deep breath and look back out into the world. I go for six breaths in a row, using my diaphragm, pulling them deep into my fifth chakra, going for some kind of yogic epiphany. Yes, the booze and breathing's starting to work. Here it comes! The Focus Roll! The Big Dissolve from the Doom Dusk of a moment ago to what I now see before me – a truly beautiful evening – a magical evening even. God's liquid miracle cruises through my veins and calms me as the sky begins to redden. It's a miracle transformation from Hell to Heaven in Two Easy Swigs.

A single ginkgo leaf dances down in front of me to the ground. It is so simple, so perfect that I feel my eyes getting moist. But before I can shed a tear, a gust of air from nowhere blows the leaf off down the path and up into the sunset. As I watch it disappear I see beyond, on the other side of the quad, my Corn-Fed Perfection looking back at me. I give her a little wave. She hugs herself as if against the cold and hurries on. More ginkgo leaves begin to fall.

'She loves me. She loves me not. She loves me . . .' I whisper to myself as my hand reaches back into my pocket for my friend.

The oak-panelled reading room of Freedom House is the colour of 25-year-old malt. In front of French windows, on a linen-covered refectory table, waits the last supper of chips, dips and raw veggies, flanked by a pretty impressive array of booze. The bottles glint, Key-Lit by a heavy-duty chandelier and Backlit by the sun's last rays.

Through the window, in the middle distance, I can see my ginkgo tree and bench, silhouetted, look safe and peaceful.

Pre-show chat fills the room. Everyone knows everyone and I don't know shit. As I set up my script on the lectern, the bearded head of English, whose name I've already forgotten since our working lunch, gives me a little wave and a thumbs-up. I notice for the first time that he has an extra little finger – a half-formed sign of the Devil.

I stand behind the lectern and take in the congregation. No one is looking at me. Hell! I could just run out now, dash to the table, grab a fifth and duck out through the French windows and into the shadows. Why not?

'*Why not? Fuck it, Noah! Don't prove them right. Stay the course.*'

'*OK, I will! But just have a wee tipple to ease things along, alright?*'

'*Noah!*'

'*Just a teensy weensy one, I promise.*'

So, I'm just sneaking my hand toward my pint of Jameson's which I have placed, in case of emergency, on the ledge in the back of the lectern, when a door in the oak panelling not ten feet from me opens, and Arthur Miller steps in zipping his fly. He gives me a nod and takes a seat slap bang in the middle of the middle row. I pull my hand back from the bottle as if I've been electrocuted. And to make sure I get that extra jolt to short-circuit any escape plans and jump-start my talk, who should walk in the back of the room and take her place by the refectory table but my Corn-Fed Perfection in the black skirt and white shirt of a waitress.

Department Head turns around and gives her a little nod as he half rises out of his seat. On his signal, Perfection draws the curtains across the French windows, leaving a gap wide enough for air but narrow enough to block my exit. She turns back and looks right at me, and this time there's no mistaking – that's a smile and that's a little low-level wave like that of a lover who knows your secret. Raising one finger from my grip on the edge of the lectern, I return her wave and start to undo her blouse. I'm just about to get into bed with her when Department Head appears at my side, raises his six-fingered hand to silence the room and starts his superlative-ridden introduction. As he drones on I glance at Arthur Miller. His eyes are shut. What the Hell is he doing here? I search the panelling where he made his entrance for some clue. There's no door that I can make out. I Zoom-In tight and, with my best director's eye, Pan Right and Left scanning the panelling to the Voice Over of the Head as he peppers the soundtrack with words like 'watershed', 'hypnotic' and 'challenging'. I spot it! – the hairline join of the author's door in the panelling just as Department Head says:

'. . . and something of an enfant terrible . . .',
claps his arm around my shoulder and laughs an academic laugh that is obediently picked up by the room. Not by Arthur Miller, though. He still has his eyes shut.

'Well fuck you, Arthur, and the horse you rode in on!'

Silence. All eyes except his are on me now. So I open my screenplay and start to read the title page: 'OBJECTS IN TIIE MIRROR ARE CLOSER THAN THEY APPEAR – a screenplay by Noah Arkwright . . . Blah, blah, blah . . .'

Now for one person to read a film script out loud to a bunch of academics makes no sense. It must be as big a torture for those listening as it is for the poor sod trying to play all the parts and be a camera at the same time. INTERIOR – ROOM – NIGHT – A FIRE BURNS IN THE GRATE – CLOSE ON FLAMES – DISSOLVE TO – E.C.U. COW'S ARSE etc, etc. You might as well have an architect show his plans for a building to a group of keep-fit instructors. No. It definitely makes no sense at all. But academics have no sense and they are paying mucho dinero for this shit, so here I am doing it, and with luck and a little help from my friend under the lectern, I'll get through.

It all seems to be going well, then I make the mistake of looking at my watch. Shit! I've been reading for only six minutes and I'm already shagged out and the audience looks like the cast of *Narcolepsy – The Movie*. Most of them have their eyes closed. Those that haven't seem to be staring intently at the top of my head. Arthur Miller's bald head is bent forward, glinting in the light from the chandelier, as he peers closely at what appears to be an Amtrak timetable.

Panic rises. I look around for a bolthole – straight ahead – no exit! To the right – ditto. I check over my left shoulder to see the way blocked by . . . ME! as I come face to face with myself in a gilt-framed mirror. Yes! that's me alright! There's the single eyebrow over eyes set too deep and too close together, dominating a 38-year-old face which sits, almost good-looking, beneath a sixteenth of an inch of alcohol bloat. The flying jacket, black T-shirt and jeans look ten years too young, but there's enough lanky height to stay this side of acceptable in academia. If it weren't for the hair. Jesus! Where is my hair? I focus on top of my head where it should be. There, instead of my scraped-back, pony-tailed dark hair sits a road-kill ginger guinea pig. Where the fuck did that come from!? I struggle to find an answer, but draw a terrible blank. I stop reading. I can feel the crowd shift its weight to the other foot. I glance back at the mirror. The guinea pig taunts me.

Then I remember! The mad-dog high-noon image-change last weekend.

I've escaped to a friend's house on the Cape to plan some edits. His 'shack' on the coast road near Wellfleet overlooks the Edward Hopper house on the dunes beyond the bayberry dells. It has the swimming pool from heaven and the custom-fitted bar to hell. I can't do a stroke of work. I swim, drink, stare at the Hopper House, feel like a talentless piece of shit, then do up a couple of lines of coke and a couple of Irish.

All of the first day, I do this over and over again like some laboratory rat, until dusk when I pop a couple of sleepers and die for the night.

Next morning it's the same routine. At noon, my blood's flowing at ninety proof, my brain's a razor blade and the sun's burning my eyes out. I escape into the summer house beside the pool and the first thing I see is a bottle of hydrogen peroxide above the sink. I grab it. Then I scan the room. I'm looking for something – I'll know what it is when I see it. There! Beside the Shaker rocking chair, on top of a Shaker sewing box – a pair of pinking shears. I pick them up like a stoned surgeon and within two minutes my pony-tail lies dead at my feet and half the bottle of peroxide has been poured over my new spike cut.

The whole afternoon of that second day I sit shriven in the sun and bake my body and brain into oblivion. But this time I don't take a single drink or drug. The day sleeps like a snake in the sun. I do nothing . . . that I can remember. Until finally, getting undressed for bed, I look in the mirror to find that my hair has turned nicotine orange – it looks interesting. Big fucking deal! I salute my new barnet, turn in and promptly forget about it until now in this Ivy League room.

Now it doesn't look interesting at all. Now it's this fluorescent beacon warning the whole gathering that there's a mad, stoned drunk underneath it. KEEP YOUR DIS-TANCE – APPROACH AT YOUR OWN RISK! Oh, Christ! Now they know. Now they know the Big Lie. I must take their focus off it. Quick, Noah. Do something, anything.

So I start to read another scene, then Mid-Shot 'acciden-tally' knock my script to the ground, give an 'oh-silly-me' apologetic look and bend to retrieve it. On the way back up I take a detour and manage to swig a triple out of the

Jameson's. I'm still wiping my chin when I rise up from behind the lectern, but I don't think anyone has noticed. Nobody is staring at my hair any longer. Arthur Miller hasn't even looked up. I've got about twenty minutes to go. If I'm lucky I'll make it with only one more script drop. With renewed Dutch courage, I take hold of my script, look back out over the room and take the kind of measured breath which inspires audience-confidence in the speaker. Then I see Perfection staring. Her look is intensely focused, but not on my head beacon. She appears to be looking through me to something behind and I turn to see what it is – nothing – just more panelling. When I look back at her, she's busy folding napkins.

I finally finish reading the extract and mutter thank you. There's a gut-crunching silence and I start to take my first steps toward the booze table when the applause breaks out. Department Head is first to his feet, grinning from ear to ear and thrusting his claps towards me as if I'd just given the best Hamlet since Olivier. The whole room follows suit. It's comforting and terrifying. There's no way I can get my drink until the clapping dies down and the honour guard disperses. But the applause keeps building – well at least I think it does – I can't be sure. Maybe it's dying down. Maybe it was never there. Of one thing I'm sure as sin – Arthur Miller's ducking along his row and off out the door.

At the Afterchat, I manage three well-spaced, nicely paced Jameson's when, just as Department Head is asking me if I could possibly get his two teenage daughters comps for the New York premiere, I go into blackout. I think I manage to squeeze in a 'yes' before I 'leave'. Now in my case 'blackout' does not mean that I pass out. It simply means that I shut down my memory bank as a safeguard against future recall of loutish behaviour. Most times it's an unnecessary pre-caution and I am told later that not a soul had guessed I was

60

drunk – that I had behaved like the perfect gentleman. Other times I wake up in a police cell, and I am not told a damn thing.

This time I wake in the middle of the night in a room that isn't mine. In that brief pain-free, lucid moment before the three a.m. hangover kicks in, I cast my slit eyes around me. I'm in an attic on a child's bunk bed on top of a Power Rangers duvet wearing only my boxer shorts and T-shirt. The room is flooded by a Hunter's Moon from SFX which bathes my body with blue. The usual boy paraphernalia litters the floor around a fluorescent lime skateboard centre-piece. The walls are full of the usual Foot/Baseball crap, but my eye is drawn to a large poster on the back of the door which says simply EASY DOES IT in large letters. Pretty Zen for a kid who rates the Power Rangers.

'WHERE THE FUCK AM I?'

I mean to only think these words but I shout them out loud and release the safety catch on the hangover and it shoots into my brain like a dumdum bullet. I feel my grey matter swell rapidly, pulsing waves of nausea through my body. I try to shut my eyes, but they won't. All I can do is groan the same question out loud, over and over like some demented dead-of-night mantra.

The door and my eyes open at the same moment – Corn-Fed Perfection enters.

'Will you keep it down in here for Christ's sake! You'll wake Gustav.'

She's in her nightie and carrying a plastic bucket. Even with my brain now thumping my vision to a blur, I take in the firm outline of her breasts and thighs, backlit by the moon. My pecker gives a little nod.

'I'm sorry. I didn't—'

I don't finish as I sit bolt upright, whack my head on the top bunk frame and vomit all over the Mighty Morphers duvet cover. Still reeling, I try to harness the recoil momentum to swing my legs over the side, but as I double over I barf a McDonald's Golden Arch in Perfection's direction. Before it can hit the floor, she has the bucket under it and bags the whole chuck. Not so much as a tomato skin hits the floor. I struggle to my feet and, swaying, start to clap.

'You play Lacrosse?' I garble through flecked lips as another wave of nausea hits and I dive for the bucket. This time it's the dry heaves and the scorching pain of a gut trying to turn itself inside-out. Perfection kneels down behind me and wraps her arms tight around my stomach. Jesus! How does she know the moves so well?

'That wasn't funny. You're not funny. You're an asshole – a very unfunny asshole.'

I can feel her breasts and stomach pushing into my back, and I'm somewhere between Heaven and Hell as I gasp, vomit and snot pouring out of my nose and tear ducts, gripping on to the bucket and muttering the World's Shortest Prayer –

'Oh, God help me'

on a two-second tape loop. She's massaging my gut and whispering in my ear:

'He can help you. And He will if you let Him.'

The next heave layers in a new taste – blood. I wipe my chin and look at the back of my hand. There's the smear, black in the moonlight, smelling sweet over the acid bile. I cover it up with my other hand so Perfection doesn't see it, and rest my head on the rim of the bucket. It digs into my brow with a distracting, pleasing pain.

'What's going on, Mom?'

I manage to turn my ten-ton head to the side and take focus on a little boy, seven or eight, standing in the doorway, Side-Lit in one of those Shots that tear your heart out.

'It's okay, Gus, honey. Mr Arkwright isn't feeling too well. You go on back to Mommy's bed and she'll be down in a minute.'

Gus nods.

'Hello,' I say as I give Gus a little bloodstained wave. But he's already a shadow on the stair.

'Oh, Christ. I am sorry. I am so sorry . . .'

'The name's Kirstin. And I don't want a sorry. Are you emptied out?'

I nod like an obedient child, puzzled by her matter-of-fact tone. What the hell is she? A nurse? She gets up, hauls me effortlessly by my armpits to my feet, leads me to the bunk bed, folds me back into it, and from nowhere produces an ice-cold Coke.

'Drink this and sleep. We'll talk in the morning.'

In a glide, she's half way out of the door. 'And so we don't have the usual morning bullshit, the answers to the questions you were going to ask me are: Yes, I undressed you and No, we didn't fuck.'

And she's gone as my head hits the pillow in an emptying spin.

Morning sunlight floods the tiny, golden kitchen through a window which overlooks the campus below. I pour myself a third cup of coffee and wonder when Kirstin will be back. I've stumbled downstairs to find a note from her held to the fridge with a Budweiser magnet telling me that she'd taken Gustav to school and to help myself to coffee and Entemann's. That was half an hour ago. If she'd still been here then, I could have presented myself, freshly shaved, Visine-eyed, and holding the shakes at bay with first-waking will power. Not now. In these last crucial thirty minutes biochemistry has taken over and I have loosened my grip – or rather, I've had it loosened for me. Now I can feel chips of tooth enamel under my tongue, a five o'clock shadow has arrived eight hours early and my hands are shaking like The Dancing Saint's. I open the Bud fridge – not a can or a bottle to be seen. So I dig the empty coke vial out of my jeans and, just as I'd done a dozen times on Amtrak yesterday, scour around its neck with my fingernail. It was empty twelve times on the train and it's just as empty now. And, unusual for me, I'm carrying no spare. I'm totally without. So, instead of using the time before Kirstin comes back to browse through her small house for those intimate clues to her life history – as any normal person would – I go for the big ransack for booze, a stash, anything to take the edge off. Not a single fucking thing. Just more slogans like the one on the back of Gustav's door. THINK THINK THINK, ONE DAY AT A TIME, and LET GO AND LET GOD. Christ! Not only is she a nurse, she's a bloody God-squadder fucking sky-pilot! But somehow that doesn't jive – not with her language, not with the Bud fridge magnet. Empty-handed I go back to the kitchen, and there on the outside of the door is a photograph of Kirstin, no older than seventeen, standing next to Hunter S. Thompson. The Gonzo Man himself! – gun-toting journalist for *Rolling Stone* who once described Hubert Humphrey's talking head as 'two iguanas in a feeding frenzy'. And there, scrawled across the pic in the manic hand of the man himself is the quote from *Fear and Loathing in Las Vegas*: 'We were somewhere around Barstow . . . when the drugs began to take hold,' and under it: 'Love Hunter'. I'm just trying to get my reeling, hurting head around this when the front door opens and Kirstin walks in.

An hour later we're in her ancient but immaculate Plymouth Valiant, turning into an Anywhere USA shopping precinct on the outskirts of town. Kirstin, looking stunning in a red leather biker jacket and sipping on a Diet Pepsi, pulls up in front of a storefront church labelled Mt Zion Evangelical Free Church. She takes a long pull on her soda and turns to me.

'Are you ready for this, Noah?'

I don't know. In the last forty-five minutes, my world has been tilted to a slightly different angle and I'm confused. Kirstin, it turns out, is not a corn-fed student. She's a 25-year-old waitress on the catering circuit who was raised on a steady diet of booze and drugs, and who got pregnant by an Oakland biker when she was seventeen – the time when the picture with Hunter was taken. By the age of nineteen she was living with a junkie car mechanic in a trailer park in southern Rhode Island, shooting speedballs and drinking lethal cocktails of Niquil and cheapo bourbon. Baby Gustav had to more or less fend for himself. When he was found by the police wandering along the road to Westerly in nothing but his nappy, it led to arrests at the trailer and Kirstin being charged with criminal neglect. She ended up in a secure detox unit in a Pawtucket nut house.

That was five years ago and she hasn't had a drink or a drug since. She turns to me and puts her hand gently over my hand.

'Remember, Noah. You don't ever have to take another drink or drug if you don't want to. And when you are in there, all you have to do is stay quiet, listen and look for the similarities not the differences.'

What the Hell is she talking about? She sounds like a walking version of her slogans. I thought I was going to an AA meeting and here I am outside a Holy Roller Church with a woman who for all I know is psychotic and a talent scout for L. Ron Hubbard or some other madman. Jesus! The sweat's pouring off me and it's a cool autumn day. I thrust my hands into my jeans pockets for a bit of ball-hugging comfort and I feel something tucked away in a seam which

65

has doubled over in the wash. A coke vial! I'd packed a spare after all. Hallelujah! I feel a smile at the corners of my mouth. I squeeze Kirstin's hand and look her in the eyes.

'Yes I am ready, Kirstin. Don't worry, I'll be just fine.'

On the way in to the meeting, Kirstin stands next to the little blue and white laminated plastic AA circle and greets her other cult friends while I nip into the men's room and, not bothering with a spoon, do up half the Colombian Cola straight out of the vial. It burns the sinuses nicely, needlepoints those pupils on cue, and goes on to freeze-dry the brainpan, giving the whole head the Tingle di tutti Tingles. I fill a palm with water from the bog tap and chase the crystals with a snort up each nostril. Then I splash my face, tug the orange guinea pig into some semblance of order, and in a tribute to Roy Scheider in *All That Jazz*, look at myself in the mirror, click my fingers and say:

'IT'S SHOWTIME.'

The words come out at about a thousand decibels and bang around the porcelain and steel room and I couldn't give a toss if anyone waiting outside hears. With Pride in my Stride and Pep in my Step I step back into the hallway to be greeted by a barrage of unsuspecting handshakes and welcoming smiles. I grin and shake like a champion. By now I am feeling no pain at all and am accelerating to Warp Factor Two and on into deep space. But at the back of my coked-up brain I begin to get a nagging suspicion that I may have overpowdered my nose.

Five minutes later I'm in a crowded basement room staring at a backlit wooden crucifix above a folding table which sports two glasses of water and a yellow slogan. With maximum effort, I give it full focus and mouth the words to myself. 'WHO YOU SEE HERE, WHAT YOU HEAR HERE, WHEN YOU LEAVE HERE, LET IT STAY HERE.' Christ, now I'm on the set of *The Magus*. My brain decides to check out and lets the coke have full rein. I'd kill for a treble of anything alcoholic to take this buzz down a notch or two. My retinas vibrate like moth wings. I spy with my little eye, something beginning with . . . There, flanking the cross, are two dangling banners made out of that stuff the world maps were made of in the stone-age schools of my childhood – some kind of waxed cotton – covered in a nonsense blur of black and red words. Of course I can read what they say – with this level of coke super-vision I could read contract small print at fifty yards – but now, spent with the effort of reading the Who, What, Whatever fucking slogan, the only word I can retain is 'God' and that word makes me clutch, white-knuckled, on to the cold metal of my school-room chair. I'm just about to bend the tubular frame when, as if on an agreed secret signal, a blue-rinse woman in her sixties and gold-chained specs takes a seat at the teacher's table next to a guy in a too-small suit and large kipper tie who's a dead ringer for Pee Wee Herman. Holy Shit! I have to get out of here. I should be in some café planning tomorrow's meeting with Ray/Blue Sky, my ex-drugmeister, now mister-efficient-clean-living cinematographer. I should be storyboarding for fuck's sake not sitting in church with the cast from a John Waters movie. Suddenly I feel an arm around my shoulder and jump through the ceiling. I whip around to see Kirstin giving me a simultaneously concerned, reproving and reassuring look which only mothers can give. I drop my speeding look from her very sober eyes to her very sober breasts which peek out from her very open shirt, and give a massive sinus snort which turns half the heads in the room.

Suddenly Blue-Rinse pipes up with a voice like a six-cylinder engine firing on five.

'Hi! My name is Marlene and I'm an alcoholic.'

Much applause followed by a unified chorus –

'Hi, Marlene!'

'I'd like to welcome you to Mt Zion Thursday lunchtime Step Meeting of Alcoholics Anonymous. Can we have a few minutes' silence please to remember why we are here and those still-suffering alcoholics who have not yet made it to these rooms.'

Everyone freezes. Some bow their heads, some stare straight ahead, some seem to be waving at someone they know across the room. I try like buggery to hold back another huge coke snort.

'Thank you. The format of this meeting is a one-hour non-smoking session at which the speaker shares on one of the Steps – this week it is Step Three – for ten to fifteen minutes after which the floor is open to raised voice-sharing and ten minutes before the end we give you shy-sharers a chance with raised hands – speaker's choice. OK? It's a tradition at this meeting that we go round the room and introduce ourselves. This is not to embarrass you but so we can put a name to a face and say "hello". And if this is your first meeting – welcome – and remember what I was told on my first time, sit back, listen, try not to be afraid, and look for the similarities not the differences.'

Fuck me gently. What the fuck is this?

I am still trying to figure this out when each person starts introducing themselves with the same introduction that Blue-Rinse gave, with only the name changed. 'Hi! My name is BLANK and I'm an alcoholic.' Oh, shit! The intro is heading towards me with the speed and enthusiasm of a Mexican wave as I sit there sniffing maniacally, trying to dislodge any rogue crystals of coke. I'm bloody terrified. Out of control, yet braced rigid in my chair against what I know's coming my way. I sniff again and this time I feel a trickle of blood run down my top lip. I'm reaching to wipe it away when I hear:

'Hi! My name is Kirstin and I'm an alcoholic.'

There's my cue! I shoot out of my seat, blood now pouring out of my nose, and hiss like a boiler which is about to blow.

'My name is MINE and you're all full of shit!'

Knocking over my chair, I scramble backwards over people who don't even try to hold me back. Some are knocked out of their seats, and as I hit the back row, I feel my flailing knee make contact with some bone or other. I tumble out of the room, scramble up the steps and race across the parking lot making a strange wounded sound. I reach the six-lane highway and start running beside it, and I keep on running and stumbling, tears now streaming down my face, faster and faster until I stumble one final time to my knees. A car pulls up just ahead. The exhaust fumes belch over me and through their haze I see a door open, legs step out, and a man's voice says:

'Hey, guy. Are you OK?'

then . . . FADE TO BLACK.

A few hours later Kirstin holds my hand as we look across an acre of polished New England walnut at her doctor who's looking at my test results. I don't know how I got here. I'm not even sure if I'm alive. I vaguely remember being poked and prodded. I could murder a whisky, failing that a cup of tea – neither seems to be on offer. Dr So-and-so looks up and looks very, very serious. Oh, fuck! Here it comes. And sure enough it does. My liver is enlarged. My prostate is enlarged. My testicles are enlarged. There's traces of blood in my urine. My nostrils are enlarged and my septum has more holes in it than an ocarina. My blood alcohol content is off the scale. But my blood pressure is low, very low, almost reptilian. Doc is mystified by this last result, but tells me that he suspects it's the only reason that I am alive.

'Let me be blunt with you, Mr Arkwright. Do not be taken in by your semi-healthy outward appearance which might fool your film friends –'

I'm about to spit out an interruption but Kirstin crunches my fingers and shoots me a death look.

'I'll be absolutely clear with you. If you do not stop this mad consumption, you will be dead within three years – four at the outside. Do you understand what I am saying?'

My mind is racing. Four years! I'd be lucky to get two more movies made, more likely only one, and that's if I stay on a roll. What if it all falls apart? What if they discover I'm really an untalented lush, a drunken flavour of the month? My head starts to spin out of orbit.

'Please somebody – give me a drink. For God's sake, I need a drink. No, you don't. Yes, I do. No, you don't.'

'Yes, I do,' I say quietly. Kirstin squeezes my hand again, this time gently.

'You need to ask yourself, Noah. "Am I sick and tired of being sick and tired?" '

Dr So-and-so nods wisely – I bet the bastard did the same when he asked Kirstin the same question – Christ, I'm stuck in Slogan Hell: I want to pour vitriol over the both of them and give them lit matches. A voice more powerful than the one usually bickering on at me in my head speaks up.

'Take a look behind those slogans, Noah, and see The Truth.'

This time I don't argue. I flip through all the slogans from EASY DOES IT in Gustav's room, through WHO YOU SEE HERE at the church up to the SICK AND TIRED in this room and there, on the back of each is the same sentence, in my handwriting, flickering in silent animation:

'My name is Noah and I'm an alcoholic.'

I want to say it out loud, but I am too sick, too tired, and all that I can muster is a slow nod and the strangled choke of a captured animal.

* * *

It's three in the morning and Kirstin holds me from behind in her bed. She breathes deep and even as our hearts beat in unison. There has been no sex between us, and since the visit to Doc So-and-so, I know there never will be. And that's just fine, bewildering but fine. I never thought I would be able to be in bed with a woman without pressing for a fuck. Now here I am with the woman who only yesterday brought on a boner with a glimpse of cleavage, her Mount of Venus pressed into my arse, and the only arousal I feel is one of deep gratitude and fear. Actually, I'm lying here, wide-eyed in this moonless room, limp-dicked and scared shitless. Somehow, in the doctor's office, somewhere in between my 'Yes, I do' and my walking out of the door, I'd agreed to check into Kirstin's trusty detox unit in Pawtucket – the secure wing so I can't change my mind and do a runner. Why the fuck did I do that? I've got my meeting with Ray. The film can't wait.

'I've got a life to live for God's sake!'

Kirstin moves in closer, holds me right across my heart, reads my mind and speaks very clearly.

'All that can wait, Noah. Just do this thing and then nothing in this world will stop you. You'll make a thousand movies.'

She pulls me even closer. For a second we are one and I am hugging myself, my fear draining away, and I am sure I have just heard the voice of God, or at least an angel. I drift into a dreamless sleep.

FOUR

They're coming to take me away. Ha! Ha!

Song title

It's eight thirty in the morning. Gustav is running round like a blue-arsed fly morphing and zapping everything in sight and Kirstin is trying to get his lunch box packed. The taxi is on its way and I'm trying to reach Ray at his motel. He drove up from New York late last night so we could drive out to some inn he knows in some quaint 'tucket' and have an edit meeting by the sea. I have the shakes. I'm on my fifth dial attempt.

Kirstin grabs the phone out of my hands.

'Here! I'll do that! Talk me through the number. Gus! Quit with the Power Rangers, get your sneakers on and check you've got your homework! Noah, you try taking a few deep breaths.'

I reel off Ray's number and obey the breathing order. My nose is useless, completely crusted up with dried blood, so I take big gulps through my mouth in between gasping out the digits. By the time Kirstin has finished dialling, I'm hyperventilating and the old familiar dry heave is flexing its muscle down in my gut. She holds the phone out to me, and I get it to my ear just as Ray answers. I shoot straight from the hip, well, shakily from the hip.

'Hello, Ray. Look, I won't be able to make our meeting

72

today. Something has come up which . . .' I race along the edge of the chasm between me and the next thought, desperate to find a place narrow enough to leap over.

'Let me make this easier for you, Noah. I've been waiting for your call. I was there yesterday lunchtime . . . at Mt Zion . . . the church . . . the AA meeting.' Ray's Brooklyn clipped words take a hundred years to sink in. Then, as if it would explain anything, 'I came up early – thought I'd catch a meeting.' Silence – then: 'I guess since you've finally come in from the cold, I can break my anonymity with you. Next month, God willing, I'll have been in the Fellowship three years – since we got back from the shoot in Greece – remember the calamari deal. I'm proud of you, man.'

My head spins. This is making no sense.

'You were at the fucking meeting?'

I glance over at Kirstin. She's got a smile on.

'What is this, a conspiracy?'

She throws up her hands and gives her slogan reply:

'THERE ARE NO COINCIDENCES.'

I start to laugh and I can't stop. I simply stand there, shaking and laughing with Ray's voice squeaking out from the phone which hangs at my side. Kirsty gently takes it from me.

'Hi, Ray. This is Kirstin. I'm a friend of Bill W's. I'm the one who took Noah to the meeting . . . that's right – blonde – red jacket . . . Yes . . . he's fine . . . well, you know . . . the usual . . . Yes . . . he's agreed to go into treatment . . . No . . . right here in Pawtucket . . . same place I detoxed. Excuse me?'

She glances over in my direction and laughs a small laugh.

'Oh, yes it's that alright . . . the cab should be here any minute . . . Well, yeah, that would be great if you think he'd go with you . . . he doesn't want me along . . . Right . . . you got a pen handy? –'

I knock the phone out of her hands on to the floor and it splits in two. I pick up the broken mouthpiece and scream down it. 'I'LL GET THERE ON MY OWN GOD DAMN YOU! YOU HEAR ME, RAY? RAY! YOU SHOULD HAVE TOLD ME, RAY . . . YOU SHOULD HAVE FUCK-ING TOLD ME!' And I'm banging the dead phone on the floor and crying like a milk baby.

'Go straight to Bradwell hospital – do not stop to collect $200 – and here's twenty for your trouble.'

Kirstin gives the cab driver twenty dollars then leans in the back window to where I sit petrified in the corner of the seat clutching my overnight bag and a cup of strong, black coffee. Over the past hour I've made a deliberate effort to behave normally, maturely, appropriate to the situation. I've apologised profusely to Kirstin, promised to buy her a new phone, showered, shaved, packed with an outward calm and even given her Ray's phone number so that the two of them can exchange slogans of concern about me. By the time I've done all this, Kirstin is convinced that I am sane enough to go alone in the taxi. The twenty bucks to the cabbie ensures her peace of mind. As the car drives off, I turn and return her caring wave with my mind on something completely different.

Heading north through town, as the driver yaks cabbie yak, I scan the ten a.m storefronts for a bar that shows signs of life. For a good five high-tension minutes there's nothing and the shops start to give way to suburban housing. I feel panic rising and resort to the prayer of the condemned man – 'Dear God, just this one last time, please, and I'll be good for ever and ever Amen.' The cab turns the next corner and there it is: The Hair of the Dog! And it's open! Hallelujah! Fifty dollars in my hand, I lunge over the front seat, thrust them in front of the driver's face, and say with the authority of a desperate man:

74

'Pull over here and wait.'

I order tequila doubles – four of them with salt and lime. I want that hard hit sandwich between the chloride and the acid. The bartender does his job and lines them up without raising an eyebrow. I do mine. Ten minutes later, I get back into the cab with four liquid worms in my gut and a small bush-fire starting in my veins. I start to hum a song from childhood – the one that never fails to fan the old flames. In a reflex response to the tune, I ask the old question – How did I get here from there?

It's embarrassing to even think about the answer – it's pure Monty Python. Those bastards! They nobbled the working-class story for good – nobbled it so well that a true northern childhood hardship story can't be told any more without Michael Palin strolling through. But the truth is I *was* a snake-belted, grey-shorted, motherless kid from the council estate in Workington whose dad, after his wife's death and unable to cope with the loneliness of it all, topped himself by jumping into a vat of molten metal at the foundry where he operated an overhead crane – cue John Cleese as the foreman! I was seven at the time. The works management was too damned cheap to respectfully bury the contents of the vat – Dad was a small man so there weren't enough minerals in him to upset the balance of the metal – and business is business! So we didn't have so much as a fucking trace of my dad to put underground and to this day he remains undead, still working for the bloody foundry. I bet he's still out there working his arse off as some bit of guttering on a Sussex barn conversion or as a turnstile on the London Underground.

I was an only child, no big sister or brother to fold me in a caring wing, so Dad's sister and her husband – Aunty Janet and Uncle Bart – took me in (cue Idle and Cleese!). Janet kept a six-foot ship's anchor in the bathtub, wore wellies all year, a tea-cosy on her head in extreme winter conditions and loved me more than Dad could have hoped for. Bart worked shifts at the foundry, and after his brother died didn't speak a word to anyone except me, and a few 'yes's and 'no's to Aunty when pressed hard.

I was not unhappy and I was not sad in my 'We lived in a hole in't road' world. I was numb to all that. Numb, that is, to anything but fear. I was terrified of what I didn't know, of the unnameable something – of Fear itself I suppose. So to protect myself, I sucked the air out from everything so I could have a bloody great vacuum around me twenty-four hours a day. I loved nothing and nobody. I hated to be touched by anyone, including myself, but I talked a good talk, pretended a good pretend, and was known by the neighbours as a polite and caring young man who would go a long way. Their opinion was confirmed one day when a gypsy, a genuine Romany-speaking Zigeuner, and her daughter came round to Aunty's door selling clothes pegs. She read my palm. After tracing her finger on it for an eon, she looked me in my child's eyes and spoke in her nomad tongue. Her daughter translated.

'He will leave this place. He will go very far. When he is in his middle years he will be very very ill.'

When the little girl said this, Aunty told her to tell her mum that was quite enough, gave her a sixpence and dragged me back into the house

'Load of mumbo jumbo . . . nothing but thievery and roasting hedgehogs. Spawn of the Devil himself!'

But how right that Zigeuner was! I've come a bloody long way in my thirty-eight years. Further than most even dream of. When I was barely eighteen, I left Aunty and Uncle and took the 'hole in't road' with me. I've carried it nearly twenty years around the world a dozen times or more, and how-ever bright-lights-and-big-city the outside has been, I have crawled back into that hole every night, drunk, drugged and feeling that nameless fear. And if I carry on with that same old shit pattern long enough, I'll do serious damage to my body and soul, get deathly ill and make the second part of the gypsy's prediction come true. If I go at it hard enough I might even drop dead mid-line, mid-swig, mid-fuck, or even all three at once.

But not just yet, I suppose. No, no, Nanette, not yet! I still must want to live or I wouldn't be in this cab right now heading for the Funny Farm and all points beyond.

As the taxi pulls off the beltway into the hospital grounds, I palm a miniature vodka from my pocket – a safety purchase from the Hair of the Dog – glance in the driver's mirror and meet his full gaze. Fuck it! What's to hide. I raise the Smirnoff in a toast and down it in one. I find the crunch of the gravel on the thousand-mile driveway calming, strengthening. I even begin to feel something like a sense of resolve creeping upon me, when the final lines of a Beckett play pop uninvited into my head. Slurring, I intone them:

Perhaps my best years are gone. When there was a chance of happiness. But I wouldn't want them back. Not with the fire in me now.

I throw my head back, laugh like a maniac and shout out loud at myself:
'YOU PRETENTIOUS CUNTING FUCKWAD!'
The driver turns to look at me, his taxi swerves on to the manicured verge, and he has to do a nifty move to bring us back on track. He mutters so I can hear him loud and clear, 'Psycho – crazy Limey asshole!' and pulls on to the statue-guarded forecourt.

The hospital is colonial and columned with the biggest wraparound porch in America. Gnarled wisteria roots hug the base of the clapboards and that old fire-red Virginia creeper cascades from the guttering. I could be arriving at a Newport mansion for that next movie fund-raiser, to drown myself in Dom Perignon and lusty society women. But any hopes in that direction are shattered when the gracious front door opens, a man bounds down the steps, trots over to the cab and opens my door with a flourish. I can't believe my eyes. The cab driver can't stifle his laugh which says 'We're at the fucking loony bin alright!' My greeter is wearing a Doctor Kildare jacket, a red clown's nose and a straw boater with a huge sunflower rammed in its band. I'm just about to tell the cabbie to get the hell out of there when the clown leans in and grins at me.

'You must be Noah. Kirstin called an hour ago to say you were on your way. We were just starting to get worried.' Then he clocks my bewildered, fearful stare, breaks out laughing and points at his nose. 'Oh, this. Gee! I forget I'm wearing it. Sorry if I scared you. We're having our Smile Revolution Week – a laugh a day keeps the doctor away!' He then does an amazing pirouette, followed by a thunderous fart which must have come from some gizmo squeezed in his pocket, grabs my arm, yanks, and I'm out on the forecourt, bag in hand, watching the cab pull away. The driver puts his arm out of the window and gives me the finger. I scream loud enough to open heaven –

'FUCK YOU!'

Then I just stand there swaying in the Perfect Colonial Breeze shaking with anger and terror until . . . A hand grasps my arm gently but firmly.

'Come along, Noah.'

Harry, that's Sunflower's name, walks me up the front steps through an open front door, into a blood-red foyer, through some swing doors and down a long, light-filled corridor edged with flowers and paintings.

'These, Noah, are the work of our guests. Wonderful, aren't they?'

'Is that what I am now, Harry? A guest?'

'Not until you've been processed by Don.'

'Who's Don?'

'You'll see.'

I'm chewing this over when a stumpy nurse wearing rabbit ears passes by wheeling a drug cart.

'Hi, Harry!'

'Hi, Doll!'

Harry squeezes a second pocket gizmo and his sunflower squirts Thumper right in the face. She laughs and walks on. I crane my neck to get a better look at the 'sweet trolley' selection – mmm, looks interesting.

Outside the triage room, Harry shakes my hand and palms me a red nose.

'It's optional.'

He takes a few steps then turns back to me.

'You'll be fine, Noah, don't worry. We take our jobs here very seriously.'

I nod and watch Harry walk away. As he turns the corner he does another little spin and fart. Despite myself, I start to laugh. A hysterical edge is beginning to creep in on top of it when a mechanical voice says: 'Come in, please.'

Inside the triage office is a tiny crumpled man in a tiny wheelchair. He's not exactly Stephen Hawking, but this man has not tripped the light fandango in a long time. His greeting has come from the microphone he holds near a tracheotomy hole in his throat. He also wears a red nose and a huge rosette which reads: 'Hello, my name is Don. I'm your triage nurse. Tell me your problem.'

Well, in for a penny, in for a pound! I pop on my red nose and give Don a little wave.

'Hello, my name is Noah. I'm an alcoholic, drug-crazy arsehole.'

Don pops the mike back over his throat hole.

'Would that be a . . . r . . . s . . . e, or a . . . s . . . s . . . hole, Noah?'

He looks me straight in the eye, smiles and winks.

Now I don't know whether to laugh or cry. I stand outside the scene and put my director's eye on it. Fantastic stuff – the kind of prime footage you kill for. So here I am – the Whizz-Kid film maker furiously making mental notes, investing in my future as if I dealt in pork bellies, while a mechanical quadriplegic midget checks me into a mental hospital.

The small voice at the back of my mind is repeating over and over, firmly:

'This is insane, Noah. Stop being a total shithead.'

It is interrupted by Don's electronic voice, which – incredibly – has taken on a soothing tone. (How the Hell can he do that?)

'Don't be so tough on yourself, Noah. The next few days are going to be hard enough. Now why don't you tell me something about yourself?'

I'm stuck. Without words or even an image to go on. The tequila worm is busy in my brain, sucking, vacuuming up every thought around. I want to talk, but I don't want to run off another smart-arsed platitude. Don gives me a kind look which in any other circumstance would make me puke. But this is genuine, encouraging, trying to help me over the hurdle.

'What about a funny story?'

'A funny story?'

'A funny story.'

Funny story? I scan the brain file – nothing funny at all – too drunk. Suddenly the tequila worms turn and I flash back to South Carolina. It's all there in wide-screen high-resolution Technicolor stock, projecting itself on the inside of the front of my aching skull. I start telling Don what I see. I feel 'on', clear and lucid. There's not a hint of a slur in my voice.

'It's 1972, and Blue Sky and I were on the interstate just north of Charleston in a VW microbus painted acid-green with orange polka dots. I'd been in the States for two years. I'd come over to do a Rockumentary on Black Sabbath in the park in Atlanta as soon as I came out of film school and I'd been in the Deep South, deep-stoned, ever since. I met Blue during the Sabbath shoot when, as I was filming some filler of a Cajun Rock warm-up band, he came out of the crowd with his hundred-pound Dobermann on a leash. The dog was wearing a blue-print bandanna. Toking heavily on the thinnest joint in the universe, Blue told me that all the dogs in my movie must have bandannas on. If I didn't get every dog in sight bandannad up by the time Black Sabbath hit the stage in a couple of hours, the project karma would be fucked and every foot of film I was shooting would be fogged. I was about to tell him to get fucked, when he handed me the joint which I took like Pavlov's dog. One hit and I jumped over into Blue's universe where he was making perfect sense. I put the shoot on hold, gave him cash and sent him off to get enough bandannas to cover a canine invasion.

'An hour and a half later Blue hasn't come back. Serves me right. How could I have been so stupid, so fucking gullible to give a guy who smokes the thinnest, strongest joints in the universe thirty dollars to buy bandannas. I cursed myself and him, locked the Bolex in the boot of my hired Oldsmobile and went looking for Blue. I had thirty minutes, forty-five maximum, before Black Sabbath came on and I had to start shooting again. Fucking karma. I'd give the bastard karma – karmfuckingrama! I was coming out of my third Head shop on my Peachtree search when I saw him across the street, sitting outside the C&S bank on the corner of thirteenth. On top of the bank was a billboard painted in Kosmik Kolours. It showed a naked longhair curled up in the foetal position inside a hypodermic which was engulfed in flames and the naughty, naughty hippie was coyly covering his dick and screaming for his useless degenerate little life. Underneath, feeding the flames, was the slogan: H IS FOR HELL!

'As I am taking in this propaganda, I am suddenly drowned in sound and almost flattened to the pavement by a powerhouse downdraft. I cover my ears and look up to see a helicopter hovering above the bank, just above a kind of flag-pole with a large canvas C&S bag hanging off it. The co-pilot leans out of the chopper, unclips the bag and the copter veers off like a dragonfly from Hell. Blue is on his back on the pavement below screaming, tearing at his hair, with his dog nuzzling him like a Stalag 17 nursemaid. I run over. He's shouting at the sky. "MOTHER FUCKER! YOU CALL THAT FUCKIN' FLYING? MOTHER FUCKING PECKERWOOD . . . I COULD FLY! I COULD FLY AND LAY DOWN THAT NAPALM LIKE I WAS FLAMBÉING A FUCKING CRÊPE!" I try to get near him but the dog snarls at me. Its teeth glint in the sunlight! Christ! It's got metal teeth. It's got bloody stainless-steel choppers. He suddenly reaches inside his jean jacket and whips out a brown paper bag from the Piggly Wiggly Supermarket and empties twenty or thirty multi-coloured bandannas on to the ground. He picks them up and starts throwing them at passers-by. "ALRIGHT, YOU GOOK MOTHERS – HERE'S YOUR FUCKING HEADBANDS – STRAP 'EM ON, YOU SONS OF BITCHES, AND LET ME SEE WHAT YOU'RE FUCKIN' MADE OF!" And he reaches behind his back and comes out with a ten-inch combat knife and starts making random, flashing slashes through the air.

'The cops appear from nowhere, and Blue seems to instantly evaporate in their midst. One minute he was back in Vietnam on the pavement and the next his waist-long hair is flowing out of the open window of the police cruiser as it heads, wailing, downtown.

'I'm left standing there, short of breath and shaking, when I realise I'm holding Stalag the Dobermann on his rainbow-braided rope leash. He's whimpering and shivering harder than I am, when suddenly he looks up to the sky and starts to growl – baring those teeth. I follow his gaze to see what's spooked him and there, on the top of the building on the opposite corner, above the Wholemeal Veggie restaurant is another billboard, facing the C&S junkie billboard. This one is painted à la Norman Rockwell. Again there's flames in it. Only this time they come from the roof of an All-American suburban ranch-style house. A young boy in his pyjamas is being carried out of the burning building by a cop with blond hair, no beer gut, and a uniform straight from the dry cleaner's. I swear he's even managing a smile to the camera as he gives the child mouth-to-mouth resuscitation. Underneath in two hundred-point Helvetica Bold are the words: AND SOME DARE TO CALL HIM PIG.

'Stalag starts barking furiously at the cop in the sky and I feel a rush of affection for this Hellhound. I risk patting him on the head.

' "I know just how you feel, boy."

'Miraculously he calms right down and nuzzles into my inside leg, disturbingly near my crotch. I ease myself away and start to pick up the bandannas from the pavement. Stalag gets beside me, picks one up and looks at me for approval. Christ! If it wasn't for the metal smile, he could be on the lid of a chocolate box.

'Just then a mighty roar goes up in the park as Black Sabbath hit the stage and break into their opening number.

And where is the dedicated, Whizz-Kid Rockumentary film maker? He's taking a bandanna out of the mouth of a dog with steel teeth ten blocks from his camera which is locked away sensibly in his sensibly locked car.'

I pause. I'm out of breath telling the story. Don is taking notes but pretending not to. Normally this would make me furious, but it doesn't. In fact, it feels like a compliment. He looks me in the eye and smiles. I can't tell if he's engaged or fucked-off.

'That's a bitter-sweet story, Noah – a funny bitter-sweet story.'

'Well, actually Don, that was only "roll credits" stuff. I should have cut to the chase earlier – that's the really funny bit.'

And before Don can stop me, I'm off again, motor-mouthing. Perhaps if I can spin this story out long enough, I won't ever have to leave this room in which I feel curiously safe.

'So we're on I-95 – me, Blue Sky – real name Ray Molina – and Cupcake – a.k.a. Stalag – and we are stoned out of our skulls – a six-pack of malt liquor between us, a couple of Thinnies of Mauie-zowie sinsemilla dope and a tab of window pane acid apiece. I've come to trust Blue's driving under any conditions. He said that he'd flown Huey missions in Vietnam so fucked up they'd had to lift him into the chopper and strap him in. This mission we're on now is to hook up with some basket weavers who, somewhere on the roadside south of Charleston, tout their wares in Gulla, a dialect which is a direct descendant of the mother tongue of their ancestors in Angola. We're to shoot a short documen-tary for Public Television. I take care of the camera, and Blue, the quickest learner in the Tropic of Cancer, is my sound man, grip, best boy, gaffer all in a glorious one. We're a good team. But there's a major difference between us – he can work stoned – I can't. So tonight we'll have to find some Monkey Farm, Alligatorland, Peanut Motel so I can catch a few hours' stoned kip. Blue won't sleep. He'll sit through the night toking, going through stoned to some kind of working plateau beyond.

'The Stones' *Exile on Main Street* is blasting out, the whole bus is a sound box. It's like sitting in the heart of a two hundred-watt speaker. Blue is driving steady, but the rest of the night traffic is crazy. Trucks overtake us too fast. Cars scream by with horns being leaned on. Blue shoots them birds as they go by, but they still keep on coming, fast and furious.

'Then there's the blue whirligig light as the State Troopers cruise up behind us. Blue pulls over, cuts the stereo and the engine and tells me to stay cool. After what seems like a century the trooper taps on my window. I roll it down, trying to get some rhythm to my breathing.

'Smokey leans his scrawny face into the bus and says:

' "What the fuck do you boys think you are doing?"

'Blue puts on his best college boy voice and apologises:

' "Sorry, officer. Was I going a tad over the speed limit?"

'The cop tilts back his hat.

' "You stoned out motherfucking hippie piece of shit! You ain't doing no speed. You are standing still in the goddam fast lane of goddam Interstate 95."

'He points his flashlight into the rear of the bus and Cupcake snarls at him, teeth glinting. The trooper leaps back ten feet, shits himself, calls for backup, rebounds to the open window and thrusts his 347 service revolver through the window and, one eye on Cupcake, asks us ever so slowly, ever so politely, to step down from the veehickel.

'It seems the cop was right. We were standing still on the highway. We must have run out of petrol, gasoline, juice, and been tripping so hard we hadn't noticed. For god knows how long we'd been sitting there, listening to *Exile on Main Street* while countless tons of metal swerved past us at a trillion miles an hour. And there was not so much as a scratch on our orange polka dots.

'This I need to remember whenever I'm tempted to say I'm unlucky in life.

'So the judge at the Charleston County Court looks Blue and I square in the eye, his face a trimixture of loathing, disbelief and repressed laughter. He shakes his head and says: "I swear to God, I don't know what to charge you boys with." Then he shuffles his legal briefs, thinks for a moment and breaks into a bilious smile. "I got it" (he goes for a big dramatic pause here), "I'll charge you with Dangerous Parking." '

I drop my hands to my knees like a schoolboy who's just read out an essay and scan Don's face for a response. For a second he's impassive and then he chuckles, but not for long enough and I feel cheated, disappointed by him. But before I can get too resentful Don extends a three-fingered right hand in which he holds a paper and I notice that the skin on the deformed hand is beautiful. I am seized with an urge to kiss it. As if he senses this, Don activates a button on his desk with his left foot and jabs the paper at me. I take it. It's my admission form.

'Please sign on the bottom line.'

In no-nonsense instruction mode, Don's voice sounds like the talking lifts at Covent Garden Tube, and I find myself stifling a nervous, frightened laugh as I sign the document which says I voluntarily commit myself, agree to any necessary administrating of drugs (yes please!), and will not wet the bed or be rude to nurses blah, blah, blah . . .

As I hand Don back the paper, Harry appears at the door and Don hands it on to him.

'There, Noah. You're signed and sealed, now Harry will deliver you.'

And he holds out his hand again. I take it in mine. His grip is strong and his skin is as smooth as it looks. I feel drained, insignificant, unworthy, and incapable of letting go.

'That was a fine story, Noah. A fine and funny story. Thank you.'

Again Don gives me that smile and that wink. Then he tries to reclaim his hand from mine, but like the man being dangled out of the burning building by the fireman and told to jump, I tighten my grip – scared shitless to let go.

'Could you please help me, Harry?' says Don calmly and mechanically.

Harry nods, firmly prises my hand off Don's and gently frog-marches me out into the corridor and trots me towards an elevator whose doors are closing. We nip in just in time and Harry presses floor seven, leans back against the wall, takes off his red nose and disconnects his sunflower from the water reservoir in his pocket. He shoots me an unfunny smile, reaches over and takes my nose off too.

'No tricks or noses on the seventh floor – house rules.'

Christ! I've never seen a bloke change so quickly! There's not even a hint of a joke in Harry as he stands hard and impassive against the stainless-steel wall of the elevator. This is the guy who half an hour ago greeted me like his long-lost child. Now he can't even look at me. He remains completely rigid, his face broadcasting far and wide that he is now on very serious business, until, as we pass by the fourth floor, he gives his upper lip an Elvis twitch and lets out a very real, humourless fart – a serious, stinking fart of the first order. And the bastard doesn't even acknowledge his action, never mind apologise for it.

I'm reeling, gagging on booze and bumhole methane when number seven lights up and the elevator doors ping open letting in vital oxygen. As I gulp down fresh air with a hint of disinfectant, Harry puts his hand firmly in the middle of my back and shunts me out into the corridor.

'Here we are!' he says flatly as he presses the red button beside a door which looks like it leads to a nuclear bunker. As a million electronic locks slide back and the door glides heavily open, I get the distinct feeling that this is not going to be a rerun of *Country Club Detox*, the lightweight movie that I starred in in Wiltshire two years ago, or *The Baby Who Didn't Cry*, that tear-jerker about my post-partum detox thirty-eight years ago. In fact, my gut tells me this film I've been cast in has been scripted by William Burroughs and is to be directed by Idi Amin. My job? I'll be playing a shit support role – one of the tortured and the damned who's sitting in the corner of the cell, nameless and without any lines.

When the door shuts as seriously as Harry behind me, my suspicions deepen. This definitely looks more like a psych ward than a detox unit. For starters, beyond a plate-glass window in what I take to be the recreation room, a guy with a pink mohawk plays table tennis with himself. He's zipping back and forth, hardly missing a shot. God knows what his problem is, but one thing is certain, he isn't here because he likes his sherry too much. Then I remember my own orange-spiked coiffure. I reach up to check that it's still there and a young woman slides past wearing yard-long braids and kangaroo slippers. Maybe I'm wrong. Maybe this isn't a psychiatric ward. Maybe it's some kind of club for people with strange hair. I don't know. I don't really know where the hell I am. But wherever it is, I wish the fuck I wasn't here.

I become aware of a squeeze on my arm and jump nervously to see a young black nurse, who by the patient look on her face has been standing beside me the whole while I've been trying to decide where I am. She takes my duffel bag which I must have been carrying all the time and smiles warmly at me.

'Come along . . .' she glances down at my admission sheet, 'Noah . . . I'll show you to your room and introduce you to Jim.'

She takes me by the hand, and leads me across the sunlit public area which, with its stylish birch furniture and potted plants, looks like a half acre of deluxe doctor's waiting room. I see from the name plate on her breast that my guiding nurse is called Althea and that three inches to the right she has a deep cleavage as smooth and dark as Bournville Cocoa paste. If only she would take me now and bury my head in her bosom, I would be just fine. In fact I'd be totally cured – wouldn't need another drink ever again. Even if she'd let me slip my hand inside her starched blouse, I'd be OK till tea time or the first shot of IV Librium or whichever comes first.

As if she can read my mind, Althea glances sharply up at me and pulls her blouse over my medicine tit.

'*Bitch! Now I'll never get better! Now I want a fifth of Jameson's on a bloody great rock of unstepped-on coke. And if I don't get it now, I'll rip this fucking nurse's windpipe out! I'll rip it out and –*'

I hear myself and stop dead in my venomous thoughts and look around the bright, flower-filled room, down to my shaking hands and back to Althea's wary face. Yes – this is a psych ward alright, and I'm definitely in the right place.

In silence we enter a neat red-curtained room with neat red-covered twin beds, from the nearest of which a small grey-haired man rises to greet me wearing an expensive suit. His handshake is like a limp dick and he speaks with the cod English accent of the Boston brahmin.

'How do you do? I'm James. I'm a schizophrenic suicidal.'

How long I stood there holding Jimmie Boy's self-destructive hand I don't know. I remember Althea gave me a huge whack of IV Librium, somewhere along the line. Exactly how long ago that was I haven't a clue. I certainly don't remember having tea.

I must have let go of James's hand at some point as it's now dark outside and I'm sitting on the edge of my bed in T-shirt and boxers with a book on my lap. It's a publisher's proof copy of the screenplay for *Shoah*, Claude Lanzmann's masterpiece Holocaust film, which a friend of mine at Pantheon sent to me asking if I might want to contribute a quote. That was three months ago and I haven't looked at it yet. I thought I'd finally get to it on the train journey up from New York, but . . .

I'm shaking badly now, not outwardly, but a deep inside shaking as my skin runs cold then hot and sweaty, then both. I don't know how much Librium they gave me, but it is only just keeping The Beast at bay as I try to keep some kind of focus by watching Jimmie in his black silk pyjamas, his back to me at the sink.

He carefully takes a handkerchief from his pocket and stuffs it into the plug hole – the sinks in here are plugless – and turns on the tap.

Totally still, he watches the sink fill, then turns off the tap and seems to stiffen for a moment. Then he slowly immerses his head until it is fully submerged and water cascades over the edge of the sink on to the red-carpeted floor. I start to count. By the time I've reached seventy, Jimmie's showing no sign of surfacing. At eighty, his head starts to come up, but he reaches round with both hands and pushes it back down under the water. Two minutes and he's still under. I'm riveted, feeling almost calm, wishing I had a Bolex and a couple of hundred feet of fast film. The stupid bugger is actually trying to drown himself. Two minutes twenty and his head is fighting for air, but his hands keep pushing it back under. I could swear I'm watching two separate people – the murderer and his victim. A split second before two minutes thirty, the head throws off the hands and catapults out of the sink, spraying me with water. I look down at the droplets on the cover of *Shoah* as Jimmie collapses to the floor sobbing.

I return my attention back to *Shoah* and open it at an early page – an interview with Mordechai Podchlebnik, a survivor who now lives in Israel.

'What died in him at Chelmno?'
'Everything died. But he's only human, and he wants to live. So he must forget. He thanks God for what remains, and that he can forget. And let's not talk about that.'

I look down at Jimmie. In between massive gasps for air he's whimpering.

'At times he felt as if he were dead, because he never thought he'd survive, but . . . he's alive.'
'Why does he smile all the time?'
'What do you want him to do, cry? Sometimes you smile, sometimes you cry. And if you're alive, it's better to smile.'

I glance back at my new room mate. Christ! He's stopped whimpering, his eyes are closed and there's a hint of a smile on his face. This is freaky, the kind of coincidence which only happens at the edge of madness. I start to sweat heavily and can feel the deep shake start to spread out towards my hands and feet.

And I don't know when the next drugs are going to get here. Perhaps if I can do something, get active, I can short-circuit the wiring to whatever part of my brain controls the shakes in my outer extremities. That's clinical rubbishspeak

I'm sure, but anything's worth a shot in my condition. I could write something. That's it! I'll get the fingers busy with words. My pen! Where the hell's my pen? Aha! There on the bedside table! Althea, God Bless Her Cleavage, has put my personal effects on my bedside table. I scramble back over the bed to my effects. Some extra-strong mints, my address book, a packet of condoms – watch out, Althea – two quarters, a nickel, a fifty-pence piece, but no pen. My goddam pen isn't here! Of course it isn't, Noah, you fucking idiot! She's not going to leave you with your trusty Bic when you might use it to do a tracheotomy on yourself or, better still, suggest it to Jimmie Boy as an effective alternative to drowning himself.

This is now a life-and-death issue. I must have that pen. My panic surges and the first twitches hit my fingertips. Then the word 'hole' pops into my head and with a prayer on my lips I dive for the clothes closet by the window. My prayer is answered. Althea, God Bless Her Cleavage again, has dutifully hung my leather jacket away on a sturdy metal hanger. I reach into the inner pocket and through the hole in the lining, blindly fumbling along the inside seam of the bottom of the jacket, and there it is – SpareBic! I wrench it out through the pocket, tearing the lining further, hold the twenty-cent piece of plastic up to the light like it was the Holy Grail and kiss it.

My pulse is already dropping as, Bic in hand, I sit back down on the bed. But now I realise have no paper, and I know I have none of that stashed in any of my linings. My pulse rises again. What to do? I don't really even want to write anything any longer, but I know I must apply pen to paper, complete the action, or I will never get out of this place alive. Maybe Jimmie has some. I can't ask him as he's now hard asleep on the floor where he fell, snoring up a storm. So I step over him and open his bedside cupboard.

Inside it's bare except for a copy of the Gideon Bible and a perfectly folded pair of dark-green silk pyjamas with a matching silk sleep mask placed on top. Jesus! Do they leave the lights on in here all night? I scan the room. Nothing. Then my eyes come back once again to *Shoah* on my bed. I leap over, grab the Bic and the book. I am a desperate man. I'm sure Claude Lanzmann will understand if I press a page or two into service. I open the book at random and am about to press the ball to the paper when I see him.

Staring up at me from page 102 in a single frame reproduced from the documentary is Simon Srebnik, a survivor of the ovens. I remember him from the film: the boy who had escaped immediate extermination because he'd won jumping contests and speed races organised by the SS for their chained prisoners. In the photograph, this full-haired, full-faced man, now middle-aged, is framed against the church of Chelmno, the town in which his mother had died in the gas ovens. I wonder if he is hearing his beautiful boy voice which had further kept him alive when he serenaded SS officers as he rowed them in their flat-bottomed boats to the fields at the edge of the village to harvest alfalfa for their rabbits which were also destined for the ovens. Those officers had loved Simon's song about a little white house, but in the end, as Russian troops approached the death camp, the SS had shot Simon through the head and left him for dead.

That poorly reproduced single frame from the movie has jump-started a projection of the whole film in my mind. But I don't want this right now. I do not. I only want to freeze-frame on my own thoughts for a moment – to jot them down and move on, perhaps to sleep. I am not ready for a rerun of this full eight-hour journey into the heart of darkness. I force myself to look at the book again, panning right to page 103 and Simon Srebnik's words.

But I dreamed too that if I survive, I'll be the only one left in the world, not another soul. Just me. One. Only me left in the world, if I get out of here.

All of a sudden I stop. What the Hell am I doing? Why aren't I writing in the bloody Gideon Bible? I have no right looking in these pages. I'm the man who never suffered any pain except that which he brought upon himself. I'm the man with the world at his fingertips and success in the palms of both hands and I try to piss it all away every day of my life. I don't know if Simon drinks or not. If he drank vodka every minute of his waking life, it would be understandable. He'd never be a drunk. But me? I'm nothing but a drunk without so much as a single excuse, an addict without reason – *c'est ça*!

I glance back over at the picture of this man who has stoked the fires of Hell, take my Bic and write in the margin above his head.

I'm sorry, Simon. Each breath I take is an insult to your suffering. This detox will be my last. I promise. It has to be. It will be my insignificant encounter with Death. I suspect you can take him by the hand only once, or maybe twice. Am I right? So, I'm going to take a deep breath, look the grim-reaping bastard in the face and spit in his eye. Then I'll stop up the last bottle with my blood and gristle and toast you in milk. Perhaps then I'll be sober. But still an arsehole. So here's to you, Simon Srebnik! *Prosit*.

Gently, I close the book on Simon and open my bedside cabinet. I take out the copy of Gideon's, put *Shoah* in its place and shut the door as if to a tabernacle. The room is silent. I can hear my own blood rushing in my veins. Somewhere on this floor, far away, someone is crying softly.

Jimmie has stopped snoring. His face is tear-streaked and his skin waxy. He sleeps like a worried child. I take the red cover off his bed, put it over him, put my Gideon Bible on top of the one in his cabinet then lie down on my own bed. I manage to take one very deep breath.

But before I can exhale, the shakes hit me full like a midnight freight train.

I'm sitting near the nurses' station with packed bag beside me and my copy of *Shoah* on my lap. Opposite, on the station counter, is a plastic piss pot full of lavender roses and down the corridor and around the corner the TV is blaring out morning crap. Any minute now Ray should be here to pick me up – or so they tell me. I am not sure how long I've been on this seventh floor, six days or six weeks. The last couple of days have been clearer, but my brain feels fried, or washed, or reprogrammed or something. I'm light-headed. The shakes stopped some time ago, and though I don't crave a drink or a drug, or even want one, I feel empty, numb and cheated in some way that I can't find the words for now. In fact my only words at this moment are these in my head. My spoken words have drifted away. I don't think I've said more than ten words since that first night when Jimmie was dunking himself in the sink. I've written some – a few more than those in the margins of *Shoah*. These are on a single sheet from a yellow legal pad which I suppose Althea must have given me and which I can see sticking out from the side pouch of my duffel bag as I wait here for Ray. I don't know. It's been very confusing. In fact, it's been Hell.

Althea walks by, cleavage intact.

'Morning, Noah. So this is it, huh? Gonna miss you, you son of a gun.'

She laughs, chucks me under my chin and kisses me on my cheek.

Son of a gun? What have I done? I nod, smile and as she sashays in the direction of the TV room, I take out the yellow page and read.

Lots of fat people in here. An Arab camp with a few anorexics – Laura, Koala Bear slippers, dreams of Australia and tells me they have sharp teeth. I only thought they had gums and ate gums – eucalyptus, the best embrocation for whatever ails you.

Shrink interview – told her to get fucked.

Laura gave me a blow-job for my Percodans – if you say you're so smart and love is like death, then how come you haven't died? See! Shows you don't love me!

Tried to call Kirstin – engaged. Again – answer machine – no message.

I hear the murmur of visitor patients all lovey-dovey and the patter on the window. I AM NOT A FILM MAKER!

'Shrink' Again Fuck off 2 U 2.

AA meeting in basement. Night. Played it cool – no fool – Hi! I'm Noah, Lord of the High Seas – I'm an alcoholic.

The fuckers watch *Ripley's Believe It or Not* with Jack Palance, what a sight all in a row in silence watching how Hitler hanged the bombers with piano wire and African ostrich people have only 2 toes – did you know CROquet was banned in Boston in the eighteenth century?

Every morning at ten the suitcase lady packs and waits for somebody to come for her. At ten thirty-three she unpacks and empties every ashtray in the day room.

Shrink wrapped again. NO COMMENT

But in here they won't let you have aerosol shaving cream. If you tie yourself to the canister and put it on the hot radiator – BOOM!

The pink punk still plays table tennis.

More AA – lousy coffee. Good material for movie of the week.

Louisiana red worms eat 150 pounds of raw sewage a day and renew themselves 2,000,000 on a ton of shit and their droppings are fertiliser. They grow hibiscus on that and animals eat it. So I suppose that rubbish is in the eye of the beholder.

Refuse to play basketball. Sorry Chief Dan! No fucking *Cuckoo's Nest* shit for me – will try to drown Jimbo instead – asked Althea outright for a fuck. It's this time. It's this place. It's the time to slap your face. It hurt – welts on my face for a week.

I cannot remember writing one word of this stuff. It reads like a reflection. So I glance back into the mirror.

The air is losing its edges – room's darker and distances longer. Thickness like a blanket. Pull it up over your face, Noah!

AA AA AA AA AA FUCKIN' A! I'm OK!

Althea says doing well, could be out soon – little does she know!

They put Jimmie in the rubber room today and took turns looking through the two-way mirror to watch his head bounce. All the lights went out last night. Locked ward in the dark. Ten seconds of what it's really all about and then the emergency generator put the voltage back in our heads.

Mother visited me tonight.

What? Jump back, Jack! Rerun the footage! Action Replay! I'm sorry I'll read that again.

Mother visited me tonight.

Now here's something I do remember. The rest is what it is – rambling notes from the Outer Limits – all that can be said about the DT's and the fine line between the alkie and the psycho. Sometimes that line is clear, sometimes not. I suppose they weren't sure in my case, and so they put me on this locked ward. I don't know. Right now I don't give a shit. Right now I just want Ray to get his fucking arse here five minutes ago. I fold the yellow page and slip it back in between the pages of *Shoah*. And I remember *Mama*. Who was it that starred in that film? Christ! I can't remember. But I remember my Mama.

She comes early in the morning, the sun is struggling up and Jimmie boy is in an exhausted sleep after yet another suicide attempt. I am lying awake listening to a bird singing when she taps gently at the door and walks in. I recognise her immediately, not from the Brownie black-and-white snapshot I carry of her in my wallet, but from an immediate surge of sense memory that would have done Stanislavski proud. Even though she is dressed in 1980s jeans and jean jacket, with hair swept up casually in a top-knot, I am in no doubt that this is the woman who, thirty-eight years ago, gave birth to me and died before my cord was even cut.

She comes and sits at the foot of my bed and pulls out a pack of Lucky Strikes.

'Mind if I smoke?'

'Not allowed in the rooms.'

She nods as if to say 'I might have guessed', lights up anyway and takes a deep drag.

'How long are you in here for, Noah?'

I can't speak. I can't take my eyes off her, the fine jaw-line, the blue-black hair and the olive, smooth skin. Her eyebrows meet in the middle and her ears are the mould for mine. The first rays of the late autumn sun highlight cheekbones which any model from the Elite Agency would kill for. This is my mother! I shake my head from side to side, I think I make some kind of low noise in my throat. She leans forward and takes my hand.

'Don't let the cat take your tongue. It could be a long time before I get to do this again, if ever. Speak to me.'

I look into her navy eyes. The light from deep inside coaxes me to say something.

'How did you get here? Are you really –'

She puts her fingers to my lips, they are warm. I can feel the pulse of her body.

'Ask me the question you want to ask, the question I want to answer.'

My throat tightens and I feel the pressure of my lifetime behind my eyes. I nod. When at last I speak, I'm not sure if any words come out. But the question is clear.

'Why did you die?'

She lifts her T-shirt to just below her breasts. Above the waist line of her jeans is a good six inches of railway line scar, crisscrossed with two ridges of puckered, raised tissue. Her clothing may be today's, but this scarring is from a time of much more primitive surgery, before the micro stitch and the laser.

'I had been in labour for thirty-three hours. There had been a mix-up, my notes had been mislaid. They told me later

I had no birth canal. I should have had immediate surgery. By the time I was on the table I was too tired from the pain, too full of morphine. I had lost a lot of blood. You had lost strength along with me. I could feel you struggling for life. There was even a moment when I was sure I could feel your unborn fingernails clawing at the inside of my blocked womb, desperate to get out before you died. But perhaps I only imagined you. I was numb from the waist down. I was very drowsy. But I heard the surgeon very clearly when he said that he could save only one life. It was not a difficult choice.'

'But you . . .'

She lowers her shirt on the past and there's silence.

Until Jimmie Boy turns over in his bed and grunts. I glance over at him and then back to the foot of my bed. I half expect my mother to have gone, but she's still there.

'I lived long enough to see you held up to me. You were sucking in breath but you didn't cry. There was blood running down your face.'

She looks around the room, as if for an answer. As her eye passes over me I speak.

'I was addicted to morphine in your womb. I had to be detoxed at birth. It was seven days until I cried. The blood? The scalpel had come through your belly and into my cheek, just here, below my right eye.'

'I didn't know that.'

Her voice is inaudible, crushed flat by the weight of the dead years. Softly, she pulls me to her and looks closely at my face, scanning. I take her finger and trace it along the top of my cheek across my birth scar. For a moment she lets her finger rest, then wraps her arms around me. I can feel her breath on my neck as she speaks gently into my ear which is a double of her own.

'Perhaps I shouldn't have come. But you were in such

agony. I had to make the journey to see you – to do what I could to take away your pain. I only hope I have helped a little. Now I must go. Be strong, my son. And let me leave you with this promise. If you are ever suffering this much again, and I am unable to come, I will send an angel to you.'

She holds my head with both hands, at half arm's length, and looks deep into me. Then with a gentle downward stroke of her fingers, she closes my eyes and kisses me lightly on each lid. And she sings a song, a song thirty-eight years unsung, the song which she used to send down through her belly to me as she paced the bedroom, unable to sleep with my weight in her, up earlier than the earliest bird. I mouth the words as she sings them now. They flow in my blood.

> I leaned my back up against some oak.
> I thought it was a trusty tree.
> But first it bended and then it broke,
> And so did my false love for me.

> Oh, love be tender and love be mild.
> Bright as a jewel when first it's new.
> But love grows cold and then grows old,
> And she fades away like the morning dew . . .

When I open my eyes again, my mother has gone.

And Ray is standing there with Kirstin at his side. She's holding his hand. There's a very uncomfortable silence until Kirstin, beaming, chirps up.

'Well done, Noah! We knew you could do it, didn't we, Ray?' Then, with the touch of a mother, she draws me gently to my feet, pins a ONE DAY AT A TIME badge on my lapel, and pecks me warmly on the cheek. Over her shoulder, through the glass panel in the bunker door, I can see Don in his wheelchair, sipping a Diet Coke through a straw. Harry stands beside the wheelchair like an extra from *The God-father* watching over Dr Strangelove.

Kirstin's kiss is still warm on my cheek as I open the door to the corridor in my mind, take out my Kalashnikov and fire from the hip in a combat arc, severing Don's head from his body and studding bloody rubies across Harry's waist. Then Ray, right on cue, saves their lives by dropping Kirstin's hand, grabbing my holdall and with his free hand giving me one half of a sober bear hug.

'Okay, motherfucker, time to rock'n'roll! You've been certified sane and sober.'

He breaks away, bows deeply and makes a sweeping gesture toward the exit.

'So, if you please, step through that door and into your future.'

PART TWO

Roll Focus! Close On!

It is not an arbitrary 'decree of God' but in the nature of man, that a veil shuts down on the facts of tomorrow; for the soul will not have us read any other cipher but that of cause and effect.

Emerson, *Essays*, 'Heroism'

FIVE

You don't need a weatherman to know which way the wind blows.

Bob Dylan, 'Subterranean Homesick Blues'

Speeding through Camden Town, February 1997

The screaming ambulance slows down a fraction as it hits the junction of Parkway and Camden High Street. Outside, something hits a side panel with a thud – a bottle, hard projectile vomit, a rampant slamdancer? The ambulance driver shouts FUCK OFF! and puts a foot down. The vehicle lurches off up Kentish Town Road and the green arm of the paramedic steadies me on my narrow ledge of a bed. Out of the corner of my eye, through the darkened back windows, I can see a floodlight Doc Marten's boot, the size of a Volkswagen in the sky. I fight the pain by trying to keep focus on this outsized footwear as we speed away, but I can't because of the blinding headlights of the car on our bumper. That'll be Etta, riding our tail like a bitch on a bitch. Clare, still in her off-the-shoulder number, her cello case at her feet, is holding on to my hand so tightly that I can't feel it. She keeps jumping in and out of focus as each wave of pain breaks through my body. It feels as if my bladder is in my head, and any minute now it will explode, rupture my eardrums, blow my eyes out of their sockets, and blast piss and blood at a million foot pounds pressure out of my coke-scarred nostrils.

'I'm here, darling – don't worry. You'll be alright.'

It's all Clare in her terror can think to say. And she's been saying those same words over and over again in random permutations since they slid me into the ambulance at Wigmore Hall and gave me a hospital pee bottle to hold over the end of my severely blood-clot-blocked urethra.

'Darling, don't worry. You'll be alright, I'm here.' 'You'll be alright – darling – don't worry – alright, don't worry, darling – here I am, worry don't alright, here, I'm darling don't I'm be here alright worry –'

And on and on and the outside is whirling by under bridges and the pain is screaming with the screaming siren and flashing blue and red and molten. Clare's mouth is moving and mine is biting itself shut and I can taste my blood filling my mouth. I want to scream but daren't make a sound. If I do I will invoke spirits and demons such as the world has not seen in ten thousand years. I am sucked under bridges, and I pull my knees to my chin – worry don't darling, alright I'm here going. And she smiles and holds my hand tighter.

FUCK OFF!

in my head as we fly over the shit-filled lock of the Camden River Styx, Dingwalls beside and past Doner Kebabs and the Roundhouse – Vanilla Fudge and the Doors and sodium lights and the whole screeching world of shit and misery whizzes by as the pain in my body breaks all boundaries just as the ambulance hits a pothole. My body arches up off the stretcher bed and the piss pot flies out of my hand into the air.

My brain and eyes are instantly clear and I notch down to the extreme slo-mo of the accident. As I lurch upwards in an arc, I can feel the air filling my lungs cc by cc and my lumbar muscles contracting cell by cell, bracing themselves to cradle the spine for when it hits the stretcher again. I can feel the blocking blood clot easing itself along my urethra and my bladder wall stretch to its biological limit. For a nanosecond, I hang in the air like an over-ripe fruit in mid-fall. I look down and I see the top of Newton's head under my tree and can just make out his jottings and, as I fall past him, I see that they are the beginnings of an equation. Then I hit the earth and split wide open at his feet.

A clot the size of a lamb's liver shoots from my dick and past Clare who is frozen, open-mouthed, her palms to her scarlet cheeks in a cartoon of ecstatic delight at this ejaculation from Hell. Blood jets behind the liver splattering Clare, her cello, the paramedic, his driver mate and the pristine white ceiling of the ambulance with blood-red polka dots about the size of the ones I'd helped Blue Sky paint on his microbus back in '72.

A massive breath shudders out of me. Now I am one huge, empty, bruised bladder. I close my eyes. The pain subsides. I fumble around for Clare's hand, hold it gently and whisper.

'I'm here, darling. Don't worry. You'll be alright.'

Her grip tightens and I can feel her smile with temporary relief. The paramedic slips the pee bottle back into my free hand and I recover my 'manhood'.

And as the ambulance speeds on up through a north London which is starting to put itself to bed, I drift, almost luxuriate, in my pain-free reprieve and the sirens sound to me like a lullaby.

SIX

I deny the accident.

Jackson Pollock

New York City, February 1985

I'm sitting in the Cozy Soup'n'Burger on Broadway opposite
Astor Place sipping a cup of coffee, nibbling a cheese Danish
and waiting for Ray.

I'm desperate for a real drink. It's been six months since I
got out of detox in Pawtucket – six months since I stepped
through that seventh floor door and into my future – five
since my last drink. It was early morning in New Haven,
Connecticut, in some block of flats housing students, somewhere near the drama school where I'd given a lecture on
film structure to playwrights the night before and had gone
home with a raven-haired student who'd asked a question
about film language to which I'd given a creamy answer. I
went with her and her whole group of budding Stoppards to
some punk dive and jerked around to some band called
Beast. Raven and I went back to her place without apology,
she drunk and stoned and me sober and horny-horny. It was
a zipless fuck and fun in a calculated, athletic way. In the
morning I'd planned to take a piss, have a sleepy-eyed fuck,
tape a sweet note to the fridge and leave. The piss was
uneventful, but on my way back to the bedroom I had to pass

a sideboard. On this sideboard was an unopened bottle of Bombay gin. I had no thoughts of taking a drink. Suddenly, as I drew level with the sideboard, my right hand flashed out and grabbed the gin. Before the action had even registered in my brain, the top was off the bottle and I was standing there in this stranger's flat, naked as the day I was born, penis dangling like the flag of a defeated regiment, guzzling neat gin like a fucking maniac.

That night I vomited and pissed blood. And somewhere along the line there was a stomach pump.

Since that day I've been in a kind of low-key Hell. With white knuckles and red eyes and a little help from a string of girlfriends up and down the East Coast from Boston to Washington DC, I've managed to not pick up a drink. I am not drunk. But I am not sober. I'd like to think I am – I often say I am, but I'm not. I haven't really dealt with my addiction, I have simply shifted it sideways. I still take all the other escape routes. I smoke at least twenty Marlboro Reds a day, smoke dope, snort coke, drink Coke and called it a temporary path to sobriety. On the surface it all looks fine. On the surface it looks very, very fine indeed. Three weeks ago I wrapped the shoot on *The Edge*, a gritty bio-pic of Jackson Pollock which even in the can is smelling of success and pricking up a lot of ears around town and on the coast. The current *New Yorker* carries a feature by Pauline Kael entitled 'Noah Arkwright – Cutting Edge Brit/Antediluvian Grit. I'm regarded as an arbiter of taste in the tasteless business. From where the public sits, my skin looks clear and so does my future. But I am three thousand miles from home and a billion miles from my soul. I'm not a happy camper. In fact I am an extremely unhappy camper and it's getting worse. 'So what's new?' as they say over here – fuck all.

Except AA, Alcoholics Anonymous, The Fellowship, The

Friends of Bill W. That's new like a pair of new hiking boots is new. That first meeting with Kirstin, and the obligatory ones in the loony bin, established in me a deep aversion for the 'Club', so deep that I even phoned back to England and changed membership from the Automobile Association to the RAC. Of course common sense tells me that those fucking meetings are, like those good hiking boots, necessary for the comfortable long-haul, but when you put them on and start walking, all you can hear is the creak and all you can feel is the pain of the rub which you know will be a weeping blister by night time. Despite my fear and loathing, I have made it to about a dozen meetings in these six months. And last week, Monday to be precise, I decided to go to Flask Street, the notorious West Village AA meeting.

I arrive early and get myself a coffee from a chic latte joint near the meeting. I am sipping my drink and trying to look casual as I turn the corner on Flask Street to find a gaggle of know-each-other sobers standing around some fetid dust-bins outside a derelict-looking building the size of a shoe box. A few turn and look at me and then return to their Alkiechat.

'Fuck this for a game of soldiers!'

I go into the dark room which looks like the foyer of a tiny flop house, nicotine-stained and smelling strangely of the finest perfume and old BO. I take a chair against a wall and facing what looks like a dock in a backstreet Victorian courtroom. Behind it hang the Twelve Steps of Alcoholics Anonymous. People start to drift in and take their seats. A social X-ray wearing *Vogue* from head to toe and make-up courtesy of Ivana Trump sits on my left and takes out a box of Tic-Tacs. A middle-aged chap wearing a polyester jump-suit and looking like a cross between Bela Lugosi and Bugs Bunny sits on my right and scratches his crotch. A Wall Street Suit takes the witness stand and the meeting is opened by a handsome young bloke who could be a PE teacher. During the opening Blah Blah I don't bow my head and spare a thought for any drunk who's still out there, I look back up at the Twelve-Step banner and my eyes come to rest on Step Two: WE CAME TO BELIEVE THAT A POWER GREATER THAN OURSELVES COULD RESTORE US TO SANITY.

Something in me snaps. Some resistance deep inside cracks. I am suddenly there – sick and tired of being sick and tired and willing to be a slogan if it will take the pain away.

So when the happy confessional introduction goes round the room and reaches me, I take a deep breath and say in a surprisingly loud and clear voice –

'Hi . . . my name is Noah and I'm an alcoholic.'

The truth at last!

As all the others in that shit-hole of a room tap into the collective unconscious of the alcoholic, they can hear the 'first time' in my voice and applaud me gently.

Looking back on it, that admission brought me intense relief and pissed me off at the same time. I always thought that my first public declaration would be floodlit, filmic – with a soaring soundtrack, an extreme close-up and a richly bass-boosted voice. It would be a scene of painful perfection, prompting critics on both sides of the Atlantic to spend column feet rocketing me into orbit to circle the firmament alongside the great truth-telling auteurs of film. But no. My entering exit was more like a silent fart than a blast on a golden horn. Some benevolent syzygy must have been at work that day, because in that cramped West Village room with its fetid air and its slogans and filthy ashtrays, I really meant what I said. Something, somehow had made me look up at that grease-stained Twelve-Step banner at that moment and read that Second Step with fresh eyes. Right there and then I knew the game as I had known it for over twenty years was up and that I would have to confess my alcoholism in that Flask Street room.

Does this mean I will never take another drink? I might. I hope to God I don't, but I might. But I will never be able to enjoy booze again, not even the tiniest sip, because from here to eternity, Guilt will always now be peeking over my shoulder and whispering in my ear:

'Remember, Noah! it's the first drink which gets you drunk . . . Cheers!'

The smug bastard! He'll also always be there now when I take a toke or lay down a line, but this time with a cheesy chuckle:

'Now, now, Noah. Don't you know you can't be high and sober?'

Well fuck you, Guilt! You won't catch me on that one! I didn't just *read* the First Step. I know it by heart – WE ADMITTED WE WERE POWERLESS OVER *ALCOHOL* – THAT OUR LIVES HAD BECOME UNMANAGEABLE. And I am powerless over alcohol, and my life, my life had become unmanageable. Booze was fucking up everything. But drugs are a different thing with me – always have been. Even in detox I could handle them. I can take them or leave them. With them my life is manageable. Look at me now. I have a little buzz on from some workingman's weed, but I am in the Cozy Soup'n'Burger sipping a coffee, alert and prepared for my meeting with Ray who should walk through that door any minute now. Come to think of it, where the Hell is he? He said eight forty-five, it's now nine o'clock. Jesus! He's the one who's always telling me on location that I'm a slack dick with time-keeping and where is he now? – probably up on 79th and Riverside zipping up his fly at Kirstin's perfect little apartment – 4RMS-R/View.

Kirstin moved to New York. It happened only two days

after she and Ray collected me from the loony bin. It wasn't so much a move as a relocation with military strategy and precision. She simply walked into Classic Caterers and told them she wouldn't be coming to work any more, jumped on the train and rode down the East Coast clutching a portfolio of Polaroids she's taken of the finest meals she's served and the exclusive locations in which she's served them. Still holding tight to her food pics, she takes a taxi from Penn Station to the Upper West Side and Zabar's Deli. Then she walks in bold as brass and demands to see the manager of this illustrious store. Within the hour she talked him into a lucrative deal involving what could best be described as an Epicurean Kosher/Non-Kosher Meals on Wheels for Yuppies on the Upper West Side. Before sunset she'd completed the even more impossible task of getting her name on the lease on the bijou apartment.

Next day a truck arrived with her stuff and by nightfall Kirstin was her own first customer for the Zabar's project. Ray was her guinea pig guest for the meal. He was a willing client – very willing! Christ! He's been on her like a dog on a bone ever since. Ray may be sober but he's an even bigger sex junkie than I am. They probably get through a six-pack of KY Jelly a week. But in public butter wouldn't melt in their mouths. In public the two of them are AA Blissfolk, daily regulars at the Armchair Lunchtime meeting on the Upper West Side, sharing platitudes, smiling all day and Twelve Stepping the universe. In private they spend every waking hour taking the art of sober fucking to new heights. Who am I to talk? – the man whom a German actress once called Der Fuckmeister? But to rabbit-screw when drunk is one thing – par for the course – but to hyperfuck with a clean and sober head is embarrassing, verging on distasteful – and it makes you late for appointments! It's a half hour ride from 79th, for God's sake, and we're due in the editing suite at ten thirty and we only have it until one a.m. I knew it was a mistake to let him go after this morning's session. Shit! This coffee is cold and stewed. Why is it that back in London they think you get good Java in New York? Big Apple coffee is for shit.

And this Danish I've been chewing on hasn't seen the inside of a baker's oven in a week. Where the fuck is he? What is it with lighting cameramen – sorry – cinematographers? I always get it wrong, I have that latter-day hippie skill with the Mid-Atlantic jargon, but it never flows well for me like it does for Keef or Mick. That's one of the big obstacles for me with Alcoholics Anonymous – it's so fucking American Jargonspeak. Listen to me! I owe my career to this country. Without America I'd still be a spotty NFT graduate making some p.c. documentary about teeenybop singers in the workingmen's clubs of Buttfuck Workington. It's jargon like 'Let's do lunch' and 'My people will call your people' and the gob-smackingly awesome 'Hey, Noah, let's make this goddam movie!' which has given me the courage to fire up my rocket and say 'Fuck the Moon! Let's go to Venus!' My life unmanageable? Not on your Nelly! But I wish I had a line or two now to smooth off the edges. 9.03! Come on, Ray, for fuck's sake!

Some woman in some bar somewhere once asked me if coke was physically addictive. I laughed and told her that when I did up a nice chubby line of coke it made me feel like a new man, and that new man wants another line of cocaine. She didn't get it. Hell! I don't want coke, I want a drink and I want it NOW and if Ray doesn't get here in the next few –

There's the bastard now, crossing over from Astor Place, past the three-dollar hairdressers where they'll give you anything from a mohawk to a number-one buzzcut in under fifteen minutes. He's arm in arm with Kirstin, and through the window and across Broadway, I can tell they've been hard at it in the sack. I can look right through their perfect His and Her L.L. Bean sheepskins and see her perfect nipples still engorged, her perfect puffy labia under her Saks Fifth Avenue kilt, and his semi-erect dick still spasmodically jerking around under his J. Crew cords.

They are jay-walking when they suddenly stop next to a belching steam vent and kiss deeply.

A downtown-bound yellow cab, horn blasting, screeches to a halt an inch from the Kissyfaces causing a dreadlocked bicycle courier to slam into its back. The cab driver leaps out and starts to shout at the already gathered rubbernecks in Brooklyn Rumanian – Armenian – whatever. He rushes towards Ray stabbing a finger, spins mid-stab and flies at the skinny black messenger boy who is running to meet the cabbie, his bike with its twisted front wheel held in front of him like a police barrier. A Cozy Soup waiter has opened the diner door to gawk so a blast of twenty-degree wind is bringing to me the full sound on this picture. The cabbie is yelling some indecipherable anger – the bike boy is blasting back at him with

'YOU WANT TO MIX IT UP ON THE STREET, MOTHERFUCKER!?'

He's darting forwards and backwards into the driver's face like a cock in fight warm-up. Suddenly the black guy leaps on to the hood of the cab, his bike held high, and screams:

'HOW TOUGH ARE YOU, ASSHOLE? HOW TOUGH'S YOUR FUCKIN' WINDSHIELD?'

And he smashes his wheels right through the cab's windscreen, does a Rocky triumphal salute, leaps off the taxi and hotfoots it down Astor Place toward the East Village. The crowd is cheering. The cabbie is close to tears. Ray reaches in his coat, pulls out some folding money, then with perfect AA selflessness and serenity thrusts a couple of notes into the cabbie's jean jacket pocket and ferries a white-faced Kirstin over to the west side of the street. Jesus! It all makes for a bloody good film moment, but it's the last thing I need right now – the both of them in here, shaken but not stirred, retelling the whole story with attitude and platitude. Shit! I told Ray to come alone. We'll never finish the edit on *The Edge.*

As Ray and Kirstin hit the pavement outside the diner, I play it cool, pick up my coffee and roll my eye-focus into the middle distance a few degrees south so I don't make eye-contact with them. I do not want them to come into the diner. But why not? What's the problem? They're here now. Lighten up, Noah – stay cool. But how? Aha! I know. I mutter the Serenity Prayer under my breath.

'*God grant me the Serenity to accept the things I cannot change, courage to change the things I can and wisdom to know the difference.*'

It's not working. I start the shakes. I grip my coffee cup hard with both hands but I can't disguise them. I'm sweating. Jesus Christ – the prayer shifts gear –

'*Oh, God! If you really give a shit – if you have any love in you at all for me, stop these shakes now. Do what you have to – swallow me up, spit me out in pieces over the plains of this fucked-up world—*'

'Hi, Noah, sweetie.'

Jesus! At the sound of Kirstin's voice, Peter Pecker gives a wee nod 'Hello' even before she pecks the top of my head and her vanilla scent pumps him up to his usual full-blown greeting.

'Hey, Noah!'

Ray slides in opposite. Kirstin slides in beside him. A simple act of sitting down, but when they do it, it looks like fucking, and the Voyeur goes rock hard. I hate this shit. Ever since I've been out of the funny farm it has been hyperresponsive – and the more tired and strung out I am, the more hyper the response.

I was in Dunkin' Donuts last week. I hadn't slept in three nights, trying to wrap the Pollock piece, to walk the dry tightrope, to hide my mini drug consumption from Ray – so knackered I felt like I was dragging my arse around on a sledge. I ordered a large coffee, a cruller and a donut. The spotty teen with shredded cuticles plopped the order in front of me. Whether he was trying to fuck with me or not, I couldn't tell – his face screamed 'I'M A DUMBO!' to the world. But the cruller had been placed so that it was just about to enter the hole of the chocolate-coated. I stared hard at this sugared still life. It was an out-take from the movie *Un Chien Andalou* – a cut away from Buñuel's priest pedalling his bicycle in the sunny street below, just before the piano is pulled across the room. I stared harder. I got a hard on. I looked up and the boy was staring blankly at me. All this in a room painted in orange, pink and white stripes, designed to limit the stay of the average customer to four minutes. In a flash, in my mind, I was back in a bathroom when I was fourteen.

I'm sitting on the edge of the bath, my bare arse nudging Aunty's ship's anchor, my right hand clutching J.P. Donleavy's *The Ginger Man* open at the worn pages of the bare bums slapping scene, my left hand Bashing the Bishop. Just as my pubescent watery wad is soaring high over the linoleum, Uncle Bart opens the door. I drop the book, Bart picks it up and whacks me over the head, driving me bare-arsed through the kitchen, past his baking wife, into the garden and up to the compost heap, where with one final whack he sends me sprawling into the stinking heap of horse shit and kitchen sludge.

I was out of Dunkin' Donuts in three and a half minutes flat.

'Happy Birthday!'

Kirstin plops a small purple velvet bag on the table in front of me. The neck of the bag is closed with a drawstring. It looks like it should contain a half-gram coke rock. What the fuck is it?

'It's not my birthday, K.'

Ray chirps up with a laugh. 'Not your birthday birthday – your AA birthday, man!'

Before I can figure that one out, Kirstin pushes the velvet nearer to me. There's a shiny slart on the inside of her index finger that looks like dried jism – or maybe clear nail-polish. She leans over with a pout and chucks me under my chin. I'm seized with an urge to kiss her full on the lips. In fact I want to shoot Ray then kiss Kirstin for ever.

'I am so proud of you, Noah A.'

'G'head. Open it!' says Ray as he beckons the waiter. 'Can we get coffee over here?'

I pick up my birthday bag and fumble with the drawstring. Ray winks at me. Kirstin's fingers are drumming the table in anticipation, the jism glinting in the bright lights of the diner. Cozy Stavros appears with the crap coffee and two cups. Kirstin blocks him as he tries to put a cup in front of her and mouths the word 'water' to him so seductively that my concentration is broken again with another rush of blood to its already swollen head.

Ray slurps deeply on his coffee. I now have the bag open and I turn it up into my palm. Out drops a bronze coin thing a bit bigger than the old half crown.

'It's a six-month chip,' Kirstin says like a child telling you what she's bought you. She sees the blank expression on my face.

'You did get out of detox September fifteenth, right?'

I nod as I examine the 'chip'. It has a triangle punched on its face with one word for each side: UNITY – SERVICE – RECOVERY. Christ! It is the slogan for the Automobile

Association. Arching over the triangle are six words which are garlic to a drinking vampire – TO THINE OWN SELF BE TRUE.

'You've done so well, Noah. I know it's been hard for you since that very first meeting. But you're doing it – you're staying clean and sober.'

'But –'

'No buts. You're making meetings, you've got yourself a sponsor, you are doing what you can, and that right now is enough, isn't it, Ray?'

'She's right, man. Look at you. I can't remember you looking so good. And you're working like a son of a bitch – best work you've done since I forgot when. Things are looking up. You're on another threshold – on the edge of something bigger than ever.'

Kirstin jumps in. 'You have luck stamped all over you. You've got the moon and stars on your head, Noah.' Moon and stars? 'Your bellybutton birthday's on March thirtieth, right?'

'Yes it is.' *Bellybutton birthday!*

'1947, right?'

'Correct.'

'Well, did you know that you were born on the very same day that the Fellowship went to England! You're an AA baby, Noah.'

She leans over and kisses me firmly on my mouth.

'And I love every inch of you for it!'

If only she knew!

Laughing with embarrassment, I turn the chip over in my hand. The Serenity Prayer is embossed on the back. Right now I need it. I'm trapped in some kind of squishy 'Goodnight, John Boy' world of pink love, presents and coincidence with a boner the size of the Empire State – or perhaps the Woolworth Building – and a drug-guilty conscience as big as the UK. And I've got a film to finish editing before tomorrow. Silently, I intone the words to the prayer as I say other words out loud.

'Thanks, Kirstin. I shall treasure this.'

With a flourish, Kirstin whips out a tiny fairy cake with half a candle stuck in the top of it, places it on my plate next to my Danish debris, lights the candle and starts to sing 'Happy Birthday'. Ray takes Kirstin's hand and joins in the singing as each reaches over and takes one of my hands in one of theirs. Stavros arrives with the water and adds his voice to the singing. When they finish the song Kirstin and Ray speak at the exact same instant.

'Blow!'

I puff at the single candle at the same time as the diner door opens sending a counter breeze. The candle stays lit. I lick my forefinger and thumb and nip out the flame. Stavros puts down the water, says Happy Birthday and goes to pick up another order.

There's an uneasy silence as we watch the thin blue plume of acrid smoke rise from the extinguished candle.

'Well, guys. I'm out of here.'

Kirstin eases herself out of the booth.

'I know you've got work to do.'

'You don't have to go, Kirstin. Stay and eat. We've plenty of time,' I lie.

'Thanks but no thanks.'

She makes a sweeping gesture in the direction of the diner counter.

'Meat. I'll grab some pasta round at Pain et Chocolat and plan my weekend food deliveries.'

She kisses Ray on the forehead, me on the top of my head again – another blood surge to my dick – and swirls out on to the street like an exiting AA fairy godmother.

Ray looks after her.

'Jesus, Noah! Look at that woman! I could fuck her all day.'

I'm about to say 'Me too' and think better of it.

'Yes. She's great. You've done well for yourself there, Ray.'

'Yep! Love that gal to bits! Couldn't have done it without you, man!'

He raises his Java in a sober toast. I toast back with Kirstin's water, imagining where her lips might have touched the glass if she'd taken a sip, which she hadn't.

In a sudden move which scares the shit out of me, Ray comes around to my side of the booth, slides in beside me, puts one arm around my shoulder and plops a folded-up page of the *New York Times* in front of me.

'Happy birthday from me, motherfucker,' he says in his Godfather Queen's English and then calls back Stavros and orders a cheeseburger with large fries and an extra dill pickle.

Before me is a page from the 'Arts and Leisure' section – music – classical. Staring out at me is a doe-eyed woman with a cello between her knees and a cleavage to be immortalised in marble.

'Noah Arkwright, meet Clare Mathesson – the woman for you.'

I push the clipping back in front of Ray with a snort.

'Ray – I've got the film student at RISD, I've the inventor in New Haven, I've the wardrobe twins in Tribeca. The last thing I need right now is another woman.' Except Kirstin.

'Bullshit, my friend. Those women are the tail-end of your addiction.' He stabs his finger at the page. 'This woman is your partner for a sober future.'

I look back at the photograph and deep inside me something shifts sideways. I want to run out of the café. Sweat beads on to my forehead. I try to take a sip of coffee but it's spilling like the proverbial beans. Ray knows something about Truth and he's not a joker. He's a squat, balding, Brooklyn-born Irishman who lost faith in magic and the little people when his father pinned his mother to the kitchen door of their railroad apartment with a carving knife when Ray was five years old. Ray spent the rest of his childhood in a boys' home on Staten Island which made him hungry in many ways. A film unit was shooting in Great Kills when he was fifteen. That was in 1962. Ray hung around and got a job as a gofer and was hooked. By the time he was twenty-one he was one of the best gaffers around. Two years later he was behind the camera and building a reputation as a lighting cameraman.

But rock'n'roll also ran in Ray's veins and when he found booze and drugs he became Blue Sky and in 1970 put his film career on the back burner – or rather it was put on the back burner for him by two tours in Vietnam.

He survived. And when I met him at the Black Sabbath concert in Atlanta he hadn't forgotten a thing either, because after I went downtown and bailed him out, he came back to the park with me and picked up that Bolex and shot some of the best footage I'd ever seen.

Today Rock'n'Roll Blue Sky is Rock-solid Ray – solid as a fire hydrant and just as practical. Ray has been sober for three years. He calls himself my sponsor and calls me his boss. There's no paradox in this for him like there is for me. He sees it as his mission to lead me by the nose down the Twelve-Stepped path to spiritual enlightenment or awakening as they call it in The Programme. It's only been a couple of weeks since, during a lull on the set, he told me that he understands my sexual addiction as he's a real fuck-merchant himself – well, used to be anyway until he hooked up with Perfection – used to play any field – anywhere, anytime. And then he comes out with this argument that in the early days of sobriety, although fucking around is not the wisest course of action, it is infinitely preferable to getting deeply involved with one particular partner.

But I've been 'sober' only six months. We've just celebrated it for fuck's sake! So what the hell is going on here with this cellist with the golden breasts? Is this some kind of sobriety test?

'Don't fuck with me, Ray. I'm too tired – too strung out – and we've work to do.'

Ray shoves the page back in front of me.

'I know. I know. And as your sponsor, I should be shot for this. But as your friend of thirteen years I should also tell you that rules are made to be broken, man. Anyhow, there aren't any rules in AA, only suggestions, right? Whatever! This is something else, Noah. I can't explain it. I was skimming through to the movie section and she looked straight at me. It sounds like bullshit, but she actually spoke to me, told me about her life.'

I snort another snort, the kind of snort that only a practised coke-snorter can snort.

'OK, Ray. You've had your joke. Now can we go over some of these cuts? I want to break the back of the first fifteen minutes tonight.'

Stavros drops the cheeseburger and fries in front of Ray who pours on relish and ketchup by touch without losing eye-contact with me. He bites into a dill pickle.

'I don't know, maybe I was doing some kind of unconscious reading as I stared at her picture, but when I started to read the article, there it was – the story she'd been telling me.'

He pushes the cutting closer to me again.

'Take a good luck for Chrissakes – she's from your home town!'

And he tells me the whole story as I'm reading it on the page. She's thirty years old, a child cello prodigy from Faraday Road, Workington, just the other side of the park from our house. When I was at the NFT she was eleven and illuminating the school concerts at my old school. When *Knickerbocker*, my first short, was released, she was at the Guildhall around the corner from me in London. Now here she is playing with the Kairos Quartet at Alice Tully Hall and knocking their socks off – toast of the city's music aficionados and drop-dead beautiful. And here I am in the Cozy Soup'n'Burger, flavour of the month for the movie crowd and as ugly as the day I was born! There are a few parallels in our stories but not enough to make her really interesting to me. And if music be the food of love then pack up your instruments and go home because my all-time favourite album is *The Who Live at Leeds* – a far cry from Schoenberg which Ms Mathesson says in this interview is her passion.

I continue the game of shuffle board and pass the clipping back to Ray. He places his hand over mine and holds it firm to the Formica top. I'm sure he can feel my shaking. He turns me to face him with a James Caan-Godfather kind of cheek-pinch action and gives me the most serious look of my life.

'You're a long time dead, Noah. So what are you going to do about her?'

I look down and fiddle with the purple velvet 'chip' bag. I glimpse something white inside. It's a paper label sewn into the seam. It reads – BAG (ONLY) MADE IN CHINA. It seems like a strange omen which will explain itself only in the sweetness of time.

Somewhere in my brain-stem I must have believed Ray's prediction about the Workington Cellist – or at least wanted to believe it – because right there and then in the Cozy Soup'n'Burger I agreed to write a note to her on the back of a shooting schedule introducing myself and asking her to join me for a cup of tea after her matinee recital at Alice Tully Hall tomorrow afternoon – Saturday. It would have to be after the matinee as I was slated to do a night shoot. The shoot, in fact, on which I was writing the note. It's a 'Say No to Drugs' Public Service Short which Miramax had all but blackmailed me into doing gratis – grainy B&W 'Night In The Life Of' a junkie in Alphabet City. What I wrote was an awkward note which centred on the fact that we were both from the same town and both went to the same school with a P.S. asking if she remembered Mr Oliver. As soon as I'd written it I wished I hadn't and would have torn up the note if Ray hadn't grabbed the sheet, scribbled my phone number on it and shoved it in an envelope which he'd already addressed to my future partner 'care of' Alice Tully Hall, Lincoln Center – the bastard! Then he looked me right in the eye.

'I'll drop this in by hand and pick up a matinee ticket for one. You will meet this woman, Noah. Tomorrow is going to be a day full of coincidences – I can feel it in my bones.'

'"THERE ARE NO COINCIDENCES", Ray, remember?'

But as I pushed the newspaper clipping back to him for the last time, Clare Mathesson looked up from the page into my eyes, and I swear to God she winked at me.

SEVEN

The road of excess leads to the palace of wisdom.

William Blake, 'Proverbs of Hell'

The morning after, February 1985

I'm being drawn up from the depths of the sleep of the dead by a familiar high-pitched beeping. I lash out in the direction of the bedside table. There's a crash and the beeping accelerates to a higher rate and a higher frequency. I concentrate all my half-awake energy on getting the 'Open Sesame!' command from my brain to my eyes, but somewhere along the route the wires get crossed and my sphincter contracts instead, letting out an enormous, hissing SBD fart. My second signal attempt is more successful. My eyes struggle open to painful slits and blearily scan the floorboards for the alarm. There's the bastard! Nestled in the crotch of my jauntily discarded boxer shorts. Suddenly I make a cobra move and slam my fist down on the clock as though it's a cockroach. Its manic beeping stops. I whisper smugly to myself:

'The Roach Motel – they check in but they don't check out!'

And then I check the time – it reads 00.00. Ground Zero! The starting point for a Brave New World! Think Think Think! Today is the first day of the rest of your life, Noah! Take It Easy! First Things First! Easy Does It! A Day at a

Time! It's the first drink which gets you drunk! Fuck! I'm being sucked into Sloganland – the country of no return! Shit! I shake the alarm – nothing moves.

'Come on, you little sod! Tick or Tock or whatever the fuck it is that you digital buggers do!'

Still 00.00 – so I whack the clock against the floor and Hey Presto! the first second pops up and Time is up and running.

'*And a good morning to you too, Noah!*'

Six and seven and eight and nine and ten and . . . warm light touches my naked shoulder. I turn my head sharply toward its source and a red flash of pain shoots behind my eyes – the old Red Dawn Warning of the impending arrival of Big Thumper.

Through the window the sun is just peeking over the top of the green copper crumbling replica of the Bridge of Sighs which connects two warehouses across the Tribeca alleyway opposite and its beams are raking down the full length of this seventy-five-foot loft. Clusters of costumes on mannequins shimmer in the backlight, and the table which overflows with the remains of last night's drinking meal is silhouetted like a burnt-out building. The rays highlight bits and pieces of discarded clothing as they head towards the bed where they hit its ornate polished footboard, edging it with fire before reaching their final destination and blushing pink the identical naked arses of the Tribeca Wardrobe Sisters. The twins, fast asleep, lie face-down, side by side, arms across each other's back, faces almost touching, their syncopated breaths ruffling wisps of each other's flame-red hair. They look peaceful and refreshed. They sleep the sleep of innocence and rebirth – amazing considering they round-robin fucked all last night and did up more coke in six hours than a farmhouse Aga does in a month. I, of course, was right in there with them – Robin Redbreast himself – snorting and shagging my nose and arse off in an insane backlash against the Pink Cloud AA 'birthday' celebration with Ray and Kirstin Perfect in the Cozy Soup'n'Burger that afternoon. I, though, have not slept the sleep of innocence or rebirth. I have not slept much at all. In fact, I have lain here since that last four a.m. dribble of an ejaculation, bathed in the blue of the city night light coming through the window, listening to my heart, to my head, and to the night-stalking garbage trucks of Lower Manhattan.

One of the twins, Rita (I think), moves her thighs apart and I find myself looking at a burning bush that would have done Moses proud. Under my gaze her shell-pink labia open to the warmth of the morning sun and smile at me. Within five seconds, Connie (I think) adjusts herself to the exact same position and adds her smile to her sister's.

'*You're a cunt, Noah. So why aren't you smiling?*'

The Voice is so clear and loud I jerk around to see who is there. Nobody. But the rapid movement dislodges the morning-after metal ball from the back of my brain-pan. It rolls forwards and hits the inside of my skull behind my eyes, sending bone shrapnel flying into adjacent soft tissue. A wave of nausea rises, but stops short of my gullet. I take as deep and as calm a breath as I can and try to figure it out – this puzzlement, this confusion, this unnameable fear I have been feeling throughout the wee hours of last night since Ray and I wrapped the edit.

It's a couple of minutes after one. Ray and I have come in under the wire – the first fifteen minutes of *The Edge* are in the bag and I am pleased as Punch's Prick. When we step out into Delancey it's sleeting down and a Siberian wind is whipping over from the East River. I am just about to suggest to Ray that we take a cab over to the EAR bar for a coffee when this loving beep comes from across the street. I look over and there's Kirstin at the wheel of her Cute

Classic – her Oldsmobile Cutlass convertible – all beckoning and glowing warm under the interior courtesy light. For the first time since I set eyes on Perfect Kirstin on that perfect campus walkway over a year ago, my Pecker doesn't rise to the occasion. Then for a second or two I must have fallen through a pavement crack into a blank time zone, because the next thing I know, Ray is opening the passenger door of K's car and ushering me in.

'C'mon, Noah – it'll be a blast. It's the only all-night AA meeting in Manhattan – it's like a fucking George Romero movie!'

'And then we can drive over to the Empire Diner for coffee and cake.'

When Peter hears these simpering words from Kirstin inside the Olds, he actually droops.

'Thanks but no thanks, K. It's been a long day. I think I'll just go home.'

And I try to walk away, but now Ray thrusts my head into the car, flips down the front seat and tries to bundle me in from behind like a kidnap victim.

I can hear the freezing rain thwacking on the Classic Canvas roof as Kirstin's sickly-sweet words riding on her sickly-sweet perfume hit me full in the face.

'Alone is only for the lonely, Noah. Your head is a dangerous neighbourhood, remember? Come with us . . . pretty please.'

Christ! What has happened to this woman – this tough-assed waitress from Rhode Island who cut through bullshit like it was cream cheese and who could catch drunk vomit in a bucket from five yards without spilling a drop? If this change from Wonderwoman to Sugar Plum Fairy is the kind of miracle on offer at AA, then pour me a treble Jameson's and lay me out some chubby lines.

I forcibly resist Ray's push and, bent-double, look eastwards through the back window of the Olds. Not a car in sight. I crane my neck to look through the windscreen and, as Kirstin's lips peck my cheek, I see the yellow cab pull out from Second Avenue and head our way.

'*Thank you, God!*'

In a flash I return Kirstin's kiss, and with a surge of superhuman strength back Ray out from behind me and run down the street with my arm raised like Rocky's. The cab pulls over and I duck in shouting a 'Goodnight' which blows west as the door slams shut behind me and I breathe out a sigh of relief and in a lungful of dope smoke. The cab driver – Jesus Jiminez according to the medallion – is smoking a joint the size of Nelson's Column as if it was a Marlboro. I tell Jesus to head for Greenwich Street below Canal. He nods and offers me the joint. Without hesitating I take a hit as Jesus turns up the radio so his cab bulges at the seams with the beat of Los Lobos and screeches into a U turn. Thrown against the cab door, my nose pressed against the window, I find myself forced to look back at the parked Cutlass where Ray stands alone and bewildered in the swirling sleet.

The Triangle Below Canal, Tribeca is pioneer country, but I'll lay five to one that within ten years it will be the 'in' place to be, the new SoHo. But as of today it's still a run-down semi-industrial wasteland between the southern outposts of the Village and the glass and steel canyons of the financial district. It's home to countless seedy shipping companies and a few broke artists who judge the post-apocalyptic deserted nighttime streets a risky but worthwhile trade-off for cheap rent and a long lease on two thousand square feet of loft space. It's true that Tribeca has good 'Art' light, but when the wind's blowing off the Hudson in January it can feel like Fairbanks, Alaska, on those cross-streets. And there is not a tree to be seen in the whole bloody triangle.

Three years ago I could have had fifteen hundred square feet on Harrison Street in a disused warehouse with cast-iron Doric columns, but I viewed it on one of those January nights at ten thirty and didn't have the guts to go for it. I opted instead for the safety of a fifth-floor walk-up studio in a building on the corner of 21st and Broadway with a mansard roof and a coffee shop on the ground floor. It reminded me a bit of my flat in Kilburn and it's been my home from home ever since.

Ruben Blades's salsa shit is blasting out as we pull up in front of the loading bay of a warehouse on Greenwich; I pay off Jesus and shout for him to keep the two or three dollars change. Jesus thrusts the money back into my hand and, nodding to the beat like a stoned woodpecker, digs into a hole in the seat between his legs and pulls out a fat joint which he gives to me, then turns back to the radio and turns it up even louder. He hasn't said a word the whole trip. I scream THANK YOU over the music, but Jesus doesn't turn round. He simply raises his fist in a *Venceremos!* salute and notches his nod up into double time. So I simply return his salute, pocket the spliff and get out. The taxi spins its wheels in the slush and, burning rubber, screeches into the night, thumping to its bass beat.

I can still hear the cab pounding a block away as I look up to the third floor of the building – the lights are on. Down on loading-bay level a shit-brown metal door is unlit by a broken bulb. But in the overspill street light, I can make out the five door-bells and their nameplates. The bottom two are blank. The fourth is illegible and the fifth reads Sabra Imports. The third, in sixteen-point Helvetica Bold, says TWIN COSTUMES. I press the button. A chirpy female voice comes over the intercom asking, 'Who is it, please?' as though it were two o'clock in the afternoon in suburbia.

'It's me, Noah. I'm sorry. Is it too late? I was over on

Delancey doing some editing and I thought that being as I was in the area and –'

God, I'm nervous. I'm never nervous on a Twin Visit! For some reason tonight I am. Maybe it was something in Jesus's dope? Anyway, whatever the reason, I'm just about to take this stupid stoned apology into hyperwarp when the buzzer goes off at a thousand decibels and the lock clicks open on the door and I nearly shit myself. I am so fucking freaked that I don't get to the door-handle soon enough. The lock locks back. I feel like I've been caught playing truant or shoplifting. But my libido is strong enough to re-raise my finger, and I'm just about to ring the doorbell again when I lose courage, turn like lightning on my heel and hop down the loading-bay steps. I land on the sleet-slick pavement and am about to head back up Greenwich when the intercom crackles seductively back into life.

'Don't be shy, Noah. Come on up and read us a bedtime story.'

The buzzer goes again and the lock draws back. Like a criminal, I glance up and down the street and am surprised to see a man in a dressing gown, beret and wellington boots walking two shih-tzus on leads around the corner into Harrison Street. Behind me the buzzer is now buzzing louder than a chainsaw. And I'm standing there torn between acute horniness and some weird kind of apologetic embarrassment when the voice screams out from the intercom, almost blasting it off the wall.

'NOAH! GET YOUR CUTE BRIT ASS UP HERE FOR A THREE-WAY FUCK!'

Shih-tzuman turns so quickly that he almost loses his balance, then rights himself, reins in his little dogs and shouts over to me in a surprising basso profundo.

'Go for it, guy! And put one in for me, why don't you?!'

I give him the thumbs up, leap back on to the loading bay

and open the heavy metal door to Shagger's Heaven half a second before the buzzing stops.

The metal industrial staircase is lit by a solitary 100-watt bulb circa 1936 which is casting me a huge Nosferatu shadow as I clang upwards towards the ladies-in-waiting. This will be about the thirtieth time in as many months that I have climbed these stairs for purposes other than business business.

I first met Rita and Connie when I was making *Downtown Surf Story*, my first US film since the disastrous Black Sabbath movie – that pretentious piece of post-film-school shit whose only artistic legacy was Ray, my Sven Nykvist, lighting cameraman on every movie I've made ever since, and now also chief hair up my arse and watchdog over my alcohol and drug consumption.

Anyway, it was 1982 and I was back in the States to make my second and last Rockumentary, or Punkalogue as Ray called it. It was a twenty-minute short to be shot in one night at the newly opened Pyramid Club and featuring the Butt-hole Surfers – the only band to rival the Dead Kennedys in the name department. A friend of mine who was the State-side stringer for the *New Musical Express* called me one Wednesday and told me to get over to New York on the Saturday and shoot the Buttholes while they were still raw and bloody. I had nothing going on at the time, so I phoned Blue Sky/Ray to see if he was up for it. He was, so on the Saturday I hopped on a plane to New York, took a cab to Avenue A and walked into the Pyramid to find Ray already shooting with an Arriflex in one hand and a sound boom in the other. The club was narrow as an alleyway and there were more drugs in the air than oxygen. The floor was heaving with stoned punks jerking to the arrhythmic beat of a manic dirge belted out at two hundred decibels from a narrow stage by three skinny guitarists wearing Warhol wigs. I tunnelled to the bar and ordered a triple Jameson's from a guy with a third eye tattooed in the middle of his forehead and wearing a spiked dog collar. When the drink came I shouted an apology and handed the bartender a fifty-dollar bill. He took it, casually reached under the bar and put in front of me a small vial of coke with a spoon chained to it. My kind of club! As I surfed the jostling to avoid spillage and was doing up the second spoonful of marching powder, a Quaalude-muted roar went up from the floor. The coke was icing in nicely as I turned towards the stage expecting to see the notorious Buttholes. Instead I was met by a sight that did something I had long thought impossible – it shocked me.

Onstage two stunningly beautiful identical redheads were dancing in sensual spasmodic movements to the offbeat of the Warhol guitarists who were now doing an incredibly bizarre interpretation of 'The Sound of Music'. Both women were dressed as nuns, but they had only one habit between them. One was naked from the waist up, the other from the waist down, and they mirrored each other's movements in a strange, sexy, split-screen dance. It was pornography, but these amazing twins were managing the impossible and keeping their performance loaded with a tantalising eroticism. At that moment I would have taken any odds against there being a soft cock or a dry cunt in the room.

I turned to where Ray had been a minute ago to shout to him to make sure he was getting this moment on film, but he was already nearing the stage, ploughing through the crowd with his camera held aloft and aimed at the redheads who suddenly raised their arms as if on the cross and began to spin into a Whirling Dervish parody of Julie Andrews on the hillside in the opening sequence of the Von Trapp Crap saga. The crowd went wild and was soon spinning up a storm, and as I started up a twirl of my own, I could see Ray's Arriflex whirling over the heads of the punks nearest the stage.

That was my introduction to Rita and Connie – a.k.a. Christie and Christie Himmelfart – the Tribeca Twins. In the wee hours of the morning after the Buttholes had done their stuff and we had enough footage in the can, Ray and I approached the sisters. They were dancing together to Lou Reed's 'Waves of Fear' which was blasting over the sound system. They were now fully clothed in identical black lamé body-suits and red berets sporting tiny penises on top where that little felt whatsit should be. We asked them to sign a release and this led to a conversation which finished over breakfast in a coffee shop somewhere in Alphabet City.

It turned out that Rita and Connie O'Hearn were graduates of the Fashion Institute over on Sixth Avenue, and had combined their love of design with their love of avant-garde music and had risen to fringe stardom in the microclimate of the downtown New York punk scene. They made all their own costumes.

'Say, would you guys like to see some more of our designs?' said Rita (I think), wiping up the last of her maple syrup with the last bite of waffle.

'We'd be happy to model them for you,' said Connie (I think) as she finished the last of her coffee.

They then simultaneously smiled at Ray and myself with a child-like innocence which, curiously, didn't seem at odds with the penises on their heads.

Back at their newly occupied Tribeca loft the twins modelled their costumes for Ray and myself. Their designs were mind-boggling, ranging from leather gear which topped anything worn by Mel Gibson in *Mad Max II* to little cashmere suits which would have set Doris Day cooing. And all of them sexy beyond sexy. As I watched those dazzling, talented red-headed sisters sashay up and down the length of loft, I knew there and then that I had found the costume designers for all my future films. So I asked them to come on board and they agreed without even asking me a single question about my work. Ray slapped the celebration coke on the table and a couple of lines later we were all in the twins' newly assembled cherry bed fucking like the Flying Burrito Brothers – and Sisters! And we laughed! We got up to such outrageous and ridiculous antics that even after we were shagged-out, the four of us – the director, the camera-man and the costume designers – lay naked on that huge bed in the fading afternoon light laughing like drains.

Since that day, whenever I've been feeling down or con-fused or simply in need of a guilt-free laugh, I've popped down to Tribeca and climbed these stairs I'm climbing now, my head reeling from Jesus the cab driver's Very Serious Shit!

I'm just about to rap on the twins' purple metal door when the lone light bulb fifty foot below pops, plunging me into darkness. By the time the sound from this reaches my fucked-up brain it has become a minor nuclear explosion. The aftershock rams my ribcage against my heart and lungs so that I open my mouth to scream in stoned terror just as Connie and Rita open the door. They are wearing identical red-check gingham dresses and look as though they have been interrupted in the hostessing of their Tupperware party. I make a desperate grab for humour.

'Ding-dong! Avon Lady!'

The sisters smile sweetly and each take one of my hands.

'Come in, dear lady, and show us your wares.'

They lead me inside and give me a chaste stereo peck on the cheek.

'Would you care for a cup of tea?'

On the table in the middle of the loft, there sits a porcelain teapot – Spode or perhaps Minton – with the most delicate flower tracery, three matching cups and saucers and silver apostle spoons, a sugar bowl with sugar cubes and a fragile little milk jug. Beside these, standing on a mirror, is another saucer on which is piled a good half ounce of cocaine with a fourth apostle spoon stuck delicately into it, beside this an unopened bottle of tequila and three glasses ready-salted on the rim, and beside all of it, incongruous yet somehow perfectly balancing the composition, a six-pack of Schlitz Malt Liquor.

One of the twins pours tea while the other scans through the music collection, picks out *Mario Lanza Sings Caruso* and puts it on. As the first aria hits the air, I'm laying out three fat lines on the mirror and the twins, in between sips of tea, are undoing the buttons of their fifties frocks.

The rest is, as they say, history.

So here I sit on the edge of this bed, the sun inching up and my hangover rising with it. And I am feeling puzzled and thrown by the events of last night. In the past the Fuckfest has never failed to work. One night with Rita and Connie with their insatiable sexual appetites and impish sense of fun has always put a new perspective on things, sometimes even bringing a bit of hope to what has seemed to be a hopeless situation, and if not that then at least a bit of a laugh to tide things over.

But not this time. No revitalising, no shagged-out tabula rasa, not even a giggle – just a lot of sweat work with a nagging feeling of guilt at the back of my drunk and stoned mind. And God knows it wasn't through lack of trying. There was one time during the mêlée when I could have sworn I was sucking my own dick, ejaculating over a set of standing nipples and fucking a flaming bush all at the same time. At one point in the proceedings, in what must have been a last-ditch stand by the twins to make me laugh, I retreated from their tailgates and flipped them over for frontal fun to find that they had somehow donned Groucho Marx glasses, noses and moustaches.

Both opened their legs wide and said simultaneously: 'Fuck Soup!'

Then they burst out laughing and pulled me down on to them. I didn't laugh. I struggled, trying to stay in my skin. They had bloody terrified me. I think I was on the edge of tears when things faded to black, and the dead-night-cold. And that's where I stayed until a few minutes ago – now.

I struggle off the bed and retrieve my scattered clothes. Getting dressed is like being flayed alive in reverse, every touch of cloth puts another burning layer on top of my skin. My sinuses are blocked and I feel as if I have been disembowelled. I have no strength at all as I try to lift my twenty-ton leather jacket off the floor. When I finally do, an envelope drops out. In one of those flashes of clarity that pepper really lethal hangovers, I am able to make out the Lincoln Center logo on the front and it all comes flooding in. This is the envelope containing the ticket for the concert in which the woman of my life will be playing. Ray had tucked it into my inside pocket just before we left the editing suite last night. The bastard! Who the fuck does he think he is anyway? God?

I stare at the envelope for a millennium, poised on the edge, knowing that even if I wait for the polar ice-cap to melt, I will eventually pick up that ticket to my future. When I finally make the inevitable move, taking a deep breath and diving in slo-mo through the thick morning-after air to retrieve the envelope, a drop of blood falls from my nose and marks the paper like an ancient wax seal.

'*WATER!*'

The emergency signal zaps through my system. I shuffle, keeping as level and silent as I can, to the fridge, pulling on my jacket and placing the envelope in the inside pocket which doesn't have the hole. I open the fridge to find that the only bottle in it is an unopened fifth of Beefeater's. Don't even think about it, Noah! Find water! Not a bottle in sight. I look over at the sink. Fuck it! It'll have to be City Water. Now ever since I read somewhere that New York City tap water has been through the human body an average of seven times, I have had a little difficulty in drinking it. The only way is if it is ice-cold, cold enough to mask the chemicals and fool me. I am dehydrating by the minute. The twins are snoring softly now. Ice! I open the freezer compartment to get an ice tray only to find it empty apart from a tattered copy of *Our Bodies Ourselves*, the sixties feminist doctor-yourself manual, and a rack of about a dozen test tubes. Four of them are labelled and contain about a half inch of frozen greyish matter.

'What the fuck . . .?'

I take one of the tubes and read: ANDY WARHOL '79. The second one says: RAYMOND CARVER '83. And the third WALTER CRONKITE '84. Walter the anchorman? Where? How? The mind boggles at the thought of Mr NBC himself with the Tribeca Twins. I close the freezer compartment flap on Rita and Connie's unborn children. When I try to shut the main fridge door, it sticks a little and I give it a good shove. The fridge rocks. A large, full bottle of Evian water falls from on top, hits my bare foot and rolls across the floor towards the bed. The pain is off the scale and a glob of bile shoots up to my mouth. In a sickening reflex action I trap the acid oyster behind my teeth and swallow it again as I reel over to the bed just as the bottle disappears under it. I bend to see it nestled among the dust bunnies, several old unidentifiable bits of clothing and about a decade's worth of discarded newspapers. I flatten myself on the debris and retrieve the Evian, but as I come out from under the bed, I crack the back of my head and, as the twins stir above, another wave of bile rises, but this time I fail to contain it and it splats over a photograph of Walter Cronkite in the 'Arts and Leisure' section of a 1984 *New York Times*.

'There are no coincidences, Noah!'

'Fuck you, Kirstin!' I hiss as I struggle to my feet and check that the twins are still asleep. They have opened their legs a little wider, but are showing no signs of waking.

I rummage in my jacket, find a couple of Co-dydramol, pop them and chase them down with half the bottle of water. I feel absolutely fucking terrible, just this side of a corpse. In fact, I would love to be a corpse right now, to be free of this total body pain which seems to be trying to turn me inside-out for my sins. From the lining of my jacket I dig out my trusty SpareBic, shuffle over to the bedside table, find a discarded envelope in a pile of post and pen the following:

Dearest both – thanks for last night or rather THE last night. You've been wonderful to me. I'll explain more on the P.S.A. shoot next week. Twin kisses – Noah X X.

Then I fold the envelope neatly and tear it in two. Like a ghost I lean over the sleeping sisters, and with my heart in my throat, tuck one half of the note into the crack of Rita's arse, the other half into the crack of Connie's, and head for the door where my boots are waiting.

As I pass the fridge the idea sneaks uninvited into my head and before I know it one of the test tubes from the freezer is in my hand and I'm making a detour to the toilet.

The jerking-off ritual is short but agonising, involving a bathroom mirror angled to reflect the naked sisters and some Oil of Ulay. I climax and a lightning bolt shoots through my skull leaving me semi-blind in my right eye. I bend down my still-hard penis and take a post-ejaculatory piss – it's streaked with blood.

'What the fuck's that?'

'Cranberries.'

'Cranberries?'

'Yes – *cranberries*.'

And I carry the test tube containing my parting shot and head back into the kitchen area.

As I stand in front of the fridge, I check the contents of the test tube – a minimal deposit, but the most this hangover will allow me to muster. So with my biro I write NOAH '85 on the label and pop that cc or so of myself back into the freezer between Andy and Raymond.

'*Probably strained yourself – burst a small blood vessel.*'

'*What?*'

'*The blood in the piss, Noah. Probably nothing to worry about.*'

'Of course – cranberry juice.'

I say these last four words out loud to myself as I slip my boots on, take one last look at Rita and Connie and leave. As the metal loft door shuts slowly and heavily behind me, the air it pushes out into the stairwell sounds like the last breath of a dying man.

EIGHT

You kiss my blood and the blood kiss me.
                    The Incredible String Band, 'Air'

North London hospital, February 1997

The ambulance doors open and the grey metallic light of the Accident and Emergency forecourt floods over the paramedics as they slide me out on my stretcher and on to the gurney. The pain in my bladder is back with a vengeance now. I can't tell up from down. But I can see Clare clearly beside me, holding the piss pot over my dick, trying her sweet damnedest to maintain my dignity by keeping all hidden under the bloodstained blanket. Her face is covered in so much of my blood that she looks like a walking wounded, as much a candidate for A&E processing as I do. She's smiling at me, sadly, anxiously, as we glide quickly through the automatic doors. Out of the corner of my eye, I catch a glimpse of Etta, standing on the edge of the scene – half in, half out, watching and girding herself for a long wait. She seems very small.

As I am rolled into the bright, harder lights of the inside of the hospital, a wave of nausea suddenly wells up through me and I feel myself drifting out of consciousness. I don't fight it. I opt for oblivion and the painless place.

The sun is already hotter than an English summer's day as

I step on to the veranda of the white-washed lodge. Bou-gainvillaea and frangipani scent the air and a band of pink cloud cuts the summit of Mount Kenya off from its base in the valley below, beyond this garden filled with flashing birds, plants of dreams and butterflies as big as your fist. I look back through the French doors and I can see Clare sleeping, shrouded in the morning mist of the mosquito netting – a beautiful ghost, sleeping the deep sleep of Africa.

I hear drumming in the distance, not from any one direction but all around me. I glance around the grounds. A starched black maid laden with sheets disappears into another lodge in a corner of the garden and then all is deserted – the coast is clear. I let my white towelling bath-robe fall to the floor, walk down the veranda steps and on to the lawn still heavy with dew. The drums are louder now. I break into a brisk trot, my legs strong, my back straight, and my flaccid penis beating time against my lower belly. I am smiling the smile of childhood and as I look up to see the sun glint off the snow-covered peak of the mountain, I let out a yell of pure delight.

Without breaking stride, like a coursing hare, I side-step through the lovingly-cared-for garden beds. I break out from the cultivated boundary, dash across a grassy no-man's-land and crash into the dense undergrowth and semi-darkness of jungle. I'm in an Henri Rousseau painting: foliage I don't recognise, leaves longer than my legs and hanging blossoms the size of babies. At the point where the stench of death of the forest floor, stirred by my pounding feet, meets the giddy flower scent just above my head, the air is thick – almost tangible – and as I stumble on, sharp growths cut into me and blood runs in tiny rivulets down my body. In the undergrowth, unseen animals grunt and screech, and on the canopy a hundred feet above birds shriek and monkeys chatter. The drums are nearer now, and a deep, massive roaring has been added to their polyrhythmic call. I run faster and faster and soon I am leaping and bounding through the jungle, naked and bleeding as when they cut me out of my mother, shouting at the top of my voice in primal whoops and hollers, drawn on by the beating of the heart of Africa.

Shafts of light break through to the forest floor ahead and the drumming is almost drowned by the roaring which is now so close it is inside my head. My lungs are almost bursting, gasping in razor-sharp air to feed my heart which is beating ten to the bar as it pushes the blood around my body and out through the wounds on my feet into the earth itself.

I crash out of the forest and into the blinding light. I stop dead in my tracks, wracked with pain, bent double with my head between my knees and my eyes closed, gasping. The roar is now so deafening I am inside it. I feel a cool dampness wrap itself around me and I force my eyes open. I am standing on the very edge of a precipice looking across a deep gorge to a waterfall that cascades a thousand feet into a boiling lake. Iridescent parrots fly from edge to edge in a choreographed air dance, and a hundred feet under them, in the rising mist spray, a rainbow shimmers, starting on the far flank of the falls and describing almost a full circle before disappearing back under the cataract.

The tom-tom's beat, now barely audible, seems to be coming up out of the whirlpool at the bottom of the gorge. My heart has slowed and is now pumping in time to the drums. I pull myself up to full height, put my palms together and stretch my arms to the sky above my head. I draw one massive breath deep into my loins, open my mouth in a silent scream and dive off, scattering parrots east and west, plunging through the three-quarter rainbow into the fevered pool far below.

In the deep turquoise, twenty feet underwater, I twist and turn like a seal. Shafts of sunlight penetrate from above and dance around me. I dart in and out of them. I want to laugh. I have no urge to strike for the air above. Bright fishes join me. They nibble my toes and dart playfully for cover into tropical underwater fronds. I will stay here and grow gills. I will drop my blood temperature and live in this water for ever.

Suddenly, out of the corner of my eye, I glimpse a fractured figure through the surface of the water, standing on what must be the bank. It raises an arm and lunges. The water surface breaks and something flashes towards me. A harpoon! As it nears, it seems to slow to a crawl. I try to swim out of the way, but I am moving even slower. I can count the barbs as they glint in the underwater sun, heading lazily towards my groin. Six – and needle-sharp. They hit their mark and shroud me in a cloud of dark pink.

As I roll belly-up three fathoms underwater, eyes closed, I hear Clare's voice.

'Just like that sun south of Mombasa, you will rise again big as the horizon, with enough energy to fuel a thousand worlds.'

I open my eyes.

Clare's face is six inches from mine, and she is clutching my hand hard in hers, close to her breast.

'Do you hear me, Noah? You have an ancient name. You have old blood. As old as Africa, where we ran on that white beach at Twiga. You were so strong. This bloody cancer wouldn't have dared to touch you then.'

As Clare raises my right hand to kiss it, I notice a fleck of blood on her top lip, beginning to congeal. My blood. When the kiss is finished, I see that fleck on my palm. So I bring my hand back to my own mouth and lick it.

'You will be that strong again.'

I swallow hard and force a smile.

'I will.'

Exhausted, I turn my head to one side and notice for the first time the IV in the back of my left hand, and see the doctor at the side of the bed making the final adjustments to a catheter the size of the Blackwall Tunnel which is sticking out of the end of my dick and running into a bag which looks like it is filled with the contents of the Black Lagoon. I can't make out a single distinguishing feature on the A&E house doctor's face. His mouth doesn't seem to open at all as he speaks to me in a monotone.

'We've found a bed for you on Elizabeth Ward, Noah. So we'll have you up there as quickly as we can and in the morning we'll have a look inside and see what's going on. Alright?'

He pats me on the thigh and his mouth twitches to something like a smile. Who the fuck does he think he is! He can't be more than twenty-five, for God's sake! I want to leap off the bed and head-butt the bastard in his smug, post-pubescent flat face! But all I do is nod slowly and squeeze Clare's hand as the doctor draws back the curtains around the bed and exits, letting in a sickeningly bright fluorescent light.

NINE

Step on a crack – break your mama's back!

Children's rhyme

The morning after, a minute later, February 1985

I step out on to Greenwich into one of those crisp, sub-zero, sunny winter days that seem possible only in Manhattan. The freezing wind is biting on everything in sight as it whips over from Jersey, icing down even more as it crosses the Hudson and hits me full on the back. My leather jacket, jeans and thin jumper can do little but prevent frostbite, and the only chance of any body warmth is to ditch the hangover shuffle and, as Ray would say, haul ass over towards West Broadway. I'm just getting up to cruising speed along Harrison Street when a patch of last night's sleet, now sheet ice, brings me down flat on my back with a dead weight thud which sends my head rolling across the street screaming.

'Fuck! Oh FUCK my luck! Oh Jesus! Jesus fuck!'

My back feels as if it's broken. I just lie there, looking up at the sun overhead and thinking it must be about eleven o'clock. With a pain-wracked sigh, I let out what little breath there is left in me and close my eyes. Perhaps it would be better all round if I just died here, the Captain Oates of Tribeca – 'Just think of the movies he might have gone on to make!' All of a sudden I feel licking on my face and open my eyes to come face to face with two shih-tzus as a familiar deep voice speaks.

147

'Oh, my Aunt! Are you alright? I saw you fall from across the street and from the sound you made I thought –'

It's Shih-tzuman! His face is right in mine and his breath smells of Belgian chocolates. He pushes his dogs out of the way and moves to cradle me into a pietà scene, but in a surprisingly swift move I duck under his arm and find myself sitting in front of him trying to look dignified. A dribble of snot runs out of my coke nose and freezes before it reaches my lip. Shih-tzuman peers closely at me.

'Say! Aren't you the fellow from last night?'

I struggle to my feet and brush off whatever filthy ice I can see. I raise a smile.

'No – he's my twin. He's the lazy one. He's still in bed.'

He reins in the dogs to his feet, winks and smiles at me. His teeth are covered with chocolate.

'Say no more – say no more – nudge nudge wink wink! I just love those Python guys, don't you?'

'No.'

'But that is an English accent I can hear, isn't it?'

'It is.'

I get up and start to walk away. I feel very uncomfortable with this man. I'm being rude, I know, but I don't give a monkey's toss.

'I thought all you guys loved those guys.'

Without turning round, I raise my hand in clench-fist salute and head off briskly with an over-the-shoulder shout to Shih-tzuman.

'Thanks for coming over and checking on me. Have a nice day!'

He screams after me, 'But I guess you don't watch too much TV, huh? Too busy fucking, huh? Well fuck you, asshole! I hope your goddam winky drops off!'

'*Winky?*'

I shake my head to myself and quicken my pace. Manhattan – God Bless Her – nothing, but nothing is what it first appears to be on this island. You walk through her, shifting your perceptions at every corner – now you see it, now you don't! She's a film maker's paradise, but she is also his Hell. Because Manhattan is a place that screams out to be shot, but is too much a movie herself to be captured effectively on celluloid. *Taxi Driver*? *The French Connection*? Great movies! Great Manhattan! But the Manhattan of your dreams and fantasies – the city of your head. The one I'm walking through now would need more than Travis Bickle to whip it into shape for release in the shopping malls of Peoria.

At the wasteland junction of West Broadway and Canal, the wind-chill drops another few degrees and I pull my useless collar up high and head east through a four-block army and navy store. This is the stretch of Canal where you can buy anything from a 'Black Tickler' condom to a 'USED ONCE ONLY' grenade launcher – I settle for a woolly longshoreman's hat as worn by Brando in *On the Waterfront*. I also buy an Incredible Hulk acrylic scarf for a couple of dollars. I'll ditch that before I reach Lincoln Center. If I ever reach Lincoln Center. I feel in my inside pocket for the envelope containing the recital ticket. Maybe I've lost it! No such luck! There it is, right over my heart. Oh, shit! This is terrifying stuff. Why the Hell did Ray ever bring that bloody article on Clare Whatshername!

'Come on, Noah! Don't pretend you don't know her full name. It was burned into your brain by the time you left the Cozy Soup'n'Burger. So say it! Come on!'

'Clare Mathesson,' I whisper to myself as I hit the northern edge of Chinatown.

'You can do better than that! Shout it out, lad!'

I pass by a Peking Duck house with steaming vats in the window –

'Fuck soup!'

I start to laugh a little. My ears are warming. My neck is

being protected from the chill by the Hulk. All around me the air is filled with the sing-song of Chinese buying and selling lychees, tofu and fish by the ton. The cold air is full of the colour of life lived permanently on the edge of a carnival.

'*Go on – shout it out!*'

'CLARE MATHESSON!'

I scream her name so loudly that the wizened vendor on the veggie stall I am passing misses his scales and drops a large order of beansprouts to the floor. He shouts at me and waves his fist.

'YOU FUCKIN' FIRECRACKERHEAD! YOU PAY FOR THAT, MOTHERFUCKER!'

I stand there, stunned by the blast of my own voice.

'ONE DOLLAR! YOU SON BITCH!'

The vendor is about to leap over his stall at me. He's old but he's wiry, and who knows what he's got tucked under that padded jacket. So quick as silver, I whip out two dollar bills and drop them on top of his Chinese cabbage and walk off quickly, trying to stay cool as Bruce Lee and a Tong gang waving cleavers give chase to kickbox me into the gutter for having broken some ancient Chinese market law.

I cross Canal on to Mulberry Street. I'm in another country. I look back over the road – no sign of Bruce and the boys. I quicken my step – a new man with a purpose. Screaming Clare's name out loud back there at the vegetable stall must have really focused me. My head is still throbbing, but I know now exactly where I am heading – what I have to do – who I have to talk to. I walk even faster. I have to catch Tiny before he does his daily Rescue Ride on his chopper.

Little Italy belies its name. Hardly any Italians actually live behind or above the coffee bars of the kind which grace at least one obligatory scene in any Mafia movie – they've all long gone to Jersey or to Bensonhurst, Flatlands or Canarsie. But they return for marriages and funerals to this Lower East Side neighbourhood of Beginnings and Dreams. And on one day in September it seems as if every Italian in the five boroughs converges on Little Italy for the feast of San Gennaro, to gorge themselves on pasta e fagiole, manicotti, or any of the ten thousand Old Country dishes sold on Mulberry, which for twenty-four hours is a vast al fresco ristorante whose air is filled with the nostalgic songs of the likes of Carlo Butti, the Neapolitan butcher turned tenor. It is said that this feast day is a favourite with that other butcher made good, John Gotti – the Teflon Don (nothing but nothing sticks!) who, it is rumoured, sits in the rear of a certain Mulberry Street café, sipping coffee near the gleaming and hissing Bella Macchina, shedding God-father tears for his departed sons.

Today the street is almost deserted, the cafés haven't yet opened for lunch and the grocery stores are mostly dark behind their window barricades of jars of sun-dried toma-toes, olives, hanging salami and boxes of pannctonc. The cars are still sleeping, parked on the east side of the street only. I stand still for a second and take in this rare moment of Manhattan stillness and quiet – I realise that my head has stopped throbbing. For a hanging moment I savour this bliss – then the air is broken by a screeching.

Up ahead a grey stretch limousine with darkened windows barrels out from Hester Street and shoots uptown, pulling into its slipstream that fragile peace and stripping my nerves raw. A split second later there's a shattering behind me as a young man as big as an ox throws up the metal shuttering on a deli. A few yards in front the two steel hatches to the basement of a café fly upwards and crash down on to the pavement sending a shudder through the ground, up through the soles of my shoes and on into my head which instantly starts to thump again. A young woman with big hair and big breasts rises up on the lift from the basement like some gum-chewing mechanical Venus. She nods at me.

'How ya doin'?'

Blood is flooding in behind my eyes washing the scene in Titian red. I'm in the opening scene of *Mean Streets*. A car pulls up and Harvey Keitel and Robert De Niro hop out and head towards the café without looking at me.

'Hey Bobby! Hi Harvey!'

'Hey, Christina! You talking to me?'

De Niro laughs and gives her a wave as he claps his arm around Harvey and they both disappear inside the building. Somewhere over towards Lafayette blood-curdling sirens are clearing the streets for fire engines responding to a three-bell alarm.

'Watch out, Noah. You're losing it.'

'I know. I know. I know.'

'So fucking do something!'

I give my head one massive shake and snort like a raging bull. I paw the ground, ready to make the big move forward.

'Hey, fellah! You OK?'

Christina is still rising up to ground level, looking at me like I'm a street dog she's not too sure about. I try to tell her I'm fine, but all that comes out is another snort. Christina's eyes widen: she quickly presses the button on the lift frame and starts to sink back down into the basement.

'You're sick, man. Get some help, why don't you?'

'WHAT THE HELL DO YOU THINK I'M DOING? WAITING FOR A FUCKING BUS?'

'FUCK YOU!'

And she disappears into the darkness below. I walk over to the gaping hole and shout down into it.

'Christina! Christina! I'm sorry. I shouldn't have shouted like that . . . it's just that . . . Christina! . . .'

But the only reply is my own echo coming back to me as a whisper.

'Keep a hold on yourself, Noah. You're not insane, just

hungover. Don't stop now. Think film – CUT TO THE CHASE.'

So I walk up as far as Kenmare Street, cut over to the Bowery and head north towards the Tea Room, and I pray that Tiny is still there. Tiny is a six-foot-four biker who rode for ten years with the Oakland Chapter and was the only man that Charlie the Child Molester confessed to being afraid of. He was one of the punishment squad that stomped Hunter Thompson for the crap he put in his book about the Hell's Angels, and he was three-time winner of the 'Colors' quarter-mile drag race – blindfolded. In the spring of 1982, stoned out of his skull, Tiny was heading down the California coastal highway to do a major dope deal with a border gang called The Banditos when his Harley exploded under him. His comrades were still looking up, waiting for bits of Tiny to fall out of the sky when he walked up out of the roadside gully without a bruise or a scratch on him.

From that moment on he didn't touch another drink or drug. He moved to New York City and made a name for himself in security. He also opened the Tea Room, a basement on the Bowery, furnished – so as not to intimidate the clientele – with second-hand sofas and easy chairs, a few old kitchen tables and a couple of trompe-l'oeil windows framed with flowered curtains. In one corner a bottomless biscuit tin stands on a shelf behind a makeshift serving counter. Nearby, the ever-ready tea urn and coffee pot sit on an illegally installed wood-burning stove. A sign over the door reads: YOU ARE ENTERING A NO-DANGER ZONE – PLEASE LEAVE YOUR BOOZE, DRUGS AND FEAR OUTSIDE. It's a safe and cosy home from no home which Tiny leaves every day at noon, fires up his bike and does his rounds of all the shooting galleries in a ten-block radius, dispensing free needles and methadone which are supplied to him by Beth Israel hospital through an arrangement he clinched by sweet-talking the Detox Unit.

Tiny came into my life when I was shooting *Downtown Surf Story* and he turned up on the set and offered his services for 'crowd control'. There was no crowd to be controlled on our low-budget indie shoot, and when I looked at the tattooed giant asking me for a job, it triggered a rerun in my head of that infamous footage from the film *Gimme Shelter* which shows Hell's Angels hired by The Stones killing a man who knocked over one of their bikes.

'Don't worry, man. I can see what you're thinking.'

'*Psychic Alert! Psycho Alert!*'

'I ain't gonna pull no Altamont shit!'

Then he laughed and slapped me on my back, separating a couple of vertebrae. I hired him.

We only worked together once more before Tiny moved on to the more lucrative business of guarding the bodies of rock stars and we lost touch until I ran into him two months ago at the Fireside Lunchtime AA meeting up at the YMCA on Sixty-third Street. Since then I've been dropping into the Tea Room from time to time to have a mug of Tetley and a chat which is constantly interrupted as Tiny welcomes another drunk or dope addict who's heard on the grapevine that the biker in the basement is good for a cup of tea or coffee, a few biscuits and sometimes a dollar or two. If he thinks the time is right, Tiny will sometimes tell a drunk or a junkie the story of his Damascus Road experience on Highway One, but he never pushes the issue of being clean and sober. If he's asked a question, he answers it – wisely, without judgment. I suppose in his windowless basement, which looks like cross between a chintz tea room and a shooting gallery, Tiny is the closest thing the Bowery has to a resident oracle.

Half a block ahead of me, something glints in the sunlight. I squint against my headache and make out the chrome handle-bars of Tiny's chopped Harley sticking up behind a pile of rubbish. Great! He's not left on his rounds yet. I trot on.

'Hey, guy!'

I almost trip over him. He's lying on some grating with steam rising from beneath. His booze-drawn face is framed by matted tails of hair and is sticking out of the neck of a filthy Yogi Bear suit which must have been discarded after some parade or other. Yogi's smiling head sits next to a bottle of Thunderbird wine, his straw hat battered and his white collar filthy.

'Keep walking, Noah. The bastard's going to ask you for money!'

Too late! My hand is already digging into my pocket. I'm not that far gone. I can still be compassionate. I can still be benevolent. I clutch on to some crumpled bills. Whatever it is – two dollars or fifty – Yogi can have it.

'You're going to regret this – move on now!'

'Hey, guy! You got a bottle? I bet you got a bottle. Crack it open, brother, and sit awhile – I got central heating.'

I look at his shrunken head looking at me, seeing me, recognising me. I turn away and come face to face with my reflection in the darkened window of a disused barber shop offering haircuts for fifty cents. There he is – Nosferatu himself, vomit-flecked and bloodstained from last night's feasting. His eyes are deep in his skull and his transparent skin is stretched to breaking point over his bones which are trying to escape his wrecked body. He's terrifying.

'Bullshit! Vampire? Through a glass darkly? Bergman? Fuck that! You're a common or garden drunk, Noah – and Yogi's got your number.'

'You think you're so sodding clever, don't you! Well FUCK YOU!'

And I throw down the paper money and walk off in the common or garden huff of a child who refuses to hear the truth.

'FUCKING A, MAN! THERE'S SEVENTY BUCKS

155

HERE! HEY, FELLAH! THERE'S SEVENTY FUCKIN' BUCKS HERE.'

I glance over my shoulder to see Yogi stuffing the bills into his bear's head. He laughs to himself and shouts after me as I move on again.

'COME BACK HERE, GUY! I'LL GODDAM FLY! I'LL FUCKIN' BUY! WE'LL PARTY ALL FRIGGIN' YEAR!'

'*Sounds good to me.*'

I stop in my tracks but don't look back. I try to step forward, but I can't move. Oh my God! It's like that time on that perfect brick path outside Freedom House, the night of the reading when I met Kirstin. But this is a trillion times worse. Then I had a bottle in my pocket. Then I managed to fix myself and move on. This time the bottle is behind me, in the hands of a Bowery bum, and I am standing here once again collapsing into the jaws of hell without a lifeline, the whole mess of my life being sucked into where I stand on this turd-strewn street of a foreign land into an emotional and spiritual void – my own Black Hole. I think this must be it! This is what the AAs mean by 'rock bottom'. This is where I have to 'get off the down elevator' or plunge through basement, down through the earth's crust, through the magma, through layer upon burning layer, until I break through to the point of my own singularity and crawl into that bed and a living death in the glass room at the end of *2001 – A Space Odyssey*.

'C'MON BACK HERE, GUY. THE DRINKS ARE ON ME!'

'*Oh, shit! What the fuck are you going to do now, cleverdick?*'

'*Don't ask me this time, Noah. You are on your own for this.*'

I feel a rapid movement behind me and hear a roaring. I turn to see Yogi Bear, now with his head on, charging towards me. I try to side-step him, but I stumble, and before

I can regain my balance I am in the iron lock of his bear hug. I can hardly get my breath. What few gasps of air I manage to suck in stink of rotting flesh and stale booze. Yogi presses his face into mine, his yellow teeth stained with blood. He tightens his grip, cracking my ribs, and hisses into my ear.

'I want you to have a fucking drink with me, you stuck-up son of a bitch!'

I summon every ounce of strength in me to gasp my acceptance to Yogi's invitation. I'm shocked when the slogan, clear and measured, comes out instead:

'THY WILL NOT MINE BE DONE!'

'Fuck that shit, you asshole!'

Yogi lets out a mighty roar, squeezes even harder and I see his teeth heading for my cheek. Suddenly the bear is yanked skywards and air rushes into my bursting lungs.

'What the Hell you think you're doing, Harry!? This is my friend, here – leave him the fuck alone!'

And there's Tiny, dangling Yogi in one hand and yanking the bear head off with the other. Harry hangs there in the giant biker's hand, looking as though he is about to burst into tears.

'I'm sorry, Tiny. I just wanted the guy to have a drink with me. I didn't know he was a friend of yours.'

'Friend or no friend, Harry – don't make a difference. How many times do I have to tell you to cut the bear crap? One day it's gonna get you in deep shit. You hear me?'

Harry nods as Tiny lowers him to the ground and gives him back his head.

'You want a drink, Harry?'

Harry nods.

'Then cool off for a while then come to the Tea Room. I got Lapsang – your favourite . . . OK?'

'OK.'

Harry comes over to me and offers me his hand.

'Maybe some other time, huh?'

Bewildered, I shake his hand and grunt something. He shuffles back towards his grating. Tiny takes me gently by the shoulders and squares me to face him.

'Good thing I came out when I did. Harry don't know his own strength. Some guy tapped him playful on the head one time. Harry tapped him back and broke his fucking neck.'

He laughs. I laugh with him, but it's not what I want. What do I want? I don't know. Isn't that why I'm here to see Tiny?

'So, Limey . . . they let you out the editing room?'

'I need to talk to you, Tiny.'

My voice has an edge to it. I'm shaking from head to toe. Nothing visible on the outside, but inside I'm vibrating like a dynamo on the blink. Tiny clocks my shakes with that sixth sense of his, and he knows they have nothing to do with the attack from Yogi Harry. So with the touch of a mother, he puts his arm around my shoulder and starts walking me towards his Tea Room. I'm unsteady on my feet – like a loaded drunk – so loaded that when we reach the steps down to the basement, Tiny throws me over his shoulder in a fireman's lift, ducks through the door, flips the sign to 'CLOSED' and plops me down on a battered sofa.

'So talk.'

And he throws off his leather jacket, puts on the kettle and reaches under the counter to bring out two Royal Worcester bone-china cups and a couple of mismatched saucers. He wipes them on the hem of his T-shirt, which I now see has FUCK YOU! printed in sixty-point white letters on his chest. When he turns around and reaches for a tartan biscuit tin from the shelf, the back of the shirt reads AND FUCK YOU TOO! I laugh aloud and feel the hard floor of the basement, solid and safe under my feet. Tiny holds up a tiny milk jug decorated with purple violets.

'Milk no sugar, right?'

'Right.'

I start to talk and find myself telling Tiny about Dad's death in the kind of detail I thought I had forgotten. Words start to pour out of me like water from a dam sluice. My life comes pouring out on fast-forward, and Tiny just keeps pouring tea and listening in silence.

I don't know how many cups later it is that I finally get to telling him about the three-way fuck with the twins and this afternoon's recital by the woman Ray has deemed to be my future.

'So here I am, Tiny, and I don't have a fucking clue what I should do.'

Tiny takes a slow sip of tea and puts his cup down daintily.

'That's bullshit and you know it.'

The verbal punch hits me hard on the side of my head. I struggle for a reply, but I'm not quick enough.

'You know what to do. Everybody always knows what to do – they just don't got the nuts to admit it. Shit-scared they might get what they want; and then what the fuck they gonna do – what they gonna bitch about then?'

'But –'

'Don't "but" me, Noah. Just think 'bout the last time you was in a "I loves her – I loves her not"-type situation. It's driving you crazy, tearing them daisy petals trying to find out if you do or don't. But the answer's simple. All you gotta do is this. You get buck-naked and you go to your bed that night and ask yourself that question then pop that light out. In that split second you plunge into dark you listen hard and you'll have your answer. And any guy who says he don't is a motherfucking liar.'

Silence. He pours himself a drop more tea and then reaches over to pour me some. I put my hand over the top of my cup.

'But . . . I don't have a night to wait. The recital is this afternoon. I have the ticket right here in my pocket.'

'Let me see that.'

I pass Tiny the envelope and he takes out the ticket and stares hard at it. Then he stands and takes my cup and his over to the counter, throws his bike jacket back on and glances at his watch.

'On your feet, my little Limey Filmmaker, we got less than an hour.'

The next thing I know, I'm perched high on the back seat of Tiny's chopped Harley, easing past City Hall and on to the approach ramp to the Manhattan Bridge. As soon as we hit the bridge itself, the icy wind off the East River hits us full-force. Tiny's long greasy hair whips me in the face like a cat-o'-nine-tails. I shut my eyes tight as Tiny lets out a whoop and opens up the throttle. I get some idea of what it must have been like to race that Colors Quarter Mile blindfolded. Christ! Tiny must have been a complete fucking maniac. Yet . . . as I hear the throaty roar of the 1000-cc engine, feel the heat from the flying exhausts through my leather jacket and the give of the suspended road under us, I can see the pull in it – this blind riding. Hunter Thompson claims to do it all the time – drop some major drug and take the old Black Shadow out on to the coastal highway, close his eyes and open her up full. I wonder? There's only his word for it – it could be the Nyquil and booze cocktails talking Gonzo. Tiny, though, has a trophy to prove he did it – and he stomped Hunter into the bargain.

'FUCKING BEAUTIFUL, MAN!'

I open my teary eyes to slits and see Tiny pointing one finger straight up like a Jesus freak. I tilt my head back and the airflow parts at my nose allowing me to open my eyes to see the web of spun steel above glinting in the cold afternoon sun. It's a stock footage film moment. Suddenly, over in Brooklyn, the sun flashes off a window like a distress signal. From the ghost of Washington Roebling – that obsessed bridge builder, still in his sickbed, paralysed with caisson disease, looking out of that same window from which he directed the completion of his father's vision to the screams of men in agony from the bends? Today, undead, he counts cars and makes stress calculations, trying to predict the date when traffic overload will snap the steel cables from their Gothic arches and send the roadbed plunging to the dark waters below. Another flash. Is he warning us now to get off the bridge? Is this the moment of critical mass?

'Jesus Christ, Tiny! Get a fucking move on – the bridge is about to collapse.'

Tiny reads my mind and puts the hammer down some more. We must be doing seventy-five as we come off the bridge into Brooklyn. I glance over my shoulder, half expecting to see the whole magnificent structure collapsing behind us. But the bridge is standing in all its glory and my faith in Truth, Justice and the American Way is still intact as Tiny pulls off Front Street, into Water Street and into the cesspit area called DUMBO – Down Under Manhattan Bridge. This area is so run-down, so uninhabited, so damp and dark, it goes beyond fatal attraction into the pure fear zone.

Tiny pulls up in front of a building so brutal that even graffiti taggers have steered clear of it. Except for one sociopath who had painted the wall with the silhouette of a man standing over the cringing form of another, knife raised high above his head, ready to strike the death blow. Next to this masterpiece is a metal bunker door with a speakeasy shutter.

'Drink?'

Tiny dismounts and heads for the Hellmouth. I hesitate.

'Or you can wait here. Keep an eye on the sickle.'

I take one look around the wasteland, feel that rare city silence for the second time today and hop down sharpish from the Harley. Tiny knocks on the bunker, the shutter slides back, he whispers something and the door opens. I follow Tiny into a black, windowless interior, lit by blue light and with a bar running the length of one wall. Written over the bar in fluorescent letters a foot high is the name of the establishment – THE SHIT HOLE. There are perhaps twenty misfits in the room, it's hard to count as it is so bloody dark. What I can see is that these men – I can't see a woman in the place – are quite simply the ugliest most evil-looking people I have ever seen in my none-too-sheltered life. They make the shuffling cast of *Night of the Living Dead* look fit and wholesome. The room is also curiously quiet. There should be music, I suppose, but the Wurlitzer Juke in the corner has the wheel and front forks of a motorcycle sticking out of the display panel.

Tiny approaches the bar. The barman stays down the other end, back to us, his shaved head blue and the folds of his bull neck hiding his dangerous thoughts.

'Yo, barkeep!'

Tiny slams his palm on the counter. The Cro-Magnon turns and actually says –

'You talking to me?'

'Yeah, I'm talking to you. Gimme a drink. You want a drink, Noah?'

'No thanks. I'm fine. But you have one – go ahead, please.'

I can feel every evil eye in the room focused obliquely on us. I am literally shaking in my boots. I am dying for a leak but can see no door leading to anywhere, and even if there was one, I'd piss myself rather than walk over to it.

'What you need?'

The bartender is a Janus. His face doesn't match the back of his head. He has the small delicate features of a banker. But, and it's a huge 'but', he actually has a bone through his septum – the bone from a chicken leg, I think. I don't look long enough to confirm this.

'You got any milk?'

'Yeah, we got milk – for coffee.'

'I don't want coffee. I want a pint of milk. You got a carton?'

Bonio looks up and down the bar and shakes his head as if to say 'I don't believe this shit'. There's a couple of laughs from the shadows. Tiny leans over the counter, taking the barman's space.

'You got a problem with that?'

'What I got, you don't need. Now why don't you just fuck off back to Manhattan and stop pulling my fucking chain.'

'You want me to go back to Third Street and bring back the Three Stooges? Just get me my milk, OK?'

The barman hesitates a moment too long. Tiny grabs him by the hand and starts to squeeze. From where I'm looking, my giant doesn't seem to be putting on much pressure, but Bonio's eyeballs start rolling back in their sockets. Nobody makes a move.

'Now I'll ask you nicely. Could you please, pretty please give me a glass of milk?'

The dairy pint appears as if from nowhere and Tiny downs it in one draught, wipes his lip with his sleeve, lets out a satisfied sigh and turns to the inmates.

'Stare on, motherfuckers. Any asshole can belly up to the bar and order a beer. It takes a man to order a milk. Any of you gentlemen care to join me?'

Silence.

'Some other time then.'

He puts a five-dollar bill on the bar.

'Keep the change.'

Then Tiny puts his arm around my shoulder and leads me out of the door smiling like the proverbial cat who just ate the proverbial cream, and I can hear him purring like a pussy.

TEN

If music be the food of love . . .
                          Shakespeare, *Twelfth Night*

As the Harley pulls up outside Lincoln Center, cabs are disgorging the well-heeled for the various matinees. They are well-dressed in that particular New York Pucci, Gucci, Fiorucci way which sets them apart from European society dressers like sartorial sore thumbs. We look like sales reps from Hell's department store – Tiny of the Fallen Angels Boutique and me of the Down and Out Menswear floor. Tiny keeps the engine running. The concert goers avert their gazes. I check my close-up in the bike wing mirror. I had hoped I might pass my stubbled gauntness off as designer chic. But no – what stares back at me from the mirror is subhuman, reptilian, a tight shot of a dead rat's arsehole. Jesus Christ! I can't be seen like this. I keep staring at my reflection and make no move to get off the motorcycle. Tiny puts his hand over the mirror and turns to me.

'Get off the bike, Limey.'

He revs the engine high. I still don't budge. And I'm about to go into my old alkie paralysis routine when Tiny suddenly thrusts his face within a half inch of mine.

'Get off my fuckin' sickle, man!'

I dismount *tout de suite* and stand there like a scolded dog. Tiny gives me a Paddington Bear hard stare.

'Go for the milk, my friend.'

Then he winks and lets out the clutch and throttles so hard that the Harley tears up Broadway like an ethyl dragster on the quarter-mile.

'*Let go and let God, Noah.*'

'Alright! I hear you! So fuck off and let me get on with it!'

This turns a few blue-rinsed heads. I ignore them, turn on my heel and cut over to Alice Tully Hall muttering under my breath.

'Who the Hell is Alice Tully?'

As I enter the lobby the doors to the recital hall are just closing. I sprint, and the usher looks terrified as I barrel down on him, a leather-jacketed madman waving a ticket. I can feel every eye in the house drilling into me as I squeeze myself thin and, as the lights dim, shuffle like an apologetic crab, banging knees and treading on toes to my mid-row scat.

The cartilage in my knee clicks and sounds like the ricochet of a high-powered rifle shot. Three seats over on the row in front a balding man turns and shoots me a Death's-head look, the dimming lights glint off his glasses like warning flares. Christ! It's Arthur Miller again! And beside him, in Cosa Nostra camel-hair coat and perfect swept-back hair, I catch the Roman Emperor profile of Martin Scorsese. No, no – this cannot be – this is some peripheral vision vision. Then, as if he could read my thoughts, Marty turns and nods in my direction, catching the final ray of stage light as the auditorium Fades to Black.

Any further speculation on my part is drowned out by the applause as the Kairos Quartet, instruments in hand, walk onstage and head for four utilitarian chairs set in a semi-circle around a squat arrangement of hyacinths. As they sit they push the air in front of them out over the flowers, carrying their heady scent to the expectant audience.

Kairos is a handsome foursome of two men and two women, which I will learn later is an unusual combo – quartets tend to be single-sex. One violinist is a young, androgynous man who could be anywhere from twenty to thirty years old. His red hair is plaited in a single braid at the back of a fine head which is fronted by a face of rock-star good looks. He fails only in one department – height. He's probably about the same height as Scorsese, which is the same as saying he is never going to play professional basket-ball. The other violinist is a coffee-coloured beauty who takes her seat with grace, rooting herself through the earth to some Pacific island home on the other side. The viola is in the large hand of a large man who could be dismissed as fat if it weren't for a presence to rival Orson Welles. He smiles as he sits and makes his face handsome. All three are good-looking – but all three of them rolled into one large, dark-skinned bisexual could not hold a candle to the woman who sits last and eases between her legs a cello made out of wood so rich and red that it seems to be on fire.

This woman – this Clare Mathesson of Ray's matchmaking and the *New York Times* 'Arts and Leisure' section – seems to float between Heaven and Earth, a willowy, gossamer creature whose tall, slender body fights against substance and refuses to define its own edges. Her huge eyes glint as she casts a look over her audience sitting in the dark. And then she smiles a smile which is so fleeting it hardly happens, but which afterwards hovers around her head like a wraith. She wears a dove-grey silk dress which when she moves shimmers and seems to kiss her. Then there are the hands. Her hands are those of an El Greco Madonna – so long, so delicate they seem to have an extra joint. I cannot take my eyes off them. They adjust the neck of the cello, they take up the bow – they work with the touch of a lover – fluid alabaster.

The musicians settle into their chairs. Clare cranes her neck forwards, smells the hyacinths, then makes a final adjustment to her cello. The androgynous boy tucks his violin under his chin and the Pacific island beauty follows his lead. After a brief pause Orson grips his viola with his substantial chin. The air hangs in the balance. Suddenly the boy nods at Clare and all four players whack their bows on to their strings with such ferocity that I'm thrown back in my seat. This attack is followed immediately by a plunging silence and then a quiet chord which tears out a piece of my heart.

I hold my programme at an angle to catch the stage light and I read: Beethoven, Opus 59 – number 3. Old Ludwig Van – Mr Clockwork Orange himself in full swing – and my head fills with Droogies and a marble penis – a woman in a jump-suit – scissors – a cut! Tits pop out! – bowler hat boot boys ready for action – LIGHTS – CAMERA – ACTION!

'*GET OUT OF THE FUCKING FILM, NOAH! GO FOR THE MILK!*'

'*Milk – milk – milk bar – CUT! DIRECTOR'S CUT!*'

And I'm out – leaving Mr McDowell and his rapists to their film footage. I'm shaking, I could murder a drink, but I have escaped. I am back inside Alice Tully, looking at Clare Mathesson's hands arcing and sweeping, slicing and caressing as they play the triumphal entry march for the First Day of The Rest of My Life.

Fuck you, Ray, you clever, clairvoyant bastard!

The rest of the recital is a sound blur of something by Ravel in F with lots of plucking and Haydn's five millionth thing for strings. For me it's the soundtrack to the movie *Quartet*. I sit in the dark watching those hands, those exquisite, incomparable hands. And I am taken back to 'Sunday Night at the London Palladium' on Uncle Bart's Philips telly with the ten-inch screen in a cabinet as big as a

New York fridge. I must have been about ten. This particular night there was an act with white gloves dancing in the dark, or against a black curtain or something. I remember nothing else about the show but hands, many hands, performing some kind of magical, mysterious ballet for me as I sat in my tartan dressing-gown, sipping hot cocoa, ready for bed. That night those white hands came into my dreams. Then they must have tucked themselves away in some corner of my brain until today; to be summoned by these angel hands playing before me now, to dance inside my head together like some disembodied semaphore giving me signals which I don't fully understand but which at one and the same time arouse me and fill me with fear.

HURRAH! BRAVO!

The applause brings everyone to their feet – except me. I sit there with a wall of clapping towering around me. I feel drained, beaten. I could sleep for a year, but I know I must make a move and somehow I struggle to my feet, just in time to catch Arthur Miller as he ducks along the row in front clutching his trusty Amtrak timetable. I look at the stage. It is empty. A wave of nausea hits me and I grip the back of the seat in front. The audience around me is flowing out of the auditorium like lava, bubbling, fiery. Marty is doing up his Don coat. He turns and sees me clutching the seat back.

'Need any help?'

I shake my head and try to avoid his look.

'No thanks – I'm fine. Just went a bit dizzy.'

Marty looks at me hard.

'We've met, right?'

'I don't think so,' I lie. Actually we met a screening in LA last year.

'Sure we have – some screening – LA. You directed that movie –'

But I don't let him finish. I turn my back and I slip into the lava flow and out into the lobby. Fuck! I don't believe I did that. I just lied to Martin Scorsese then turned my back on him.

'*You can say that again, you stupid little shit. You gave the director of* Taxi Driver *the cold shoulder when he tried to help you – you silly, silly bugger!*'

My head is now thumping again. I beetle about among the glitterati like some demented wino – which is what I am – looking for a way out. I come face to face with myself in a full-length mirror. Bloody Hell! No wonder Marty looked concerned. I look like I have been exhumed and set into motion by some sinister hand. My eyes sunk deep into my skull, the almost grown-out guinea pig on my head is trying to scurry away and my bone-white face is framed by two days of filthy stubble. And I had said in my letter to Clare that I would meet her after the show.

'*No, no! Can't be done . . . simply can't – cannot!*'

There's no arguing that one – there's no way I can turn up to meet her looking like I do.

I lean against a plinth, take out my ticket stub, and write in tight manic tiny script:

'*You've enough people to see. Thanks for your playing. Tomorrow? Tea? 3? Polish café opp. St John the Divine? Noah Arkwright.*'

I shove the stub back into the envelope, scribble her name on the front and give it to an usher who says she'll take it backstage to Ms Mathesson.

As I slither out of Alice Tully into the bustle and early evening lights of Broadway and Columbus, I hiss.

'She won't get it – I know it! Fat chance! Pissing in the wind.'

There's a fine drizzle coming down and umbrellas thwack open around me like launching vampire bats as I'm swept toward the curbside by the Tully magma which is being joined from the right by the lava flow from the Metropolitan Opera. I could drown in this mass of people, but I feel sickeningly alone, and lonely – abandoned by somebody I haven't even met yet, and probably never will now now that I've blown my big chance like a . . . a . . .? I search for the word.

'*A simple-minded, self-destructive twit.*'

That's right! Nothing more or less than a common or garden twit. I turn to an axe-faced Social X-ray tottering along on my left and make a walking confession to her.

'I'm a twit – a simple-minded, self-destructive twit.'

She twitches and smiles a cover smile as she digs in her pocket for her canister of Mace. Before she can blind me, I slip sideways into the crowd and, over the shoulder of a distinguished silver-haired man wearing a dinner jacket, I see Tiny languishing on his chopped hog, oblivious to the rain, drinking from the neck of a Perrier bottle as if it was Thunderbird Wine. He doesn't see me. And for the third time that night, I do a Judas turn and betray another person, myself, and the whole fucking situation. But I just can't face Tiny giving me a bollocking for not having 'gone for the milk'. There's a coffee shop on the corner of Ninth Avenue and Fifty-seventh. I'll get a drink and something to eat. I'll hide out and let the dust settle – work out a contingency plan for when Clare Mathesson doesn't turn up tomorrow – then go down to the Lower East Side for the drug shoot.

PART THREE

Cut to the Chase

ELEVEN

You better run for your life if you can, little girl. Hide your
head in the sand, little girl –

> The Beatles, 'Run for Your Life'

Welcome to the first day of the rest of your life

> Cloying cliché

New York City, February 1985

It's almost three o'clock and I am sitting at a window table in
the coffee shop on the corner of 111th and Amsterdam,
opposite St John the Divine, just as I said I would on the
ticket stub to Ms Mathesson which I know the usher threw
in the rubbish bin where it belongs. I look across the street,
through the snow flurries to the largest gothic cathedral in
the world. It's still unfinished, one third of it yet to be
completed. Unlike me – I'm finished – knackered and
pissed-off in extremis.

The filming last night outside a shooting gallery on Avenue C and East 7th was a nightmare and a washout – not to
mention a human tragedy. It was to have been a simple scene
in which a young junkie is queuing outside the dope den
when he accidentally stumbles against the guy in front and
gets a knife in his belly. We were using a local kid that Tiny
had been giving tea and methadone to, and he seemed chirpy
and bright when he appeared on the set just before midnight.
His nickname was Bullseye, he never missed a vein and he

173

weighed about an ounce, but looked clean. He drank coffee constantly and ate about a dozen doughnuts during the first four takes and was fascinated by the trick knife with the retractable blade which the extra in front of Bullseye used to stab him. His mood was steady. He even laughed once or twice. But I should have known that you can never judge a junkie by his cover. Because . . .

Before the fifth take Bullseye threw up all the doughnuts and coffee at Ray's feet, who handled it like a true friend of Bill W. by giving the boy a hug from which he broke free like a weasel and jumped back into his place in the queue to be stabbed. Bullseye was even paler than before and very shaky, and it sickens me to say it now, but I was really chuffed about that – the camera would lap it up. He really looked as though he could die any second. Which is exactly what he did. Just before the guy in front whirled round with the prop knife, Bullseye swayed one big metronome sway, fell into the gutter, gave one massive convulsion, vomited a stream of bile and went still.

CUT!

Ray and I reached Bullseye about the same time. He was dead as a dodo.

I pulled the boy's face out of the shit-filled gutter and placed it in my lap. To the crew it looked like a gesture of kindness, a move of caring respect for the dead. But I didn't feel a fucking thing except anger. If I'd know Bullseye was going to pull this selfish trick, I would have cancelled the shoot. I would have exchanged my matinee ticket and taken the time yesterday afternoon to clean myself up, have a meal before going to Clare's evening performance. If Bullseye had been considerate enough to warn me of his final exit, I could have been prepared to meet the love of my life. She would have been bowled over by my freshness and charm, my healthy confidence. Hell, we would probably have driven upstate to some Catskills lodge and made passionate, tender love till dawn and agreed to marry that very Monday at City Hall.

I wanted to drop Bullseye's head back into the gutter. But I made the mistake of turning his face to mine. Lifeless he looked like a worn-out ten-year-old. Only his dark eyelashes, luxuriant and thick, seemed unravaged by smack. I lowered them over his dead eyes, held him close to my chest and strangled a sob as it rose from deep inside me.

Ray put his hand on my shoulder then walked back to the camera, calmly unloaded the reel and tore it out of its canister, exposing it to the night.

In the stoneyard adjacent to the cathedral, young potential Bullseyes from the dangerzone of Morningside Heights only a block away are being trained in the stone-carving methods of the Middle Ages, in the hopes of saving their souls and immortalising them in figures yet to be carved on portals of the West Front.

I take a sip of strong coffee, take out a yellow legal pad and pen, and try to schedule tonight's retakes of the death in the shooting gallery queue. But my heart isn't in it. In fact, all I can do is write the same thing over and over again like Jack Nicholson did at his hotel lobby table in *The Shining*. But instead of '*All work and no play makes Jack a dull boy*', I write simply '*Bullseye's dead . . . dead Bullseyes . . . Bullseye's dead . . . dead Bullseyes*'.

'Noah! Noah Arkwright?'

I turn to the source of my name. There's Clare Mathesson standing by the café door calling out my name bold as brass. She's wearing tight jeans, a fleecy-lined denim jacket, and on her feet, despite the February weather, a pair of old-fashioned English school plimsolls. Her hair is scraped up in a top knot. She looks like a ballerina.

Our eyes meet and I wave. She crosses over to my table

and pulls back a chair which makes a chalk-board scrape on the floor. The hair on the back of my neck shoots up and a shudder runs down my spine. Her hands are covered in skin-tight, ox-blood leather gloves. She peels off the right one and extends her hand for me to shake.

'Clare Mathesson.'

When I take her hand in mine, for a second I flash back to Don the quadriplegic – perfect skin. Clare has a firm, zero bullshit tolerance grip which she releases almost immediately, and goes on to remove her jean jacket, drapes it on the back of the chair and beckons the waitress. The sweater she's wearing is white cashmere with a cowl neck. It fits her snugly and makes a perfect whaleback arc across her perfect chest. I look at her breasts a moment too long.

'I waited for you yesterday evening.'

I look up to her face. I'm flushed with embarrassment and a kind of sexual arousal I've never felt before.

'I left a note with an usher. He promised he'd give it to you.'

For a nanosecond Clare looks right through my brain then speaks flatly.

'He did. Fifteen minutes after the recital finished.'

Before I can answer, the waitress arrives to take Clare's order. I want to disappear off the face of the earth.

'I'll have an English breakfast tea, please.'

'Alrighty!' says the waitress as she turns on her heel.

'But just a minute.' The waitress stops.

'Would you please make sure the water for the tea is on a rolling boil – a boil boil – and that you pour it directly on to the tea bag and rush the brew back over here like it was an emergency case?'

The waitress takes this in, nods and says more slowly, less confidently – 'Alrighty.' Clare turns back to me.

'I should tell you right now that I am the only person on this planet who hasn't seen a single one of your films.'

'That's OK. Yesterday was the first time I'd been to a chamber music recital.'

I sound like a total wally. A brief silence. The tea arrives. Clare thanks the waitress, puts milk into her cup and says firmly, 'Good – then we don't have to talk about movies or music.'

She takes a sip of tea and looks long and hard at me.

'You look like you have one hell of a hangover.'

'Go for it, Noah. Turn it around now. Tell her – first things first – tabula rasa – clean slate right from the beginning!'

'I wish. I'm exhausted, that's all – had to pull an all-nighter after I left your concert.'

'Well, you look like death. You need a brandy with that coffee.'

'Thanks but no thanks. I don't drink.'

'Well done, lad!'

'Oh, really.'

'Really – drink and drugs and me don't mix. I gave them up a couple of years ago.'

'Oh, Noah, you silly, silly man – you stupid twit!'

'I take my hat off to you.'

She raises her teacup in a toast. I can't read her face. I want to look back at her breasts. I feel very, very uncomfortable.

'I was sure you wouldn't come.'

She laughs an enigmatic laugh.

'I had to meet the man who was rude enough and cowardly enough to pay me the insult of standing me up after I'd played myself inside-out for two hours for him.'

'Not just for me – please don't say that. I feel bad enough already.'

'For you – for everyone – my audiences are both whole and discrete – in the musical sense.'

'I'm sorry.'

'So you should be. You really pissed me off. But apology accepted.'

And for the first time since she crossed to my table, she smiles.

'So what do you have planned for us this afternoon, Noah? I have to be at the concert hall by six.'

This woman is throwing me off-balance at every turn. Is she toying with me? I can't read her.

'*She's just being honest, Noah. Try it sometime!*'

'*Fuck you!*'

'*In your dreams, Noah. In your dreams.*'

'I . . . I . . . have you been to the cathedral?'

'No, I haven't.'

'Would you like to take a look around?'

'With you?'

Christ! Why did I tell her anything about me and booze? Why the fuck didn't I let her buy the brandy – a double? I could be plain-sailing through these shark waters now if I'd taken the edge off. How in God's name does *anyone* do *anything* sober?!

My reply comes out like a bullet.

'Yes with me.'

'Good! Then let's do it!' She downs her tea in one gulp, throws her jacket over her shoulders, a ten-dollar bill on to the table and heads for the door. I scramble behind like a puppy keen to be played with some more and then petted. It's a very new role for me and I am totally confused by it.

By the time I'm outside, Clare is on the south-west corner of 111th and pulling on her left glove. The wind is whipping across from the Hudson three blocks away and it feels like about a hundred below zero. I hunch down inside my useless motorcycle jacket and trot after her as she stands erect and casually buttons up her Levi jacket with one hand. With the other she grabs my arm as I arrive beside her.

'My God! Look at that!'

She turns me through a quarter-turn and points her red-gloved hand like a scarlet THIS WAY sign which my eye follows. I can't believe what I see. There, being led up the cathedral steps opposite, are two camels, followed by two ostriches, two zebras, a couple of dogs and a baby elephant. Ahead of the camels, disappearing through the west wing door I can just make out the rear ends of a pair of cows.

'So, did you park the ark inside, Noah?'

She starts laughing and I just stand there gobsmacked. I don't find it funny at all. In fact I find the whole thing frightening. Clare drops my arm and heads across the street toward the cathedral. She shouts over her shoulder:

'Come on! Before you get a parking ticket!'

Obediently, I step off the curb into the path of a thumping Salsamobile heading uptown at about seventy-five. I jump back but I feel the car graze my jacket. A Hispanic guy wearing a polka-dot bandanna leans out of the window.

'MOTHERFUCKER!'

I don't even shout back. I stand there swaying on the edge of defeat. Suddenly a pain shoots up through my penis and into my bladder. I clench every muscle. I bend double. In little more than a second the wave of agony has passed. What the Hell was that?! Have I pissed myself . . . No, I haven't. Tears of shock and relief well up. Dodging beeping traffic, Clare rushes back over to me.

'Are you alright?'

I can't find a reply. Instead, my tears spill over and right there in that windswept gutter of Upper Manhattan Clare hugs me to her and I bury my face in her shoulder.

TWELVE

We are gathered here in the presence of God . . .

Inside the cathedral the air stinks of animal dung. The vast nave is filled with every creature imaginable – even an ant-eater held on a leash by a huge black guy wearing a satin do-rag and a muscle shirt. All the animals have handlers – all the handlers are chatting with each other like owners strolling their pooches in the park on a Sunday morning. I stand there, Clare beside me, wondering if I am having some kind of flashback. I can't be – it was Clare who pointed out the menagerie to me – she saw it too. And besides this smell of shit is real – very real. So what the devil is going on? I see an Episcopal priest talking to a tiny lady in pearls holding a koala bear. I'll trot over and ask him.

Clare beats me to it.

'Wait here a second.'

A minute later she's back looking very, very serious.

'It seems we've stumbled into the gathering of God's animals to be blessed. It's an annual ritual. The priest apologises for any inconvenience – any interruption to our private worship. He assures me that everything will be scooped, disinfected and back to normal in a couple of hours. It's *not* good enough, Noah. I *hate* having my private worship interrupted!'

I am riveted by her as she stands there in the narthex, her

undisguised Cumbrian vowels echoing around her, bathed in the light from the stained-glass window of the Creation. I tremble. Suddenly her serious look breaks and she laughs a loud, irreverent staccato laugh which startles the animals. The priest turns his head to see Clare doubled as if in pain.

'Oh, God! Oh my God!'

The priest rushes over just as Clare straightens up with a huge intake of air. He speaks with a voice full of concern.

'Are you alright? I am so sorry if I upset you –'

Clare struggles to bring her laugh under control. She does well. In less than ten seconds her face settles except for a twitch at one corner of her mouth, and her laugh is reduced to a strangled, gulping snort. Almost composed, she meets the priest's eye and is about to say something, when one of the larger beasts lets out a huge fart.

The suppressed laugh explodes from Clare, spraying the priest in the face with spittle. He ducks to save himself from a second blast. Clare clasps her hand to her mouth and, under the critical stare of dozens of people and almost a hundred animals, she scuttles over to me, takes me by the arm, hurries us over to the south aisle and turns us left towards the transept. Only when we have passed the choir and reached the shelter of the baptistery do we stop and stand under the vaulted dome panting like two schoolkids who have knocked on the local curmudgeon's door and run like hell.

We face each other. Our chests are heaving and we are grinning from ear to ear. From a niche over Clare's shoulder, looking down on us with a rebuking look, is a statue of old peg-leg Stuyvesant, the exterminating Dutch governor of this island when it was New Amsterdam. Nearly three hundred years ago Stuyvesant drove out the Indians between Broadway and the East River creating what is now Alphabet City where last night Bullseye choked on his own vomit. The old bastard looks like he could kill us now for disturbing his peace.

I place my hand on the small of Clare's back and gently move her out of the line of Peg-Leg's evil gaze. As I do this she turns her head and looks at me quizzically. Her eyes catch a shaft of light from the lantern above and flash. We stare at each other – scanning each other's face for some clue as to what is going on. And, as corny as it sounds, this scene is advancing frame by frame – time is being held in a flickering balance. Beyond the altar a horse whinnies. From somewhere deep in the cathedral I can hear a harpsichord playing.

'Bach – *Fantasia and Fugue in A minor*,' she says.

I say nothing. I simply listen, willing the music to me, amplifying the notes as they cross the cool and holy cathedral air and into my soul. All the time I cannot take my eyes off Clare. She smiles, almost imperceptibly, as if she is about to ask a question. As though in answer I nod and as the music seems to fade under and hold, I grasp the truth of the moment. I am standing in limbo, straddling a fulcrum, standing at a major crossroads, etc., etc. If I tip this way rather than that, choose this direction over that other, I could fuck up in a big way – live the rest of my life in a state of regret. But if I tip the other way, choose the other road? Christ! There'll be no going back. I'll have to move forwards, on and on and on for ever and ever Amen.

'*You wouldn't be alone, Noah.*'

But I like being alone – sometimes. Oh, shit! This is a nightmare – an exquisite and beautiful nightmare. And Clare stands there exquisite and beautiful – is she reading my mind? Does she know the turmoil I am in? Is she aware of the fact that in between my gentle touch on her back and this very moment I have fallen deeply and irreversibly in love with her? Well, I have. There! That's it! I've said it. The truth is out in all its glory.

'*Well done, lad! Now what are you going to do?*'

'*Do? I'll tell you what I want to do! I want to scream I LOVE YOU at the top of my lungs, loud enough to shatter stained-glass and rain it down on our heads like confetti. I want to hold close this woman predicted for me, close to the point where innocence and lust meet. I want to feign a dead faint at her feet and peek through slitted eyes as she gives me the kiss of life.*'

Instead I give a little shudder and pull my leather jacket across my chest. And when I speak my words sound like an order.

'It's chilly here. Let's move on.'

She shows no readable emotion.

'Fine. Which way?'

I put my arm around Clare's shoulder and turn her in the direction of the Greek Orthodox chapel. My grip is firm, brotherly, disguising my new-found love. Actually it's to steady me as I walk beside her on jelly legs.

After just a couple of steps, I become aware of somebody, something, behind me and I look over my right shoulder to see Stuyvesant, stone hat in stone hand, bowing low. He speaks in Dutch.

'Bloed en melch, Brit! Da's een gezengend howelijk.'

What the fuck is the old Fascist saying – Bloed en melch? – what the Hell does that mean when it's at home?

'*What the fuck is he saying?! What the fuck are you saying, Noah? It's a bloody statue for pity's sake!*'

'*That's right! It's a statue, Noah. You're tired. You've got a Class-A hangover. You've just fallen in Capital "L" Love. You're delicate – very delicate around the edges. Keep cool. Keep focused. Keep walking with this woman and don't look back again – ever!*'

'Noah?'

Clare takes my hand firmly and stops us just as we reach

the wrought-iron tracery of the Orthodox Chapel gate. She looks up at me, tilting her head to one side like a question mark.

'You went a bit pale back there. I thought you were going to pass out.'

My God! She hasn't rumbled me. My whole universe has been tilted on its axis. My heart is engorged with heady blood. I would have thought that I had L-O-V-E tattooed on my forehead. But no! Clare thinks I've just had a dizzy spell. And she is concerned about me. I can tell from this look on her face that she cares for me beyond the casual, but the word love is not even on the horizon for her. Or if it is, she's a better actress than any I've ever worked with. So take it easy, Noah. Stay cool and keep the inside on the inside. Now you've chosen the fork to take, don't fell a bloody great tree across the road before you've even started the journey.

'Must have drunk too much coffee – it does that to me sometimes – makes me a bit light-headed.'

'It winds me too tight – and gives me acid.'

'Me too. I'm alright now, though. Thanks for asking.'

'My pleasure.'

Clare squeezes my hand and lets go. It feels almost like a kiss. She looks through the metal grille into the chapel. I am about to say that we should go in when she senses my intention, puts her finger to her lips to silence me, then she points inside to where a Greek Orthodox monk in his black robes and stovepipe hat kneels deep in prayer at the altar. The late afternoon light is dove-grey and the smell of cinnamon fills the air. The sanctuary looks like a filigree icon wrought from the purest silver, intricate and yet curiously simple and unadorned. I have loved this baby chapel hidden deep behind the altar of the Mother Cathedral ever since I discovered it as a tourist on my first visit to New York. It was the quietest place I had ever been to in this city or any other, the only place where I felt that there was a hope in Hell of hearing the whisper of God. It still is. I have never shared it with anyone – have never wanted to until now. Now I want to share it with Clare and I can't because some Archbishop Makarios lookalike has invaded my place with his shamanic mumblings!

I'm just about to go in there and drag the Greek bastard screaming and kicking from the altar when I notice that Clare has her head bowed in prayer. I feel shame and embarrassment rise in a flush from the soles of my feet and I walk a respectful distance away and lean against a column. A woman carrying a lemur in a baby sling scurries by and nods in my direction. I close my eyes and try to make some sense of what has happened to me in the past hour. I can't. It's clear that I've fallen in love. But why? Why now? Why here? Why me? I'm too raw for all of this. I've only just admitted that I've lost the plot of my life. And just when I've taken a couple of baby steps to retrace it and carry on, this bloody great reversal has been written in by The Great Scriptwriter. Cue The Huge Obstacle! Force The Protagonist to take action and reveal Deep Character! I don't know – I don't think I'm ready for this. I shake my head from side to side – something crinkles behind it. I turn to investigate and see, taped to the column at head height, a small poster displaying five words.

LET GO AND LET GOD.

I tear it down, screw it into a ball and tuck it deep into the recesses of my leather jacket. Clare arrives at my shoulder.

'What was that?'

'Nothing.'

I lie to Clare for the second time and feel myself going pink. For a second she's poised on the edge of pursuing the subject then, like an adult, chooses not to. She glances at her watch.

'I must be going.'

I glance at mine. It's only four fifteen.

'But it's only four fifteen. You don't have to be there till six you said.'

Christ! This is not going right at all. In this first minute, the new love of my life has caught me in an act of vandalism, I've blushed, I've lied, and now I'm acting like a petulant thirteen-year-old.

'Let go, Noah! Let go and let G –'

'– God, I know! I'm sorry . . . I forgot . . . I –'

Clare smiles and touches me gently on the cheek.

'It's alright. I've had a lovely time. It's just that I like to eat before a recital. Then I like to take a little time for myself – deep breathing, chanting, three Salutes to The Sun – you know how we performers are.'

'Yes, right, of course.'

She bursts out laughing.

'Actually I have a half-hour kip in the green room and a single belt of vodka when I wake up.'

I find this funny but don't know whether to laugh or cry – the word 'vodka' has thrown me. If only Clare knew how I could murder a dozen single belts right now and slide down in oblivion on to the cool marble of this cathedral floor.

I don't really remember much about the journey back downtown. We walk over to 110th and Broadway to find the subway station closed due to some Act of God or other. It's almost dark and the wind-chill factor is about ten below. There isn't a taxi to be had, so Clare and I put our heads down into the wind and walk down to 96th Street. Around 105th, Clare slips one red-gloved hand through my arm, and with the other pulls her coat tight across her chest.

'Are you alright?'

She nods – 'Yes.'

Those are the only words we speak for the whole sixteen

blocks. But it feels natural and comfortable in spite of the Brass Monkey cold.

The 96th Street subway station is a Manhattan major divide. It's where 90 per cent of the white people get off the train, and the other 10 per cent transfer from the Uptown Express to the Number 1 Broadway Local. To stay on the express is to be whisked north and east into the Heart of Darkness. If White makes this mistake once, he'll never make it again. I know. I made it on one of my first visits to New York. I was taking the subway up to Columbia University to give a talk.

I was jet-lagged and hungover, so I gave myself over to the rock'n'roll sway of the train affectionately known as the Broadway Beast and nodded off.

I am woken by a massive lurch just as the train screams through a blur of a station, its interior lights flashing on and off and the juddering of its wheels shaking my brainpan. The carriage is so crowded that my face is jammed against the snot-streaked window, and the roar of the Beast is so loud that it drowns out all other sounds. I am the only Caucasian in sight, hurtling down a black tunnel with a million black people into a nightmare region of New York City which I have only seen on film. It awakens a primal fear in me that takes hold and will not let go. I want to vomit this racist bile out of me, but I am too scared even to retch. I haven't a clue where the train is headed, but I know that even if I can open my terrified mouth and ask, I will only succeed in unleashing against myself a collective revenge for every brutal act of imperial thuggery throughout history and be torn apart Mau Mau-style, to be fed to a savage god as the ghosts of a billion dead slaves ululate their approval.

So I wait until the next stop – 135th Street – get off the train and scan the dimly lit, graffiti-scrawled station for the way across to the downtown platform. I'm still looking for some kind of London Underground internal passage or bridge after everyone has left the subway, and it becomes nut-numbingly clear to me that the only way to cross over to the other side of the tracks is to go outside!

At the bottom of the exit flight of stairs, I can hear the polyrhythmic bass beats of a thousand boom-boxes. I am actually shaking with fear as I near the top. The night air is sultry. The sky in the gaping entrance hole above is blue-black. I look down at my feet. Oh, fuck! I'm wearing a pair of English brogues, punched ox-blood leather, polished to a mirror and the turnups of my double-breasted chalk-stripe suit trousers break perfectly over the tongues of my shoes. I am wearing a pseudo club tie. In short, I am in my lecture uniform which I use to announce my Englishness and on which I have traded shamelessly in trying to get a foot in the American film camp.

I hate striped suits. I hate lace-up low shoes. And I fucking abhor ties of any kind. I shouldn't have been a traitor to my taste, because now this arsehole disguise of mine could actually get me killed.

I step out into the heat of the night on to the corner of 135th Street and Lennox Avenue. I can't focus on a damned thing. All I am aware of is a wall of loud music and a crowd of people milling around drinking and talking and shouting. The air is thick with dope smoke. Out of the corner of my right eye I see a neighbourhood basketball court flooded with light. Gang warfare with a ball is taking place. I fix my gaze firmly on the other side of the street – on the entrance back down into the subway – and head to the edge of the pavement. A deep voice stops me in my tracks.

'Yo, man! How much you pay for that bitchin' suit?!'

Frozen with fear, I can't even turn to look at my interrogator. I feel like I'm going to piss myself. I find myself thinking of the dead mother I never knew and of my father tossing himself into the vat of molten metal. Did he dive, or did he go feet-first?

'I bet you pay two hunnerd dollar for 'em, right, man? Now why would you wanna pay two hunnerd sweet greens to get yo white ass laughed at, Crazee Motherfucker?'

He laughs a deep belly laugh and is joined by a whole chorus as I dash across the road, dodging traffic, and arrive panting at the top of the downtown subway. I hear the sound of a train deep underground, but heading which way? The train is pushing warm air ahead of itself, and from deep in the tunnel below it blows up and over me like the foul breath of a shit-eater. I look down the steps to the ticket booth and the turnstiles glinting in the poor light – I am standing in the jaws of Hell.

Suddenly a huge black forearm reaches horizontally across me at throat level and stops me from moving forward. I look up to see the World's Largest Man leaning against the subway wall in front of me, blocking my way. He is naked from the waist up and looks like a fucking giant Nubian slave. He stares at me. The whites of his eyes are yellow. Oh, shit! He's on PCP or some other insane drug! He wants to chase me down into his subterranean maze and play minotaurs. The sound of the train is getting closer. I'm pouring sweat and fear. Any second now I'll hear the screech of brakes as my only chance of escape pulls into the station. I'll have to make a run for it. Take the risk of being torn limb from limb. The Minotaur puts its face to within an inch of mine and the lips twist into – a smile! He grins an open grin, laughs a belly laugh and pats me kindly on my shoulder.

'Keep comin' back, bro' It gets better!'

I stand rooted – in shock – and start to tremble. The ground shakes. The train is pulling in below. Bull takes the dozen or so steps in two leaps, shouting over his shoulder:

'Move your ass, mo'fo!'

He leaps the barrier and on to the train where he easily holds the doors open with one hand as I struggle at the turnstile with my token like a good citizen. The train man is screaming patois abuse at Bull as I jump into the carriage and take a seat. Breathless, I turn to thank my hero, but he has gone and a voice is crackling over the intercom.

'Asshole niggah! Jive muthafuckin' turkey!'

Twenty minutes later, I'm still shaking with fear and self-loathing as I climb the steps out of 96th Street station. About six steps from street level I stumble and bang my shin on the metal lip of the concrete step. The pain shoots through my leg up my spine and explodes in my brain-stem. I suck in air and sway like a drunk about to fall. A woman's hand steadies me by the arm. It's gloved in red leather.

'Are you alright?'

Asks a man's voice – kind, tired – familiar. I can't look up to see His and Her faces, but I nod.

'I'm fine, thank you.'

'Well, take care of yourself – goodnight.'

I nod again. Then with great effort I steady myself, climb out onto Broadway and breathe in deeply the night air.

It's starting to sleet as Clare and I reach the subway entrance on the north-west corner of 96th and Broadway. The liquid ice is blowing down into the station and the top steps are treacherous. We hold tight to each other as we start our descent. Suddenly a guy with a short pony-tail and a Bertie Wooster suit stumbles on his way up and cracks his shin on the edge of a step. The sound is sickening – loud enough to be heard over the city sound. Clare rushes forward and steadies him. I ask him if he's alright. He mumbles something and without looking up pushes past us and on to street level. It's a strange moment, and for some reason I get a flash of the opening sequence of Kurosawa's epic movie *Kagemusha*.

Clare leaves the train at Columbus Circle, firmly refusing my offer to escort her to Alice Tully. But just before she gets out, she leans down and pecks me on the cheek.

'Thank you for this afternoon. It's been lovely.'

And she ducks out. I shout after her through the closing doors:

'When can I see you again?'

The doors shut before Clare can answer, but as the train leaves her behind on the platform, I can see she is mouthing the word 'Sunday'.

THIRTEEN

Don't want to end up no cartoon in no cartoon
graveyard.

Paul Simon, 'Graceland'

North London hospital, February 1997

I open one eye to a slit. Everything is undefined. Time and
place are in the balance. What and Who I am is an inexplic-
able conundrum. Like Schrödinger's Quantum Cat, I am
both dead and alive in a space without a name. I exist only as
a potentiality, and only when I am observed, or maybe only
when I am aware of being observed, will the potential Me
take the form of a living or dead Noah.

I stare out of my voodoo eyes and gradually the picture
comes into focus. My head is tilted hard to the left, and
diagonally across the room I see in a bed a man wearing an
oxygen mask. His bile drains into a bag hanging on the
bedframe. His forearms are heavily tattooed. Saline drips
into the back of his right hand. His left hand is cuffed and a
chain runs from it to the wrist of a uniformed prison officer
who sits in a chair at the foot of the bed reading a comic.
Neither of them see me.

I can't hear any sounds. I can't feel any pain. In fact I can
feel nothing. I must be on some serious painkillers. Or
perhaps I'm not on anything at all. Perhaps I am undead.

Perhaps this is the future – and I'm in a horrific hospital Limbo for Ever and Ever but no Amen.

My head seems heavy. I try to move it and it surprises me by sliding weightlessly over to the right. I open my other eye to a slit, and there, half-silhouetted against the window barricaded with flowers, I see Clare and Etta, side by side on plastic upholstered 'easy' chairs. Etta has her hand on Clare's knee. My turning head turns Clare's and she looks over to me. He mouth opens and closes. She is saying something but I can hear nothing. She looks like a fish underwater. Etta glances at me, stands up, gives Clare a kiss on the cheek and walks out of my line of vision.

There's a gurgling in my groin and with great difficulty I pull back the sheet to see my battered penis, blood-caked and bruised. This sight of my blood flicks the pain switch and in an instant my dick, my balls, my urethra and my bladder are on fire. The Potentiality has taken on Form. I am no longer the Quantum Cat – I am Noah. I am alive. I am very much in this hospital ward. And I don't have to be a quantum physicist to know that there aren't enough opiates in my system to make this hurt bearable.

'Welcome back – Fine Man.'

While I was busy observing myself and taking shape, Clare has moved to a chair by my bed, taken my hand in hers and is bent to my ear talking. I must have been out a fair while because, in between my admission and now, she's been home and changed out of her performance dress into jeans and sweater. There's a hint of mothball coming from her. Or is it some theatre stuff on me – some anti-something or other?

'How do you feel?'

The question is flat, fixed by rote over the years. Clare knows exactly how I fucking feel.

'Alright', comes my rote reply.

She squeezes my hand tightly and with her free hand turns

my face gently to her and looks deeper into my eyes than I can ever remember her having done before. A shadow passes over us. And I can hear the beating of wings.

Clare is about to say something else when Mr Norman Baker, my Big Cheese urological consultant, appears at her shoulder. It takes me a moment to recognise him because he is wearing full hunting pink – apart from the riding hat. He carries a crop in his left hand and the light glints off the chrome leather of his boots. I am not shocked. Why shouldn't he be? This is the man who, on the day he was off to scale eight Lake District peaks to raise money for a CT scanner, held clinic dressed in very serious mountain-climbing gear – his pitons and ice axes piled in a corner behind the examining couch. I like this man. His eccentricities appeal to me. He spends his working life grubbing around inside people's piss pipes and sumps. To relax he rides to hunt and climbs the Himalayas. There's a balance in this which I find very reassuring.

Clare likes him because he looks her in the eye when he speaks to her.

Which is what he does now as he puts his non-crop hand on her shoulder.

'Excuse the attire, Mrs Arkwright – addressing a farmers' dinner this evening – no time to go home and change.'

'Fox steaks?'

'Pardon?'

'On the menu – tonight?'

'Oh Good Lord no. Nothing like that. They don't feel a thing, you know – at the kill.'

Spoken like a true surgeon! He doesn't crack a smile. Because Norman Baker is also a man totally without irony. Clare – God bless her soul – is simply trying to maintain what is known irreverently in cancer circles as A Sense of Tumour and Stormin' Norman doesn't get it – he thinks she's serious.

One look at her and I can see that she is on the edge of tears, fighting back a scream with every ounce of her energy. What does she know that I don't? What has Norman said to her on the QT while I was struggling for the surface of consciousness, fighting the Pentothal undertow? Something's gone on, that's for certain, because they look at each other now as though they have reached an unpredicted impasse. They are frozen, my standing consultant in his hunting outfit behind my seated cellist, his hand on her shoulder in some bizarre parody of a Victorian photographic portrait.

Norman thinks I don't notice when he gives Clare a barely perceptible nod. This must be her cue, agreed upon in their secret Carer's Chat before I woke. He takes his hand from her shoulder. She stands and leans over me again.

'I'll come back later tonight. You get some rest. I love you.'

Then she gets up, kisses me on the forehead and leaves the room – quickly. But not quickly enough – not before a single tear has dropped from her eye on to my cheek. I instinctively reach up to wipe it away and almost rip out the IV in the bruised back of my hand. I gasp and shut tight my eyes.

When I open them, Norman is in the seat Clare was in. He places his riding crop deliberately on the thin eau-de-Nil cotton bedspread and clears his throat nervously.

'I'm afraid it looks bad in there, Noah. Almost all bloody tumour – not much of a bladder left. Bugger's struggled for you, though – and we tried our best to keep him in – but it's come to that time, yes?'

He looks at me as though expecting some kind of reply or question. I don't move a muscle. I will not make this easy for him. Let the sod struggle – feel a bit of the terror of the fox when he has nowhere to run and nowhere to hide.

'Well, it has. The whole nature of the cancer has changed – it's very aggressive now – and it's fast. We'll have to have the bladder out – as soon as possible, alright?'

I still don't give an inch. Then he hits me with his Big One.

'Look – we're going to do our damnedest – yes? I'll need a couple of weeks to get organised – want to get the best team together. I want you to go home – eat red meat – lots of it – none of that soya rubbish – I want blood in you. And . . .'

Here he hesitates, picks up his crop and fiddles with it. He shifts slightly in his seat.

'You might want to make sure your affairs are in order – will – that sort of thing . . . and you could perhaps write a letter to each of those girls of yours – something they could open at a future date.'

He bends and brushes some invisible speck of dust off his gleaming right boot. He's got me! The bastard! The words come out of my mouth like a snake hiss.

'What are you telling me?'

He looks me square in the eye. The fox has gone to ground.

'I'm simply telling you to make sure your will is order and to write a couple of letters, Noah.'

Then this huntsman, this mountaineer, this speleologist of the tiny tunnels of the human urinary system does something he has not done in the whole seven years I have known him – he touches me lightly yet intimately on the back of my hand. Then he withdraws it quickly, guiltily, as if admitting to a breach of some unwritten law governing the relationship between a surgeon and his patient. When I look back at his face his cheeks are on fire. He stands with military speed and buttons again his jacket and his formality, and as he turns on his heel I hear him say as if to himself –

'I'm so sorry.'

Then he is gone, there is nothing. I am the undead Quantum Cat once again. I could simply choose to observe myself now – define myself as dead and save everyone a lot of time and effort. But before I can even make the choice to make a choice, I hear the loud rattle of chains and roll my head back to my sinister side to see the patient prisoner being led off down the corridor, wheeling his drainage and saline bags on a stand, still chained to his guard who is a few steps ahead of him talking on a mobile phone.

FOURTEEN

O, from what power hast thou this powerful might . . .?
William Shakespeare, Sonnet 150

New York City, February 1985

It's half past eleven in the morning of that next 'Sunday' mouthed to me by Clare through the window of the Broadway Local one week ago. I'm turning on to Prince from Broadway into SoHo. There's a bitter wind but the sun is bright in a TV Chromakey blue sky. The streets have had a Sunday morning wash and Manhattan feels almost virginal. I am freshly showered and shaved and for almost the whole walk down from 21st Street I've been whistling Bach's *Fantasia* in that smug through-the-teeth way that I can't stand. I look well. I haven't had a drink or a drug since the Tribeca Twin fiasco which feels like ten years not ten days ago.

Not that I haven't felt like one. For the first three days I had to exert astronomical foot poundage of energy to resist either bullishly going up to Alice Tully and carrying off Clare like Europa, or going over to the EAR Bar and getting stoked and smoked into an all-time high. Only Ray and three AA meetings kept me on some kind of straight and narrow – on the outside at least. My head – in Recoveryspeak – was a neighbourhood more dangerous than 135th and Lennox. I was teetering between my new-found love for Clare and my old-time self-hatred, between boundless hope and incapacitating despair. Somehow I managed to work and we wrapped the Drug PSA on Tuesday night. On Wednesday morning Ray and I and a few of the crew drove out to the Quaker cemetery in Prospect Park for Bullseye's burial – it turns out that he came from a long line of Friends dating back to the Pilgrim Fathers, and even in his darkest days the poor sod had still been sneaking back to various Meeting Houses in Manhattan. If he was looking for a way out he didn't find it in those rooms. Quakers may be experts at turning guns into ploughshares, but it seems that a bit more know-how about how young boys of faith turn into junkies would have been more help to the native son they buried in the silence and the snow in Brooklyn.

Driving back down Flatbush after the funeral, I was spitting venom at anything and everybody. I was angry and I was going ten rounds with the Unnameable Fear. If some street pusher had approached us at the next stop light and offered me acid called Cancer, I would have bought two hits right there and done them up through my eyeballs – the fastest track there is to tripping. But the only person to come near the car on a red was a scrawny wino with a Squeegee and a mouthful of abuse whom Ray told to leave his goddam windshield alone.

Actually I know what I really wanted in that car and it wasn't a Jameson's or acid or any of the above bullshit. I simply wanted to hear from Clare who had been silent since our visit to the cathedral. As soon as we'd got on the train at 96th Street I'd given her my phone number as casually as I could, so she knew where to reach me. I had thought she might leave it for a day – two at the most – but by Tuesday night I was beginning to suspect that I was not going to hear from her ever again. She had seen through me after all and clocked me as the arsehole I really am. But then why did she kiss me as she left the train and tell me she'd had a wonderful time? Why did she let me fall in love with her in front of Stuyvesant? It was her who led me behind the altar, wasn't it? I would have been alright staying with the camels and the small primates for the ceremony. Fuck it is what I say!

'Fuck her!' is what I said.

Ray heard this and turned to me deliberately – one hand on the wheel.

'You're too wired, man. Let's swing up through midtown and catch the Fireside meeting.'

No! I wasn't having any of that shit. That was too sensible a suggestion.

'Just drop me off at Twenty-first Street, alright?'

Ray shrugged and turned his attention back to the road.

'It's your call, Noah – it's your call, my friend.'

At the flat, there was a message from Clare on the answer machine leaving her number and asking me to call her back the next morning – Thursday. Instantly I felt better. The transformation was so quick it was frightening – pathological. But I didn't care. I was feeling so good then that I almost phoned Ray on his carphone to tell him I'd see him at the Fireside meeting after all, but thought better of it and instead rounded up all my dirty clothes and herded them down to the Laundromat Corral.

I finally got Clare on the phone late on Thursday afternoon and she told me that she had a chock-a-block week, that her recitals had been going well and could I meet her at a pub in SoHo on Sunday morning . . . and oh! By the way, she'd had a really nice time at the cathedral with me. And oh! By the way, she was leaving for England on the following Tuesday. This second 'by the way' threw me for a while after the phone hit the cradle, but within the hour I'd hit upon a strategy for our ongoing relationship – an offer Clare cannot possibly refuse.

200

I have been spending the last three days organising this deal, and it's all looking sweet – very sweet. That's the real reason behind my irritating whistle as I round this corner on to Prince and see a block ahead of me on the south-west corner of its junction with Greene Street the red and white sign of Fanelli's Bar.

I glance at my watch – ten fifty-three – seven minutes early. I'll take a stroll down to West Broadway, back around a couple of blocks and arrive on the dot all neat and tidy.

However, as I pass by the rendezvous window, I make the mistake of peeking in, not to see if Clare is already there – at least not consciously, but simply an alcoholic's reflex response to bars which look inviting. And with its corner windows and gingham curtains on brass rods, Fanelli's looks very inviting. It reeks of Homburgs, cigars and parked Packards and seems frozen in the years of Post-Prohibition celebration drinking.

I cup my hands against the glass and peer in. My eyes adjust to the darker light of the interior.

There's Clare! At a window table tucked in between the front and back rooms. Across from her sits Kairos's beautiful coffee-coloured violinist whose name Clare mentioned but I've forgotten. They are drinking coffee. The violinist, who is wearing a cloche hat and smoking a cigarette, looks like Lady Day in her heyday. Clare is animated, eye-to-eye with her fellow musician and talking purposefully. Suddenly they both burst out laughing. The couple at the adjacent table glance over their shoulders at the two women as Lady Day now gently takes my new love's wrist, turns it and checks the time on her watch. Then she gathers up her handbag, leans forward and kisses Clare on the cheek before putting on a full-length black astrakhan coat and heading for the door.

There is nothing out of the ordinary in all this, but it has the effect of filling me with a jealousy so strong that I want to run into the bar and rip out Lady Day's beautiful throat.

I don't of course. Instead I whip back from the window so that Clare won't see me as she watches her friend leave, then jump back on to the pavement and manage to look as though I'm just dropping into the pub as my coffee-coloured nemesis comes out of the door, blissfully unaware of how close she just came to being killed.

She smiles as she passes me and glides up towards Broadway like a silent film star.

So much for my walk around the block and a neat and tidy arrival! It's three minutes to eleven now and I feel all churned up. There's beads of sweat on my upper lip. And if that isn't bad enough, in order to reach Clare, I'll have to run the gauntlet of the bar.

'*Remember the milk, Limey!*'

'*I hear you, Tiny.*'

But right now, the thought of going through the door into Fanelli's fills me with more terror than entering The Shit Hole in DUMBO.

Yet from somewhere deep inside or high above, somehow I find the courage, put my hand on the doorknob and push myself inside the bar. I needn't have worried. Clare spots me immediately and waves and her smile guides me safely past the bar and into the seat recently occupied by Lady Day. We lean across the table and peck, and I slide my jacket off and on to the back of the chair. The outside cold hovers around me for a moment or two before being consumed by the warm air of the room which bustles with brunch and chatter, with cool jazz, coffee and beer.

I glance around me. It's a happy Sunday scene. I have my back to the bar – that's good – that's safe.

'*You can do this, Noah.*'

I nod ever so slightly to myself and smile widely at Clare. She smiles back warmly and speaks.

'You just missed Etta.'

'Etta?'

'Our beautiful Second Violin.'

'Ah, yes. I remember now – you told me her name.'

'I'm surprised you didn't bump into each other.'

'Yes,' I say, side-stepping a lie.

'You'd really like her – she's as talented and interesting as she is lovely.'

I pick up the menu and try to sound casual and genuine.

'I'm sure. I look forward to meeting her some day.'

A waitress who looks about twelve with the figure of a boy appears at my side as if by magic. She says nothing but simply stands there, pen poised over her order pad.

'I'll have corned beef hash and eggs over medium, whole wheat toast and coffee – and some A1 steak sauce if you have it. Anything for you, Clare?'

She shakes her head.

'Then that'll be all – thank you.'

'Okeedokee' is all the Girlboy says as she turns on her heel.

'Healthy appetite,' says Clare: and that's the start of several minutes of chat which lasts until my order arrives.

My brunch now sits in front of me and I'm sad to say I can't remember anything we've said during the wait for it. I was and still am too concerned about how and when to reveal my plan to listen to small-talk, even from the one I love. Suddenly I ambush myself and launch into phase one of the operation.

'I know you're going to England on Tuesday, but I was wondering when your next work commitment was.'

'The middle of April – we're doing a mini-tour of Holland.'

'*YES!*'

'Well . . . I know we've only just met . . . and that Fools rush in and so on . . . but I was wondering . . .'

'Yes?'

'For the last six months I've been working putting the pieces in place for a film – it's called *Kobo*. The finance is looking good – Fox is behind me all way – and Danny Glover – who's hot and promising more heat – will commit to the title role.'

This is almost all rubbish. I have no finance. I haven't spoken to Fox. I don't have a script. What I do have is the bare bones of a story that's been tickling me for years and a title I made up yesterday.

'That sounds exciting. What's it about . . . or am I not supposed to ask?'

She takes the bait like a pet carp, and I'm off and reeling in like Hemingway in *Islands in the Stream*.

'Kobo is a renegade student leader in Nairobi who is thrown out of Kenya by President Moi. He seeks asylum in Britain and is refused, but does manage to get into the US where he turns his astute organisational mind to the import/export trade with his native continent. It's coffee mainly on the Africa/US leg and agricultural equipment on the return. Kobo does well – extremely well – and the coffee boys in Little Italy get pissed-off with this uppity nigger – their term not mine – with an ape's name. La Cosa Nostra try to close him down and try a drive-by shooting at Kobo's Tribeca warehouse. First Big Mistake – our Kenyan kid cut his teeth on Mau Mau and the deadly serious business of African student politics – with the emphasis on deadly. Etc. Etc.'

I take a bite of hash browns – Clare seems poised for me to continue with the story. I'll go to the heart of the matter.

'Anyway, ninety per cent of the story takes place in New York City, but there's a prologue in which Kobo the tribal child becomes the Manfighter. These scenes will be intercut with stock Mau Mau footage to form a long title sequence. The upshot of this is there'll be some second unit stuff to be shot in Kenya. And I won't be able to lock down the budget until I've done a recce in Africa. It's a one-man job, but I was wondering if you'd come with me . . . I'm leaving the last week in March.'

I tuck into my eggs with feigned nonchalance. No reply. If Clare, for dramatic emphasis, is using a pregnant pause, this one is going to give birth to quads. After I've finished half an egg, I look up and take a sip of coffee. When Clare has my eye, she speaks.

'There's a man who follows my career very closely. So closely that he sends me a single red rose every performance night – has done for nearly two years now. I've never met him.'

What the fuck is she telling me this for now? I look into her face for a clue and can't find one.

'His name is James.'

'So?'

I pop another bite of egg in with a jerk of defiance. But I lose the moment and a slart of yolk dribbles down my chin. I wipe it away with my napkin and try a short laugh to change the energy of the situation which is not going according to plan at all. I should be in the driver's seat right now, but instead I feel relegated to the back seat, curiously tired, defeated before the Big Event of the scene.

'He's a South African lawyer –'

I let out a snort of derision which I immediately try to disguise as a bit-of-food-stuck-on-the-epiglottis hack. But Clare stiffens and I'm sure lowers me a couple of notches in her estimation.

'Actually he's a great admirer of my playing. He wants me to meet him.'

'In Africa?'

'No. He has a flat in Paris. I've told him I'll visit him there.'

'Really? When?'

'I'll go after I sort a few things out in London – weekend after next perhaps.'

'For how long?'

'That depends.'

On what? You want me to ask that, don't you – well I won't. 'I'll go!'? Just like that! No discussion with me?

Pure unadulterated venom rises into my gullet.

Paris! Great admirer! Fucking Afrikaaner! A fucking red rose every performance. I'll kill the motherfucker – the smug, self-satisfied rich bastard. Yes, rich! He has to be because to send a single fucking rose from Paris to New York or wherever costs near as dammit the same as a dozen. Christ All Fucking Mighty! I know what I'll do! I'll beat Clare to Paris and headbutt the smarmy shit into his parquet fucking flooring in his chintzy fucking bijou boîte above the Rue fucking St Jaques!

'Sounds nice,' I say. 'Paris is a beautiful place – even in March.'

I force down another bite. I can't look up. Clare reaches over and places her hand on mine. Her palm is cool and draws just a little of the heat from me; then she exerts enough pressure to make me look her in the eye.

'I've only just decided to do this, Noah. And it is something I must do.'

I look back at my plate.

'Look at me, Noah!' I look back at her. 'Something has happened between us that could become very big. You felt it in the cathedral, didn't you?'

'Yes, I felt it.'

'Then you will know that I must go to Paris. I must see this man and find out . . .'

She's doing it again, leaving the story dangling at the crucial point – wanting me to ask the question and make it easy for her. Well, we'll sit right here in Fanelli's until Armageddon before I'll do that. But I must do something. So what is it that Clare is least expecting me to do now? I think very fast and then simply lean over and kiss her gently on the cheek. CUE Robert Doisneau! Snap this photo, you French Fuck, and slap it in your ALBUM DE PARIS!

'Thank you.' She sighs with relief. 'For a moment there I thought you were going to handle it badly.'

FIFTEEN
THE STORYBOARD FOR
GETTING TO KNOW YOU – THE MOVIE

Up in this high air you breathed easily, drawing in a vital
assurance and a lightness of heart.

Isak Dinesen, *Out of Africa*

Over Africa, 29 March 1985

I've abandoned New York in a hurry. The only flight I could
get to Kenya at such late notice was on Air Sudan out of
London. Ray was pissed-off at me for leaving him to finish
the Drug PSA and thought I was an idiot to test my sobriety
by doing such a huge geographical with a woman I hardly
knew. I took great pleasure in reminding him that if he
hadn't plopped that 'Arts and Leisure' section in front of me
in the Cozy Soup'n'Burger I wouldn't be going to bloody
Africa in the first place. Kirstin was more sympathetic and as
I was leaving for JFK gave me a copy of the AA International
'Where to Find' and a smackeroony kiss on the mouth which
affected my libido not in the slightest. Our affair is definitely
over. Two days ago, over a cuppa, Tiny gave me his blessing,
but as I was leaving the Tea Room he gave me a bear hug and
said:

'When I said to go for the milk, Limey, I meant a pint or
two, not the whole fucking dairy!'

From the airport I called the Tribeca Twins and left a message on their answer machine telling them about Clare and our trip to Africa, assuring them that they were still on board for the next film project and I would be in touch. As soon as I'd put the phone down I regretted having rung – I must have sounded like a pretentious fucking arsehole.

And that's how I feel right now – like I've just used and abused everyone, dropped them all in the shit and left town without a thought for anybody but myself. Even this so-called recce is a cheat – a sly method of getting Clare on her own in an exotic location guaranteed to win a smile and influence a tender heart – a heart which seems to be opening up to me already. Clare did go to Paris to see the Afrikaaner, but I know no details. All I know is that I reached her on her London number and she told me that she was ready to go to Kenya with me. She's flying out to Nairobi the day after tomorrow on BA – God knows how she managed to get the ticket – and we will have two weeks together. I telephoned her from Heathrow as I made my connection, but she wasn't in. The message I left on her machine was awkward with the awkwardness of strangers. It couldn't have been anything else because I know nothing more about us now than I did when we walked out of Fanelli's two weeks ago, and that was little enough. In fact, as I fly at six hundred miles per hour at thirty thousand feet over the desert, all I really know is that Clare and myself are two people with a spark between who have agreed to meet at a point in darkest Africa. It's crazy. It's a long shot. Anything could happen – I'm on the cutting edge, and the sado-masochistic alkie in me loves it that way.

But the sober me is so terrified, so insecure, that his eyeballs are aching.

I'm holding nausea at bay. My stomach is empty, not because I want it that way but because the food served a couple of hours ago – some kind of unidentifiable meat and half boiled rice in a fetid gravy – was actually inedible: not simply unappetising, but able to swell up in the back of the mouth so that was physically impossible to swallow it. Keeping a lid on the heaves is made more difficult because the air in the plane is sweet with the same sickly perfume that comes from air fresheners dangled from rear-view mirrors by middle-eastern cab drivers in New York. And when I try to distract myself by looking out of the window, perhaps to glimpse the Nile below, the sunlight arcs like a welding torch off the wing, blinding me for a good twenty seconds. I'm also boiling – the air conditioning is either on the blink or it's so bloody hot even six miles up that the system is struggling against all odds. A cold beer would be good right now, but I know it wouldn't. Besides, there's no alcohol served on Muslim planes, or rather planes flown by Muslims. I can't even chat to someone to take my mind off how bloody awful I feel. I seem to be the only non-Muslim on board. Half of the passengers, crisp white in their djibbahs and turbans, appear to be mullahs who boarded the plane in Cairo; the other half are businessmen, some in traditional robes, some in suits. Six of these sit in three rows across the aisle from me, each wearing a grey silk suit, each topped off with a plum-coloured fez.

I'm wearing jeans and a T-shirt with a crumpled linen jacket and a pair of pale-green Converse high-tops. The two seats next to me are very empty.

I suddenly have to take a leak. This has been happening a lot to me lately – ever since the jerk-off donation at the Tribeca Twins' loft. The urge to pee has not come upon me gradually as the bladder swells, but quickly and without warning. And the pissing has been painful. But I've been putting it down to tension and each time I've pushed my penis back into my pants, I've pushed any worry into the back of my mind.

As I put my hand on the handle of a door to the rear toilet of the plane, an air hostess rushes up and grabs me by the arm. There's panic and anger in her voice as she shouts in Arabic. She obviously doesn't want me to open the bog door. But despite her iron grip my hand turns the knob. The door flies open and a hundred soiled food trays fly out with the force of machine-gun bullets, splattering half-chewed bits of inedible meat and lumps of coagulated rice and gravy over the ceiling, the floor, the stewardess and myself: I promptly vomit the vomit which I've so diligently held down since we were somewhere over the pyramid of Cheops.

Everyone in the plane looks around and with such visible disgust that I'm sure I've broken some law, some rule so fundamental that I will be killed here and now on Air Sudan flight 600, thus finally satisfying the desire for revenge which has been smouldering since General Gordon, from the walls of a besieged Khartoum in 1884, denounced the Mahdi as a false prophet.

There's a whirlwind of a commotion, Arabic fills the air and I am pulled in all directions in something between a heavy armaments attack and a clean-up operation. In the middle of it all, somebody puts a hand down the back of my pants and has a quick fondle of my bum.

At last the stewardess plops me back into my seat and gives me something that looks and smells suspiciously like a Baby Wet Wipe. I look ahead of me. All seems to be in order – mullahs eyes-front; businessmen all nicely fezzed and with their heads in newspapers. Nobody is looking at me. I glance backwards down the aisle – no sign of the Attack of the Killer Food Trays. Did I imagine it all? Is this scent in the cabin air some dynamite kind of hash oil? I'm sweating. I dab my top lip with the Baby Wipe, bend forward and retch a little. There just above the knee on my jeans is a fleck of vomit next to the ubiquitous tomato skin. No! This is not a figment of my cinematic imagination but a full-blown bizarre crisis over the desert which Air Sudan has taken every step to cover up.

I rummage in my bag and pull out a fresh Accupad – one of those wonderful yellow, larger than A4 American legal pads which writers often die clutching in their written-out hands – and draw a cartoon sketch of me opening the bog door. In a large schoolboy hand I write underneath: ALWAYS FINISH WHAT'S ON YOUR PLATE – THE DIRECTOR LEARNS A LESSON.

I look at what I've put on paper and at once feel a little better. It also gives me an idea for a way forward over the next two weeks. Sketches and film-maker jottings might just give me enough distance from unfolding events to keep me afloat – to provide me with an African Queen for any emotional rapids that might lie ahead. *Is that a leech on your thigh, Mr Allnut? Or are you just pleased to see me?*

Nairobi, 30 March

It's three in the afternoon at Jomo Kenyatta airport, and I'm waiting at the barrier for Clare. If there is an air conditioning system in here, something is really wrong with it. My jeans and T-shirt feel like a wet suit, and the air is so humid that I could be underwater. My Love's plane landed thirty minutes ago but not a single passenger has emerged; and like an idiot I've left the Ngong Taxicabs driver waiting at the Arrivals Bay holding 100 Kenyan shillings – I'm sure he's fucked off back to town by now. I'm pretty fucked-off myself. I'm beginning to wish I'd listened to Ray. What the Hell am I doing here on a lie of a recce, on the equator in the hottest month of the tropical year, making a rendezvous with a woman who is 90 per cent stranger? I'm tired. I'm hungry and hot – I'm in a foreign place and I'm playing with the fire

212

of new love and lust. This is the most dangerous scenario an alcoholic addict can set up for himself. I should just go over to the ticket desk now and, whatever it costs, book myself on the next flight out of here. I'm just about to put my worst foot forward when . . .

Clare comes through the arrivals gate like a dream come true.

She's wearing black drawstring trousers, white T-shirt, a beat-up jean jacket and a baseball cap with a peak worthy of Bruce Willis's approval. But she isn't wearing a smile. In fact she looks really worried, or afraid, or simply pissed-off.

Then she sees me and her face lights up, but there's something of the mask in the resulting broad grin.

Oh shit! Worst-case scenario confirmation!! Ray *was* right! Clare hates me – has done since the moment we met and she's flown to Africa to deal the death blow – hit me hard here on the equator and leave me stranded with my lies, my sun-block and my fictitious recce.

Before I can run any further down Paranoid Alley, I'm stopped dead in my tracks with an embrace. Clare's lips are on my cheek and her hands – *those* hands – are on my shoulders, and my hands are on the as-yet-unexplored Terra Extrafirma of her Glutei Maximi. Suddenly all is in order and I'm the most loved man on the planet – Noah the Normal – the man every girl's mother loves, meeting her lucky daughter for a romantic tropical jaunt. I was wrong as usual – getting all bent out of shape for what? I mean to say – if Clare had not been pleased to see me, she wouldn't be embracing me like this. If she hadn't wanted to come to Africa, she wouldn't have come – right?

'*If you say so, Noah.*'

'*I say so.*'

So I hold her at arm's length and say in my 'double cream' voice:

'I've really missed you, Clare.'

She looks into my eyes and an indecipherable something flickers across hers. What the fuck is that? I'm about to step back into The Alley again when Clare takes me by the hand.

'Come on. Let's get a taxi.'

'I left one waiting, but he's probably long gone by now.'

Wrong again! When Clare and I step out of the building into the hundred degree heat, the Ngong Taxicab driver is leaning cool as a cucumber against his car waiting – trusting bugger! As soon as he sees us he trots over and with a sweeping gesture takes Clare's bag. In one swift movement he open the boot, pops in the bag, slams shut the lid and smiles.

'Habari, Mama. Welcome to Kenya.'

Then he gives Clare a little bow and opens the rusting door of his rusting Cortina as if it were a State Occasion. Clare steps into the jalopy like a queen and I duck in behind her.

The director, the cellist and the leper

Fifteen minutes later we're almost back to Nairobi on the Mombasa Road. King Sunny Adé belts out a high-energy beat out of the taxi's tinny radio and the sun belts down on the taxi's tin roof. Even at fifty miles an hour with all the windows down the heat in the cab is stifling. Clare sits with her back half turned to me looking out of the window. A single rivulet of perspiration runs down the fine line of her jaw. It drops from her chin just as she takes off her baseball cap, thrusts her head out of the window and closes her eyes against the wind – searching for cool. She looks different somehow. What is it that's changed about her? Her hair! She's cut her hair – Christ! Has she cut her hair! – cropped it all over to a half inch. On that last date in New York, with her hair in a chignon, Clare had been a ballerina. Now she's a time-warped, transplanted sixty-four Mod with her stubble buzzing in the window wind of an African taxi.

'*I love you, Clare.*'

'*Not now, Noah, you fucking idiot! The woman's jet-lagged – she's hot – she's not even sure if she's done the right thing in coming here – take it easy – let it unfold, OK?*'

'*OK.*'

Suddenly the sky opens with a mighty thwack and a waterfall fills the air. In the split second it takes for Clare to pull back into the taxi, she is drenched – as wet as if she had put her head into a bucket of water. Streams cascade down her face and she laughs like a ten-year-old. I hold her close to me and I can feel her laughter reverberating through my body like sobbing, her wetness soaking my shoulder like a lifetime of tears.

'*Don't fuck up this moment, Noah. Keep your mouth shut and hold it.*'

'*I can hear you. I'll do my best.*'

So I don't say a thing for what seems like the whole of history, until Clare's laughter subsides and the full weight of her head rests heavy on me. I can feel the throbbing of the vein in her neck against mine, and the drumming of the little monsoon on the roof of the car drowns out the music from the radio in this mobile sauna. The air is hot. The air is wet. We are wet and pulse with the potential – our opposites almost in conjunction, moving toward a pure syzygy. It can happen, and it will any moment now – *if* I simply stay in the moment and let it be.

'*Hang in there, Noah!*'

'*How?*'

'*Let go! YESTERDAY'S HISTORY – TOMORROW'S A MYSTERY – remember?*'

But I don't remember; and how the hell can I hang on and

let go at the same time? All those AAs are fucking liars – it can't be done. And I sure as shit can't do it now in the stifling heat of this taxi which is about to suffocate both of us before we've even started our bloody relationship. It's time to move this thing on – be a man and take some initiative – put a stop to this entropy. So I whisper into Clare's ear:

'How was Paris?'

Immediately she stiffens, lifts her head from my shoulder, gives me a 'fuck you' look and turns back to the window just as the sun comes out again and the taxi turns on to the Harry Thuku Road. I try to scramble out of the hole I've just dug but only bring more earth down upon myself.

'I'm sorry. It's just that when we talked in New York, it . . . he . . . James seemed very important . . . to you . . . and I didn't think that you'd . . . well . . . you know . . . come . . . and I was just wondering if . . .'

Clare turns like a cobra.

'If I fucked him?'

'Well . . . yes.'

'You'll never know.'

And she turns her back once more and puts her face out of the window. It blazes in the sun and her cropped hair shimmers around her head like a halo. I feel like poison.

The taxi hits a pothole and the chassis slams into my arse and up into my skull. There's a vicious pain in the small of my back which shoots down from the kidneys to the end of my dick – dick head.

'*Dick head!*'

I'm about to vomit or faint or both, but before I can execute either of these attractive responses to Clare's reply to my Paris question, the taxi pulls up in front of the understated colonial grandeur of the Norfolk Hotel. This should turn things around. I've booked us two adjoining rooms in this elegant town lodge, the most prestigious address in

Nairobi for over a century – with its hideaway teak and rattan rooms – with hot and cold running servants – peeking on to the turquoise oasis of its swimming pool.

I nip out sharpish and pay off the driver, who already has Clare's bags on the pavement, with an 'Asante' and a twenty-shilling tip, and he actually tugs embarrassingly at his wiry forelock and says, 'Asante Bwana – kwaheri,' then nips around and opens Clare's door for her. She doesn't get out of the car, but stares instead at a point in the middle distance. I follow her gaze to a point a few yards up the pavement from the hotel entrance steps where a woman sits begging under a hibiscus bush. At first glance she appears to be hunched-down small into a ball, but then I see that she has no legs at all. She is simply a torso and she is sitting on a home-made skateboard. Her hands are bandaged across the knuckles with filthy strips of cloth and her face is half eaten away. Where her nose should be, two black holes pierce scarred tissue, and the whites of her eyes stare blind and yellow up to the passers-by who pass by without putting anything in the hollowed-out half of a gourd which sits on the ground in front of her. Our taxi driver also clocks Clare's gaze.

'Bad woman, Mama. Greedy woman.'

Clare gets out of the taxi and pushes the door back hard, almost knocking the driver over. She walks over to the leper, digs into her shoulder bag and takes out a fistful of paper money, and instead of putting it in the gourd, she gently takes hold of the woman's hand and folds the money into it. As Clare is doing this, the uniformed Norfolk doorman storms up and barks something nasty in Swahili at the beggar. Terrified, she picks up her gourd and, holding it between her teeth, scoots away, propelling herself with her filthy bandaged knuckles.

The black doorman turns to Clare with a smug look on his

face and is just about to extend his hand for a tip when she brushes past him and comes straight over to me.

'You've booked me into this hotel?'

I don't have time to reply.

'Well, I will not stay here!'

And she gets back into the taxi shouting at the bewildered driver.

'Let's go!'

'Where to, Mama?'

'Anywhere but here . . . somewhere . . . anywhere that's cheap.'

The taxidriver looks over at me for help. I nod for him to get on with it and he gets back behind his wheel and cranks up the engine. I stand there like a jilted lover, still holding Clare's bag. She shouts out of the window to me:

'You can stay here or come with me. I don't mind. Just throw my stuff in the boot if you're not coming!'

I hesitate for a second then trot over to the doorman, tell him to cancel the reservations for Arkwright, slip him ten shillings and jump into the Ngong Taxicab. Clare doesn't look pleased with my decision to come along.

'You gave him a tip. Didn't you? You gave that fascist fucker a tip!'

She stares at me in disgust, waiting for my sorry excuse. I have none. This time it's my turn to turn my head away. The driver feels the venom in the air and turns on his radio – Frank Sinatra is singing 'My kinda town . . .' I snap over my shoulder, 'Turn that bloody radio off!'

Five minutes later the Ngong cab stops in front of the Terminus Hotel on Moktar Daddah Street. It's a sixties cube affair with a group of backpackers sitting outside on top of their Aussie-flagged rucksacks. Our driver turns into the guidebook he's learned by rote.

'Terminus – most reliable and safe budget choice – friendly staff – clean rooms –'

'*And no lepers, right?*'

'And handy for the station,' I quip, hoping that a little irony might lighten the atmosphere a little, but it drops like a lead bubble from my lips. Clare isn't even in the cab to hear them. She's snuck out under cover of darkness, taken her bag out of the boot and is leaning in through the driver's window paying him off. I stumble out into the street like a drunk puppy and am almost killed by a brightly coloured Nissan Matatu with at least a hundred passengers clinging to the outside and top, waving and grinning at me like I was some lost white uncle. When the dust has settled, the Ngong taxi has gone and Clare is disappearing into the Terminus. For the first time since I said 'Hi, my name is Noah and I'm an alcoholic' in that Perry Street room in Manhattan, I wished myself back in one of those smoke-filled meetings, surrounded by other alkies who would listen to my insanity, nod sagely and say SNAFU! – Situation Normal – All Fucked Up!

31 March – MEA CULPA! MEA CULPA!

The Terminus Hotel café is like a school canteen. It's almost half past ten in the morning and I sit at a Formica-top table, under humming fluorescent lights, drinking a cup of coffee, eating a slice of buttered toast and staring at a poster advertising Tusker beer. The toast is cold and the 'butter' rancid, but, this being Kenya, the coffee is excellent and is clearing my head which is thick and muddled. I feel hungover. But I didn't take a drink last night. I didn't sleep either – not a bloody wink. Hour after hour I lay on my paper-thin mattress in my spartan single room listening to the mosquitoes circling me in the dark, waiting for their high-pitched buzzes to stop, signalling a landing on me, then slapping myself hard again and again like flagellant insomniac.

In between blows, I did a lot of thinking and, just before dawn, I came to a decision, got out of bed and scribbled a note to Clare. In the half light I crept down the spartan hall and slipped my billet semi-doux under her spartan door.

That was nearly four hours ago and I am waiting patiently. Clare will no doubt be knackered and lagged – in no hurry to get out of bed, let alone to see me. But if all goes according to plan, she'll read my note, melt a little, or at least be curious and will make the rendezvous with me.

Then I'll be able to get it all off my chest. I've got it all planned out. I'm going to tell her about my alcoholism and then I'm going to tell her that I fabricated the recce. I'll confess to all and then let the chips fall where they may. I don't know how Clare's going to take it. She could sweep me into her arms, smother me with kisses, say that I deserve a medal for bravery and that she's hopelessly in love with me – has been since the moment she first saw me. She could make me the happiest man in the Terminus Hotel. Or she could throw Kenyan coffee in my face, piss off there and then, never to be seen by me again, and break my heart and send me to Hell. It's big risk, but a risk I have to take, because to try and get through the next twelve days with the tension that has been with us since that first look at the airport would be a living Hell beyond all other Hells.

I try to light a cigarette, but I can't because I'm shaking as hard as if I had the DTs. My lower gut is in knots and I feel as if I have to piss, but that must be nerves because I took a leak about ten minutes ago. I shift focus from my bladder. I stare harder at the Tusker beer poster and like some high and dry free-diver try to slow my breathing and my heart rate. It doesn't work. The bull elephant stares me down, fans his ears out full and emits a blood-chilling trumpet. He begins to charge at me. The ground trembles and my coffee cup rattles on its saucer. Cigarette dangling unlit in my lips, I grip tightly on to the edge of my Formica table, shut my eyes tight and intone:

> God grant me
> the serenity to accept the
> things I cannot change,
> courage to change the
> things I can, and
> wisdom to know the difference.

God knows how many times I repeat these words as I fight to hold the elephant at bay. All reaches a crescendo when the prayer and the thunder of the charging beast fight for the space in my head which feels as if it will split asunder. Then suddenly the noise stops and, after a century, the shaking stops too and I open my eyes to find that the dust has settled, Jumbo has gone back to being a beer label, and Clare is sitting opposite me.

'You look dreadful.'

I take her hand in mine. She makes no move to take it away.

'Clare . . . I have an confession to make – a couple of confessions in fact.'

'Yes?'

'Do you remember when we were in the café across from St John the Divine, and I looked so awful you offered to buy me a brandy to go with my coffee?'

'Yes.'

'I told you that drink and drugs and me didn't mix, and that I'd given them up a couple of years ago? . . .'

Clare nods.

'Well, that wasn't exactly the truth –'

And I'm off and running at the mouth.

It's almost eleven fifteen when I finish with what turned out to be a full-blown confession – a no-holds-barred drunkalogue which would have done any AA meeting proud, ending it with the guilty revelation that there is no movie recce, that this African trip is nothing more than a contrivance.

What is Clare's reaction? Miraculously she has left her hand under mine. Or is it simply trapped there? I search her face for clues. Again that indecipherable something crosses her eyes. But this time, before I can run down Paranoia Alley, instead of taking hold of my hand as she did at the airport, Clare takes hers from under mine and nods slowly. Then with that same hand she reaches for my cigarettes, takes one, lights it, and inhaling deeply looks over her shoulder at the Tusker poster. I can feel her slipping away from me. I can't measure the moment. Should I speak or not speak? I speak.

'I didn't know you smoked.'

She turns back, slowly takes another drag, exhales and smiles just a hint of a smile before speaking.

'I don't. I gave it up a couple of years ago.'

Then she inhales once more, stubs out the cigarette and looks straight at me.

'Take me to the ocean, Noah.'

SIXTEEN

You say it's your birthday – Happy Birthday to you.

The Beatles, 'Birthday'

1 April

It's early evening and still ninety degrees. The pavements are steaming from the afternoon rain as Clare and I head along Haile Selassie Avenue in the direction of the railway station. She thinks we're walking back to the Terminus Hotel. I have other plans for us. While we were in Uhuru Park this afternoon, feeding the flamingos on the ornamental lake and watching Up-country tribal dancers, our Ngong Taxicab driver was taking our bags to the station and putting them in the left luggage office. Actually, Clare knows I've something up my sleeve because before we left the hotel this morning I asked her to make sure that her bag was packed and ready. In the light of that request, she doesn't have to be Poirot to deduce that we're going somewhere, and in the light of her response to my confessions, that somewhere might be the ocean. And she'd be right. I've booked us on to the overnight train to Nairobi-by-the-Sea, Kenya's former capital – Mombasa.

I'm hoping against hope that I've got it all right – that this *fait accompli* will present itself to Clare as a wonderful, romantic surprise and not as a self-serving alkie deceit.

It's been a good day so far. Things between us have been

cordial – warm even, and there appears to be a freshness in the air despite the clinging humidity and hundred-degree temperature. And as we walk together now, I have my arm around Clare's shoulder and she's making no attempt to bolt.

We haven't spoken a word about yesterday morning. In fact we've spoken hardly a word at all as we played tourist, buying a couple of bright cotton-print kangas – sarongs for the sea – in the City Market, being refused entry to the Jamia Mosque and viewing paintings of primitive maritime scenes from Lamu in the cool of the Gallery Watatu. In a hole-in-the-wall café off Mama Ngina Street we bought a takeaway lunch of nyama choma – barbecued nameless meat, some mashed green plantains – matoke, and a mango. We were just leaving the premises when Clare nipped back, bought a couple of passion fruit and returned to my side without comment. I took it as a good sign.

We ate our lunch in silence beside the lake in Uhuru Park, whose name means freedom. And there was a freedom in it too, the two of us side by side under the scorching sun of a foreign land, eating food with foreign names, saying little, cautiously building a new language of our own.

When we had finished eating, I went to buy bottled water from a vendor wearing ragged shorts and a ten-ton ice chest around his neck. Clare went down to the water's edge and threw our leftovers to the flamingos who waded over like salmon-coloured hit men and shovelled up the bits of meat and mango as they sank to the bottom.

When we returned to our picnic site, several dozen men and women had gathered a hundred yards or so down the shore. Some of them appeared to be stripping off their clothes, while others were bending down to open suitcases taking out items too far away for me to make out. There was a lot of shouting and laughter. Then a couple of drums started talking to each other. They were soon joined by an instrument so unexpected in a park in Nairobi that I couldn't place it until another joined in and it became clear that I was hearing two accordions playing a polka. But a polka unlike any I had ever heard. This was Tribal-Tyrol, a high-energy blend of the Royal Burundi Drummers and a Schweizer deutsch Oompah band. By now the suitcases were shut and cast aside, and a central square of dancers had formed, flanked by half a dozen drummers and at least as many accordion players.

As Clare and myself moved in closer we could see that the dancers, who were short and blue-black, were wearing a mixture of Tribal and Marks and Sparks – grass and animal hide over black bras and Aertex vests. From head to knee they had painted themselves with white polka dots the size of jam-jar lids, and to bottom this off all wore black wellingtons decorated the same as their skins. Cued by the single blast of a whistle, the dancers started stepping. What followed was a complex choreography that involved pairs of men and women stamping and leaping through a human tunnel in a dance which must have started life in the colonial era as an Alpine Strip the Willow.

It was the most bizarre – the most culturally alien – event I had ever encountered. And this fabulous formation, this beautiful homage to Terpsichore, seemed to have to no other end than its own existence. There certainly wasn't an audience that I could see – only myself and Clare, the drinks vendor, and two or three drunks laughing among themselves and drinking Tusker. Some passers-by glanced for a moment as they passed, and three middle-aged black women wearing pink fifties sun-dresses, outlining bottoms so high they seemed to be bustled, gingerly danced a few steps, laughed, hugged each other and walked on.

The second dance started and Clare slipped her arm through mine. The temperature soared. For an instant the sun was so hot that it seemed to be inside my head, and then it was gone and the sky opened. Rain came down as straight and hard as stair rods, and by the time Clare and I reached the shelter of a large baobab tree we were soaked to our souls. But the tribal polka, muted, still came to us and through the waterfall we could see that the dancers were still dancing.

I couldn't say how long Clare and I stayed there under that Faraway Tree listening to the faraway music and watching the faraway dancers, but when the sun came out again, so did we. The show was over. Laughing and shouting once more, the drenched men and women were changing back into civvies and the musicians were shoving the drums and accordions back into drawstring sacks. We walked over until we were only a few feet from the dancers.

Remembering the woman on the skateboard outside the Norfolk Hotel, I turned to Clare.

'Should I give them some money?'

She shook her head to say no, walked over to one of the women and shook her hand.

'Asante, Mama . . . thank you.'

The woman smiled and then turned to get on with the business of packing up. Clare came back to where I was standing, put her arm through mine and in silence we walked off in the direction of the east gate, left the park and turned south on to the Uhuru Highway.

That was about fifteen minutes ago. Now we are almost at the entrance to Nairobi station, and I'm suddenly very, very nervous about what will happen when I lead Clare into the station and reveal my plan. If she takes it the wrong way, mistaking my intentions, then I might as well kiss her good-bye there and then, go back to the Terminus and let Tusker out of his poster again to stamp the shit out of me once and for all.

*   *   *

226

Three minutes later, we're standing on the low platform, looking up at the chocolate-brown door of compartment 22 on the Nairobi to Mombasa sleeper. An immaculate porter points proudly at a brass holder which holds a buff card on which is written in chocolate-brown ink and beautiful copperplate *MR and MRS N. ARKWRIGHT*.

Clare leans forward to take a closer look.

'*Oh, shit! That's torn it, Noah!*'

I nod. Mr and Mrs is bad enough, but my *surname* and my first *initial* – I'll kill the misogynist Edwardian throwback who's done this to me! If I live to execute the deed. Christ! when Clare's finished with me I'll be lucky if –

But 'if' doesn't happen, because when Clare turns from inspecting the nameplate, she looks pleased, or moved, or perhaps a little touched, or none of the above, but she definitely does not look pissed-off or even slightly peeved.

'*Praise the Lord and pass the ammunition!*'

'Did you write this?' Clare asks the porter.

'Yes, Mama.'

'It's very beautiful – thank you.'

She turns to me and smiles.

As the porter opens the door and helps Clare step up into our compartment, I look over his shoulder, further down the train to where two men are loading the large luggage into the guard's van. The particular item which catches my eye is a black instrument case, which, even from three carriages away, I know contains a cello.

I lean in close to our porter and speak softly and hand him ten shillings. He nods, touches the peak of his cap and heads off in the direction of the guard's van. I leap up the carriage steps like Springheel Jack.

The compartment is art deco, all green leather and glowing sapele wood. Along one wall the two bunk-beds are already in place and made up with crisp white linen; along the other is a writing table and two small leather armchairs. On the wall next to them is a service bell. Above this, flanking a bevelled mirror, are two fan-shaped light sconces in the style of Lalique. A bowl of blood-red flowers on the table scents the room with a blend of cinnamon and orange. Our bags have been placed intimately together beside the beds.

Clare is sitting on one of the chairs. On the table in front of her is an opened half bottle of red wine and a couple of stem glasses. Clare turns one of the glasses upside down, pours herself wine and raises a toast in my direction.

'Compliments of the house . . . the train . . . you . . . cheers!'

I pick up the bottle and clink it against her glass. Clare's eyes dart from the bottle in my hand to my mouth. Will he or won't he?

'Well, will you or won't you, Noah?'

The weight of the bottle feels good, but light. I toss it gingerly in the air spinning it a half turn, then catching it my palm. Like a pro I don't spill a drop. It would be so easy now to suck this baby down in one go and then order six more – full bottles, none of this half-bottle-nancy-boy-hardly-wet-your-whistle shit. I could get arseholed right now and ride this train to oblivion in the safety of a blackout. For the longest second on record it all hangs in the balance. Under the scent of the flowers, under the bouquet of the wine, the smell of pure alcohol makes my million nasal cilia bristle in anticipation. My hand twitches. The neck of the bottle angles upward and my elbow begins to bend.

I take one last look at Clare and I freeze. The look in her eyes is a cocktail of terror and disdain with a twist of curiosity. My stomach turns. I look back down at the bottle in my hand.

'Lake Naivasha – they say it's the only decent Kenyan wine.'

I place the bottle back on the table and touch Clare lightly on the back of the hand.

'Cheers . . . and thanks.'

'For what?'

I tap the top of the wine bottle.

'Would you like me to ring and order you something soft?'

'No thanks . . . I'll wait till dinner.'

Taking out my cigarettes, I sit down opposite Clare and offer her one. She gives a little laugh and shakes her head as I light up and inhale deeply. I feel light-headed and a little shaken, as though I have just leapt over a wide and deep chasm. I exhale slowly before I speak and once more risk getting it wrong.

'I tipped the porter ten shillings.'

Clare takes a deep sip of wine, then runs her tongue ever so slightly over her lips. The act is practical not seductive.

'Good – I'm glad you did.'

It's past nine when Clare and I return from the dining car which looks as if it was designed by Charles Rennie Mackintosh. The meal was superb, a very tasty blend of English and African food. It centred on a main course of roast pork, roast tatties, kale and Irio, a vegetable mash of peas, maize and potatoes. The pork sported crackling that the factory-farmed pigs at home can't deliver, the kale had some kind of vinegar on it, and the Irio withstood our taste test very well indeed. All this was topped off by the Gravy Grandma Makes, and followed by crème brûlée and a platter of pineapple, mango, papaya and watermelon. Clare had only one glass of wine and I had two large bottles of fizzy water which I gulped down as if they were lager. And we talked and talked about . . . food. As the train clickety-clacked across the Athi Plains, we yacked and yacked, each rattling off foods precious to our stomachs and souls: Yorkshire puddings, rice puddings, Christmas puddings, mince pies, smoked mackerel, black olives, lemon curd, malt loaf, roast lamb, roast duck, roast parsnip, garlic roasted or raw, sago, apples, plums, crumpets in season, fish and chips from anywhere north of Sheffield, liquorice root, pork pies from Melton Mowbray, nan bread, bhindi bhaji, aloo mateer, and cold sesame noodles from the Number One Son Noodle house on La Guardia Place in NYC. Only twice did we dislike the other's choice. I balked at Clare's uncrisp bacon fat, and she turned her nose up at my hard roe. At one point – we both pointed at exactly the same moment and shouted, 'CORNED BEEF HASH!' and laughed so loud that the whole dining compartment turned to look at us. So we dropped our voices, leaned in towards each other and whispered 'with eggs' giggling like a couple of schoolchildren. When we got a hold of ourselves, we asked for coffee to be served in our compartment and, much to the relief of the other diners, left.

We're still heady now, holding hands as we sway back along the corridor. I feel full. I feel drunk. I feel happy. I feel sober. I feel empty. I am a man of contradictions with a shit-eating grin on his face. Clare stops and puts her face to the dark of the window, and I can feel seriousness fill her body. I put my forehead to the glass beside her head. It feels cool and it slows my heartbeat. We stand there side by side, still within the moving train which, as it goes over each expansion gap in the rails, sends vibrations up through our bodies like encoded passion signals from the heart of this vast continent.

Outside the window the land passes, grey and vast in the moonlight. It looks like a moving cyclorama. I think this and realise that it is the first movie thought to cross my mind since the food tray attack on Air Sudan. My mind, which is driven by film analogies, visual references and possible image systems for future use, has been empty of them for over three days and . . . I haven't missed them one jot.

'Beautiful, isn't it? – like a film,' says Clare, and I laugh.

'What's so funny?'

'Nothing's funny, Clare. You're right, it's beautiful . . . like a film . . . like Africa.'

I turn her face to mine to create a moment where a kiss is possible, but it is broken by a lurch of the train which throws us against each other and beyond the point of embrace.

When we enter compartment 22, even though nobody passed us in the corridor, our coffee and petits fours have miraculously appeared on the table.

A minute later, I'm pouring cream into Clare's coffee when there's a tap at our door. My heart leaps against my ribcage. Oh, Christ! I hope I've done the right thing.

'So open the fucking door, Noah, and find out!'

When I do, the ten-shilling-tip porter is there with the cello case. For a moment I think about using my body to block the view, but before I can even try that Ten Bob has lugged the cello into our little room.

'Where shall I put it, sir?'

I look around for an answer – there's very little space in here. Then Clare pipes up.

'Why don't you put it on the bed?'

Bob puts the black case on the lower bunk. Clare tips him some change and he leaves with a smile and a touch of his peak. I sit back at the table and take up where I left off with Clare's cream which I stir into her coffee.

'So, Noah . . . if you were a betting man, how would you say the odds stack up?'

'Fuck you!'

With a trembling hand I finish the task. Rock-steady, Clare picks up her cup, sips, then takes a petit four and bites into it. Only when she has swallowed does she speak.

'Well, this is a surprise, Noah.'

Her voice gives nothing away – I can't read this woman. What is clear is that this is a potentially explosive situation, so I go for the light touch and hope to defuse it before it blows.

'It seemed like a good idea at the time, but then so did the *Graf Zeppelin*.'

Clare looks long and hard at the case on the bed, then takes another sip of coffee.

'To the cellist, her cello is her child. She loves him as if he were born of her flesh and blood, and he gives her both her most exquisite moments and her most frustrating. Like a child, her cello is utterly unpredictable. One day he will sing for her with perfect resonance, the next he won't even speak to her. She constantly worries about him. In the hot concert hall, is he sweating – feverish? On the aeroplane flight, is he dehydrating – losing his voice? Day after day, hour after hour, like Jocasta she straddles her musical Oedipus. Like Jocasta she is a jealous mother. She will have no other son. She shares him with no one. She will have no one else even touch him.'

She puts her coffee cup down. I want to go over to the bed and pull the blanket up over the cello in its case – to protect it. When Clare speaks again it's with the voice of a pragmatist.

'A Stradivarius cello can cost five million pounds. A Guadagnini from the late eighteenth century will set you back a million. You can pay eighty thousand pounds for a top-quality French bow!'

'My God! That's movie money!'

'That's right. And even if only out of financial consideration, no self-respecting cellist, taking a train journey, would put her cello in the guard's van.'

The train whistle sounds long and low in the night as Clare goes over to the lower bunk and pats the cello case.

'What I think we have here is an abandoned child.'

She tries the case locks, they snap open, Clare lifts the lid and gingerly slides out the cello without hitting the top bunk.

She stands the instrument upright and holds it by the neck at arm's length.

'Worse than I thought – this is an orphan. He's probably lived his whole life in an institution . . . most probably a school. Does he look sad to you?'

I look at the cello. Even I can see it's pretty shoddy, the wood has no glow to it and the whole of one side of it looks as though it has been replaced at one time in the distant past.

Clare reaches back into the case, takes out a battered bow and points at me.

'Why don't you sit down, have a coffee and a cigarette?'

I do, and as I'm pouring and lighting up, she settles the orphan cello between her legs, tightens the bow and begins to tune up.

'Not as bad as I thought,' she says, her fingers working nimbly on the neck, the pegs and the strings. I bet she could load a camera like a pro.

'When you play a cello not your own, for the first moments you hear the voice of the last person who played it and you have to gently coax it into singing with yours – and that's true for a Grande Dame of a Stradivari or a nameless orphan like this one.

Then Clare begins to play and the room fills with a sound which is so full, so present, so achingly beautiful that not only my ear but my whole body is caught unawares. To hear a cello in a concert hall is one thing, but to hear it in a small, resonating room which seems at once to move with the strings is a shock. It is to be wrapped by the sound, picked up and taken to its centre – to a hallowed place where you are both guest of honour and worshipper.

I watch Clare as she dips and weaves, gaining the trust of the neglected cello, which must also be in a state of shock at being in her magical hands. She leans close into the cello's neck and seems to whisper, then pulls her head back, turning her face away as if pierced by the instrument's reply. I am transfixed, on the verge of tears. So I close my eyes against them and lean my head back – the chair leather is cool against the warm of the music – and for the first time since the morning of my arrival at the Rhode Island hospital last year, some words from old Sam Beckett ride into my head on the easy rhythm of this Mombasa-bound train.

'*But under us all moved, and moved us, gently, up and down, and from side to side.*'

As soon as I close my eyes, I see projected as clearly as a Showreel, the image of a lake, covered with mist, and on that colours lie like a giant multicoloured halo. In a split second it is gone. And as the music builds around me, I shut my eyes harder and try and try to bring the picture back, but it's useless – all I can see now on the red screen of my lids is the shifting pattern of electric impulses firing from my rods and cones.

The music has stopped.

I open my eyes again to discover that there has been a little Editing going on while they were shut. A little Editing? – a bloody-great jump cut! I am still sitting in the chair, but my coffee sits untouched in my cup and in the ashtray my cigarette has burned down and out. The cello is back in its case and standing in the corner like a dunce.

On the bottom bed where the case should be Clare is lying looking at me. How long has she been there? A minute? An hour? A dozen lifetimes? I open my mouth to say something, perhaps to ask her how long. What those words were going to be I will never know, because Clare, sensing that I am about to break the silence, puts her finger to her lips like Mata Hari on a mission.

In a Quick Dissolve I am on the bed beside her and we are kissing a kiss that makes love-making inevitable, and as with all things inevitable this is terrifying and comforting at the same time – as heady as the ozone layer and as grounded as Mother Earth herself. Soon we are naked and exploring each other's body with the combined skills of Isabelle Eberhardt and Mungo Park. Every movement is so beautiful, so deeply felt, so carefully considered yet at the same time abandoned, driven by passions unlocked from a place so deep within that it seems to be without, beyond us, beyond this earth and this time in a parallel universe not of our making. There is a moment when Clare puts her hand in the small of my back and draws me to her when I realise that I, Noah, Der Fuckmeister, the man who in the smallest emotional storm would dock his cock in any vaginal port, have never made love like this to a woman before. In fact, from the way I feel now, I would say that I've never *made love* to a woman in my whole life. This realisation puts a dark factor into the equation, and when our moment of ecstasy is reached, blurring all distinctions between us, behind the blinding intensity of my ecstasy there's a shadow of sadness, of regret for the lies of my past.

Afterwards, we lie naked side by side and the feeling of vulnerability in the hot air is almost tangible, but we make no effort to cover ourselves, obeying instead the primitive urge when threatened to make for high ground. We climb up on to the top bunk where it is even hotter, and the view from the window takes away what little breath we have left. The moon is even brighter than when we last looked out from the corridor, and beyond the silver plains of the Nyiri Desert, the peak of Mount Kilimanjaro glints like a Masai spear. There are no animals to be seen, but in my mind I populate those plains and distant foothills with the giraffe, gazelle, lions and elephants from the story books of my childhood. A herd of wildebeest charges across the moonlit grass and I can hear the drumming of five thousand hooves, as through the mattress under me, I can feel the pounding of Clare's heart as loud and strong as the engine which pulls us through the night and into a future which neither of us can know.

'YESTERDAY'S HISTORY – TOMORROW'S A MYS-TERY! Please, Noah! Spare me the violins.'

'Stay out of this, alright?'

'Was it good for you too, Noah?'

'Piss off!'

'Happy Birthday to you too!'

Clare kisses me gently on the cheek.

'Penny for them.'

'I was just remembering that today's my birthday.'

She laughs softly and moves in even closer.

'And that makes me the April Fool, I suppose?'

'No, there were no fools that day, only losers . . . my mother died a few moments after I was born, well, according to Macbeth, not born at all – just torn from his mother's womb.'

I can feel Clare let the breath out of her body and shrink in my arms.

'Nice one, Noah – still got the old velvet touch, I see.'

'I'm sorry, Clare, that was rough of me. I don't even know why I said it.'

'Safety Sabotage.'

'What?'

'Men do it all the time. They let themselves be intimate, feel the happiness that comes with letting go – for a few moments – before they panic and press the Control button, firing a rocket right into the heart of it all. When the dust settles after the explosion, they find themselves back in the comfort of the Safety Zone.'

She pulls the blanket up over herself and pulls away from me just a fraction. For the second time this evening I start to say something, and for the second time Clare puts her finger gently to my lips.

'Goodnight, Noah . . . Happy Birthday.'

I couldn't say how long I've been lying here in emotional limbo with the clickety-clack below and the moonlight pouring over me. Clare has her back turned to me but I don't feel any anger radiating in my direction on the Alpha waves of her deep sleep. This confuses me because in the past, if there has been the slightest upset with a woman before Lights Out, I have not been able to sleep a wink, lying awake till dawn, tortured by her REM vengeance. And I would feel so guilty that I wouldn't even take myself out of the line of fire by decamping to a sofa or floor, choosing rather to add self-loathing to the already excruciating punishment. Tonight it is different. Clare, naked and spent, sleeps beside me, and I, naked and spent, am awake beside her. I don't feel good, but neither do I feel bad. I feel empty and in a state of expectation – a tabula rasa with a limp dick. I am aware of something at the edges of my empty mind and I don't have to look too closely to know what it is: it's Fear, skulking around with his tail between his legs waiting for me to fall off to sleep so he can do his stuff. Clackity-clack, clackity-clack and the long low whistle – clackity-clack and my eyelids begin to droop. I fight it. I pull the Chi up into my head. I draw breath deep into my fifth chakra. I say the Lord's Prayer – the Serenity Prayer – Ohm Namah Shivayah. I try everything to keep my consciousness alert. But it's no good – sleep wins and the wagging finger of the Director's subconscious starts to write the Script from Hell.

I'm on the blue and red train from Green Eggs and Ham, sitting there next to Sam I Am, and just before we disappear into a tunnel, I become aware of a presence behind me and I turn my head to see The Beast sitting in the last open car. He has the body of a human giant, covered in dark scales, and a head which is a cross between that of a jackal and the Creature from the Black Lagoon. His teeth, which are bared, are as long as a man's finger and his eyes have no pupils. Deep inside his nostrils I can see the eternal fires, and his breath is straight from the bowels of Hell. I turn to cling to Sam I Am, but he is no longer there. He has gone along with all the Green Eggs and Ham Gang. The train has gone, the tracks in the air and the mountain ahead, and I am in a deserted railway cutting hewn out of dark granite. I am naked, and all around me the wail of Banshees fills the air. The stone blocks of the walls are covered in slime and my naked feet sink in a silt of human excrement. Suddenly I am grabbed by razor-sharp hands which cut my flesh then drag me to iron rings in the wall and fetter me. The hands belong to small creatures who instinct tells me are children, but children turned inside out, their dark hearts beating outside their rib cages, their intestines purple in the sick moonlight, the backs of their eyes staring blankly at me. They gurgle hideously as they press me flat against the icy rock. One of them holds something aloft which glints; another, low down, an object with a handle. The moon disappears behind a cloud and for a few seconds I am blind in the fetid darkness. When it reappears, I see a metal spike an inch from my groin and a hammer head arcing towards it. The pain when it finds its mark is blinding. Blood spurts, showering the inverted children who laugh in hysteric ecstasy and dance a dance of celebration. I take advantage of the moment and throw my full weight forward, tearing myself from my groin, leaving my bleeding genitals hanging on a spike behind me, stumbling and falling down the cutting, the Devil's Children chasing behind me. But I run and I run and I outrun them to find myself on the edge of a precipice looking down on to a black, fast-moving river of putrefying corpses. A girder bridge stretches half way across the river, then stops, a broken span plunging into the 'waters' below. The gas from the rotting bodies rises and clogs my every pore. Only the pain cutting my body in half keeps me from passing out, from falling off the edge and tumbling down the magma of rotting flesh. The children are closing in behind me – I can hear the bones of their feet clickety-clacking. I leap on to the bridge and run, bleeding and screaming, a hurting, hurtling, terrified body of pain – until I reach the mangled end of the middle span, where I pull myself up abruptly and, panting and whimpering like an animal run to ground, I pace back and forth along the edge watched from below by the dead eyes of the million corpses floating by, knowing that to jump is my only hope.

Suddenly, miraculously, just as the first sharp bones of an infant pursuer claw at my back, the broken bridge rises up and mends itself. And coming jauntily towards me I see the Dr Seuss train. I laugh out loud with relief and start to run along the gleaming track to meet it. Then I see who is at the controls – The Beast himself, stoking the firebox with one hand, pulling the whistle with the other, and singing an old Country Gospel song in a key from beyond the grave.

> Life is like a mountain railroad
> With an engineer that's fine.
> Keep your hand upon that throttle
> And your eye upon that line.
> Blessed Saviour . . .

He stops singing, lets out a shriek to freeze blood and opens his stinking mouth wider and wider as he races toward me, faster, faster and faster until his maw is the size of a galaxy and the Black Hole of his throat is sucking me in.

'Jesus Christ, Noah!'

I can just make out Clare's voice in the distance and feel something or someone reaching across the vast gulf, trying to take hold of me.

'NOAH, WAKE UP!'

As I break through the surface into consciousness, I gulp in air, gasping and shaking my head like a diver from deep space, to find myself soaked in sweat in Clare's arms.

'I'm here, darling – don't worry.'

'*Darling*.'

'*That's what she said*.'

I can't remember any woman ever calling me darling. I thought it was a fictional term of endearment – so sweet that any script I ever read that contained the 'D' word was automatically rejected as sugarcrap. And now here it is being spoken in full Sensurround by Clare to me, not as a tender coochee-coo, but as a tough word to bring me back from that place of the undead – a needle shooting adrenalin straight into the heart.

My tongue fills my mouth so that I can say nothing as I lie in Clare's arms, aching from head to toe as if Tusker and all his mates had trampled me underfoot. This scene is both familiar and totally new to me. Countless times in the past I have woken from some nightmare in the middle of the night in a woman's arms, disorientated, sweating, wracked with pain and unable to speak. But all those times, it was a sure bet that I'd been totally fucking wasted and had collapsed into bed in a blackout, and it was odds-on that the woman beside me in the bed was a total stranger. There'd have been a nightmare too, but I wouldn't have remembered it when I woke up – not as I can remember tonight's nightmare now, so vivid that I fear that it might run for ever in my head on an infernal, eternal video loop. I hold closer to Clare. In the past, I would never have done this either. Terrified, I would get dressed without saying a word, and leave whoever it was bewildered in the four a.m. bed, wondering if somehow she had done something wrong. I wouldn't care about that, in fact it would suit me for the blame to be shifted so that I could nurse my hangover the next morning in my usual state of denial.

Tonight, as far as I can see, there's no blame to be laid. I don't think I've done anything wrong, except perhaps the low blow about my mother's death; and Clare has been perfection itself. And I wasn't drunk. So why the dream from Hades? Why me?

'*Why the fuck not you, Noah?*'

I move in even closer to Clare and whisper,

'Yes . . . why not me?'

Ever so slightly, she turns from me so that she is flat on her back, and when I squint open one eye, I can see the profile of her face, dark and beautiful, staring at the ceiling which is only a foot or so above her. And that's how we have stayed, side by side, silent as the train climbed through the Chyulu Hills, rolled across the Tsavo National Park and started to pull up the Taita bluffs on the edge of the coastal plain. Clare fell asleep about an hour ago. I felt the exact moment that she went, when her weight doubled against my side; since then I have been listening to her breathing, regular and deep, the nightmare has ridden off over the horizon, and a heavy warmth has filled my body. I don't even feel tired. During the last half hour or so, the light has become dove-grey. The land will be revealing herself, but I haven't dared to lean over to look out of the window for fear of waking Sleeping Beauty.

Suddenly a single shaft of first light sweeps across the carriage. As it touches Clare's face she puts her hand across her eyes and slightly arches her back. She wets her dry lips with her tongue and, even though she's still half-asleep, speaks as clearly as if she were ordering lunch.

'Oh, fuck it! I love you.'

Then she pulls the blanket up over her head and presses herself hard against the wall just as the sun pours into our room, turning everything into gold from King Solomon's mines.

SEVENTEEN

Hear no Evil. See no Evil. Speak no Evil.
Chuck Berry, 'Too Much Monkey Business'

The director, the Coke and the Cortina

As the train pulls into Mombasa Central and heaves a sigh of relief, I stick my head out of the window. The air is already stifling and it's not even eight thirty in the morning. Along the length of the train, people step down on to the platform, men in crisp white djibbahs, women wearing bright dresses and turbans, babies slung across their hips and battered suitcases on their heads, very few white people. Everybody moves slowly in the heat except for some twenty or thirty who run like rabbits with a purpose toward the station exit.

Suddenly there's a beating of wings and a shadow passes over the crowd. I look up to see a flock of flamingos, black against the sun, necks pointing north-west like flying compass needles. Everyone except the rabbits has stopped and is also looking up. This is a very unusual sight – flamingos are not coastal birds – they live on Lake Bogoria up beyond the Aberdare Range. What are they doing down here? Perhaps the lake waters can't support their increasing millions. Perhaps they are planning a massive exodus brought on by a collective understanding of impending starvation. Perhaps they are about to do the Darwin Quickstep and move

242

down to the beaches where they will shovel the oceanside sand with their beaks for transparent shrimp, tiny crabs and fragments of coral to keep them pink. It's possible. This flying roseate wedge which is now half a mile north of the station, glinting salmon in the morning light, could well be a recce team on its way home to report on possible coastal relocations.

Clare's arms wrap around my waist from behind, and she nuzzles her head into the back of my neck and for the second time since midnight tries to get a bargain.

'Penny for them.'

I turn and pull her close to my chest, put her head under my chin and speak into her cropped hair.

'Funny, isn't it? how people are so ready to pay you a penny for your thoughts and yet they won't give you tuppence for your opinion.'

'Mmm – the roots of capitalism.'

We kiss a Morning-After kiss – one of those kisses which, like the tiniest fragment of the hologram which has in it the complete image of the whole, contains all of last night's love-making. It's heady stuff, and if we let it linger a moment too long, we'll be back in the bunk coupling while Thomas the Tank Engine is uncoupling and handing over to Gordon for the long, slow pull back up to Nairobi.

Clare breaks away with a smile, reaches into the money pouch hanging between her breasts and pulls out a hundred-shilling note. I hold up my hands and shake my head in mock affront.

'No money, please! What do you take me for?'

'Arsehole!'

Laughing, Clare goes to the table, scribbles something on a paper coaster then goes over to the cello case in the corner and opens it. She tucks the bill and the coaster note under the strings, pats the instrument, closes the case and turns to me.

'For a new set of strings – a little thank you.'

As she picks up her knapsack and slings it over her shoulder, Clare looks full, radiant with last night's music, with this morning's light, with anticipation of her rendez-vous with the ocean, and perhaps with a little of me. She pecks me on the cheek, pushes gently past, opens the carriage door and steps down from the train. I grab my bag and am just about to follow her when a knitting needle is suddenly jammed up into my body between my scrotum and my arse. It's gone before I know what's hit me, and I am left with a burning need to piss.

'I'll be right with you, Clare. Got to pee.'

I nip into our tiny en-suite just as I'm about to wet myself, whip out and let out a nightful of recycled carbonated water and coffee and . . .?

'*What the fuck's that?*'

'*C'mon, Noah! You remember, don't you? Cranberries.*'

'*Cranberries?*'

'*You heard – cranberries!*'

Cranberries my arse! I drank no cranberry juice last night. What I see sinking through the pee water in the toilet are a couple of clots of my blood about the size of large match heads.

'*Ejaculatory strain?*'

'*What?*'

'*It happens all the time – you shoot a big fuckwad and bust some small blood vessel or other.*'

I stare at the clots spiralling down in slo-mo and I nod sagely to myself. Ejaculatory strain – that's it! of course. After last night's love-making it's a wonder there's not a whole toilet bowl full of clots! No problem, Noah, my son – *pas de probleme* – no problema – nothing to fret about at all on this sun-filled Mombasa morning. So with a smile I flush away any lingering worries, zip up, shut the loo door on it all, and jauntily hop down on to the platform where Clare is waiting.

On the wide forecourt of the station there's not a soul in sight and there's not a taxi to be seen. Now I understand what all the rabbits had been running for. The light is blinding and the heat has doubled in the last ten minutes and seems to be coming from below rather than above, generated by the concrete and asphalt not the sun. I am dying of thirst. I look around and spot an ancient Coke machine shaped like a juke box sitting at the end of the station wall.

'Drink?'

Clare shakes her head and wipes her brow with her forearm.

'No thanks. I'll have a sip of yours.'

As I drop a coin into the Wurlitzer drinks machine the air is filled with spluttering, and I turn to see through a cloud of dust the most dilapidated Ford Cortina I have ever clapped eyes on rattling across the plaza. After a ten-megaton explosion from its exhaust, the 'taxi' collapses in a heap of wreckage at the kerbside next to Clare just as a bottle of Coke, stubby and frosted, thuds down the machine chute and into my hand. By the time I reach the Cortina, our bags are in the boot and Clare is chatting to the driver who is wearing a Yankees baseball cap and must be eighty if he's a day. She gives me the thumbs up as she ducks into the wreck and pats the seat for me to get in beside her. I hesitate. I who have ridden ten-up and fucked-up in a slant six Plymouth Valiant with no brakes, I hesitate. Only love could make me this nervous – this careful. Fuck it!

'It sounds like Tiwi beach is the place we want – it's tucked away down a jungle path about twenty miles south of here – no tourists.'

Sounds like a *fait accompli* to me! The driver is already starting the Cortina with two hot wires he has taped to the side of the steering column, and even from inside the car

Clare's happiness fills the air like a glorious infection. I let it catch me, button my mouth and duck in beside her. She takes my hand in hers and places it on top of her leg above her knee – her skin is curiously cool.

'Tiwi it is then. Let's go, Ishmael!'

Call me Ishmael! First-name terms in less than a minute – that's my girl!

Ishmael turns, grins and says 'Okeedokee'. Then he sees the Coke in my hand, reaches up and grabs a bottle opener which I have not noticed and which is dangling on a bit of coiled telephone flex from the rear-view mirror. He stretches it to me with a knowing wink. A knowing wink? What the fuck does he know! More than me that's for sure, because when I open the bottle and take a swig, nothing comes out – the Coke has frozen – plugged the neck. After a moment a single drop wets my lips and christens me Tantalus. Ishmael starts to laugh and Clare laughs with him. For a split second I want to dive out of the car and lob a grenade back into it, but instead I raise the bottle again to my lips and this time the plug gives way, shooting into the back of my mouth, followed by half a bottle of coca pop under about ten atmospheres of pressure. I spray the inside of the cab with cold soda and, half-choking, start to laugh like a half-wit. It's one of those Movie Moments that the director has to get on the first take.

The dead monkey

If it hadn't been for the dead monkey, we would still probably be drinking fresh coconut milk in the shade of the walls of the Kongo Mosque at the end of Tiwi beach, not crammed into the back two seats of a Piper Comanche, six thousand feet above Lake Magadi, heading towards a towering thunderhead at a hundred and fifty miles an hour.

Five days ago, fifty minutes after I sprayed his cab with Coke, Ishmael drops us at Twiga Lodge, a no-frills collection of mud-built bandas nestled under the shade of huge baobab trees beside a crunchy white beach. Skyscraper palms dot the edge of the tide mark, and a quarter-mile off the shore, the turquoise water is edged with a coral ridge. The lodge has everything we need. There's a hole-in-the wall shop for fags and mags, an outdoor barbecue where nightly fresh fish is cooked on a grill, there's a palm-thatched bar by which I can trip lightly and pretend that I've been sober for years, and there's a gazebo overlooking the sea in which you can sit on rattan chairs and read and sip tea delivered the hundred yards from the restaurant by a handyman-cum-waiter named Kobo.

'Excuse me?'

I look up from my *Rough Guide to Kenya* which Barry of Oz from the banda next door has lent me.

'Did you say your name is Kobo?'

'Yes, bwana. Is this OK with you?'

I flush with embarrassment. Clare looks up from her copy of Jean Rhys's *Sleep It Off, Lady*.

'Kobo – isn't that the name of your character in –'

I interrupt with a stuttered reply.

'Yes . . . no . . . I mean, yes of course it's OK with me. Everything is more than OK – the tea, the beach, this fabulous breeze which tells me to my face that I am a very lucky man – to be alive – to be here . . . in this gazebo . . . on this glorious coast – in Africa. I don't know, Kobo – I'm sorry . . . what I'm really trying to say is . . .'

Both Clare and Kobo are looking at me as though I'm totally fucking mad, which for this moment I am. Meeting Kobo face-to-face, not *my* fictitious Kobo of course, but a Kobo none the less, has brought me up with a jolt to face my lying. I crawl with shame to think that to serve my base needs

247

I have hijacked the name of this perfectly respectable man who makes the best cuppa in East Africa. Alright! I know that I came clean with Clare at the Terminus Hotel, but perhaps that was all part of a ruse as well – just some clever-dick calculated move to bump up the empathy, draw a veil of truth and romance over my brainless urge for a fuck. I don't fucking know! That's a lie! I do know. I know that right now I could go over to the palm beach bar and drink it so dry it would lower the water table of the whole coastline between here and the island of Zanzibar.

And I know that I am shaking like a fault line. Clare touches the back of my hand.

'Are you alright, darling?'

'*Darling – dangerous! – darling.*'

'I'm fine. I'm sorry. It must be the heat. I feel a bit woozy.'

I top the first lie off nicely with that lie and pull a twenty-shilling note out of my shirt pocket. Kobo looks taken aback and then hurt. With his hand he folds mine back over the money.

'I have a wage, sir. I am a happy man – thank you.'

As he walks off, proud and erect, I feel tears welling up – tears of self-pity – fuck it! I take hold of Clare's hand and pull her towards me.

'Hold me, Clare . . . please . . . and don't let go.'

The next thing I remember is waking with a stiff neck, still nestled against Clare's shoulder who has almost finished *Sleep It Off, Lady* which she is reading by the light of a lantern hanging from the rafters of the gazebo – lit I assume by Kobo. Sparks fly upwards into the night from the barbecue grill and the cook is silhouetted against a rising moon which fills half the Prussian blue night sky. Soweto jive drifts over from the bar on the offshore breeze and I feel as though I have aged a hundred years. In fact, like Rip van Winkle, I am not sure if I'm the same man that fell asleep those hours ago. Clare seems to read my mind.

'You slept. You look years younger.'

She strokes my hair with one hand and flips her book shut with the other. Then she eases me gently off her shoulder, laughing and wincing with pain at the same time.

'Ouch! My side slept with you.'

I lean back in, kiss her ribs and whisper, 'Wakey, wakey.'

Later that night, full of fish and fresh fruit, and after Clare read to me the title story from Jean Rhys's book, we make deep love in our banda on a thin, starched mattress under a humming mosquito net. In our mud room on this Moorish coast we move behind our protective scrim like film lovers, the sheik and the desert maiden entwined in a complex arabesque. Outside the tree frogs and cicadas serenade us to the back-beat of the breaking waves. I am reminded of something an aging Director of Photography said to me when I was fresh out of college. He was at least ninety years old – his name was George and he'd cut his teeth in the silent movie gold rush. I'd found myself talking to him after a screening of Kurosawa's *The Seven Samurai* and in the middle of my making some wanking comment, George turned to me and said, 'Bullshit! Do you think anyone ever sat on the point at Mendocino, watching the whales blow in the Pacific sunset and said, "Gee, it's pretty but it's a real visual cliché!"' How right he was, Old George, because whenever, as now, I try to express the true heart of the matter, the dividing line between the deepest emotion and the Hallmark card is a very, very fine one.

After we make love, Clare falls asleep in my arms as she did on the train, but this time there's no nightmare for me. I just lie there, listening to the night and feeling the breeze through the banda windows which are simply holes in the walls through which the SFX moonlight falls across our bed.

My skin is blue, but not my spirit. I am a contented man. I hum to myself that song that my mother sang to me in the womb and when she visited me in the Pawtucket detox.

> I put my finger to a bush,
> I thought I'd find a lovely flower . . .

Then I hear a scratching noise and low throaty sounds coming from the direction of a window opening above my head and a little to the right. I feel my heart beat a little faster, but I am curious not afraid. For a second I see nothing, and then the silhouettes of two small monkeys, outlined in electric blue by the moonlight, appear on the ledge. They sit discussing whether or not the coast is clear. One of them stares down at us and I find myself actually closing my eyes and pretending to be asleep. When I open them again cautiously, the two monkeys have hopped down on to the rough-hewn table and I understand their mission. They are sitting on either side of a wooden fruit bowl which yesterday afternoon Clare had piled high with fruits: mangoes, pineapples, dwarf bananas, and some rough-skinned pear lookalikes. One monkey strips the rind off a mango with its teeth, tears off neat pieces and hands them to his mate who in turn is peeling a banana and placing chunks at the first monkey's feet. The rhythm between them is smooth and the exchange loving. The act is so simple, so honest that it takes a hypnotic hold on my gaze, and I can feel my heart, which I thought already full, expand to fill just a little more.

After they have consumed the mango and the banana, the monkeys look over in my direction, take two bananas each, slide down from the table, and in two silent leaps, leave by the same window opening through which they entered. I lay my head back on the pillow and look up at the ceiling rafters. Clare turns in her sleep and her breasts brush my arm.

'Good night, World – sleep tight,' I whisper and within seconds I am deep into a dreamless sleep.

I wake with the dawn to Clare's snoring. It is music to my ears – an atonal confirmation that she is mortal. A sweet little fart from her right now would finish the job nicely and guarantee that I would never put her on a marble pedestal. I lean over and touch my lips to her hair then slip out of bed, pull on a pair of shorts, grab a packet of fags and my lighter, and slide out into the first light of morning. The sea is pink – the sky streaked with wisps of salmon. The birds are still sleeping and the only sounds are the palms rustling high above and the waves booming softly on to the still-dark sands. I light a cigarette and head along the path into the dark shadows under the baobab tree.

The silence is suddenly broken by a manic screeching, and the sound of panic and a wild crashing up through the branches of the huge tree. It scares the shit out of me. And it all happens so quickly that I don't catch sight of whatever made the sound, but the screeching sounded to me like monkeys.

I recoil and stumble backwards. The back of my head thumps into something heavy and soft. When I spin around, I'm hit again in the face and my lips brush against fur. I take out my cigarette lighter to shed some light on the subject, but I already know what I am going to see, and my stomach is already rising as I flip the Zippo top and spin the flint wheel.

The dead monkey is hanging by a length of thin blue nylon rope, and in its mouth the hangman has stuffed four un-peeled bananas, dislocating the poor animal's jaw and thrusting its eyes out like organ stops. The body spins slowly and when its back is turned to me, it looks for all the world like a limp human baby in a snow-suit.

Cursing under my breath, I burn through the rope with the lighter flame and take the monkey down in a perverse parody of the Descent from the Cross. I cradle his lifeless body and head towards the beach where it is now almost light. I am crying with anger. Who the fuck could have done this? With the end of a palm stalk, I dig a pit in the sand, remove the fruit from the monkey's mouth and place him in the hole. When I have back-filled the shallow grave, I find myself quietly singing an old blues song:

> In my time of dying, Lord,
> Don't want nobody to moan.
> All I want for you to do,
> is to take my body home.
> So meet me, Jesus, meet me.
> Meet me in the middle of the air . . .

My voice trails off when I realise that I am sitting on a beach beside the Indian Ocean singing a song of mourning to a dead monkey. Enough! I pat the sand on the grave, light another cigarette and walk to the water's edge, vowing to myself that if I find out who killed the monkey, I'll headbutt the bastard.

Clare and the vagina shell

Four days later we're still at Tiwi, and on the surface things have been going smoothly. Clare and I have swum with angel fish in coral pools, split coconuts on an upturned sharpened stake and poured the cool, sweet milk down each other's throat, watched the moon rise each night and made passionate love beneath the frangipani tree down by the old mosque. We've said nothing about films or string quartets – in fact, we've said little at all to each other. This must be a good way to proceed, because, unless I am imagining things,

Clare's eyes are sparkling with life and flashing with high-lights of new love.

I'm watching her now, as she looks at bright shells displayed on the rough plank shelves of a beach kiosk made out of four bamboo poles and a roof of palm fronds. Her hair is bleached lighter by the sun and salt water, and her long back is turning golden. She's wearing only a black and yellow kanga tied in a single knot above her breasts. Two days ago I bought it for her at the Twiga fags and mags and she's worn nothing else since. Further along the beach, a group of young Norwegians are playing a loud game of volley ball – they arrived yesterday afternoon on a leg of their Cairo to Cape-town lorry trek for the mediumly well-off young white adventurer. They and their 'hoodi hadi hoda' shouting will be gone by tomorrow, thank God. Back up near the bar/restaurant, Barry of Oz is squatting next to a fire he's built in a ring of beach stones. He's wearing a bandanna and laugh-ing with Kobo. They are both chewing mira – the speed grass favoured by Kenyan youngblood men. Some kind of large sea bird, perhaps an albatross, rides the up-draft far above, and out beyond the reef, a dhow, mainsail billowing, heads north to Mombasa like a pregnant coastal woman. All seems to be in a kind of order.

I should be very happy, and 90 per cent of me is; but there's been a shadow in me ever since I found the monkey hanging from the baobab tree. I try to pretend the terrible thing never happened, and for a while I get away with it, unless I am within sight of the tree and I see the blue nylon rope still hanging – its end black and deformed where the flame from my lighter burned through it. Then Paradise is touched with evil.

I had to pass by the baobab a few moments ago to buy some fresh fish from the vendor who every afternoon pushes his bike draped with the catch of the day along the path in front of the bandas. I bought a couple of red snapper which Clare and I will cook on an open fire tonight at the north end of the beach, under the shelter of the vine-hung cliffs. I dumped the fish in a bucket of water outside our door, glanced back in the direction of the tree, and started whistling to push the dead monkey to the back of my mind. At the bar I bought a Coke and took it to the gazebo where I am now sitting taking in the scene.

'Noah!'

Clare beckons me to come over to the 'souvenir shop'. For a moment I hesitate, and that split second is invaded by a feeling of dread, then it is gone just as a 'Yadahooa!' goes up from a goal-scoring Norwegian.

'Aren't they beautiful?'

They are. The twenty or so shells range from a simple blush-pink, single-hinged carapace which I recognise as a type of scallop, to a large deep purple and red whale-back of a shell with spines as long as a man's forefinger which looks like a figment of the imagination. Clare picks up one and shows it to me. It's a large cowrie which fills her palm. Its apricot, rounded back is covered with a distorted leopard-skin pattern, gleaming in the sun. Just under the glaze, a blue-grey wreathes around the design like trapped sea smoke. She turns it over to reveal a pinky-white underbelly which looks exactly like a vagina, complete with clitoris sheath.

'I was thinking it would make the perfect present for Etta. What do you think?'

What do I think?

'What do I think?'

'Yes. Do you think she'd like it?'

'I've never met her, remember?'

Clare laughs.

'That's right! You haven't, have you. That seems impossible – that the two people who are most precious to me haven't met. Oh, you'll love her, Noah. She's a spirit of the sky, born out of the sea – air and water – a flying mermaid. And she loves me. She would do – has done – anything for me.'

She holds up the cunt shell again – labia facing out.

I'm jealous and it's a very particular jealousy. It's the same as I'd felt when I saw Etta and Clare at the table through the window at Fanelli's – how close she'd come to being shot in the back of the head when she brushed past me on the way out. Why the fuck does she have this effect on me?

'Face the facts, Noah! You know what the score is.'

Facts? There are no facts. There's no ground for anything as far as Etta is concerned. Clare simply wants to buy her Second Violin girlfriend a gift from Africa, and she wants my advice.

'Yeah, yeah, yeah! . . . she wants your . . . advice, Noah.'

I don't know what to say. I just stare down at the vulva in Clare's hand and my imagination starts building Etta around it, starting with her curly jet pubes, then her golden, parted thighs, her flat smooth belly, her . . .

I tear my eyes away, panning around for a legit distraction. Barry of Oz and Kobo are looking over in our direction, but high above our heads. Kobo points and I see that Barry is aiming a high-velocity hunting catapult into the top of the palm tree behind the shell kiosk. Suddenly he lets the sling loose, there's a scream above and a monkey drops to the beach with a thud a couple of feet outside the makeshift shop where we stand. It convulses for a moment, the goes still, a drop of blood trickling from its nose. Barry and Kobo are laughing. Clare is standing, palms on her cheeks, mouth open in a silent scream. The cowrie lies at her feet. Now I know! With a roar I charge at the Australian, covering the fifty feet between us in about three seconds.

'YOU MURDERING BASTARD!'

And I'm on him, headbutting him to the sand like a crazed woodpecker.

'You hanged that poor fucking monkey!'

I whack my forehead down again and feel his septum collapse under the blow. Barry is trying to scream something at me, but I can't hear a word he's saying. All I can think about is battering his face to a pulp. But before I can get the next butt in, Kobo grabs me from behind and slams the scene into slow motion reverse as I fly upwards and backwards on to my feet, and he holds me in a vice-like grip. Barry's balled up on the ground, his face streaming blood. He wipes his hand across his split mouth and spits.

'What the fuck're you doing, you crazy cunt?'

He spits blood again.

'What monkey? . . . What fucking hanging?'

'Don't fuck with me! You know what I'm talking about.'

Kobo loosens his grip and firmly but gently leads me in the direction of the bar.

'Come, bwana . . . have a drink and calm down.'

With a surge of superhuman strength, I break free and spin on my heel to face him.

'I don't drink! You understand me? I . . . don't . . . drink. Save your freebies for your friend the monkey killer.'

Shaking with after-shock, I walk back towards the banda. I glance over to the shell stall to see that Clare is still standing where I left her, cowrie shell at her feet, watching me in disbelief. The Norwegians are all standing in silence by the volley ball net staring at me like a bunch of lost Vikings in shorts, and I shout over to them as I duck into our doorway:

'Show's over, lads! Play on! Hoodie hoodie!'

It's cool and dark inside. I flop down on the bed and reach in my T-shirt pocket for my fags and lighter. Gone . . . dammit! Lost in the struggle!

'You really blew it this time, Noah!'

'*I don't think so. For once I took the moral high ground –
she'll understand.*'

'*You beat the living daylights out of him . . . and you don't
even know if he killed the bloody monkey.*'

'*Once a Mod always a Mod . . . and he killed it alright.*'

Clare appears in the doorway, silhouetted against the
turquoise sea. I give her a sheepish wave.

'Hi! . . . you alright?'

'I'm fine . . . thank you.'

She comes in and holds up a packet of Marlboro with my
lighter held to it by a rubber band.

'You dropped these. Want one?'

I nod and she takes out two cigarettes from the packet,
puts them in her mouth and lights them with a single deft flip
of the lighter. She comes over to me and hands me one,
inhales deeply on the other she's kept for herself and sits on
the side of the bed.

'Now, would you like to tell me what all that was about?'

EIGHTEEN

One toke over the line, Sweet Jesus . . .

Up, up and away!

The private airstrip just outside Msambweni, thirty miles down the coast from Tiwi, is a quarter-mile grass path in the middle of a banana plantation. The customs office is a large, creosoted garden shed. A stamped metal label on the doorpost reads: *Eridge Garden Dwellings, Braughing, Herts* – you've come a long way, baby! Next to it, under a palm-leaf awning, somebody has lovingly placed a bottle of Johnnie Walker Red, a packet of Senior Service untipped and a packet of Marlboro Reds. A sign hangs from the crossbar – DUTY FREE SHOP. I look wistfully at Johnnie Red, then drop a couple of shillings in the honesty box, pick up the packet of Marlboro, and head with Clare to where the Piper Comanche sits on the grass runway with its door open, like an extra from *Biggles and the Flying Doctor*. I should be bent low and running, pulling Clare behind me, the beautiful missionaries' daughter whom I've rescued from the Fuzzy-Wuzzies, throwing her into the plane and leaping into the pilot's seat to fire up the engine just as the natives break into the clearing and launch a salvo of spears and poisoned arrows.

Instead, an Indian pilot in a dirty short-sleeve shirt with epaulettes leans against the wing of his brown and cream plane sipping a Coke. He looks as though he might drop off to sleep at any moment.

'Hello! Is this the flight to Kiganjo?'

The pilot doesn't look at me; he just nods, waves a hand in the direction of the open door.

The plane looks like it could do with a damn good overhaul. Rivets on the wings are rusty, the fuselage is streaked with oil, and the tyres don't seem to have a lot of tread on them. I laugh nervously and go for a quip.

'Are you sure the old rustbucket's up to it?'

He still doesn't look up, but takes a final swig of Coke, crumples the can and shoves it in his trouser pocket. When he finally speaks it a cocktail of Oxbridge and Delhi.

'This "old rustbucket" is the very same Comanche PA-24-250 which in 1959 flew Max Conrad from Casablanca to Los Angeles – 7668 miles – non-stop in 58 hours 38 minutes, at an average speed of 130.9 miles per hour.'

He finally looks at me and flashes a smile.

'She'll get you to the top of Mount Kenya if you ask her nicely.'

Then he pats the wing beside him where there is a step-up and extends a hand to Clare to help her up. She takes it and climbs into the plane. I follow and we take our seats in the row behind the pilot. At first I think we're the only passengers until I become aware of a wheezing and turn to see the rear two seats almost totally filled by a huge Arab businessman wearing a shiny midnight-blue suit and a plum-coloured fez. His hands are clasped in front of his huge belly and he appears to be asleep.

The engine kicks into life, and I look out to see the rivets rattling nicely on the rust-streaked wing. Another plane lands at the end of the runway, and by the time our pilot has put on his sunglasses and had a deep pick of his nose, it taxis next to us. Bengal Biggles pokes his head out of his window and shouts to the other pilot:

'What's the weather like up ahead?'

I hear the reply all too clearly.

'Bad storms – just keep to the right of the thunderhead!'

Clare must have heard it too because she leans over and kisses me full on the mouth, then after an hour or so breaks away.

'Just in case anything happens, which of course it won't.'

'It won't.'

'Promise?'

'I promise.'

As the pilot lets out the clutch, or whatever they do in a plane, Clare and I are both thrown back against our seats, and the craft hurtles off down the runway, bumping and leaping like a goose trying to take off from land, until suddenly we're airborne and clearing the trees with about an inch to spare, then rising up, up and away northwards with the Indian Ocean glinting behind us.

Why are we flying to Kiganjo, a tiny town in the foothills of Mount Kenya? First, I had to leave Twiga Lodge as soon as possible to get the Dead Monkey off my back. Second, Kiganjo is the destination for that region of Simba Air, our carrier of choice – the only 'jungle line' which would fly us at a minute's notice. Third, Kobo was born in that region – not Kobo the accomplice to Barry the Monkey-Killer but Kobo the title character of my non-existent movie. When I was lying awake the night before last, dwelling on the monkey murder and the cunt shell, I remembered a slogan on the wall of some AA meeting in New York: YOUR HEAD IS A DANGEROUS NEIGHBOURHOOD! and it suddenly became obvious to me that I must get out of that head, get out of Twiga and get on with the recce which was the foundation lie of this whole trip, which was in danger of going very, very wrong.

I told all this to Clare who said she would come along with me but stressed that it was not because she wanted *anything* to do with my guilty conscience but because she too had been thrown by the monkey incident and was ready too for a change of scenery. When I pressed for a little more assurance that it was OK to leave the sea and go to the mountains – that I wasn't being an arsehole – for her to give her seal of approval to my alkie geographical shift, Clare turned to me and spoke clearly and slowly.

'If I had wanted to be with a boy, Noah, I would have found myself a boy. I thought that with you I was getting a man. So be one – make your choice and go with it. If I want to come along I will, and as I have already told you, I want to, and only because *I want to* and for no other reason. When I want to be a mother, I'll get pregnant.'

And that was that and here we are. I think if I'd said anything at all in reply, Clare would not be sitting beside me now, and in maintaining my silence I learned that sometimes 'going for the milk' means knowing when not to. I must remember to tell Tiny that, although the cleverdick will probably nod a slow nod which says 'I was wondering how long it would take you to reach that conclusion, you fuckin' brain surgeon!'

Clare pulls at my sleeve and points out of her window.

'Look! Flamingos!'

I lean across, brushing her pert breasts and for a split-second wonder if there's any way we can have a quick fuck at five thousand feet, before dragging my attention to a small lake below where a flock of flamingos is feeding near the edge. The pilot reads my mind.

'Shall we swoop down for a quick *butcher's*?'

He stresses the last word, proud of his bit of Cockney. Clare makes a little whooping sound and answers with child-like enthusiasm.

'Oh, could we?'

I glance over my shoulder at the Arab businessman – he's fast asleep.

'Okeedokee!'

The pilot doesn't mess about and suddenly thrusts the plane's nose down and we start the descent at a forty-five-degree angle. There's a grunt from behind and I look over my shoulder to see the Arab, still fast asleep with his fez resting on the bridge of his nose. In no time at all we're no more than a couple of hundred feet above the lake and I can see the flamingos clearly, shovelling the silt of the shallows, as yet unaware of our approach. I wonder if these are our recce friends who gave us the Welcome Fly Past at Mombasa Station? As if in reply, the birds suddenly rise up into the air as one and for a brief instant we are all flying together, the director, the cellist, the Arab, their pilot and the flamingos, flashing silver and pink above the deep blue of the lake below which falls further and further away as we rise back up steeply and come face to face with the biggest fucking thundercloud I have ever seen in my life!

'Bad storms! Just keep to the right of the thunderhead!'

No shit, Sherlock! From where I'm sitting, we seem to be about a hundred yards from a wall of dark-blue brick. I glance over at Clare, she's looking down and behind us, and from the back seat comes the sound of deep occidental snoring. Our pilot seems unfazed and simply lifts his sunglasses back on top of his head like a model, produces a bottle of Coke from somewhere under his seat, takes a swig and with a flick of the wrist banks the Comanche up and to the right like the pro I hope he is.

Clare is thrown against me just as the plane begins to toss like a cork on the currents. The Arab wakes up with a start and shouts something in full voice at the pilot who looks over his shoulder at us and grins.

'Hold on to your hats, Ladies and Gents – time to rock'n'roll!'

'LIGHTS! CAMERA! ACTION!'

The forked lightning is zapping around the cumulo-nimbus and the air is turning a strange shade of green as the pilot steers us along the side of the cloud as if it were the wall of a canyon. One bolt of lightning is so close that I hear a sizzling along the length of the fuselage followed by a sickening drop down as the tiny plane hits some kind of vacuum. Clare's fingernails are digging into the back of my hand. The Arab is intoning a loud prayer over and over. And the pilot is singing a pretty convincing version of the Stones' 'Route 66'. I am trying my damnedest not to piss in my pants, cursing myself for not having taken another leak before take-off. The Comanche lurches again, this time shooting upwards as though being plucked out of the sky by some giant hand. Fuck it! If you can't beat 'em! I start to sing along as the pilot brings the number back around to the first verse.

'. . . IF YOU EVER PLAN TO MOTOR WEST,
JUST TAKE MY WAY, IT'S THE HIGHWAY, IT'S
   THE BEST!
GET YOUR KICKS ON ROUTE SIXTY-SIX!'

Clare joins in on the last line and we're off, rocking on to the next verse and when we hit the beginning of the third, the plane is buffeted hard from the side, the Arab all of a sudden stops praying and starts to drum the back-beat of the song like Charlie Watts himself.

Hello! I'm Doghead – remember me?

After an hour's drive down through the coffee plantation foothills from Kiganjo, our taxi arrives at the gates to the Outspan, about a mile down a dusty road outside the small market town of Nyeri. At the entrance to the hotel grounds, next to the gate pillar, a woman in an acid-yellow dress and a young girl in jeans have set up a battered old card table which is laden with carved wooden souvenirs and a few dozen strands of glass trade beads. The driver is about to whiz past but something in my gut tells me to ask him to pull over and I do.

'You do not want this, bwana. Only rubbish.'

But I insist he park and I get out. Clare watches from the car. The carvings are 'rubbish' – nasty, clumsy attempts at lions, giraffes, elephants and some shapeless blobs which the young girl tells me with a grin are wart-hogs. The necklaces are sad too – the cheapest, chipped reject beads from the Venetian slave trinket factories, strung on to fraying parcel string. I'm just about to turn on my heel and get back into the taxi when the woman speaks for the first time.

'Wait!'

And she bends down behind her little table, rummages around, brings out something about a nine inches long wrapped in hessian and holds it out to me.

'This is for you.'

I hesitate then take the cloth package from her and reach for my wallet. The woman's hand shoots upward, palm forward like a traffic cop.

'No money. Free for you.'

She cocks her head slightly to one side and gives a little coded nod which I don't understand. She nods again in the direction of the gift in my hand and slowly I unfold the wrapping. What I see there makes me suck in my breath so hard that I'm sure the pilot of our Comanche, now half-way back to the coast, is having to take evasive action to deal with the pressure drop I'm creating. Lying in my hand is an exquisite carving of The Beast from my Dr Seuss nightmare on the Mombasa train. It has the perfect ebony form of a young black male, muscled and shining, and the head of a jackal, teeth bared and eyes set with two tiny emeralds.

'He is Anubo.'

Anubo! Of course! Why hadn't I recognised him? Anubo – Anubis the jackal-headed Egyptian God of the Dead – the Great Destroyer – dismemberer of men, women and children – the darkest vision behind the darkest vision beyond the grave. I look the woman in the eye, searching for some clue, some sign of a plot or a trick – nothing but an open smile.

'Asante, Mama.'

Carefully, I wrap Anubis in his cloth, put him in my trouser pocket and get back in the car. Clare looks puzzled.

'What was all that about?'

I pat my pocket.

'Souvenir for a friend.'

I tell the driver to go on and we pull through the gates and up the long, manicured driveway, and past the lodge where Baden-Powell spent the last years of his life waiting for old Anubo to come and chew down on his bones before dragging him off to the Great Scout Hut in the Sky.

The guidebook tells me that the Outspan is a 'charming old colonial hotel with spacious rooms and all the trimmings'. Despite the Norfolk Hotel fiasco, I've decided to take a chance and book a bit of luxury, banking on Clare having had enough rough'n'ready for her to risk a quick dip back into the world of the Other Half. So I'm holding my breath as the taxi pulls up in front of the faded elegance of the entrance. Not a peep from Clare as she lets the doorman open the door for her and places a travel-weary foot on to the cool gravel of the hotel forecourt.

The medicine man and the bowl of piss

The eucalyptus trees which line the dusty road from the Outspan to Nyeri must be a hundred feet tall. Golden hot sunlight filters through them and dapples the floor at my feet. Of all the people walking the way, I seem to be the only one walking *towards* the town, and I also seem to be the only man. I am definitely the only white person. On the other side of the road, on top of an embankment going away from town, there's a continuous stream of black women of all ages, all bent double carrying massive loads of cane, hay, heavy sacks of what I take to be grain, and huge bundles of cord-wood. One woman who must be at least sixty is balancing a Baby Belling cooker on her head and carrying at least twelve feet of copper pipe in each hand. They file by easily, chatting and laughing over their shoulders to each other, ignoring me totally. It doesn't feel like a deliberate exclusion, as if notice has been taken then dismissed as unworthy of further attention. I simply don't exist in the same time and space as these women. I am wholly insignificant, not slightly marginalised, not at the edge of the frame, but completely out of the fucking picture. In fact, if this was one of my movies, I'd have to edit myself out on the First Cut.

This realisation makes me feel absolutely alone, so alone that it's going to take every ounce of what little maturity I have to stop me from turning on my heel and going back to Clare whom I left soaking contentedly in The World's Largest Bathtub. It stands on a raised podium of large quarry tiles and is at least seven feet long and two foot six deep, surrounded by massive wall hangings of bold, rough fabrics dyed with the rich colours of vegetables and roots. Everything in our Out of Africa suite is huge – the fireplace, the ceiling fan, the parquet floors and the full-wall windows overlooking the great spread of manicured tropical garden to the massive peak of Mount Kenya beyond, rising above its lower slopes which in turn rise above its foothills and the thick forest below. The half-acre coffee table is supported by four carved elephants and our carved teak bed is the size of a championship billiard table. On the porch the huge view is viewed from rattan armchairs as big and comfortable as small English cottages.

Clare was perched on one of these cottages just half an hour ago when she turned to me and made her big announcement –

'You know something, Noah? Right now, I'd like nothing better than to fill that huge tub with steaming water, slide in, lie back and smoke the biggest fucking joint in Africa!'

My reply bounced back like Pavlov's dog.

'Sounds good to me.'

'But you can't, can you? Smoke a joint?'

I looked up to the summit of Mount Kenya glinting in the pure sunlight and the pure air and launched into one of my porkies.

' "*WE ADMITTED WE WERE POWERLESS OVER ALCOHOL!*" Alcohol is my problem, Clare – always has been. Drugs I've always been able to take or leave –'

'Really? For some reason, I'd always thought that –'

I broke in with a staccato laugh.

'Fuck, no! If we had a joint now, I could smoke it with you and not give it another thought for God-Knows-How-Long.'

'Well, that's great – that's really great. Do you think we can find anything?'

'Is the Pope Catholic? You run that bath and get in and I'll nip into town for a shufti,' I said as I grabbed my sunglasses and wallet and hopped lightly down the huge veranda steps on the first leg of the Quest for the Huge Joint.

So if I'm honest about it, as I walk along this road toward Nyeri, I feel pretty fucking guilty as well as alone because I know I'll track down some weed, I know I'll toast my brains and I know that for all the good it will do me, I might as well shoot pure Irish into my veins.

'Slippin' and a slidin'
Peekin' and a hidin''

Little Richard's song is blaring out from a cheap transistor radio next to a skinny young man wearing a vest who is sitting on top of a wall outside a building whose sign declares it to be Nyeri Courthouse. The man is one of about a dozen, all sitting on the wall, all wearing vests and all topped off with a Trilby hat which must have been part of a job lot dumped by some cheapjack store on Kilburn High Road. They don't say a word to each other, and they stare with dead eyes at my passing.

Two turns and a couple of minutes later I reach the top of Nyeri High Street. The shop-fronts are a dilapidated mixture of sixties English prefab, tribal mud hut and Wild West boardwalk. Everything needs painting and the red mud from the unpaved road is splattered half way up walls and over windows. The place is curiously empty. I become aware of something heavy in my trouser pocket and reach down to find the carving of Anubis, wrapped in his blanket and nestled against my crotch. There's a cold comfort in his presence.

Beyond the corner of my eye I can feel somebody staring and I turn to see Africa's answer to Hopalong Cassidy beckoning me. Giving Anubis a little reflex pat, I head over to this blue-black guy, at least six-four, who's wearing a black ten-gallon Stetson, black double-fronted shirt with silver buttons, black pants and chaps and a pair of black snakeskin cowboy boots with a set of spurs the size of saw-mill blades. He is standing beside an old glass-fronted pharmacy display counter which he has put on wheels and painted blood-red and crammed with watches, shoe laces, cigarettes and lighters. When I reach him, Hopalong breaks into a wide, genuine smile before speaking with a treacle voice.

'Smoke, my friend?'

I see that he has Capstan Full Strength. I haven't had one of those in years.

'I'll have twenty Capstan, please.'

With a quick draw flourish Hopalong opens the back of his case, gets the cigs and, as he hands them to me, speaks without breaking his smile.

'You want something stronger, man? Something to knock your dick into your watch pocket?'

I can hardly believe my ears – my luck.

'Yes – OK. You're sure it's good stuff?'

He recoils slightly, putting his hand across his heart as if wounded by my question.

'One toke no joke – all bud no fucking seeds! Cowboy's honour, man!'

I look around to make sure I'm not being watched and then give him a nod. He reaches into his display, comes out with a kitchen-size box of matches, puts them in a brown paper bag with the fags and holds it out to me.

'That'll be ten bob – nine for the matches.'

'Thank you.'

I give him the money, take the bag and start to walk away when Hopalong calls after me:

'You here with the BBC?'

Puzzled at the question I turn back to him and he nods down to the bottom of the High Street just as a bank of Klieg lights come on, 'Action' is called over a loud hailer and dozens of extras dressed in nineteen thirties clothes start to crisscross the road as an old bull-nosed Morris sweeps in from a side street and parks in front of a hardware store which I can see has been dressed to perfection for a film. The Morris door opens and I recognise Denholm Elliott as he gets out and is greeted by a young woman in a white suit who looks so much like Clare that my heart actually skips a beat. I turn back to Hopalong.

'No, actually I'm not with them. What film are they making?'

'The Happy Valley story – posh people taking drugs and murdering.'

He laughs.

'No work for me – no call for cowboys.'

I laugh.

'They've got all the cowboys they need, believe me.'

We're both laughing uproariously – the kind of laugh that breaks down huge barriers – when I am once again aware of something beyond the corner of my eye. I turn just enough to see, coming out of a fabric shop two doors down, and dressed in matching pale-pink safari suits and pale-pink pith helmets, Rita and Connie the Tribeca Wardrobe Twins! Oh, shit! In a flash I turn my back on them and run, clutching my stash like a fugitive, down a filthy alleyway where I stop and lean my back against a wall, my head and heart pounding like steam hammers.

I don't know how long I wait for the coast to clear, or even why it's so important that it does. Why don't I just go back on to the street, catch up with the Twins and say '*Hi there, girls – fancy meeting you here!*' What could be so dreadful about that?

'*You'd never get out of here alive!*'

I don't even bother to question the answer. I know in my thumping heart-of-hearts that it is right. Leaning back hard against the alley wall, I can feel my own blood pumping in my veins. I flatten myself harder against the wall until I am just a shadow and try to take measure of my situation. Here I am in a back alley of a shit town in the Central Highlands of Kenya, a matchbox full of killer dope in my hand and a fetish of a Death God in my pocket, hiding from identical twins dressed in pink safari suits whom I fucked less than month ago in New York. I'm in Africa under false pretences, pretending to be on a recce for a non-existent movie, and as if to rub my nose into my lie, the fucking Beeb are shooting a real film not five hundred yards away. And back at the hotel, the new love of my life is in the bath, waiting for me to return so that we can get wrecked – something which will only deepen my paranoia about my relationship with the universe which already has me shaking in my boots, and might just trigger a junket of addictive behaviour which could bring the whole fucking lot tumbling down around my ears and consign my relationship with Clare to an entry in the History of My Self-Destruction. I could change all that right now by simply coming clean. I could go back to the hotel and tell Clare that I've got some grass but that I can't smoke it with her – that she was right – I can't be high and sober. Then I could tell her about running into Rita and Connie, and about the BBC and suggest that we go into Nyeri together and see who we can see. It could be a lot of fun. But no! That would be too simple a solution for a mind as complex and deep as mine! KEEP IT SIMPLE! Fuck that! CUE THE THESAURUS! *Simple, foolish, silly, muddle-headed, undiscerning, unenlightened, unphilosophical, bigoted, narrow-minded, pig-headed, mulish, stick-in-the-mud, unballasted, ridiculous, barmy, daft!* Me simple!? Me daft!? Ha!

Ha bloody Ha! And I start to laugh to myself like a fucking idiot.

Suddenly, without any warning, the old knitting-needle pain shoots up through my groin and I double over, clutching at my crotch, pulling my fly down for a piss. When I reach for my cock, I feel something squirming and I look down to see Anubis, his ebony back arched over and his jaws clamped on to my penis. I thrash out to knock him off, but his teeth are buried deep in my flesh. He turns his head and looks up at me, his emerald eyes flashing in the dark, blood and saliva dripping from his sharp teeth, then with an evil hiss bites deeper into me. Like a mad dog, I shake my head back and forth and somehow I manage to throw off the pain. When I look back down, Anubis is nowhere to be seen. My fly isn't even undone. And when I feel in my right pocket, there's the wood carving of old Doghead, still wrapped in his security blanket, safe as houses.

Pulling myself together, I notice for the first time that I am not trapped, that the alley is open at both ends. Hopalong's Stetson is still casting a shadow across the High Street end, so I opt to leave the back way. The narrow side street I come out on to is made up almost entirely of butchers' shops, all painted sky-blue with bloody red carcasses hanging in their unglazed windows. Only the tiny storefront directly opposite the alley is not festooned with meat. Its freshly painted black and white front is mock-Tudor and there's a tiny bow window which is right out of *Little Dorrit*. Across the window in meticulous gold leaf copperplate is written *DR M. NUBI M.D., CAN-TAB*. I cross over, knock on the door and open it to the sound of a tinkling bell. The room is bare and immaculate apart from an old leather examining couch, a crisp white linen bed-screen, a small desk and a range of wall cupboards containing phar-maceutical bottles whose deep blues, greens and golds are mysteriously and beautifully backlit. A coal fire flickers in a small Edwardian grate and in a wing-back chair next to it sits a large black man wearing a suit, his face resting in his hands and the top of his head glistening in the firelight. Very slowly he becomes aware of my presence and looks up.

'Good afternoon. What can I do for you?'

There is something about this ersatz Dickensian room that reminds me of Tiny's tea room on the Bowery and it has the same effect of making me want to sit down and pour out my heart and soul.

'You wouldn't have a cup of tea, would you?'

He nods slowly, raises his great bulk out of the chair and goes behind his screen.

In less than no time, Dr Nubi is back with tea in cups and saucers decorated with tiny violets which would set the Bowery Oracle aflutter. Abernethy biscuits appear from nowhere and before I know it I'm unfolding my medical history to this complete stranger.

Half an hour later when I've finished, the doctor leans down, pokes the fire and throws on a little more coal. Then he opens one of his wall cabinets, takes out a shallow wooden bowl and hands it to me. He nods in the direction of the screen.

'A urine sample, if you don't mind.'

Behind the curtain, next to the gas ring, kettle and tea caddy, I pee a good stream into the bowl, take it back out and hand it to the doctor, who thanks me as casually as if I've just refilled his teacup, holds it up to his nose and takes a deep breath. Then he leans very close and stares at my piss for a long time before swilling it around like wine in a taster's glass. He holds the bowl even closer to his nose and sniffs little short sniffs like a dog at a tree stump, then he takes the bowl over and places it gently on his desk before taking out of a drawer something which looks like a pair of ebony chopsticks. With these he whisks up the contents of the bowl just as if he's preparing a urine omelette, then he puts the bowl back under his nose, inhales very deeply and closes his eyes.

When he finally opens them he looks me squarely in the face. He looks very sad.

'Mr. . . .?'

'Arkwright – Noah Arkwright.'

'Mr Arkwright. I'm only a country doctor –'

'Your degree's from Cambridge. You –'

'It impresses the locals.'

'So impress me. Did you find anything?'

Dr Nubi carries the bowl over and stands by the fire.

'The Gabon pygmy has a saying – "*Tomorrow is empty and naked for the Maker is no more there, is no more the host at the hearth.*" Go home, Mr Arkwright.'

He then pours my piss from the bowl on to the fire and as a cloud of acrid steam rises up and envelops him, I slip back out of the surgery door into Butchers' Row, take Anubis out of my pocket and toss him into the gutter.

You kiss my blood and the blood kisses me

When I get back to the Outspan, Clare is still in the tub. She is floating, arms slightly away from her sides, her eyes closed, her nipples breaking through the water like tiny tropical islands, and below them her belly is a golden sand-bar rising and falling under the surface with tides of her breathing. The longer I stare at her, the less she seems to be breathing at all, the more she looks like dead Ophelia, and I start to feel a perverse flirtation with necrophilia. So I turn to leave the bathroom. Clare speaks.

'I thought you were never coming back.'

Then she sinks under the water and emerges a second later spouting like a dolphin.

'I got some stuff.'

'Great! Pass me the towel, will you?'

As she stands up in the tub, I put a towel the size of a football pitch around her shoulders and she kisses me on the lips. Only half of me receives her kiss – the other half is still in Dr Nubi's office watching him pour my piss on his fire. Clare senses something is out of balance, holds me under the chin and looks me in the eye.

'What's wrong?'

'Nothing.'

'Noah!'

'Mission accomplished – got the stuff.'

Then, like a mother swaddling a child, I pull the towel tight around her and peck her on the cheek.

'You get dressed. I'll roll us a joint.'

That was well over an hour ago. The spliff I rolled was one of the skinny ones favoured by New Yorkers, and thank God it was only a thinny. 'One toke no joke!' Fuck! One toke of Hopalong's special was like smoking a pellet of opium – real Dream Machine stuff which turns your body into lead and your mind into waters under the pressure of ten atmospheres, driven on slow currents to the shoreline shelves of unexplored countries. We undressed. For a few brief moments, we were naked, drifting in the direction of stoned mid-afternoon sex, but without saying a word, we both opted for something less strenuous and I dragged myself into the still-warm bathwater while Clare lay down on the bed, arms crossed over her breasts like a sleeping Egyptian queen.

I floated in her water, eyes closed, riding her currents.

The sun is already hotter than an English summer's day as I step on to the veranda of the white-washed lodge. Bougainvillaea and frangipani scent the air and a band of pink cloud cuts the summit of Mount Kenya off from its base in the valley below, beyond this garden filled with flashing birds, plants of dreams and butterflies as big as your fist. I look back through the French doors and I can see Clare sleeping, shrouded in the afternoon mist of the mosquito netting – a beautiful ghost, sleeping the deep sleep of Africa.

I hear drumming in the distance, not from any one direction but all around me. I glance around the grounds. A starched black maid laden with sheets disappears into another lodge in a corner of the garden and then all is deserted – the coast is clear. I let my white towelling bathrobe fall to the floor, walk down the veranda steps and on to the lawn still heavy with dew. The drums are louder now. I break into a brisk trot, my legs strong, my back straight, and my flaccid penis beating time against my lower belly. I am smiling the smile of childhood and as I look up to see the sun glint off the snow-covered peak of the mountain, I let out a yell of pure delight.

Without breaking stride, like a coursing hare, I side-step through the lovingly-cared-for garden beds. I break out from the cultivated boundary, dash across a grassy no-man's-land and crash into the dense undergrowth and semi-darkness of jungle. I'm in an Henri Rousseau painting: foliage I don't recognise, leaves longer than my legs and hanging blossoms the size of babies. At the point where the stench of death of the forest floor, stirred by my pounding feet, meets the giddy flower scent just above my head, the air is thick – almost tangible – and as I stumble on, sharp growths cut into me and blood runs in tiny rivulets down my body. In the undergrowth, unseen animals grunt and screech, and on the canopy a hundred feet above birds shriek and monkeys chatter. The drums are nearer now, and a deep, massive roaring has been added to their polyrhythmic call. I run faster and faster and soon I am leaping and bounding through the jungle, naked and bleeding as when they cut me out of my mother, shouting at the top of my voice in primal whoops and hollers, drawn on by the beating of the heart of Africa.

Shafts of light break through to the forest floor ahead and the drumming is almost drowned by the roaring which is now so close it is inside my head. My lungs are almost bursting, gasping in razor-sharp air to feed my heart which is beating ten to the bar as it pushes the blood around my body and out through the wounds on my feet into the earth itself.

I crash out of the forest and into the blinding light. I stop dead in my tracks, wracked with pain, bent double with my head between my knees and my eyes closed, gasping. The roar is now so deafening I am inside it. I feel a cool dampness wrap itself around me and I force my eyes open. I am standing on the very edge of a precipice looking across a deep gorge to a waterfall that cascades a thousand feet into a boiling lake. Iridescent parrots fly from edge to edge in a choreographed air dance, and a hundred feet under them, in the rising mist spray, a rainbow shimmers, starting on the far flank of the falls and describing almost a full circle before disappearing back under the cataract.

The tom-toms' beat, now barely audible, seems to be

*coming up out of the whirlpool at the bottom of the gorge.
My heart has slowed and is now pumping in time to the
drums. I pull myself up to full height, put my palms together
and stretch my arms full to the sky above my head. I draw
one massive breath deep into my loins, open my mouth in a
silent scream and dive off, scattering parrots east and west,
plunging through the three-quarter rainbow into the fevered
pool far below.*

*In the deep turquoise, twenty feet underwater, I twist and
turn like a seal. Shafts of sunlight penetrate from above and
dance around me. I dart in and out of them. I want to laugh.
I have no urge to strike for the air above. Bright fishes join
me. They nibble my toes and dart playfully for cover into
tropical underwater fronds. I will stay here and grow gills. I
will drop my blood temperature and live in this water for
ever.*

*Suddenly, out of the corner of my eye, I glimpse a
fractured figure through the surface of the water, standing
on what must be the bank. It raises an arm and lunges. The
water surface breaks and something flashes towards me. A
harpoon! As it nears, it seems to slow to a crawl. I try to
swim out of the way, but I am moving even slower. I can
count the barbs as they glint in the underwater sun, heading
lazily towards my groin. Six – and needle-sharp. They hit
their mark and shroud me in a cloud of dark pink.*

*As I roll belly-up three fathoms underwater, eyes closed, I
hear Clare's voice.*

*'Just like that sun south of Mombasa, you will rise again,
big as the horizon . . .'*

NINETEEN

Tonight I am coming
to visit you in your dream . . .
Be sure to leave your door unlocked.

Man'yōhū

North London hospital, February 1997

'Just like that sun south of Mombasa, you will rise again, big as the horizon . . .'

'Clare?'

I open my eyes to the harsh fluorescent light of the ward. Clare is nowhere to be seen. The prisoner is back in the bed opposite, shackled and drugged, staring at me through half-dead eyes. Next to him an old woman wearing an oxygen mask is having her saline drip changed by a large black nurse with bandaged ankles. By the window, framed by flowers in vases, sits a young man with a bruise of tattoos on the back of each hand and a fresh one of a dotted line on his neck. I can read the words above the line very clearly – CUT HERE. He's wearing headphones and bobbing his head up and down twice a second. I strain my head round. The bed next to me is empty, perfectly made-up for the next customer, and the next bed along is surrounded by so many women visitors that I can't see who is in the bed. All of them wear head-scarves and talk in very low tones.

The pain in my groin is excruciating. I pull my legs up to my chest. The pain doubles. I know what's going on. My bladder is full and there's a clot in the plumbing and the urine has to go somewhere. So if I don't piss in the next couple of minutes, there's going to be such back pressure on the kidneys that they could explode and blow two holes in my back the size of my fists.

'*We could catheter you, Noah. But if we do that then we'll have to delay the operation and we don't have time for that. It's best if you go to any lengths to void your bladder naturally, alright?*'

From some indeterminate point in the recent past my consultant's voice echoes in the back of my head, and I nod slowly and whisper like a scared schoolboy:

'Alright, Mr Baker.'

I swing my legs over the side of the bed. My pyjama bottoms are bloodstained around the fly. I'm wearing my Road Kill Café T-shirt which was so admired by Yangos or Peter in their restaurant in Cyprus. It seems impossible that it was only last week that I was taking a dip in Aphrodite's pool and walking back along that dawn beach of Chrysochou with the sound of gunshots still ringing in my ears.

Since being admitted to hospital two, or was it three?, days ago, I've worn the Road Kill shirt as a black joke – to show the world that I still have a sense of tumour! I have also occupied myself by taking the shirt off every so often and trying to memorise the menu on the back.

I know it by heart now, and when all this is over, I've made a promise that I'll go to Sturgis, South Dakota, walk through the door of 1933 Main Street and order Smear of Deer and a large fries, or perhaps some naturally aged Bloat Goat, a Slab of Lab, a Chunk of Skunk, some Toad à la Road, a Rack of Raccoon, topped off with the Bag'n'Gag daily takeout lunch special for the road.

Thumper on a Bumper . . . Round of Hound . . . Ooze of Moose . . . Snippet of Whippet . . . I go down the menu in my head as I head toward the Patients Only toilet. This mental short-ordering usually gets a chuckle out of me but tonight I can't raise even the start of a smile – the sense of tumour is nowhere to be found.

Everyone is looking as I shuffle past, but they're not reading the menu on my shirt. They are not even looking at me. They are all looking at Death as he creeps along behind me rubbing his hands together. Some of the patients try to croak a warning as they watch Him sidle up to me, put his arm around my shoulder and open the bog door with his free hand. He ushers me in, laughs and says:

'Now that's my kind of T-shirt, Noah.'

I stiffen under His touch, take a deep breath and, defiantly brushing against Him, cross the threshold. Even with my breath held, his stench burns my nostrils and makes me gag. I do the hundred-year dash to the porcelain and finally stand in front of it, panting, Death breathing flies and maggots over my shoulder. I'm desperate to turn to him and scream 'Piss Off, Motherfucker!', but I don't have the strength. What little I have I use to lift the toilet lid and point Percy at the Porcelain, Shake Hands with My Friend, Exercise the One-Eyed Trouser Snake. Shaking, I hold my tortured, terrified dick and try to pass water. I am fucking petrified. Death chuckles to see me shake.

'*You can do it.*'

I hear the soft voice clearly under the bastard's laugh. It's the voice of Clare, Faith and Coral mixed with that of an angel.

'*Use your name to talk you through – "Noah who found grace in the eyes of the Lord . . ."*'

'Come on, Noah!' I hiss aloud.

'That's the idea, Noah,' belches the King of Halitosis. 'Piss it all away and come to me, my sweet child.'

I am on the edge of passing out.

N is for Not Again – not one more time, please God give me strength!

O is for Oramorph, for Nembutal, or pethidine or any damn thing to block this pain which, any second now, is going to redefine its own name.

I desperately try to regulate my breathing, to remember all that I have learned in sodding Yoga – Chi Gong – T'ai Chi – Acupuncture – Alexander – Feng Shui – La-La Self-Help Land. I focus all my energies on my fifth chakra, my cock, and I try to ease out the blood clot.

'*Let go – relax. Let go – relax. Let go –*'

Shove a catheter in me, for Christ's sake!

'*It's best if you go to any lengths to void your bladder naturally, alright?*'

Bladder? You call this a bladder!? It's 75 per cent cancer, 20 per cent bladder and 5 per cent hope.

'*Let go – relax – fuck – Oh, Jesus Christ – fuck – I can't do this!*'

A is for Actually You Bloody Well Can, Noah! If not for yourself, for Clare and the girls. Get this bastard clot out, and then the next one and the next. Piss them out all night if you have to, get down into that operating theatre and keep your end of the bargain.

'. . . *make sure your affairs are in order – will – that sort of thing –*'

H is for HELL NO! Never! Not over my dead body. Fuck it! I will live! This is not what my life is. I refuse to believe it. I'm a father and a film maker, for God's sake – and a good father and a good film maker at that. Right now as I stand in front of this fucking toilet, Clare will be walking the walk, crawling up the walls and praying as the two babes sleep, reminding the whole world that innocence is alive and well. You hear that, Death – you Son of a Dog? Remember what I said on that beach? I'm alive and well. I shall live for them, and you and your whole bloody army won't stop me. There's my work to do too. As I piss pain here, there's over thirty hours of footage in Soho waiting to be edited. Thirty-three hours to be exact, of a story of love and life and optimism, not this shit, or piss. This is not what I am. Ask my wife and children. This is not –

A scream tears out of me and my lower spine snaps in two as I throw my head backwards. The fluorescents blind me as I suck in half the air in the room. My fingernails dig into my penis in a Hammer Horror rerun of the Ambulance Incident as an egg-sized clot shoots out into the pan, followed by a jet-force of blood which splatters the walls to chest height. On the bloody water in the loo, small rings of tissue float like spaghetti hoops. Choking on vomit, I fall to my knees, grab hold of the toilet lid and start to bang it against the porcelain in a sobbing rhythm. Death starts to clap to my beat. In the mirror, out of the corner of my eye, I can see him clearly for the first time. No pantomime black hood and scythe for this guy. He's Warren Zevon's Werewolf of London – 'and his hair was perfect', wearing a Hugo Boss suit and hand-made Church's shoes. No hour-glass either. He's wearing a Cartier watch which he glances down at. He looks back up into my eye and blows me a kiss. In slo-mo I turn to face him and snarl –

'Get fucked'

as I collapse to the floor, pulling the emergency cord on the way down. Death kneels by my side and is starting to hum Brahms's 'Lullaby' when he sees the door handle move a fraction. Silently he slips behind the shower curtain just as the black nurse with the bandaged ankles comes in to find me mumbling in a pool of my blood. With difficulty, in pain of her own, she kneels beside me, puts my head in her lap and wipes my brow with the touch of a lover.

TWENTY

Even like the sun is your god-self.

Kahlil Gibran

On the road to Kenyatta Airport, Nairobi – the portrait of President Daniel Arap Moi, April 1985

Ishmael is singing as he drives us along the dual carriageway from Nairobi to the airport. No wonder! He must think it's his birthday because when it came time for us to leave Nyeri, neither Clare nor myself had the stomach to fly back, deciding instead to take a taxi to the capital. I was about to pop into Nyeri and ask Hopalong to point me in the right direction for the cheapest fare when Clare produces a bit of paper with a phone number on it. When I asked what it was, she told me it was Ishmael's – the Mombasa taxi driver – and that she thought it would be a nice gesture to have him drive to Nyeri and pick us up. I laughed and told her it was a mad waste of money. She didn't laugh and told me that it would cost about a third of our combined air fares and to think what a difference it would make to one man and his family. I tried once more to side-step the issue, but Clare was determined.

So here we are bouncing along in Ishmael's Cortina. The journey has been uneventful and we've made very good time. Clare's British Airways direct flight to London leaves in an hour and a half at one thirty, and at six this evening my Air

Sudan flight leaves for The Smoke via Khartoum and Cairo with a possible drop-off in Dubai. The thought of hanging around the airport for five hours without Clare before boarding the flying mosque with its quaint food-disposal system makes me want to puke. It also makes me want to scream at Ishmael to shut the fuck up with his happybunny tra-la-la!

This last week has been subdued. My fears about having to deal with the Beeb or run into the Tribeca Twins were cut short when I learned that that first day of our arrival had been the last day of the Happy Valley shoot. The dope-smoking has continued with me exercising major control and toking only enough to keep the edge off and the paranoia at bay. Clare, on the other hand, has been smoking up a storm and has notched down to a languorous pace, sending out constant sexual signals and acting on them at unexpected moments day and night. We've passed most of the time sitting on the veranda reading, strolling in the garden, dozing in the heat, fucking and falling in love.

We did take the Outspan excursion to Treetops to watch from our teak-panelled room as the animals gathered in the night around the salt-strewn edges of the floodlit water hole. We did see some elephants, a few wart-hogs and a couple of snakes come down for a sip and a dip. But their behaviour was nowhere near as interesting as that of the guests at the communal dinner table who, dressed in matching Safari gear from Abercrombie & Fitch or Burberry, oohed and aahed as the strange Lazy Susan which slid up and down the middle of the huge wooden table mysteriously delivered mysterious food to them.

The next morning Clare and I nipped down the rope ladder from the arboreal lodgings for a clandestine walk before the bus took us back to the Outspan Hotel. We were about a mile from Treetops on a dusty road when we spotted two men coming towards us. One was a Masai, a good six foot ten inches tall wearing a long orange sarong and carrying a spear, the other was a small, dark Kikuyu tribes- man wearing shorts and a pair of Converse high-top basket- ball boots. Clare and I were both wearing jeans and T-shirts – me with my two-day stubble looking like a wino and she with her sun-bleached cropped hair and slim hips looking for all the world as though she belonged to some pale, andro- gynous Rift Valley tribe. As we came alongside the two men walking towards us, the Masai stopped in his tracks, raised himself up on one leg, balanced on his spear, looked at Clare and said something in his native tongue. Then he moved on without giving me the slightest glance. Before his companion could follow, I asked him if he spoke English. He said he did so I asked what the Masai had said to Clare. The Kikuyu told me that the warrior had spoken these words:

'She has swallowed the sun.'

On the bus back to the hotel, Clare told me that the look the Masai had given her had been completely without a sexual edge – the first she'd ever experienced from a man. I tried to dismiss this, but in my heart I knew it was true. I had seen that look and I was threatened by it because I knew that I was incapable of such an uncluttered communication with a woman. Clare must have sensed what I was feeling because later, sitting on the veranda in our rattan cottage watching the sunset, she touched me on the back of the hand and said:

'Every look you give me has a sexual edge, Noah. But don't worry. I love it.'

In all, it's been a good week, but I've been a bit outside it – calm on the surface, but underneath the water I've been doing a pretty desperate doggy-paddle. I shouldn't have smoked the dope that first time, and definitely not the second, third, fourth and fifth. My jaw is tight, my eyes are edgy, and my brain is trying to seep out of my ears. Worst of all, my knuckles are showing bone-white through the flesh as I keep my fists clenched against picking up a drink. I am dying for a fucking drink! Years of practice have made my 'cool' act well-honed and polished, but I'm surprised that Clare hasn't seen through it these last few days. Then again, she's been stoned out of her gourd most of the time, and why should she read the signals that nine out of ten addicts can't decipher until it's too late and they're back in detox or dead in some back street. *'Remember we deal with alcohol, cunning, baffling and powerful.'* Sometimes that AA Big Book hits the nail right on the fucking head!

Ishmael parks the Cortina in front of the terminal, hops out, opens the door and we step into the stifling heat of the airport concrete. Even before we can break into a sweat, Ishmael has our bags on the pavement and that expectant look of somebody about to come into funds. Clare pays him the three hundred-shilling fare, then as an afterthought takes all her remaining Kenyan currency and hands it over to the gobsmacked driver who starts bobbing his head up and down and pouring out effusive thanks in Swahili. The skies suddenly open and we have to pick up our bags and dash for cover under the terminal overhang. Dripping, I look back to see Ishmael, sheltering his money under his arm, ducking back into his battered taxi, very much richer than he was a minute ago. I turn to Clare who's waving at Ishmael as he pulls away tooting his horn.

'You gave him the lot!'

'That's right – and if I'd had more I would have given him that too.'

'You must be mad.'

'I must be. I'm with you, aren't I?'

She smiles, picks up her bag, puts a soaking-wet arm through mine and leads us into the terminal building.

It's a long wait for check-in and we shuffle along the line

side by side in the kind of silence that you get only before leaving a loved one. By the time Clare has her seat allocated, it's time for her to go to the departure gate. I take her to the point of no return and we stand facing each other. A few yards away a huge photo-portrait of President Damiel Arap Moi hangs on the wall next to a picture window through which I can see the April monsoon rain bouncing eighteen inches off the tarmac. The planes are taking off regardless. Clare tucks a folded piece of paper into my jean jacket pocket.

'For later. I have to go now.'

Then she kisses me on the lips, goes over to passport control, shows her papers to a thin-faced black woman in a starched white shirt who nods and waves Clare on through to the other side where she turns and gives me a little wave.

At that very moment, a black man in a suit, passport in one hand and briefcase in the other, steps up to the control desk and hands over his documents. Just as the starched woman is opening his passport there's a barking shout behind me and automatic gunfire rends the air. The business-man screams, drops his briefcase and clutches his thigh. Stumbling, he tries to escape as four paramilitaries storm past me brandishing Kalashnikovs and screaming at people to get down.

I dive for the floor and slither towards passport control. There's more shooting and another scream. I turn to see the businessman spinning through the air in Peckinpah slo-mo, his blood splattering across the portrait of President Moi. He hits the ground with a sickening thud, convulses under another burst of gunfire, then goes still. The gunmen pounce on the body as people scream and run this way and that. About ten feet away from me a young woman lies sprawled on the marble, legs splayed, skirt hiked indecently above her waist, a trickle of blood running from her open mouth.

'CLARE!'

Screaming, I get to my feet and see Clare standing on the other side of passport control, her hand to her mouth in the reflex shock gesture. She sees me and tries to run back through passport control. Her way is blocked by one of the gunmen who waves his weapon and shouts for her to get on her plane. I dash forward.

'LEAVE HER THE FUCK ALONE!'

The gunman turns like a cobra and fires a warning round over my head. I throw my hands in the air in a gesture both defiant and helpless as Clare is bundled through some swing doors looking over her shoulder at me, terrified.

Out of Africa

It's six hours later and we're about to land in Khartoum. The flight is packed, but this time around I am not the only Westerner. Six rows in the middle of the plane are taken up with a group of Australian world trekkers whose Voice Volume Control is stuck on Full. They're obnoxious, but I thank God for them because they act as a massive decoy, drawing such attention to themselves that my sorry-arsed face won't elicit a single glance from anybody. And that's the way I want it, because right now I am in the mood to kill anyone who so much as looks at me. I'm still spinning from this afternoon's nightmare. I don't know how long I stood by the passport control desk staring at the double doors through which Clare had disappeared, but when I finally turned to leave, the bodies of the guy in the suit and the woman in the skirt were gone. They had been spirited away so quickly that if it hadn't been for the three women with buckets wiping the blood off President Moi's portrait, I might have thought that Hopalong's weed had built up in my system and finally whacked me with a massive hallucination. I even went over to the president after he'd been scrubbed down, looked very closely at the glass in his frame and found a thin line of dried blood running from the lobe of his left ear to the bridge of his nose. This last bit of evidence was the justification I needed to go to the bar and have a stiff double whisky.

I had planned for it to be the first of many drinks. I didn't give a flying fuck. But flying fucked me when the last call for boarding Air Sudan flight 602 came over the PA. I had to hoof it to the gate and only just made it in time with just that one double in me. And I was reeling, not in my body, but in my mind. It is said in AA that it's the first drink which gets you drunk. I'll drink to that! It's also said that if an alkie goes to a meeting, he might never go to another and he may never sober up, but his drinking is screwed for the rest of his life. I'll drink to that too. That double didn't give me a buzz. It didn't even taste good. All it did was prick my guilty conscience and give me this headache.

I lean my throbbing head back, close my eyes and swallow hard against the decompression as we make our descent and I try to not think of my own downfall. I tell myself over and over that nobody need know that I've taken a drink and over and over I hear that little voice telling me that I know and that's all that matters. And as this self-pitying crap throbs in my skull to the throb of the engines I am all too painfully aware that I cannot undo what is done, and I cannot unknow what I know.

Then I remember the note that Clare put in my pocket at the airport. Like a drunk struggling to get the top off that next bottle for that next fix, I fumble with the stud button on my Levi's jacket, pull out the small piece of paper and unfold it.

And so you will soon be home.
Indeed, you never really left me.
And if all the butterflies of ten thousand
Africas
Were to come together, the sound of
their wings
Could only echo the fluttering of my
heart
As I realise just how I love you.
C.

I stare at the words like a bleeding idiot. I can't compute them. My brain is on overload with images of dead monkeys, pink safari suits, dead people, pink-nipple islands in the stream, a Masai warrior and a blooded president, sex and drugs and piss-steam rising, Anubis and Baden-Powell, flamingos and thunderheads, love and fear and a deep present loneliness edged with fleeting, hopeful expectations for the future.

TWENTY-ONE

Home is where the heart is.

Sentimental adage

London, August 1985

It's the first weekend of the August after our African trip and it's my first public appearance as Clare's 'new man'. I've been back to New York, worked with Ray on the Final Cut of the Drug PSA, sub-let the 21st Street apartment, and told everyone I'm changing my base of operations to London. When people asked me 'why?', I simply patted my heart and said, 'Love.' In late July I moved back to page 45 of the *A to Z* and into the Kentish Town flat I'd had since getting out of film school. I could get rid of it for at least ninety grand and buy somewhere better, but I'm holding back in the hopes that it won't be long before Clare and I pitch in together. She has her garden flat in Fulham. If we sold both gaffs we could afford to buy something really grown-up with a garden and enough bedrooms for . . . kids?

The party is being held in Etta's place on the banks of the Thames on a bright and warm Sunday afternoon. The paved forecourt of her converted coach house – once owned by William Morris – is set up with food-laden tables – white cloths blowing in the breeze off the river. The centrepiece is an old-fashioned Italian ice-cream cart which has been converted to a bar. The sunken compartment for the gelati has been made into a huge ice bucket, glasses are stacked where the cone wafers should be, and on the four brass posts supporting the red-and-white striped awning are optics – one for each of the steeds of the Four Horsemen: Gin, Vodka, Rum and Whisky. From a PA system rigged on the eaves, Paul Simon's *Graceland* eases gently over a crowd of thirty or so sunny strangers, a hard core of whom I would come to know well over the next few years. There's a jovial queue at the bar and joints are being passed around as casually as the laughter which ripples through the air.

I'm inside the coach house on an overstuffed sofa draped with some heavy Arts and Crafts School velvet banquette talking to Etta who's sitting on the floor. Stacked casually against the wall behind her are a half-dozen or so William Morris wooden printing cylinders, carved deeply with floral wallpaper designs which I recognise from coffee-table books. They must be worth a bloody fortune. Etta is wearing an emerald-green silk scarf wound loosely around her head, a white cotton T-shirt and a Bali batik skirt which is stretched tightly across her splayed knees. She is not wearing any knickers. I try to look her in the face as she speaks, but my eyes keep dropping to her naked bush. This is not love at first sight – not even arousal. My dick doesn't give the slightest wee twitch even though Etta's vagina is perfection itself. Instead, my Little Voice tells me that this beautiful mulatto woman who seems so unaware of my gazing at her cunt knows exactly what she's doing and is throwing down a most unusual gauntlet. What the challenge is I don't know. What I do know is that although this is *not* a come-on, as sure as my name is Noah Arkwright and I'm an alcoholic, sex is sneaking around here somewhere.

'The perfect second violinist is relaxed – lazy even – and completely without ambition.'

Etta's voice is the colour of honey. I force my look to her eyes and she smiles enigmatically as I ask my question.

'Why is that?'

She laughs.

'Because solos scare the shit out of us! Oh, we have a lot to say in rehearsal and we try to get our own way. But if we don't get it, we aren't hurt enough to fight. I suppose you could say we're easy-going. Are you easy-going, Noah?'

Something flickers across her face. Where have I seen that look before? She pulls her knees together, putting away her muff, then draws them up to her chin and wraps her forearms around her shins. It's my turn to laugh.

'No I'm not. I am definitely not.'

Easy-going! At this moment my whole body is one big fucking nerve and I'm dying to visit the ice-cream cart or take a hit off a circulating joint. I don't know why I'm so wired. By rights I should feel relaxed and at home. I am at home – back in England. I'm being made welcome by Clare's musician friends, and apart from this strange interlude with Etta, this party is going well – as well as parties ever go for me these days and a million times better than I had feared. I'd been very apprehensive about this gathering, because I arrived in London to hear that my film *Downtown Surf Story* – which is something of a Cult Classic – was showing on the London art-house circuit for the umpteenth time. This could have made any gathering with me in it go pear-shaped in one of two all-too-familiar ways. There's the Bad-Case Scenario which would have been a capital-W Welcome party with me as its Guest of Honour where I'd be bombarded by inane movie questions – does Richard Gere really put gerbils up his bum? – or fawning looks accompanied by NFT ticket stubs thrust into my hand for me to sign. And there's the Worst-Case Scenario with simply a load of tiring, intelligent, in-depth discussions with the *Auteur* in arty corners with a bunch of self-important film-buff cunts. As it is, there's not a gerbil question in sight and the only cunt here is beautiful and has just disappeared under Etta's skirts.

This crowd is too good for any of that sycophantic crap. And even if there were the slightest possibility of any shit rising, it was knocked on the head as soon as Clare and I walked through the coach house gate slap into George, a giant of a man wearing a gold earring, a white sleeveless vest and a number 2 buzz cut. He was manning the ice-cream cart and the moment he saw me he poured a pint of Diet Coke over ice and handed it to me with a wink. He spoke with a Geordie accent and loud enough for anyone standing on Hammersmith Bridge to hear.

'Noah, you bastard! Welcome! Saw *Downtown Surf Story* a couple of weeks ago – fucking great, man! Bloody fucking fantastic!'

His words met with a chorus of approval and a spontaneous round of applause which was painful but, like a good tooth extraction, over in a split-second. And those words of George's were the first and last I've heard all afternoon on the subject of my films. I've been drinking Cokes non-stop and smoking a ton of cigarettes but that's nothing unusual when I'm on public view. So why I am so edgy right now, I don't know.

'*Don't talk so stupid, Limey!*'

Tiny's voice pops into my head.

'*Everybody always knows . . . they just don't got the nuts to admit it . . . any guy who says he don't is a motherfucking liar.*'

'I hear you,' I say to myself. The Bowery Oracle is right as usual. Jesus! I miss him. I miss Ray and Kirstin. I already miss everybody in New York. I miss me, and if I get naked in my mind right now, hop into bed and turn out that light switch, I know very well why I'm one big fucking nerve. I have fallen so deeply in love that I have cut all my safety nets and undertaken a massive 'geographical' back to territory which is both completely familiar and so remote that I might as well be on Pluto. That is as true for the English Terra very Firma of this coach house patio as it is for the beating of my heart which has taken on an almost indiscernible but very different rhythm. I'm about to embark on a circumnavigation of my world which has for thirty-eight years remained for the most part unexplored. Oh! For years I thought I was fucking Vasco da Gama – with drink, drugs, women and a bit of fame. I thought I was driving my 4 by 4 Soulmobile down the dangerous roads of unknown lands – moving along, discovering myself and the world I live in. Wrong! With my early attempts at sobriety came the sneaking suspicion that I hadn't really been exploring anywhere, and certainly not in any four-wheel-drive jeepster. Meeting Clare not only confirmed this suspicion but made me realise that I hadn't been driving anywhere at all. Just like that time on I-95 with Blue Sky/Ray in his VW bus when we ran out of gas and were so fucked up we didn't know we'd rolled to a standstill, I had in fact been parked very dangerously most of my life. So now I am faced with Hobson's Choice which for an alcoholic who has dedicated his life to creating choices which were never really there is the stuff of nightmares. But I must make that no-choice choice. I must move on now or die – and I must do it sober. Fuck! It would be much easier if these people were big enough arseholes to justify my taking the Big Step Backwards – hitting hard on the ice-cream cart before sodding off back to New York with a tear in my eye and a chip on my wounded shoulder as big as the Citicorp building!

I feel a kiss on top of my head and look up to see Clare leaning over me, her breasts peeking out of her flowered summer dress like two naughty schoolgirls.

'Can I drag Etta away from you for a few minutes, darling?'

Before I can answer she's pulling her friend to her feet with an easy movement she's executed many times before.

'Go ahead. I'll mill around a bit.'

'*Fat chance! I'll sit here like a bump on a log and feel sorry for myself because everything is going better than I could have ever hoped for.*'

'Everyone here thinks you're wonderful. No mean achievement, musicians are a choosy lot.'

Once more she kisses me – this time moistly and on the lips.

'I'm so proud of you, Noah.'

With that the Cello and the Second Violin go out on to the patio and sit on two little white wrought-iron chairs at a little black wrought-iron table. Almost immediately they are deep in conversation, Clare with her chin cupped in her hand, Etta smoking a cigarette with an easy rhythm, just as they were when I peeked through the window at Fanelli's in New York. Something in my gut twists and the hairs on the back of my neck bristle in that 'Me Tarzan – You Jane' kind of way. A feeling struggles to take shape, but it keeps shifting. It would be easy to say it was the old Fanelli jealousy, but this is far more complex than that. Whatever it is it carries with it the weight of my whole fucking future. Etta says something and Clare throws back her head in an arching laugh then reaches out a hand and touches Etta's cheek. Then Clare digs into her shoulder bag and takes out a small box and gives it to our hostess who opens it like an eager child on Christmas morning. She takes out the gift and even though I cannot see it clearly from this distance, I know exactly what it is. It's that sodding vagina shell from Twiga! Clare must have nipped back and bought it after the monkey had dropped dead at our feet and I'd headbutted

Barry from Oz. Etta holds up the cowrie and turns it in her hand. The sunlight glints off the shell and blinds me for a second and I look away. When I look back a young Mediterranean-looking woman in her late teens is coming through the gate with a beautiful cream-skinned baby riding high in a back pack. This must be the au pair and Maya, Etta's six-month-old baby daughter. It was only on the way to the party that Clare told me about Maya. I asked her why she hadn't told me before and she shrugged. And when I asked who the father was, she tapped the side of her nose with her finger and said:

'She's a mermaid, remember?'

Etta puts the shell back in the gift box, eases up from her chair, glides over and takes her baby from the pack to ride low on her left hip. With her free arm, she gives the young woman a hug, leads her back to Clare and indicates for her to sit in the wrought-iron chair while she stands rocking her daughter back and forth to an age-old beat. The Mediterranean girl picks up the shell and looks at it. Something is said. The three women laugh. It's a preordained ritual – a dance between women. I am mystified and drawn in, and at the same time feel as though I have no right to be watching and want to look away. I don't. Etta suddenly thrusts her baby girl high above her head, drops her and skilfully catches her at breast level. The baby screams with delight. The women laugh again. At this moment, David the First Violin arrives wearing his chestnut plait and an olive-green linen suit. Etta immediately plops Maya like a sack of spuds into Clare's lap and trots over to greet the head honcho of the Kairos Quartet. The tightness in my gut loosens and the hairs on the back of my neck lie back down, just as another pint of Coke is thrust in front of my face and George sits on the sofa beside me. He looks out to where David is giving and getting kisses all round.

'Look at him! Fucking little prick – thinks he's bloody God's gift!'

'To women?' I take a long sip of Coke.

'He thinks they adore him. Stupid twat can't see it's his music they love.'

Still seated, Clare gives David a little wave. He crosses over to her. She turns her cheek upwards. He leans down and pecks it.

'And Etta?'

'She cuts him more slack than most – says it's the price to pay for his genius and all that shite. But they're always at each other's throat. It's that First Violin/Second Violin thing.'

I dig out my best Texas drawl: 'Hey pardner! this town ain't big enough for both of us!'

George laughs, puts his arm around my shoulder and squeezes, breaking both clavicles.

'Clare's done nothing but tell us you're a canny lad since she got back from Africa. She's right.'

Then without warning he pulls my face to his and kisses me on the mouth. It's a sexless kiss, loaded with beer, cigarettes and dope – a gift from one mate to another. Then he ruffles my hair and falls quiet. I'm embarrassed, not by the kiss but by the silence which seems to go on for hours until I break it.

'Are you a musician?'

George nods and tokes heavily on a joint which has appeared in his hand.

'Which instrument?'

'Guitar.'

'Classical?'

He offers me the spliff and after a split-split second of hesitation I put my hand up like a traffic cop.

'That's right . . . you don't . . . Clare said. No, I play R&B – session man. You like Rhythm and Blues, Noah?'

'Love it.'

'Alright! Fuck yes!'

Then as magically as the joint appeared a guitar manifests itself from somewhere behind the sofa. It's a battered Gibson with a hole worn through where the scratchboard should be. George strums a chord and begins to tune up. It's a call to arms and within a minute there's two other guitars, two fiddles, an accordion, a double bass, two harmonicas, a washboard and a crowd drifting in from outside. Another minute and everyone is in tune and with a nod and a 1–2–3 from George they break into a hard-driving version of 'Kansas City' with George and his gravel voice at the helm. Clare sits at my feet tapping hers, watching every musical move. David is rocking on his violin and Etta is matching him with hers. Everyone seems to know exactly what they're doing, all taking their lead from their Geordie friend, and all playing bloody marvellously. Big George finishes the first verse, points at Etta who in turn points with her bow to Clare. Clare knows the routine. She gets up and Etta hands over her instrument to her friend in a seamless transition, then she steps forward just in time to meet the next verse and belts it out like a honey-coloured Janis Joplin. She is bloody amazing. And she is sexy. I can see now why Clare thought the vagina shell to be the perfect present for this woman.

> Going to Kansas City
> Kansas City here I come.
> They've got some pretty little women there
> And I'm gonna get me one . . .

Everyone joins in the chorus, loud and happy and as one, and I am part of it – the Old Mod and his rebel yell back home again. But then, during the last verse when everyone is taking it to the limit –

I might take a train
I might take a plane

an image cuts through my mind of a woman diving naked into a lake at dawn. She does not surface. Where this comes from I don't know – somewhere way back when or somewhere in the future. Before I can process the thought any further, Etta sings the last note, George hits the last chord, then all the musicians take a deep self-mocking bow as everybody cheers and applauds the players and themselves. I'm shouting and clapping along with them, but somewhere in the back of my mind a woman is sinking lifeless into the cold dark waters.

PART FOUR

The Unstoppable Force meets the Immovable Object.

TWENTY-TWO

I thought myself a strong man.
But the sleeves of my garment
Are wetted with tears.

Prince Otsu

London, January 1997

It's been a bugger of a morning. In New York City I shudder
at the thought of riding the Broadway Local – The Beast. But
The Beast is a pussycat compared to the Northern Line. I
have *never* travelled on the Northern Line without something shitty happening.

Take this morning. Last night I stayed at the old flat on
Inkerman Road in Kentish Town. Without the kids and
Clare, I've slept like a single man. I've had toast, coffee and a
good crap. I've even remembered to take my extra piss, and
with this precautionary piddle, I should make it to D'Arblay
Street like a regular bloke with a regular bladder.

So when I leave the flat at eight twenty I feel high and
mighty and not even the iron-grey sky sitting on my head or
the tat and litter of Kentish Town Road can take the edge off.
Even when I find that the down escalator at the tube station is
out of action, after a quick curse I nip down the steps two at a
time. On the crowded platform I whistle the music that Clare
has composed for the title sequence of *Blood and Milk*, my

latest movie, which at nine thirty I'm going to screen in Rough Cut to a bunch of film cronies for feedback before I give it a final Trim and Style to meet its public. At eight twenty-eight a Southbound via Charing Cross pulls in and I get on.

The carriage is already packed and stacked, but I handle it smoothly. I hang on a strap, close my eyes, do a bit of Chi Gong breathing and start projecting *Blood and Milk*, frame by frame, on to the back of my eyelids.

When the tube stops at Camden Town and the In Crowd gluts on, a giant of indeterminate origin bulldozes me up against the spit- and snot-smeared divider between the door and the Give-It-Up-for-a-Cripple seat. I never place myself next to that glass partition – I avoid it like the plague it carries. Still, I take a deep breath, strengthen that old Chi and try like buggery to hold on to my good mood and health. I'm doing just fine until we hit the black hole of Mornington Crescent and the train lurches to a halt. This jolt hurls me against K2 and jams my face into the toxic armpit of this six-four straphanger who's wearing no shirt and a sleeveless leather jerkin which niffs of formaldehyde. I take a deep breath and hold it. Because my wrist watch is jammed right in front of my left eyeball, I know that it is exactly one minute and twenty seconds later that I let out a gasp and come up for air. K2 shifts slightly, just enough for me to be able to catch his good eye – the other is covered with a black patch. I stare my Paddington Bear hard stare at him, hoping to hex him into removing his armpit hair from my mouth. After a blink of a standoff, he lifts his eye patch, winks at me with his watery blind eye, then clamps his huge bicep to his side and squeezes my head so hard I feel the plates of my skull grind against each other. Under this pressure, all my bodily fluids shoot down into my bladder which has till now been empty – almost serene.

In a millisecond I'm bursting for a piss. I no longer have a brain. I am no longer a film maker, husband or father, but just a gagging, hurting body trying not to wet itself. Blindly, by rote, I put the Emergency Rescue Routine into operation. Extricating my right hand which is flattened between my back and the snot screen, I reach into my shoulder bag and take out my trusty empty Volvic bottle. I'm now so blinded by pain that I don't even care if anyone notices as I blindly unscrew the cap, slip the bottle down inside my jeans and void my sorry piss. Just then the train starts again, and as it lurches forward my head shoots out from the grip of the Giant Arsehole. Desperately I clutch the bottle tight to my leg as embarrassment and gut-wrenching loneliness rush in to fill the gap left by the receding pain.

So much for a good start to my day!

It's now eleven thirty and the screening of *Blood and Milk* has gone well, or so my film cronies tell me. I thought it looked like shit – the projection system was fucked and so under-power that the film looked as though it was shot Day for Night and Clare's soaring score sounded as if it was underwater. I feel miserable, but everyone else seems to be in good spirits as they faff around with fags and coffee afterwards dropping words like gritty, challenging, stark and cutting. They sound cliché-ridden and fake. Hell, Noah! That's just not true, you ungrateful prick! Everybody here, including my agent, is genuinely complimentary and forthcoming with helpful comments and observations, but if an Oscar nomination were dropped in my hand right now, I'd probably read it as a Final Demand notice from the gas company. I can't think straight. In fact, I am more than a little bit insane at this moment and have been since I emerged from Tottenham Court Road tube station into the stinking crowd of Oxford Street. Hidden in the seething mass of cheap shoppers, I palmed my Volvic bottle out of my pants into my bag and caught enough of a glimpse of the contents to suspect that all was not well in Bladderland. Then as soon as I arrived at the D'Arblay Street screening rooms, I nipped into the toilet, took out the bottle and confirmed my suspicions – light claret – cloudy with no body – some sediment – not a good year at all! So the truth is that all I've really been thinking about during the screening is getting to my doctor immediately afterwards and then on to an AA meeting, because if I don't I might just blow the last clean and sober ten years with a fucking great quadruple Jameson's and a joint as big as that Northern Line bastard's armpit.

The film gang are all around me, but I'm in the Danger Zone, pouring that fuck-off Irish in my head when I feel a touch on my shoulder. With a start, I turn to see Etta with Jara snug, slung African-style across her back. She looks beautiful as usual – yellow and black scarf wrapped around her head, black *faux*-astrakhan coat, yellow and black cloth sling for the babe. Wait a minute! That piece of cloth looks familiar. Around its border I can make out the words Watatu . . . Ma . . . and some other word which disappears behind her sleeping baby's head. Hey! That's my kanga! I mean that's the kanga I bought in Twiga for Clare who whooped with delight when I gave it to her and said she would treasure it for ever and ever, Amen. The little green djinn starts waking up in my brain.

'*What the fuck are you doing wearing our kanga, Etta?*'

The question speeds through my rapid-response neuro-network towards my opening lips. Bloody amazing! After all these years I still don't trust her completely – not since that first time I saw her onstage at Alice Tully Hall, not since she pushed past me on her way out of Fanelli's Bar, and certainly not since I was first introduced to her at the 'do' at her gaff in Hammersmith

'*What the fuck are you doing wearing our kanga, Etta?*'

The question races round again. Shit! I've got to override it quickly before it reaches my lips otherwise I'm going to lose a lot of hard-earned ground and look a complete jerk into the bargain. So I grab the djinn on his next circuit, shove him back in his bottle, stop it up with a bit of my blood and gristle, bend down to Etta's beautiful caramel cheek and give it a gentle peck.

'Etta! What a nice surprise!'

I had pitched for low tones, but my greeting blasts out loud and Jara's eyes snap open. She takes one look at me over her mother's shoulder and starts screaming at the top of her lungs. Coffees and fags and chat are held in the balance for a split-second as all eyes turn to look at us. Jara seems to have blown a safety valve and is screaming so loudly that the air in the room hurts.

'Christ, Noah! You nearly burst her eardrums!'

Etta whips Jara out of my kanga sling and on to her tit. All eyes are still on us as the baby's loud sucking sounds like an amplified tape loop of the first spoonful out of the World's Largest Blancmange. It's Peter Blessed – one of the leads in *Blood and Milk* – who starts to laugh, followed immediately by Big George and the rest of the crowd. It's meant to be fun – I suppose. Etta's smiling – I think – and so am I on the outside. Inside my gut is half-way up my throat and I Focus Down to that tunnel vision which immediately precedes a major Dry Drunk explosion. All I can see now is the proposal that Peter has trapped between his bicep and his flank in order to free his hands to clap. I am that document, back on the Northern Line trapped in the armpit of the stinking gorilla. My eyes bulge and ROLL FOCUS! TIGHT-IN on the underarm pages so that I can read the title page from clear across the room. *Mecca Dancing – A Film Treatment by Peter Blessed and Noah Arkwright*. What the Hell does Peter think he's up to for fuck's sake!? This morning is about my *Blood and Milk* in which he has a very juicy role. So why is he creeping around with this project in his greedy little fingers? We're slated to meet for lunch tomorrow! Can't he wait until then? No! That would be too much for a bloke who always has to have a main shag lined up before dumping the last. I know his plan. He wants to ride my coat-tails all the way to the top. Well, we'll – Peter waves over at me and smiles warmly. And why not? I'm one of his favourite people and he's one of mine. I like this man a lot. He holds *Mecca Dancing* up in the air and gives me the thumbs up. Wait a minute! I take another look. The title on the script is *Blood and Milk*. Oh, shit! This is bad. Then Big George raises his hands in my direction and starts to clap.

Everyone joins in. This is very bad. Somebody whistles. Somebody else shouts Bravo! This is very, very bad. A room full of my peers, led by one of my closest friends, is giving me this amazing vote of confidence for a fucking Rough Cut and a second ago I was on the edge of machine-gunning the lot of them.

'*So fuck off, Noah!*'

'*I hear you! I'm out of here!*'

I take a deep breath and adjust my smile to as near genuine as I can and raise my hand in that sickly Bill Clinton-Getting-Off-Airforce One kind of way, mutter Thank You and feel like a totally worthless piece of shit! Then I take Etta's hand and lead her with Jara still locked on her tit towards the door. It's the kind of dramatic arse-covering withdrawal I have perfected for times of mind-boggling embarrassment and shame. This one almost works except that this exit has to be broken off by a side trip to the bog and one more painful leak to remind me of what a piss-artist I really am.

Jara is spark-out on Etta's back as we head northwards up Poland Street. Etta is telling me that she has come from an appointment with a paediatric osteopath in Cavendish Square. She had hoped it would sort out Jara's awful crying which had been so bad recently that Etta had been unable to make rehearsals so Kairos had taken on a temporary second violin and had also been working up some string trios. I know all this, for God's sake! She tells me that, as we walk and talk, Clare is rehearsing at Wigmore Hall for a Bartók recital next Wednesday. This I also know! She'll be through by two and Etta had popped into D'Arblay Street in the hopes that I might kill time with her until she could meet up with Clare for coffee. This I didn't know! But then what do I ever know about those two? She's sorry about the timing of her entrance at the screening rooms and Jara's outburst. It wasn't my fault and it could have happened any time because Jara is just a jar of nitroglycerine these days. In fact, she's so bad that the cranial osteo has never seen a case quite like it. It has all the signs of colic but if it is, then it's the worst case she's ever seen in her whole career. Had Maya been the same? she'd asked Etta. Oh, no! Maya never cried. 'You remember, don't you, Noah?'

'*Of course I bloody remember!*'

Of course I remember, Etta. Of course you do. And she continues almost as if she's alone. ' "Maya was the opposite extreme, doctor," I said, but I don't think for one minute she's a real doctor doctor. After the most nasty knock or a fall Maya would hold back from crying with a ferocity more frightening than tears.' When we reach Oxford Street, Etta is still going on and on. And on she goes until we turn into Cavendish Square and she blinks to a standstill and silence to find herself once again in front of the paediatric cranial osteopathy clinic.

'Look, Etta. I'm glad you dropped by, and I'm really sorry that I woke Jara. But she's sleeping now, so maybe you should go back in and let them take a look at her in sleeping-angel mode. I'd come in with you but I have an appointment with my consultant in fifteen minutes.'

I half-lie. I don't have an appointment, but as I'm producing rosé – Volvic Vintage – I am going to see my consultant.

'It's alright, Noah. The doctor, the osteo, told me Jara'd sleep like a log after she'd manipulated her plates. In fact, I'm surprised you woke her. I'll cruise John Lewis and then walk about a bit more. Jara definitely won't wake if I'm on the move.'

We look into each other's eyes, both of us, as usual, bewildered by the journey we've been on since that first meeting in Hammersmith. There's definitely something strong between us – not love but some mixture of respect and once-removed cherishing.

'Are you OK, Etta?'

'I'm OK. And you? What's this with the consultant?'

'Routine.'

'Good.'

'Hope so.'

I smile, but Etta doesn't smile back. She doesn't look scared, but something damned close to it. I shoot from the hip.

'Etta . . . why did you really come to the screening rooms?'

'I came to ask you to be kind to Clare.'

'*What the fuck . . .?*'

'What do you mean? Cut to the fucking chase, Etta.'

She does.

'Clare's going to tell you tonight that she and I are going down to Lulworth next weekend, and she probably won't pitch it right and you'll knee-jerk and get angry. I don't want that to happen, Noah. I want you to say it's fine and I want you to mean it. I want you to say it will be OK because it will be. OK?'

My head is whizzing around trying to find an out, a non-committal reply to this surprise piece of straight talk. Why should I be surprised? This is Etta talking. Haven't I learned by now that when it comes to the subject of Clare I should not be taken in by Etta's preambling verbiage? – even when it's heightened by genuine worry about one of her other suffering babies.

'We both know these are hard times for you, Noah. But

this cancer is taking its toll on Clare as well. I think she might crack if she doesn't get a break after this next recital and I don't want her going away on her own –'

'I could go with her . . . when the final edit's done.'

'No. That won't work. She needs to go sooner than that. And she needs to be with me. You know that, don't you?'

I'm rooted on the pavement, but I manage a slow nod. *To Hell with you, Etta! And you too, Clare! To Hell with you women and the Sea Horses you rode in on!*

'Oh, come on, Noah. Let it go, for God's sake. It's a long time ago now.'

'*Nice one, Etta, you smug bitch!*'

'Yes, Etta. It's a long time ago.'

'So it's alright with you?'

'*Why even ask me, for fuck's sake – you'll go anyway.*'

'Yep. It's alright.'

Etta touches my cheek with the back of her hand.

'You're a good man, Noah. I knew that the first time I ever saw you.'

Then she kisses me on that same cheek and walks off toward John Lewis. Jara, snugly asleep on her back, is blissfully unaware that at this moment her godfather is for the second time in his life wishing he had a gun so he could shoot her mother in the back of the head.

Almost as soon as the obscene thought enters my head I perish it, shake off its shitty residue and call after Etta.

'I could look after the kids if you want.'

Without breaking her stride, she half turns on her heel and shouts back, 'Thanks! We'll talk!'

When she reaches the pelican crossing on Henrietta Place, Etta pushes the button, and as if on her command, the little green man lights up immediately. She sails across and disappears into John Lewis, the store which is never knowingly undersold.

TWENTY-THREE

You don't look different, but you have changed.
I'm looking through you. You're not the same.
                    The Beatles, 'I'm Looking Through You'

London, January 1997

In his Harley Street surgery, Norman Baker holds my
Volvic bottle up to the light and examines its contents with
his surgeon's eye. He then crosses to the sink, pours away
my piss, pumps Hibiscrub over his hands, opens the tap
with his elbow and washes away any possibility of contamination. On the way back to his desk, he buttons his
bespoke suit and adjusts his silk tie. By the time he's back in
his leather chair, he looks like an investment banker with
bad news.

'Well, Noah. I think we'll have you in as soon as we can
have a quick shufti.'

'It doesn't look good, does it?'

'Could be just a small regrowth.'

'And if it's not?'

He interlocks his delicate fingers as if to say a prayer and
takes a breath which is ever so slightly deeper than normal.
On the wall behind him, mounted on a rosewood plaque, is
the head of a dog fox. He has a snarl on his face and a glint in
his glass eye. And from where I'm sitting, he seems to be

grafted on to the top of Stormin' Norman's head. I have to stifle a laugh.

'*If* it's not we'll deal with it.'

'More chemo?'

'Not an option I'm afraid – not after last time. How many sessions was it we had?'

'*I* had ten.'

'Right, ten. And there was multiple regrowth within the year. No, if chemotherapy is going to be effective on the bladder, it will be first time around, especially with the quantity you took on board.'

'A litre.'

'Excuse me?'

'The quantity I took on board – one hundred cc's of mitomycin per session – ten sessions. That makes one litre by my reckoning. But then again, I could be wrong. What do I know? I'm just the poor fuck who took it up the dick!'

Norman is taken aback and looks a bit scared.

'Yes, well – I don't suppose you'd want to go through that again.'

He laughs a nervous little laugh.

'But you took it on the chin like a champion. Were even able to laugh at it – kept your . . . what did you call it?'

'Sense of Tumour,' I say flatly.

'Sense of Tumour! Ha! Ha! Bloody good that! Had us in stitches for a week.'

And he goes on with some blah blah, squirming, trying to make light but it's too late. I'm not really hearing him any more. I'm back in that white and eau de nil room four years ago lying on a hospital bed bollock-naked from the waist down. Through the tall Florence Nightingale windows of this ancient Victorian ward, I watch the snow falling on the jungle of rooftops of Archway as Dr Patna the Urology Registrar slips a twenty-millimetre plastic tube into my urethra. As I suck in air through my teeth, through his he whistles the 'Triumphal March' from *Aida*. This is routine for him. For me it's not. This is only my third chemotherapy session. So far it's been easy-peasy. I haven't felt a much of anything yet. No burning, no nausea, no loss of hair or appetite. In fact, I'm curiously detached from the whole process and watch the whole thing like a film of which I'm not the director. The Irish sister at Patna's side hands him the transparent bag containing a meths-coloured liquid and, as casually as pouring a double gin, the registrar empties the mitomycin into the catheter. Clinically, I watch as it drains down the tube and disappears inside me and heads up to my bladder. I don't feel it reach its destination.

'How will I know when the chemo is doing its stuff?'

Patna finishes squeezing the last few cc's out of the bag before looking at me. He's a dead-ringer for Gandhi, not the real thing but Ben Kingsley. He takes off his specs, polishes them on the hem of his white coat and looks at the nurse. There's a scream from a faraway ward. Even over a distance, it chills the blood and all three of us glance in the direction it came from. Sister Irish takes my hand and gives it a reassuring squeeze. Patna drops the empty mitomycin bag in the Clinical Waste Only disposal and gives me that medical smile which tells you that what you are about to hear is not good for the health.

'We'll know the chemicals have bitten deep enough into the bladder muscle when you find the pain intolerable.'

He laughs. He's nervous. I'm terrified.

And the bastard was right. Today it's session ten. For the last month I've barely been able to function. After the fifth week, the chemical cystitis kicked in and since then I've been pissing burns. I've been wobbly, full of headaches and empty of energy. I can't work. And the only exercise I get is the reps I do lifting the bog seat every fifteen to twenty minutes. Uninterrupted sleep is a distant memory. Last week's session was so painful I bucked off the bed and nearly snapped my spine, so today I'm not looking forward to what I know is about to happen. A month ago, another poor bastard in line for chemo told me that mitomycin could burn a hole through an oak board in a couple of hours. I laughed at his exaggeration. Over the last few weeks I have come to believe him. I have stopped laughing. And I sure as buggery am not curiously detached! My tension is making things worse from the outset. My jaw is tight. My sphincter is tight. And my urethra is so tight that Patna, already pissed-off because Sister Irish is nowhere to be seen, is having difficulty getting the catheter in. He's very grumpy and he's muttering in Urdu under his breath. I take a stab at breaking the downward spiral.

'Now, now, Doc! Sense of tumour!'

Patna shoots me a cess pit of a look, shoves the tube hard enough for it to come out of my nose, and as I bite the bullet he picks up the sachet of chemo which looks as big as a fucking Sainsbury's placcy bag. As he's attaching it to the end of the catheter, Sister Irish bustles through the door saying sorry. She hurries over and grips my hand extra firmly just as the first cc's hit their target and I hit the ceiling, leaving my fingernails in the sheets.

'JESUS FUCK!'

Nurse leans over and takes my other hand muttering something about staying calm or it will be alright – alright on the night – shite – shag that shit! The chemo is now napalm in my bladder. I'm being disembowelled. This isn't sodding medical practice. This is what the Ton Ton Macoutes do to you in a Port-au-Prince dungeon! The exchanges move into pure cliché.

ME: 'Stop! For Christ's sake stop!'
THEM: 'Just a few cc's more, Noah!'

ME: 'Aaargh!'
THEM: 'Almost over. You can do it!'
ME: 'I CAN'T!'

I scream these two words and force my eyes open. I can't see a fucking thing. The room has disappeared. Nobody is there. I can't even feel the bed. My body has given up and walked away leaving just this ball of scalding, brain-searing pain where my bladder was. Vomit rises where my throat used to be, and tears stream out of my blinded eyes. I am falling backwards, backwards into the jaws of Hell.

Twelve hours later I'm in isolation somewhere off Emergency Ward 10 shuffling across the room wheeling a saline drip on a stand and clutching a drainage bag which is strapped to my right leg and connected to yet another catheter. The bag is filled with blood and my head is filled with pethidine. I feel like walking death.

As I inch towards a door in the corner, Sister Irish bursts in.

'What in the name of God are you doing?'

'Going for a pee.'

She half laughs.

'But sure now, you've a bag. Get back into bed, Noah, there's a good –'

I turn to her and hiss.

'I . . . am . . . going . . . to . . . piss . . . in . . . there.'

I point at the loo door. She tries again with another, more nervous laugh.

'And what if you don't?'

'I will die.'

And I inch off with as much dignity as I can muster, go to the loo, address the toilet bowl, void what I can into my trusty baggie, and shuffle out again. Sister Irish watches on: this time she says nothing. The windows which run the full length of my room are too high for me to see out of when I am lying down. Now, as I head slowly back to my bed, I look out of them for the first time and I see the angel.

Across the courtyard, looking at me through a window of the children's ward is one of God's youngest seraphs. Her head is bald from chemotherapy and she's wearing blue pyjamas printed with red sailboats. Even though I must be a good forty feet away, I can see her eyes clearly. They are the deepest, darkest blue – the blue of deep space. The angel waves at me. I wave back. A door closes behind me and without looking I know Sister Irish has left the room. I stare at the angel who suddenly puts a finger in each corner of her mouth, pulls a funny face and laughs. Then she drops out of sight below her window ledge, leaving me standing alone with the certain knowledge of two things.

(a) My journey with this cancer is not over yet and it will get more difficult before it gets easier.

(b) I will be fine in the end. What 'fine' means I don't know, but there are a few miracles in store.

Miracles did happen. I survived the chemo – that's a miracle. I managed to write a short TV film, a dark comedy which I entitled *Bite the Bullet*. Short and Curlies had commissioned it, but on reading my script said that it was just too painful to be credible and that they couldn't see the funny side of it. I found that funny. Clare, by taking on some young cellists for private lessons while cutting down on her recitals, has managed to keep some semblance of a career going while allowing her energies to drain into me – that's a miracle. Coral, now almost four, is blissfully unaware of any of these problems – that's a miracle, and a blessing.

But the Big Miracle happened eight months after I got out of hospital.

It's October 1993 and I'm in the garden of our des-res, PC, five-bedroomed, original-fireplaced, dado-railed, stripped-pine, moulded-corniced, claw-foot-bathtubbed, Jocasta Innessed, Conranned, Poggenpohled, Right-On Crouch End house. We'd bought the place just after Coral was born with the proceeds from the release of *Kobo*, which finally got made, albeit on a wing and a prayer, and the release of an album by Kairos which clocked up phenomenal sales in Japan and Australia – we jokingly call it our Occidental House.

The morning is crisp, cold and sunny and I'm at the bottom of our pocket-handkerchief garden pruning Madame Alfred Carrière, a ten-foot climbing rose. I'm a long way from Manhattan – eight years, three thousand miles and enough water under the bridge to fill a dozen Atlantic Oceans. My life now is both a completely different story and exactly the same one. I still make films. I am still with Clare. Ray is still my lighting cameraman. Tiny comes over to England once a year. And even Kirstin phones from time to time. I am still sober, or at least I am still not drinking. But the day this sodding cancer hit, my centre shifted. For a while it was completely outside me. If my life without cancer had been a glove, with cancer it was still recognisable as a glove, but gradually it turned itself inside out until the soft lining was on the outside – the resistant leather on the inside. Over the last couple of years, a day at a time and with agnostic prayer, I've managed to get the leather back on outside, but the inside isn't comfortable any more – it's ripped and torn and it doesn't keep me warm. It's gone on long enough. I know that it is now time to start thinking of changing my life from a pair of gloves to a pair of shoes and get walking down the path. It might not be the path I'd mapped out for myself, but it's the one I've got, and cancer or no cancer I'm going to have to drag my poor arse along it or drop dead here and now.

Snip! A dead head of the rose falls into the hostas below.

With each faded flower I remove, with each cluster of hips, black and hard as pebbles, Madame gains strength against the hard winter to come, storing the energy released back into her by my pruning. Ah! Madame Alfred Carrière! You old and beautiful survivor! I'll cut you hard back today, mulch you down well and tie a wind chime to your topmost branch. It will hang there and tinkle like an icicle until spring. Snip! Another dead head falls. The secateurs flash in the cool sunlight as a silver plane passes overhead laying a vapour trail. For a moment my forearm is frozen. It is gardener brown and healthy, strong and youthful – sexy even. Hard to believe that only eighteen inches away from it another part of my body is plotting to kill me. I stare at the plane as it heads for Heathrow and I laugh out loud to think that this Noah Arkwright – his life and death, his hopes and fears – is so bloody huge to me and yet someone twenty-five thousand feet overhead on Flight 101 from New York can't even see him.

Well who gives a shit!

I select a branch of Madame as thick as my thumb. It's at least ten years old, the supporter of healthy blossoms and it should be kept at all costs.

I'll show them!

I take a deep breath, and with a force which almost separates my fingers from my knuckles, I cut through the branch and watch it fall to the ground. Then I whirl around and with all my might throw the secateurs into the air. The blades whirl above me like the bone thrown skywards at the beginning of *2001: A Space Odyssey*. I watch them as they soar high above our garden wall and bisect the path of Flight 101 before landing in a large elder bush half way up the disused embankment of the old Hornsey line. The railway was built in 1872, about the same time that Madame Alfred Carrière was born, and was used to transport building materials for Ally Pally from the city, and then when the palace was completed, to ferry workers back into the city until 1952 when Dr Beeching wielded his axe. Now it's called The Parkland Walk, a oh-so-right-on linear park which runs from Finsbury Park to Muswell Hill and is full of Walkman joggers, mountain bikers, empty crisp packets and dog shite.

Suddenly I feel very cold. No bloody wonder! I'm shirtless and wearing only summer shorts and a pair of Converse high-top sneakers. My hair hangs loose on my shoulders, my bald patch is open to the sky. It's a sight to frighten the neighbours. I must be mad. A hint of sunshine and I'm all but naked in the garden. I reach down and pick up my T-shirt. A bearable pain nips up from my groin to my navel. It's no surprise. Since my chemotherapy the old bladder is a shrunken thing, lined with hypersensitive new tissue which struggles to protect the muscle which was stripped bare by the battery acid. In the blink of an eye the hurt has come and gone. But as it always does, it leaves a slight shadow of itself behind.

As I turn to go back into the house I glance up just in time to see Flight 101 disappearing into the blue and Leonard, our batty neighbour, leaning out of his second-storey window. Stripped to the waist, he's unshaven and has a roll-up dangling from the middle of his lower lip. He must have been taking in the whole scene, and as I look up at him he continues to stare down at me. I shout at him.

'What are you staring at, Leonard?! I make films. What the fuck do you do?!'

Then I disappear into my Poggenpohl kitchen and slam the door.

'*Arsehole!*'

'I'll drink to that.'

Why did I scream at Leonard like that? – the first words I've spoken since Clare left two hours ago.

'*You deserve a reward, you cruel bastard.*'

That's right, Noah! make yourself a coffee and get all self-indulgent again, waste away some more time until Clare gets back. You have every right to, you poor bugger, with your poor cancer and your piss-poor attitude. SELF PITY KILLS says the slogan. Yes, well, fuck that for a game of soldiers. I crank up *la bella macchina* – my beloved espresso machine.

Where is Clare anyway? Even if Tesco is packed to the gunwales, she should be back home by now. Perhaps Coral has thrown one of her wobblies or worse still gone walk-about. Just like the time when during the split-second that Clare was looking in disbelief at the price tag on a pair of Start-Rite with butterflies on the toe, Coral walked out of the shoe shop and disappeared into the human flotsam and jetsam of the Holloway Road. Clare had come home ten years older and still shaking, having plumbed the full depth of her love for her firstborn daughter in the fifteen tortured minutes it had taken her to find Coral. She was sitting on the pavement outside Corrigan Bros butcher's shop chatting to a chained Labrador puppy. Upon being found, Coral had looked up at her mother, smiled and introduced the dog which she'd named Twinkle. Clare screamed at her daughter then dragged her to her feet back to the shoe shop where she'd left the stroller. Both were in tears and saying 'sorry' over and over again like a Mother/Daughter mantra.

The machine clears its throat with that raspy gurgle which heralds the arrival of a coffee strong enough to flip your dick into your watch pocket. Or at least it used to. These days I can't take the caffeine, so it's Lavazza Dec'. Bugger it! I hate decaff. I suppose it's better than nothing, gives me the smell and taste of the coffee and doesn't make me piss in ten seconds. But in the end it's like chopping the rock, laying it out in a big chubby line with the Gold Amex Card, rolling the hundred-dollar bill and snorting up 99 percent Mannitol – sodding baby laxative!

This pissing thing, these bladder spasms, are getting to me now. I'm trying every way possible to deal with them. The best way I've come up with so far is to give them Brechtian banner titles – PISS BREAK!, BLADDER SPASM! or CHEMOBURN! – which I think to myself if anyone is around. But it works better if I'm alone and I can say it aloud. This naming of the beast takes the edge off the terror and it sometimes does it with some of the old sense of tumour. When this happens, I can find myself laughing while clutching at my abdomen in pain and pissing fire.

I pour the decaff and go to the French windows. Madame Alfred Carrière looks naked and a bit pissed-off. There's a missel-thrush on our PC cement birdbath – a gift from First Violin David who had it cast by a co-operative of handicapped artisans who had scraped NA loves CM in childscript on the plinth. He really is a prick – David not the thrush. The missel-thrush is a rare sight these days. He's in danger of extinction. He feeds on snails poisoned by slug pellets and dies a slow and painful death. This one on the birdbath has a snail in its beak and is about to bring it down on to the rim of the bath to break its shell. I bang on the window. The thrush drops the snail and flies off.

BLADDER SPASM!

Where the Hell is Clare?

I decide to fill the time with some work, head upstairs and when I reach the first landing –

PISS BREAK!

Well, sod Lavazza Dec'. If I'm going to do the sip&piss routine, might as well drink the real thing from now on. I wash my hands in our eau de nil, green-stencilled, 'looks really New England' bathroom and go up to my office on the top floor. It's my space – my retreat – vast, with a fireplace, books, a huge TV and VCR, stacks of videos, and walls covered with posters for Clare's concerts and recitals and a few for my films. I feel safe up here – most of the time. Other times, like now, it only serves to remind me that this boy from Workington has become one of Those his instinct from birth had told him to loathe – a well-heeled member of the Middle Class. It's true. I'm a well-known, well-off film maker living in his big sod-off house with a well-known, well-off cellist and a daughter who is well-off in all respects. Coral is only five and she rides ponies up in Totteridge every Saturday – velvet hat, jods, crop, the whole shebang. She takes piano lessons with Zeb Fontaine, a concert pianist friend of Clare's, and at the tender age of two she was on my shoulders at the opening night of Purcell's *The Fairy Queen* at the Coliseu in Lisbon. Christ! At her age I played marbles and footie and went once a year to Morcambe or Blackpool if I was lucky. Concerts? Aunty took me to see Helen Shapiro and Screaming Lord Sutch in Barrow when I was nine. I was sure Shapiro was a man in drag as she sang in a high baritone.

> Walkin' back to happiness!
> Whoop-eye-oh yeah, yeah.
> Said goodbye to loneliness!
> Whoop-eye-oh yeah, yeah.

And my aunty started crying like a baby and saying that it can't be done, over and over between sobs. I was so embarrassed I went out to the foyer. When I heard the screaming for Lord Sutch, I was about to nip back in, but ran straight into Aunty, hanky on her nose, coming out. She took me by the arm and told me angrily we were leaving. Poor bugger. I don't think her marriage to Uncle was one made in heaven. In all those years I lived with them, I don't think I ever heard him speak to her first, and I *never* saw any hint of affection from him. He had plenty for me, but none for her. If he'd been a bit nicer to my aunty, she might never have cried at those stupid Helen Shapiro lyrics, then I might have seen Screaming Lord Sutch, gone on to join the Monster Raving Loony Party at an early age and saved myself a fortune on booze and drugs.

A horn beeps outside. It sounds like Goosegog, Clare's ancient Morris 1000. I lean over the desk and look out of the window. It's not her. Pulling back from the window I knock a pile of scripts to the floor and curse. One of the downsides of success as a film maker is the avalanche of terrible scripts which pour through the letter box. They all come with The Accompanying Letter which is guaranteed to fall into one of two categories.

(a) The Formal. *Dear Mr Arkwright, I am a great admirer of your work. Not since Pasolini/Bergman/Scorsese or Spielberg (!) have I been so inspired. It would be a great honour for me if you would simply read my first screenplay which I have enclosed with a SASAE, etc. etc.*

(b) The Intimate. *Dear Noah, I caught your talk at the BFI last week. It was stunning and I told you so at the reception afterwards. Perhaps you remember me? I was the young UCLA guy who asked you if you felt that* Alphaville *had been a milestone influence on your development – and would you* ever *consider* looking *at my screenplay* FAT FUCK *which is a dark comedy set in a Shoney's Big Boy and blah, blah, blah . . .*

They all get read – many by me. None are ever any good. But I keep on reading when I can and I genuinely hope that I'll find a winner that I could make. And I hope I find one soon, because if this cancer is going to get me, I'd like to think that I had lifted one joint of one finger of my self-obsessed self to help one of the young and helpless – that in some small way I'd paid back Mr Oliver for that Kodak Super 8 camera.

I slap a tape on the deck – Clare practising Rodrigo. I make dozens of these rehearsal tapes on an old Nagra field recorder which I keep permanently set up in the living room downstairs where Clare likes to work. I love to listen to them. They make me feel very comfortable, and in a strange way a part of her process. If Sue Lawley ever asked me which disc would be my one choice for the desert island, it would be one of these rehearsal tapes – a Bach Cello Suite in D minor.

As the heat and light of Rodrigo's Spain filters out of the speakers, I pick up the first screenplay from the pile scattered across the floor and glance at the title, *Louisiana Skin*. Forced Metaphor! I can see them coming a mile away. Tear it up!

BLADDER SPASM!

I reach in my shorts pocket and pull out a screwed-up piece of tinfoil. I open it and find a tramadol pill where hash would have been back in the Stoned Age. I pop it and turn to page one of the script.

INT: A TATTOO AND PIERCING PARLOUR ON AN OIL RIG IN THE GULF – NIGHT.

Not bad. In fact that's a pretty good hook. Well, it's got me hooked, because ever since that visiting lecture I gave at NYU last year, I've been both repelled by and strongly drawn to body piercing. I was in a room full of Film School graduate students. I'd just asked them go round the room, introduce themselves and name one thing about which they were passionate.

Six students into it, we have six names and not one bloody passion. I'm getting pissed off. Then it's number seven's turn. She's a stunning young woman in a black leather bustier and skin-tight pink plastic pants. She runs her fingers through her New York Big Hair and mumbles, or rather she makes a strange cleft-paleted kind of sucking sound. I can't make out what she's saying. She tries again. Still no luck. I'm embarrassed for her. She opens her mouth as if to speak again but then opens it full and thrusts out her tongue. At the base of it, through the thickest part, is a silver stud the size of a car cylinder head. Her tongue is still swollen and bruised from the piercing. She speaks again. The shock of what I've just seen makes me more perceptive. This time I can just make out her words.

'I'm Lucrezia. My passions are drugs and fucking.'

'And body piercing,' I say. She laughs and her stud glints in the fluorescent overheads. I know there and then that I've finally come up against the Generation Gap. I can wear a thousand leather jackets, put a whole colony of dead guinea pigs on my head, but I would still be uncool to Lucrezia. When I speak again I almost whisper.

'How could you do this to yourself, Lucrezia?'

I can't make out her reply. I wait. She repeats and this time it's clear enough.

'Hey, Noah! It's art. Try it!'

I look down at my notes and there in bold script, underlined, I've written *Beauty is truth, truth beauty – that is all ye know on earth, and all ye need to know*. I take out my pen and write under it *Beauty is in the eye of the beholder*.

And my mind goes back to my trip to the Shit Hole in Dumbo with Tiny, and the bartender with the bone through his nose. I was probably in the presence of a great artist and I never knew it.

The doorbell rings downstairs and brings me back to my office and Clare calling up from outside. *Louisiana Skin* sits on my lap dead in the water. It couldn't hold up past page five – a Steven Seagal rip-off in a slick location – nothing more. I toss it back on to the floor, throw open the sash window and look down. Coral is on the pavement, scratching at something on the bonnet of the car. Clare is rummaging in her handbag. Her blonde hair is scraped back in a top-knot. I Zoom In on the nape of her neck. The nape! That most erogenous of zones – forget about nipples and earlobes and feet and bellies – give me the nape of the neck any day! There's a certain smell secreted from the base of the neck, sweet with a hint of vanilla, strongest in a new-born baby, which is irresistible. Even from three floors above, the urge to nuzzle Clare's nape is overpowering. I feel an erection twitching up.

Trina, Coral's five-year-old friend, runs down next door's path. Her hair is plaited into beaded corn rows. Her mother, June, dreadlocks pulled back in a scarlet band, nips out and catches her before she can reach the pavement. Soweto jive band beat blasts out of the open front door. Trina jumps up and down and shouts over the music.

'Mum, Mum! Can Coral come and play?'

Coral is already running to meet her friend.

'Can I, Mummy? Mummy, can I?'

'Alright with you, Clare?' June's rich voice rises up to me clearly.

I can't hear Clare's reply, but Coral is already in Trina's front garden and the two of them are hopping around to the music. June puts the latch on the front gate and as she comes back down the path, she sees me and waves. I wave back. Clare looks up. She's smiling radiantly. This is not the face of a woman who has spent an hour and a half at Tesco's with a four-year-old. And that's a very particular smile. I've seen it before – but when? My erection is now in full throb. I shout down.

'Locked out?'

'Took the wrong set – no house keys!'

Christ! If she beams any broader she'll split.

'Be right down!'

I'm feeling heady with excitement and I don't know why. Full of some of the old piss and vinegar, I bound down the stairs two-by-two, twenty-five again – well, thirty/thirty-five. I slide sidesaddle down the banister of the last flight and land in the hallway with a lusty bounce in my balls. For the last twenty seconds I have been free of cancer – just a young blood ready for sex.

The jive thumps through the wall as I open the door. Sunlight floods in, silhouetting Clare. The music swells from next door – African – female – celebratory. I feel the urge to sing along. Clare must read my mind.

'That's it, Noah! Sing!'

She wants me to sing because she's been to Tesco's?

'Sing it from the rooftops!'

My erection jerks and pushes my shorts out like a tent. I adjust it. I'm confused. I try to look Clare in the face, but the sun is blinding. Then I remember when I've seen that smile before. That bright light silhouetting her in the door frame is not the sun – it's her aura, blazing out from every pore, every hair follicle, setting the whole bloody street on fire.

'I'm pregnant, Noah.'

And the scene is frozen in time for a hundred thousand years. Such is the power of the announcement of a Grade-A, gospel-class miracle, a *Miracolo di tutti Miracoli!* This wasn't supposed to happen. The chemotherapy last winter had been a neutron bomb – a population wipe-out which left the infrastructure severely damaged but still standing amid the corpses of a billion sperm. We had given up the idea of another pregnancy. We'd talked often of adoption. Now this – the Big One, The Against-All-Odds-It-Shouldn't-Have-Happened One!

I hold Clare close and nuzzle into her neck. Our jugular veins lie next to each other and I can feel Fatherhood pulsing through mine, Motherhood through hers. I smell vanilla balm. Pulling her even closer, I whisper aloud to the Angel from the children's ward.

'Thank you. Thank you.'

Clare breathes 'Amen' into my neck and starts to sob quietly. Over her shoulder I see Trina and Coral dancing to the Township music like an animated United Colours of Benetton poster.

I want to carry Clare over the threshold, into the living room and make love to her on the swirling Punjabi rug. She's stopped crying now. She's supple in my arms – ready. Then she straightens up, sniffs, and kisses me on the end of my nose.

'Happy?'

'Like a sandboy!'

'Me too – sandgirl!'

Well, perhaps I'll just take her by the hand instead and lead her gently to the rug. Clare beats me to it, takes my hand and leads me back inside and closes the door. Then she lets my hand go, peels off into the living room and says:

'Put the kettle on, will you, Noah? I must phone Etta.'

'*Shit.*'

'Alright, love . . . tea or coffee?'

'Tea please.'

And she's already dialling Etta's number.

'*Fuck it!*'

This bit of BT bonding is going to go on for ages. The tea will be stone-cold. I'll be feeling left out – a pissed-off sperm donor. By the time she's finished, Coral will be back from next door and any chance of nookie will be gone until tonight by which time we'll both be exhausted and sex will have dropped down the agenda to somewhere below emergency midnight fire drill.

'*Leave it out, Noah! She's her best friend, for God's sake,*' I can hear Ray saying to me. And I want to reach out across the Atlantic, grab him by the neck and ask him where the Hell he is when I need him.

I bring the drinks in, put Clare's at her feet and she blows me a kiss. I sit on the sofa in the window, sip my coffee and watch her talking. She radiates happiness and looks beautiful with the light from the French windows raking across her hair. In the corner, her cello stands in its case. Can it feel her presence nearby? Does it too want to be played on by its lover? Well, tough titty, mate! Neither of us are in with a chance while the hotline to Etta is still open. From across the room I catch the odd words: 'gift', 'afraid', 'fat', and I try unsuccessfully to hear some schoolgirl whispered stuff which ends with a laugh and a look across the shoulder in my direction.

I look away and see Leonard, still stripped to the greasy waistband of his greasy polyester trousers, wandering up and down the street picking up crisp packets, empty cans of Coke and Idris ginger beer and handfuls of twigs and dead leaves. He tells me he saves these things and once a month takes a battered suitcase full of them to his mother in Dorset. I can see he's singing 'The Boy in the Balcony'. I know that's what he's singing because that's all he ever sings. He has a pretty good tenor voice. Clare says that with the right training he could have been a pro.

I look back at Clare, still deep in conversation. Another whisper. Another laugh. I feel the old rat in my gut, starting to gnaw away at my happiness which only a few minutes ago was complete. Another look in my direction – this one followed by a little wave. I realise as I observe this curious ritual that I know absolutely nothing, *nada*, *niente*, about women. Can this be the Noah Arkwright about whom it was written in the Women section of the *Guardian*: 'At last a male film maker who understands something of the female psyche . . . who can weave Yin and Yang into a whole which transcends gender'? The Noah Arkwright who inspired the editor of *Adam's Rib* to say to the director of the film *Vogue*

Patterns that *if* he was a man (which she doubted) he should contact the Los Angeles sperm bank immediately? Ha! When those women said what they said about me, I was as Proud as Punch's Prick. Now I am just a prick. If they could see me now, exposed for the gender sham I am, fighting jealousy and anger when I should be filled with pure joy. What would they write now?

Bullshit!

BLADDER SPASM!

The glass almost breaks in its frame as I hammer on the window and scream at Leonard.

'Leonard! Put a shirt on, for fuck's sake!'

'Noah!'

I turn to see Clare staring at me. She speaks into the phone.

'I've got to go. I'll speak to you later . . . yes . . . me too . . .'

And she puts the phone down, comes over and sits beside me. I can't look her in the face.

'Look at me, Noah.'

She touches my cheek softly and turns me towards her, then lets go. It's a long time before she speaks.

'Have you ever considered what Kairos means?'

'No . . . I mean . . . well, I've always assumed it was somewhere in Greece – an island.'

I flood with embarrassment. I've never actually given the word a second thought – the name of Clare's quartet, the heart of her art, and I've never once stopped to think about its meaning. Yet I expect her and every other person on God's planet to be drawn by my film titles, to ponder over them, discover them and be awed by their depth of meaning.

'The Greeks have three main words for time. There's *kronos* – plain old plod-along, time on your hands, time. There's *kairos* – the one we chose – which means exact or critical time as opposed to your bog-standard *kronos*. And then there is *kairos oxus*. *Kairos oxus* is as fine-tuned as time can be. It means 'sharp moment'. Sharp as in acute, shooting, stabbing, hot, biting . . .'

'Razor?'

'Exactly. *Kairos oxus* can be the sweetest of time, it can be exalted and radiant. It can also cut you to the quick and leave you gasping for breath, dying.'

'Better name for the quartet.'

'Takes too much time to say.'

We both give a little laugh. Clare takes my hand in hers.

'The point is, Noah, neither of us is a stranger to *kairos oxus*, so let's face this one with courage and a bit of happiness. I knew by the pull of your hand on mine in the hall that you wanted to have me, that's why I came in here and phoned Etta. I didn't really need to talk to her. I just wasn't ready for sex. The time for me was sweet enough, anything more would have made it too rich.'

I pull her to me and kiss her moistly, deeply, until I feel that faint muscle contraction in her jaw, that almost imperceptible struggle which indicates she is ready for the moment to end, and I stop and touch her half-open mouth with my finger.

'So it's all in the timing?'

She bites playfully.

'You could say that.'

Norman Baker clasps his hands together seriously on the desk in front of him. He sighs.

'I'll be frank with you, Noah. The time has come to look very closely at our options. It doesn't look good. But let's not jump the old gun. It *could* be nothing to worry about.'

I nod. 'Right.'

'*And if you believe that, Noah, you're a bigger fucking fool than I took you for!*'

332

I nod again sagely. 'Right. So how soon can we take this "shufti"?'

'Tomorrow if you want or can. God Bless BUPA, eh?'

'Yeah, right.'

He smiles. And so he bloody well should. I'm one of his best customers – probably writes off two polo ponies a year to my account. Yes, well, Mr Norman Baker, smile on, be happy and keep that hand nice and steady for tomorrow.

Clare and I did make love later that night. We were tender and slow, careful and filled with love. We fell asleep in each other's arms. In the dead of night, I was woken by the screech of an owl. The bedroom was blue with moonlight, Clare's back rising out of the sheets like chiselled Carrara marble. I kissed the nape of the neck and she stirred slightly. The screech owl shrieked again. Like a snake, I slithered out of bed, across the floor and on to the landing. On the way down to the loo, I looked in on Coral, sleeping the sleep only children can, on her back on top of the covers with arms and legs splayed, nightie up around her chest. I pulled her nightie down, eased her back under the duvet and kissed her innocent forehead. I was flooded with calm as I watched her easy three a.m. breathing.

There was no pain when I peed. But as I bent to lower the seat, I glanced down at the reservoir. Even in the moonlight, I could see clearly enough to know that this was a Big Time, razor-sharp *kairos oxus*.

TWENTY-FOUR

Alas! 'tis true I have gone here and there,
And made myself a motley to the view . . .
Shakespeare, Sonnet 110

London, January 1997

I'm frozen stiffer than a triple vodka on the rocks. I want a triple vodka on the rocks. I *need* a triple vodka on the rocks. I've walked to Chelsea from Harley Street and the night has come in on the back of an icy fog which started to creep up from the river when I was half way across Hyde Park. By the time I was crossing Rotten Row, the canvas shrouding the Albert Memorial loomed out of the mist like a becalmed galleon. I was spooked. The visit with Stormin' Norman had already thrown me, put the old nerves on edge. Not that what he said wasn't expected. In fact I was surprised he didn't whip me into hospital there and then. I wish he had. Now I have a night to kill before tomorrow's surgery. At least if I'd been checked in today I would have winkled a shot of pethidine and a couple of Valium out of Sister Irish, followed by a Temazepam night-cap if I was lucky. Instead I'm inching my way along Sloane Street in the freezing fog to sit in a roomful of alcoholics so grateful for their recovery that they make me want to scream. But it's the only place I can go. If I go home to Clare, I'll collapse at her feet, a mewling, clinging baby dumping my fears on her like nappy shite. If I go to a pub, at best I'll crawl home to Clare and do exactly the same shit only puking as well, at worst I'll end up in the ER for a hot date with the stomach pump. If I phone Big George, he'll answer on his mobile in his local and tell me to come over and join him. And that could lead right back to Clare's lap or the stomach pump or both. It's a brutal circle with nowhere to run and nowhere to hide.

The best thing, the *sensible* thing, to do would be to get in touch with Ray, have him meet me at the meeting. But where is he when I need him? The bastard's in New York trying to drum up some interest in *Blood and Milk*. So to Hell with that idea! Tits on a bull!

Wait a second! Perhaps I should just take that bull with tits by the horns, nip on to the Piccadilly Line at Knightsbridge, shoot out to Heathrow and be in Manhattan in time for a nostalgic bite at the Cozy Soup'n'Burger with Ray. Then tomorrow morning I could ride with the Bowery Oracle over the Brooklyn Bridge and blow this shit out of my head back to Buttfuck Egypt where it belongs. But just as I'm about to turn around and head back up Sloane Street, I hear Ray's and Tiny's voices coming out of the fog, muffled but very clear.

'*Drop the Geographical, Noah! Get to the goddam meeting!*'

Ten minutes later I'm outside the church where the Evening Stars greeter stands at the door greeting the drunks who emerge like ghouls out of the fog to shake his hand before stepping past him on their road to recovery. A Bentley lurks at the kerbside, which means that tonight's meeting will be living up to its nickname with the attendance of some recovering star whose own road, though not necessarily easier than that of lesser mortals, is definitely better paved.

'Hi, Noah! Good to see you,' says the greeter – a thin youth with skin care by heroin.

'Hello,' is all I can say because I haven't a clue what his name is as I scoot past him into the foyer where people are milling around in a boozeless cocktail party scene. Squatting at the base of a *faux* marble pillar and smoking a roll-up is Robbie. He's an Evening Stars regular, long greasy hair, thin jean jacket – useless against the cold – and down-at-heel cowboy boots. All the other shoes in the room are better cobbled, supporting the well-heeled Sobriety Seekers. Robbie sees me and gives a hopeful wave. I give him a fiver – not because I'm feeling generous, but because I'm feeling guilty about my decent footwear.

'Thanks, Alan . . . you're alright, you are.'

He always calls me Alan. I give him a muted smile.

'I wish, Robbie . . . I wish.'

I wish Ray were here.

Suddenly, from behind, someone gooses me deep into the crack of my arse and whispers in my ear.

'What the fuck you think you're doing, boy?'

I know that voice. I know the routine. I find my best drawl.

'Sorry, officer. Was I going a tad over the speed limit?'

Ray spins me round to face him and plops a smackeroony kiss on my forehead. He tilts back his baseball cap and pops gum like a State Trooper.

'You stoned-out mother-fucking hippie piece of shit! You ain't doing no speed at all.'

I join in and together we speak the final line of the scene.

'You are standing still in the goddam fast lane of goddam Interstate 95!'

We laugh and he hugs me hard. This has been our standard reunion greeting ever since a party last year when Ray dragged me to my feet and forced me to re-enact with him our arrest and conviction for Dangerous Parking in

South Carolina that summer when Ray was still Blue Sky and all we wanted to shoot was Rock and Roll – when fucked-up was still fun.

'Shit, Ray! I was *actually* thinking of you *right* then. What the Hell are you doing back so soon?'

'Got Miramax in the bag in one meeting – like popping a pig in a gunny sack.'

'That's great, man. That's really great.' My voice is dull – flattened by the effort of the routine.

'Are you OK, Noah?'

'No, Ray. I'm not. I'm fucking terrible.'

Before he can ask me why, the crowd, on an instinctive signal, head as one into the meeting room – a bunch of hopeful lemmings carrying Styrofoam coffee cups. Ray and I are swept along and are soon sitting side by side on plastic chairs facing a plastic-topped table flanked by plastic-coated banners of the Twelve Steps and Twelve Traditions. The place is packed, but down near the front and over to the left is more densely packed than the rest of the room. In the middle of this oily group of sardine sycophants will be this evening's star, so heavily screened that I haven't a clue who it is – but it's a pound to a penny they're in there somewhere. Haven't they read the Twelfth Tradition which is 'ever reminding us to place principles before personalities'. Obviously not. Christ! Where's my tolerance? Where's my milk of human kindness? The tits on this bull are dry tonight.

DRY DRUNK WARNING!

When I'm this self-obsessed, circling myself like a jackal, I'm dangerous. If the meeting would just get started and I could focus even 5 per cent on the speaker, then chances are I'll hear the 'something' which will deflect me from my hara-kiri flight path. But then again, I might hear something else which will make me thrust the joystick forwards and open the throttle full. But somebody better get this show on the road, because if I have to put up with one more 'kissy face how are you darling?' on this bad Robert Altman soundtrack, I might lose it and leave in a way which will make my coked-up exit from that first meeting Kirstin dragged me to look like a polite farewell. Ray puts his hand on my knee and I nearly hit the ceiling.

'That bad, huh?'

All I can do is nod and bite my lip.

'Then go back to basics, Noah. Listen for the similarities not the differences.'

I bite down harder until I taste my own blood. A bell tinkles and everybody sits down and gives full attention to the secretary, a streaked blonde Coco Chanel of a woman in her late forties. She speaks in the measured pace and earnest pitch of an anchorwoman.

'Welcome to the Chelsea Tuesday evening Step Meeting. I'm Fiona and I'm an alcoholic.'

'Hi, Fiona!' comes the standard reply in unison.

'Could we have a moment's silence please to remember why we are here and to give a thought to the still-suffering alcoholic who has not yet made it to these rooms.'

Heads down! I keep my eyes open and look around to see a few naughty alkies mouthing 'How-are-you-darling?' and taking the opportunity to give a social wave. Heads up – eyes front!

'Tonight is Step Nine. Our speaker will share on the Step for fifteen minutes, followed by raised-hand sharing . . . speaker's choice. At a quarter to, I'll open the meeting for shy sharers only.'

Then she introduces the speaker who wears a nondescript jacket and trousers, has a nondescript haircut, and a face which tells you he's between twenty-nine and fifty.

'Hello, my name is Brian. I'm an alcoholic.' His voice is flat.

'Hi, Brian!'

'Oscar Wilde once said, "I have only in my life once met a truly boring man and that fact alone made him extremely interesting." So I suppose there's hope for me yet.'

The crowd laughs. I mutter under my breath.

'Clever little shit!'

That's all I need right now – some grey bloke who's turned his sorry recovering arse into a sight-gag. Ray leans in close to me.

'Take it easy, Noah.'

'Don't give me a hard time, Ray!' I hiss.

And Brian is up and running about how he's made direct amends to everyone and his brother, not forgetting the dog, the cat and the pet iguana. But most of all 'I've made amends to myself. Only when I was able to do this was I able to love myself – that boring self which I so hated when I was drinking.' Jesus! This guy is good. Slate this shot and get those cameras rolling! Get him on film and then shoot the bastard for fuck's sake!

And he goes on and on and the more serene he gets the more I'm tearing my hair out from the inside. I'm sitting here and I'm supposed to be identifying with this man who has his life in sickeningly sweet order – who is so full of gratitude that he can actually live with his boring self, and I could be dead in six months. I know that I should be able to put my shit on a shovel and throw it over my shoulder, but it's too big a stretch right at this moment. Now Brian's talking about how today he's working on his most difficult reparation, to a neighbour whose car he set fire to because the man let his dog shit on Brian's lawn.

'Listen for the similarities not the differences.'

Sorry, can't be done right now. Try me again when I'm on my death bed. Right now as I sit here among the evening stars, making amends is the last thing on my mind. Right now all I can think of is Etta and Clare and that weekend at the cottage in Lulworth. It was in the very early spring of 1994 – the second of March to be exact.

Clare is twenty weeks pregnant but her belly is nothing but a small swell. She looks strong and magnificent. From Day One she's had no morning sickness – not even a headache. Except for me. I've been her migraine since the night of that day we learned she was pregnant, when I pissed after our celebratory love-making and saw the future – and it was bloody.

I should have gone right back to the bedroom and told Clare there and then that the cancer was back. But I didn't. Instead I fitted back in behind her drifting body like a spoon and nuzzled her neck. She reached behind herself, put her palm on my bum and whispered half-asleep:

'You alright?'

'Mmnnn,' was my noncommittal reply – my sleepy-moan insurance against that inevitable day when Clare would ask me why I lied.

'Sure?'

'Mmnn.'

I tried to stop the questioning with a kiss, but it wasn't really a kiss, it was my third denial. As I lay there in the dark listening to my blood pumping in my veins, I felt certain I could see the first light of dawn through the curtains and that at any moment a cock would crow and show me for the liar I was.

'You are happy about the baby, aren't you?'

Thank God! A chance to tell the truth.

'Of course I am.' I pull her even closer to me. 'Of course I am.'

Within seconds Clare and her minuscule baby deep within her were asleep, and I lay awake for hours listening to their deep breathing. Just before dawn the first jet of the day rumbled on its flight path three miles overhead and I heard

Coral cough in her room below. At that moment something shifted in my mind and I realised that in lying to Clare I had put myself on the outside of the pregnancy and that I would never get back in. I had cast the die and it had rolled into the danger zone. I was going to have to be very very careful. Even if I were to tell her over breakfast that the cancer was back, she would lose the baby – perhaps not immediately – but before the end of the crucial first trimester. And if I were to go too near her, let alone make love to her, my malignancy would go into her and the baby. Yes, very careful indeed and very clever. To stay well out of it, yet be there. To be intimate with Clare but not touch. To guard one and all against myself.

And for the first time in my life I was not only going to have to deal with my terror alone, but pretend into the bargain that everything was alright.

That was four months ago and I haven't been handling things well at all. In fact I've made a real cat's arse of things. In *fact* fact, the whole bloody shooting match has gone seriously pear-shaped. There was a regrowth of course – four of the buggers to be exact. I went in as a day patient and Stormin' Norman cauterised them with his trusty diathermy machine which is a kind of red-hot wart blaster he shoves up into the bladder through a catheter while I squirm around and shout abuse in a pethidine haze.

I went home that evening and told Clare I'd been at a script meeting in Birmingham. She said nothing. She went to bed early. I said I had work to do. Near midnight, Clare came downstairs for a glass of water and almost caught me disposing of my bloody underpants deep in the rubbish of the kitchen pedal bin. I managed to squirm out of it with a bit of bad acting – something about thinking I'd thrown twenty quid away with some Kleenex. She didn't believe me, but was too tired to care. And that's how it's been and still is. Me

341

terrified, convinced I'm a source of contagion, but putting on a really over-the-top 'Look how happy I am!' performance. Clare is perplexed by my behaviour, but too busy clinging on to the wheel of her hormonal-change dodgem car to spend too much energy on my driving. Coral thinks I'm acting weird. I tell her that I'm very busy trying to get a new movie off the ground and that in my own way I'm having a baby, and just like Mummy, my mind is elsewhere. I can tell that she doesn't believe me.

Getting a movie off the ground! Christ! All I do is sit upstairs in my office hour upon hour writing meaningless notes to myself to write notes to myself and making nuisance phone calls to Ray, Kirsty and Tiny. Sometimes I phone numbers I find on scraps of paper in my wallet and talk to a person with only a first name whom I've met in some AA meeting and who's anonymous enough for me to call late at night and pour out my self-pitying drivel without fear of a comeback. I feel more insane, more drunk than I ever did when I was drinking and each day reaffirms my conviction that I am a force for evil and that whereas I once parked dangerously, I am now dangerous parking personified.

Of course Clare and I haven't made love since that night. From time to time, I have forced myself to hold her, but it has been with the tenderness of a stone and she has backed away. She is convinced I am having an affair. I know this because she came right out and asked me one day when I had been up at the hospital for another Dyno-Rod extravaganza. (The tumours have been responding well to pruning and have been cropping up like evil buds of May all winter.)

'Just tell me, Noah – are you having an affair?'

I laugh and try a stone hug. She pulls away.

'Are you screwing someone else?'

'No, Clare, I'm not.'

'Then you must be drinking again.'

'No.'

She looks at me long and hard. Her voice softens.

'Everything else is alright, isn't it?'

'Here's your chance, Noah. Tell her now.'

'No!'

'Tell her!'

'I can't.'

'Why not?'

If Clare knew I wasn't well, she'd hold me and comfort me and that would be unthinkable. Because if I was a contamination risk three months ago, I'm deep-bunker radioactive now – the fucking Angel of Death for my own unborn child. So I lie yet again.

'My health is fine, Clare – A1.'

The cords on her neck pop into relief, her face reddens, and as her anger rises in her gullet like lava, I notice that her nipples are erect, huge through her tight T-shirt. The old magma bubbles in my crotch and burns me with such guilt that I wish it would erupt and incinerate me on the spot. It doesn't have to – Clare's lava does the job for it.

'THEN WHAT THE FUCK IS WRONG WITH YOU, NOAH?!'

She races around the kitchen, sweeping stuff aside, steaming.

'For God's sake! This should be one of the happiest times of our lives. We've a baby coming – all the signs are good – you're well – you've a project on the go – I'm still sawing away – money's no problem – I'm fit as a Lop – Christ, Noah! I'm even feeling horny – and every time I come near you, you act as if I'm radioactive!'

I stand there paralysed in the middle of the outburst.

'Look at you! Look at me, will you! You can't even look at me! Jesus, Noah! I have to get out of here. I'm going to Etta's. You get Coral from school. I'll be back for dinner and then I strongly suggest you get yourself to a meeting and do whatever it is you do there to change, as right now you really need to change because you are fucking impossible and you can tell them that from me!'

She exits and slams the door. I shout after her.

'Why don't you tell me like it is, Clare? Don't beat around the bush!'

She didn't come home that night. She phoned to say that it would be better all round if she stayed at Etta's and that she'd just spoken to June who said that Coral could go round for a sleep-over with Trina so there would be no excuse for me to avoid my meeting which she hoped I was still going to because she sure as Hell didn't want to be around me until I'd changed course.

Since that night, Clare's spent more and more time with Etta and less and less time with me. I don't blame her. I don't like spending time with me so why should I think anyone else would want to? I wouldn't say that I feel jealous, but I do feel left out – and really pissed-off for having put myself outside the pale. The pregnancy goes on. Clare stays small-bellied and beautiful and doesn't say anything about it to me. I don't blame her for that either. I have continued to be as remote as Tristan da Cunha. It's a vicious circle. I'm withdrawn. Clare finds company in Etta. I feel left out, so I withdraw some more. She is drawn closer to her friend. I withdraw further. It's not long before they are going away with each other for the weekend, sometimes taking Coral and Maya, sometimes not. This weekend they've gone by themselves.

They've gone down to Dorset, to the cottage in Lulworth. Rainbow's End is a tiny eighteenth-century fisherman's place which I bought one weekend with twenty-five grand from *Kobo*, which – impossibly – showed a bit of profit on the back end. The house clings to the bottom of a chine just west of the village. It is primitive and to use it in deep winter is an act of masochism. A wood-burning stove provides the only heating and any hot water that decides to flow is a bonus. The walls are white-washed, the floors flagged with stone, and the loo is still outside. In the summer it is glorious, crouched beside its own shingle beach where we can sunbathe hidden from the gaze of the stream of tourists who hoof it up the coastal path from Lulworth to the natural arch of Durdle Door. Even now, in early March, on beautiful weekends like this one, Rainbow's End traps the sun enough to coax me into shorts and tempt me to paddle, but the water is frigid and I end up stacking logs for the stove which will have to be lit as soon as the sun drops behind the top of the gully.

But I'm not there – not yet anyway. It's Saturday morning, and I'm just passing Junction 8 on the M3 going west. I've left Coral with June next door again (again!) and am heading down on a surprise visit to Clare and Etta. Sitting behind me there's a wicker hamper full of goodies which for a small fortune Bunces' deli in Crouch End made up for me. There's also a cooler loaded with Cordon Rouge for the girls and Badoit for me. Pretty bloody pretentious! Should be strapped to the dickie seat of a damned landau, not dumped in the back of an ancient Volvo Estate. Charlie Musselwhite's 'Rough News' is cranked up full volume –

> Both sides of the fence.
> Both sides of the fence.
> You can't play both sides of the fence!

Followed by the meanest blues harmonica break ever. Big George introduced me to Charlie and whenever I need a trip back to urban USA I get in the car, slap him on the tape deck extra loud, drive down the A102(M) through Hackney and pretend I'm on a Chicago 'thruway'. It's not the same. Like alcohol-free lager, it only serves to remind you of what you're missing. I knew yesterday alright what I was missing. As soon as Clare and Etta piled themselves and their instruments into Goosegog and drove off, I felt a bleeding hole in my gut. And when they waved out of the windows as they turned on to Elder Avenue, I had a terrible feeling that I would never see either of them again. I felt totally and utterly abandoned. It was my own bloody fault. Etta had actually invited me to join them, but I had made some bullshit excuse about having to bury myself in Soho to do some Post Sync work that didn't exist. I must have stood on the pavement staring down to the junction with Crouch Hill for a good five minutes before going inside and cranking up La Bella Macchina to make myself a punishing cup of fuck-off strength espresso. This would guarantee that I would spend the next few hours in a state of physical pain to match my mental ache.

I went up to my office and made a few pretend business calls, but was so unfocused that I reversed east and west, phoned my Los Angeles agent and woke her up at three a.m. She was not happy and asked me if I'd been drinking. I told her I hadn't but that I could murder a Jameson's and as I put the phone down I could hear her voice squeaking out telling me not to be so damned stupid. I should have then phoned immediately any one of those numbers on any one of those scraps of paper in my wallet. But the only AA members I wanted to have anything to do with were Ray, Tiny or even Kirstin and they were all five time-zones away and that provided me with the perfect excuse not to contact them and to sink into a morass of self-pity, fear and loathing – in London not Las Vegas. After another hour of wallowing punctuated with self-inflicted painful pisses, I knew I either had to phone somebody, take a drink or slit my wrists. Like the sensible alkie I am, I still didn't phone a sober number. Nope! On the pretence of asking him if he could make me a

tape of *Jammin' With Edward*, the legendary Ry Cooder–
Jagger studio session, I called Big George whose blood must
be eighty proof and who smokes more dope in a day than a
hundred Metallica fans smoke in a year. He'd be sure to give
me some sensible advice.

'Aren't you AA people always talking about taking action?'

'That's right.'

'Then get off your arse and take some.'

'That's all very well, George, but I don't know what action
to take.'

'Noah, what would you like to be doing right now – more
than anything else?'

'Drinking – doing up a few lines.'

'Leave it out, Noah! That's what I do. Don't avoid the
question.'

Christ! He sounds like an old-timer who's been sober for
twenty years, and yet I know he must have had at least six
Special Brew and a couple of spliffs by this time of the
afternoon. How can he do that and still make sense?

'I'd like to be with Clare and Etta.'

'Then be with them.'

'They're down at the cottage.'

I hear a big sigh which says, 'I don't fucking believe this
arsehole.'

'You know, Noah? For a bright bloke you can be thick as
dog shite. Just get a nice little something together as a gift, get
in the motor, get down there today and surprise them.'

'I can't today. I'll have to sort something out for Coral.'

'Then leave in the morning.'

'Actually, Etta did ask me if I wanted to go with them.'

'Then what the fuck are you dithering about for – get
sorted and go.'

He makes it sound so bloody simple. As I put the phone

down, I feel like a ten-year-old who's just been told off by his mum. Fuck you, George! And thank you, George!

So I took his advice and immediately scooted off to Crouch End, arranged the hamper and champers not forgetting the fizzy water. Ten minutes after I got home a bike messenger delivered a Charlie Musselwhite tape – not yet released in Britain – which is blasting out of the Volvo sound system as – at George's suggestion – I speed towards my wife and her best friend on a surprise visit which I'm praying will bring me some relief.

> You think you're bad
> But you can't have your
> Cake and eat it too . . .
> You think you're cool,
> But only a fool
> Plays both sides of the fence . . .

Charlie's harp wails as the road signs flash by! – Abbot's Worthy, Martyr Worthy, Headbourne Worthy. I feel pretty bloody worthy as I approach Junction 9 – a deserving man racing past Winchester and its magnificent cathedral spire.

It's a long haul up from Lulworth's scar of a car park. The bloody thing is half the size of the village. The hamper is heavy. I've threaded a length of old seat-belt webbing through its handles and around my forehead so that I'm carrying my load like a Shanghai porter. By the time I reach the top of the first rise, I'm sweating cobs. I've tied my Country Squire wax jacket around my waist and it feels like a bloody anaconda, and between my teeth I'm holding a plastic bag containing my few bits and bobs. Anyone coming over the hill towards me now would savour one of life's rare moments of total translucency. In a ten-denier sheer *kairos oxus* they'd see me for the lunatic that I really am.

'Hello! I'm Noah Arkwright the well-known Art House film director. Lovely day, isn't it?'

'Good morning to you, sir. And I'm Jean-Paul Sartre.'

So it's probably best that I haven't seen a soul since I pulled into Lulworth. As I continue to slog up the hill, a montage sequence pops into my head:

EXT: FANELLI'S BAR – NIGHT. Etta exits the bar. Noah side-steps her, takes out a gun and shoots her in the head. CUT TO –

INT: COACH HOUSE – AFTERNOON. A party is under way. Etta sits opposite Noah, legs apart. He stares at her crotch then pulls out a gun and shoots her. CUT TO –

EXT: COACH HOUSE – AFTERNOON. Clare takes out a shell and hands it to Etta. Etta smiles with joy. Noah emerges from the coach house with a gun and shoots them both. CUT TO –

EXT: NORTH LONDON LEAFY STREET – MORN-ING. Clare and Etta drive off down the road in a Morris Minor. They both wave at Noah who stands outside the house holding a grenade launcher. He waves back at them, then fires. The car burst into a ball of flames. CLOSE ON –

INT: NOAH'S HEAD – DAY! This is terrifying stuff in deep saturated colour, razor-sharp – hyper-real. It makes me stop in my tracks, my head spinning. It throws me so out of kilter that for a moment I think about turning on my heel and heading home. I make some slight move and flush a skylark out of a gorse bush. It sweeps in a low arc up from the ground then starts its vertical ascent, perhaps the first of the year. Up and up she rises, trilling, boring a hole in the early spring sky until she is a tiny speck a thousand feet above me. With my head tilted back the weight of my picnic load is doubled and the strap digs into my forehead. It hurts like

Hell. So I ease the hamper to the ground, open it, sit down and take out a bottle of water. For a minute or two I sit there sipping, the skylark singing overhead and the sky sparkling beyond the village below. Calm returns as I meticulously file away the painful footage deep in the archives of my director's head. Job done, I get to my feet, tuck the hamper under my arm and press on.

Just before the crest of the next rise, I drop off to the left, down a narrow path which leads to the head of Rainbow's End gully. Primroses edge the track, basking in the sun. As I near the edge, I can hear the stream which falls over the narrow ledge at the top of the ravine, and in the background the rising strains of string music. A few more steps and the cottage comes into view, far below, on its shelf next to a bright lapping sea. The windows are flung wide open and from out of them floats the music – I think it's a Paganini sonata. On the washing line strung up between the house and a scrubby pine tree are three pairs of knickers, white in the sun. A wisp of blue smoke curls from the chimney. It's an idyllic scene and I stop to take it in fully, closing my eyes and letting the music take me out over the sighing waters. The sun on my face is warm, nudging hot. The music rises to a crescendo and then stops. When I open my eyes, I see Clare and Etta coming out of the house. A reflex action makes me flatten myself against the rocky wall to watch unseen. I often wonder to this day what would have happened if I had shouted down to them at that moment, or if they had simply felt my presence, looked up and seen me. But I didn't and they didn't.

Instead I watch in hidden silence as my wife and her best friend, the cellist and the second violin, put their arms around each other and kiss a deep lover's kiss. I press myself harder against the cliff, praying now for complete invisibility. As I move I dislodge a stone and it tumbles down the gully. Though hidden, I can imagine them breaking off the embrace and looking in the direction of the sound. Then I hear screams and laughter and dare to sneak a peek to find that there's been a Jump Cut in this bloody movie and Etta and Clare, now naked, are running into the sea, spray flying off them in slo-mo. They dive in and stay underwater for an eternity before breaking the surface again like dolphins. Clare floats on her back, her belly above water, glistening. Etta swims over to her, cradles the back of her head and kisses her on the forehead. I feel a wave of guilt wash over me, and I turn away from the scene like a voyeur who has suddenly developed a conscience. I'm wounded and confused by what I've just witnessed – an episode which is so beautiful and yet fills me with such fear.

I sat there at the top of the ravine in a state of shock until the light began to fade. They could have decided to take a walk to the village and found me, but I somehow knew they wouldn't. They were bedded in down there and were not going to leave the nest. I waited until after dark, until the lights were on in the cottage and I could hear the muffled sounds of cooking, conversation and laughter, before sneaking down the ravine by the light of the moon and placing the hamper on a boulder in a prominent position. I opened the lid and took out one of the bottles of champagne before stealing back to the car park like a thief in the night, getting into the Volvo and, gripping the steering wheel like a vice, screeching off – knuckles white – in the moonlight.

Less than twenty-four hours later I'm dragging my tired arse to an AA meeting in Muswell Hill. I am angry and bewildered. As Ray would say: my head is a dangerous neighbourhood and I shouldn't be walking through it alone. I'm not alone, deep in the poacher's pocket of my country coat is the bottle of Cordon Rouge I nicked from the hamper. Why am I going to this fucking meeting? Don't know. Keeping it all in the moment like they've been telling me to do.

'*YESTERDAY'S HISTORY – TOMORROW'S A MYSTERY.*'

'No *shit, Sherlock!*'

There are about thirty people in the church basement, all looking perky, and sober, sane even.

'*DON'T COMPARE OTHER PEOPLE'S OUTSIDES TO YOUR INSIDES, NOAH!*'

'*You're fucked!*'

'No, Noah! You're fucked.'

It's one of those meetings where 'Hi! My name's Blank and I'm an alcoholic' goes round the room like an Anglo-Saxon Mexican wave. As it heads my way, I dig into the poacher's pocket and, with the skill of a bomb disposal expert, get the foil and wire off the champagne bottle and loosen the cork in its neck. Here it comes!

'Hi! My name's Tom and I'm an alcoholic.'

'Hi! My name's Bobbie and I'm an alcoholic.'

'Bill! Alcoholic!'

'My name's Gemma and I'm cross-addicted.'

Only one more to go before me. I take a firm grip on the bottle.

'Hello! I'm Fiona and I'm a grateful, recovering alcoholic.'

Here goes.

'Hi! My name's Noah and I AM AN ALCOHOLIC!'

POP! Champagne shoots out from under my coat like a massive ejaculation and I whip the bottle out from its hiding place and up to my mouth.

'CHEERS!'

And I'm sucking down the bubbly like an addictive calf on the teat. My throat can't open wide enough to take the flow and the Mumm is cascading out of my mouth and down my front. I can feel the shock in the room. I'm waiting for strong arms to grab me and eject me bodily. Out of the corner of my eye I can see Grateful Fiona, mouth wide-open, palms on her cheeks, a parody of Munch's *Scream*. Well, if they're not going to stop me, fuck 'em. Putting my thumb over the mouth of the bottle, I shake the champagne like a Formula One champion then spray the other alkies with booze. That gets the reaction. Strong arms appear. I am grabbed and ejected shouting at the top of my voice.

'DON'T GET NO KICK FROM CHAMPAGNE – FUCK YOU! FUCK YOU – YOU AND YOU – YOU SOBER FUCKERS!'

'. . . you and you and you – fuck you, you sober fuckers!' I'm aware that I'm sitting in the Evening Stars and muttering this over and over, loud enough for people to hear. I look up at the podium and see that Brian is looking straight at me. His nose is twitching as if he's just smelled shit on the sole of his shoe. He speaks slowly and deliberately.

'Sometimes, someone in a meeting behaves in such a way as to remind me of how glad I am that I am not still out there – that for some time now, a day at a time and with God's help, I have stayed away from a drink . . .'

I feel Ray's hand on my knee gripping like a vice. It hurts and stops my muttering and for a second interrupts the urge rising from my feet to jump on to the podium and headbutt that smarmy little shit to the ground. Ray tightens his grip, leans in and whispers forcefully in my ear.

'Time out, Noah. We're leaving.' Then he pulls me to my feet and leads me down the row, knocking knees and apologising while people whose faces I know well but whose names I've forgotten look at me with a mixture of sympathy and revulsion.

Outside, the chauffeur star sits in the Bentley smoking a cigarette and reading the paper. The fog is now so thick that he appears to be suspended in a square of light which hovers three feet above the kerbside, and every time he draws on his fag, it sets his face on fire. When I turn to bring this bizarre image to the attention of Ray's cinematic eye, Ray isn't there. Where he should be is the massive bulk of the Minotaur holding his captive in an iron grip, breathing mist into the fog at the mouth of his underground maze. I almost shit myself with terror. I look back to the chauffeur – for help? No chance! He's now the fire-eating God deep in the labyrinth. Any second now, his priest the Minotaur will tear out my throat and sacrifice me to him on that floating altar of light.

'*It's now or never, Noah!*'

'*Oh, shit!*'

'*Courage, mon vieux!*'

With a massive intake of air, I suck myself a clear escape route through the fog. Then I gasp a ballsy Mod Rebel Yell out of the mists of time, wrench myself away from Ray the Minotaur and run like Hell in the direction of where I think the Brompton Road should be. I glance over my shoulder. The fog closes behind me like a vaporous zipper.

The visit to the hospital the next day goes exactly as expected. Ray picks me up at the house (Clare is deep in rehearsal for a Schoenberg recital in a couple of months). I apologise for last night, he says 'Forgetaboutit', takes me to the day ward and settles me in. The nurses are all smiles and 'Hello, Noah, how are you, darling?' I undress, step into the open-backed fashion-statement hospital gown and put my things in the locker beside my bed. I'm weighed in like a jockey. The anaesthetist gives me the once-over and does the check list: 'How many legs do you have? Are you allergic to surgeons?' etc. He leaves. I read *Hello* magazine. I listen to Radio 4 on the Walkman – some crap interview with Altman. A nurse comes to tell me I'm third on Stormin' Norman's list and stays to chat for a bit. 'How are the kids? How's your wife – she's the cellist, isn't she?' She nips out and nips back in with the goodie tray. She squeezes anaesthetic gel into my urethra then puts a plastic clamp across my dick. A heavy sedative and an anti-vomit drug in one injection. Oxygen thingy up the nose. Drift off into La-la Land. Wheeled down to surgery by Barry with the tattooed forearms and bad jokes. Wait in the room adjacent to the OT. Look up to see the Mickey Mouse poster on the ceiling. He's wielding a stardust wand. Very swampy now. Feet in stirrups. Norman's voice. A glimpse of a mask from underwater. Overhead light. Sharp stabs and sharp intake of breath as the hot rod hits the target. Hands holding my arms down – cursing – mine I think. BLACKOUT – DISSOLVE TO:

The recovery room. Feeling like shit rising up from the bottom of the pool. No pain. Turn my head to see around and see the chart beside me. It's swimming. But I can make out the child's drawing of the bladder. It's dotted with dots and crosses. I close my eyes. 'Fuck!' Too many regrowths. 'You alright, Noah love?' I nod – my throat too dry to speak. Wheeled back to my bed. Cup of bad tea, two slices of white buttered toast and packet jam. Tastes like heaven. Headphones back on – Radio 3. Wait for Norman to come round and tell me what's what – but I know already.

An eon later, still drifting. The double doors to the day surgery swing open and I turn to see Arthur Miller coming through carrying a huge bouquet of flowers. I haven't seen old Arthur since that night at Alice Tully Hall. He's looking balder and so do his ancient corduroys. He heads straight for my bed and puts the flowers – Paper White narcissi – in a huge and expensive glass vase which I had not noticed before on my side table. Then he takes my hand in his, which is massive and, strangely for a writer, calloused. When he speaks, it's with a two-pack-a-day voice.

'Hang in there, my friend.'

Before I can say anything, he's leaving through the swing doors. There, waiting for him, cinnamon coat flung over his arm, is Marty Scorsese, flanked by De Niro and Harvey Keitel. As if to comfort him, Bobby reaches up and puts an arm around Arthur's shoulder while Harvey opens the outer door and the four of them leave.

The scent from the Paper Whites is heady. I turn to look at them, and as they beckon me into the sun-dappled borders of their spring garden, I drift off to sleep.

'Hello, Noah. How are you feeling?'

Stormin' Norman's voice comes to me slowly but clearly from a long way off, through thick air and my eyes crank open to see him standing at the foot of my bed surrounded by the usual retinue of young minions.

'You should be pleased. It looks wonderful in there – nothing nasty in sight at all.'

'But . . .' Remembering the chart on the bed beside me in the recovery room.

'But what about the bleeding? Could have been one of many things – bit of old scar tissue or an infection. Whatever – it's clear as a curate's conscience in there. Well done.'

He shakes my hand and is off in a whirl of open lab coats and brand new stethoscopes. I stare after him until he turns a corner and almost runs into an empty gurney which Tattooed Barry is pushing the other way. He side-steps it with a well-heeled little skip which the entourage of students copy to create a perfectly choreographed medical dance moment.

I drop my head back on the pillow and turn to my side table. No sign of the flowers from Arthur.

TWENTY-FIVE

Plus ça change, plus c'est la même chose.
                    Alphonse Karr, *Les Guêpes*

London, summer 1994

Clare is in the final weeks of pregnancy, and in her light cotton, white maternity dresses she looks like a galleon in full sail, seeming to run effortlessly before the high seas of her house and garden. Naked she looks awkward with tits as big as marrows and nipples the size of half cucumbers. Her huge belly is about to burst at the dark seam of melanin which runs from the top of her pubes, over her straining, inverted navel up to her breast bone. She looks strong, like she could give birth to the universe.

If she's a galleon and a Lilith all in one, I'm nothing but a humble boat-hook – useful only in someone else's hands. I have no sense of purpose or direction and I'm really thin. I don't think there's any link between the two. But I do appear to have lost a pound for every one Clare has gained, and seem only to take action when she or Ray or somebody suggests/insists that I do.

All things considered, Clare and myself are getting along well, better than I could ever have hoped for after Lulworth.

I'd spent the whole of the next day – Sunday – up in my office farting around nursing a hangover and a guilt-trip the size of the Isle of Wight. About four in the afternoon, I heard Goosegog futter up outside and glanced out of my study window to see Clare and Etta getting out of the car. The hamper was sitting on the back seat. As I looked down on them coming up the garden path, I was sure that within a minute – two at the most – a cess tank full of shit was going to hit the fan. I had been thinking about the shit hitting the fan all day. I *wanted* the shit to hit the fan. I *wanted* the fan blades to shatter under the turd attack, and for shards to fly left and right, slicing soft tissue and cracking bone – mine as well as Clare's and Etta's.

I didn't get what I wanted, or rather I did, but not in the way I had planned. Instead of a huge quantity of shit, there was only a gigantic full-strength fart which actually accelerated the rotation of the fan, and over the next month or two cleared the air.

When the two of them came through the door, the first thing Etta did was thank me for the hamper. When I asked how she knew I'd left it, she laughed and said smoked oysters (seafood cocaine to me). Then Clare kissed me warmly and said we all needed to talk. She fired up La Bella Macchina while Etta uncorked a bottle of plonk. They performed with calm and military precision. I was completely thrown – disarmed. By this stage of the proceedings I had planned to be in full dry-drunk rage, screaming to Heaven and Hell and the both of them about betrayal, revenge and the perversity of the Love Which Dare Not Speak Its Name – all culminating in my telling the two of them to pick up their double-ended dildo and fuck off back to Lesbos – to live out the rest of their Dyke Days diving for the hairy clam in the clear blue waters of the Aegean.

Instead I found myself with a double Lavazza in one hand, a fag in the other, sitting in the garden on my twee wrought-iron chair, under a budding Madame de la Carrière, facing my double Nemesis sitting on thcir twcc wrought-iron chairs. On the twee wrought-iron table between us stands the half-empty bottle of wine – symbol of the great divide. Rather than prompting me to confess to swigging down the champagne the day before, or to chasing it with the bottle of Jameson's after I arrived home via the off-licence, the bottle reinforced the alkie *omerta* – The Cocktail Code of Silence. As I stared at the wine, I knew that cattle prods to the gonads would never get me to spill the beans – to give Clare and Etta the satisfaction of knowing that I had been wounded by them deeply enough to fall off the wagon. Etta was saying something about being level-headed when suddenly, in a very calm, firm voice the wine bottle actually spoke to me.

'*I have a message from the Booze World for you, Noah. The Word is out on you and your shenanigans. I'm here to tell you from myself and all my friends that we're no longer going to work for you. Irish, Scotch, rum, beer – you name it – we're tired of being used and abused by you –*'

'*But –*'

'*But after last night's display, champagne called an extraordinary committee meeting during which we decided to exercise our long-standing right to opt out of any relationship which has become unmanageable. We're sorry, Noah. We've had some good times together, but we simply cannot go on with this fiasco.*'

I took a long drag on my cigarette and a slow sip on my coffee. It was not unexpected news, and in a way it came as a relief. As I looked at Etta and Clare sipping their wine and saying words I wasn't even hearing, I thought of the ignominy of last night and of the blood-flecked vomit of this morning, of my standing with my back against the rock at Rainbow's Gully – the loneliest man on God's earth – of my damaged bladder and of cancer, of coffee as strong as battery acid and of Marlboro Reds, and I knew the wine bottle had spoken the truth.

'*Hi! My name is Noah and* I AM *an alcoholic.*'

How many times had I said that before? But then as I sat in my garden with the words being projected across the inside of my skull like the News Ribbon in Times Square, for the very first time I *knew* they were true. Maybe the last drink of last night had been my last drink, maybe not. One thing I now knew for certain was that if I were to take another drink now it would be without the drink's consent. It would be a violation of the right of booze to say 'no'. In short – it would be a rape and I would be the rapist.

'*Grape rape?*'

'Are you alright, Noah?'

I looked up to see Clare and Etta looking at me strangely. I'm smiling. Then I stub out my cigarette and throw the dregs of my espresso into the flower border.

'Oh? Yes . . . fine . . . thanks. More wine?'

Leaning over, I pick up the plonk as Clare and Etta hold out their half-empty glasses like two small girls wanting more Ribena. As I pour, I can feel the bottle shaking with a knowing laughter and I start to laugh with it.

'What's so funny?' asks Etta.

'Everything, Etta. Everything is funnier than you could possibly imagine.'

Very gently, I place the empty wine bottle back in the exact centre of the twee wrought-iron table and lean back as far as my twee wrought-iron chair will allow me.

'So how *was* your weekend, girls?'

They told me and I listened. Everything came out according to the gender-politically correct textbook. I had been remote and they understood that, but my distance had made things very difficult for Clare. They had become convinced that, despite my denial, I'd been having an affair. Many evenings had been passed, sipping wine in Crouch End, comforting, analysing, questioning the possibility of a successful relationship between any man and woman. Gradually comforting took over from everything else – they'd even established their own Comfort Corner in the World Café on Crouch Hill where they'd while away afternoons over latte and Portuguese custard tarts. They weren't really angry with me, they just relegated me further and further to the edge of the picture. After a while the comfort sessions changed to Etta's place, playing music together, Cello and Violin sawing away at the underpinning of my relationship with my wife. Then one night after a bit of Schubert, they'd found themselves in each other's arms and soon after that, *in flagrante delicto*. Afterwards they had both come to the conclusion that in some way, the strength of Clare's and my relationship had given Clare the confidence to fuck Etta – that despite all the questioning and doubting, there was after all a solidity, a security in our partnership that made her feel safe to go exploring. Ha! Etta explained that she *had* really meant it when she'd asked me to go to Lulworth, after all, her relationship with Clare was not predicated on sex. It was on a much higher plane than that. Then Clare jumped in and told me that whatever was happening between her and Etta was no threat to me at all – that was something that men never understood about sex between women. Up to this point, I had actually not said a single word. I think it was throwing them a little off-balance and they were pouring out their stuff at a mind-boggling rate of knots. But when Clare said this, I almost broke my silence to suggest that The Old Three-Way Fuck might be the solution to our problem. But I knew that if I said that, I would only succeed in driving a stake through my own vampire heart, and I hadn't yet drunk my fill of blood. On and on they went, until finally they said that if I could see my way to letting this physical interlude between them run its course, I would come to know the meaning of true gratitude – that I would reap rewards beyond my wildest dreams. What the fuck were they talking about? A silence fell over the garden. Etta looked at Clare. Clare looked at Etta then touched her gently on the back of the hand. Over Etta's shoulder I glimpsed a movement and I looked up to to see Leonard looking down on us from his open sash window. He was completely naked and scratching his belly. When he saw me looking up at him, he shot me the V sign – now a curiously old-fashioned gesture. As if scratching something, I rub my middle finger up the side of my nose in reply. Leonard ducks out of sight.

Then I spoke quietly and calmly and without edge.

'You're right, Clare. I have been staying clear of you. But I haven't been having an affair – well, I have in a way – the most dangerous liaison of all. For the last five months, from the day you announced your pregnancy to be exact, the cancer has been back – several regrowths. I wanted to be near you, but I couldn't be. I felt as if I were poison – that somehow some biological law would be broken and the baby would catch cancer – or that we would make love and you would abort in natural defence. I'm sorry. I know I should have spoken about it a long time ago. I couldn't. The irony of all this is that I'd planned to this weekend.'

Looking back, it was a cruel thing to do – the cheapest of cheap shots, but I had to bring out the biggest weapon I had. Kill or be killed. Rewards beyond my wildest dreams? Bullshit! If I hadn't done something to put the brakes on Clare and Etta there and then, I would have been out of the picture before I could say 'Sappho'. It was also a cowardly shot because I knew that just as I probably had another couple of drunks in me, Clare and Etta probably wouldn't stop doing the do right away. But having realised that they'd justified having sex together on the false premise that I was being a shit and having an affair, they'd rethink things and sooner or later ease off on the physical relationship while at the same time enshrining it as the purest phase of their friendship. Probably a respectable time before the birth of the baby.

At the time, I can honestly say that none of this crossed my mind. At the time I was a man with his back against the emotional wall instinctively playing his Wild Card by telling the truth.

Over the next couple of months my subconscious prediction came true. Clare and Etta continued to spend a lot of time together. They even went back down to Rainbow's End for another weekend. What they got up to I will never know. Most days I climbed upstairs and played Film Director by digging out various megalomaniac projects from the past which never got off the ground and toying with them, knowing that, like Howard Hughes's Flying Goose, they wouldn't take off in a trillion years. Actually, I spent most of my time gardening. The garden never looked better and, one day at a time, I didn't take another drink. I went to a ton of AA meetings. Not *one* person mentioned the Muswell Hill fiasco. I had one more look-see cystoscopy and had a tiny regrowth burned out. The next day I passed a lot of blood. I continued to pass a good red rum for weeks.

About a fortnight ago I pissed out a clot the size of a sparrow's egg. It was on the day Etta came by to see me. She'd dropped by because she knew Clare was on an antenatal visit at the hospital and she wanted a word. Then she proceeded to thank me (!?) for having been so balanced and noble (!?) about her and Clare and then went on to tell me that I had nothing to worry about any more.

'Clare and I have moved on,' she said in a tone both pragmatic and sad.

Then she kissed me on the cheek and left me standing in

my dado-railed hallway feeling guilty and curiously defeated. A few minutes later I was cranking up the espresso machine and thinking of Etta's use of the word 'noble' when it dawned on me that a part of me was sorry and sad that the sexual liaison between my wife and her best friend, the cellist and the second violin, had come to end. For despite any subconscious, self-interested machinations which might have been going on in that meeting between the three of us in the garden, there had been a dignity and a maturity to it which graces very few of life's encounters.

Ten days after this, in Clare's twenty-ninth week of pregnancy, I haemorrhaged badly. I was in too much of a mess to drive, so I took a taxi to the hospital and left a note for Clare and our bulge who were at the swimming pool with Etta.

So there I was again, bleeding in the back of a car, wracked with pain and heading for the hospital and the hopefully steady hand of Norman Baker. Over the last seven months so much had changed and yet nothing had really changed at all. I was still Noah Arkwright, film maker. I was still not making films. I was still married to Clare the cellist with the Kairos Quartet. She still had her best friend, Etta the second violin. I was still an alcoholic and I still had cancer. And yet . . . something deep within, something fundamental had shifted. Whatever it was, I hoped to Hell and back that it had shifted out of that darkness which wanted to enshroud everything I touched – had shifted forwards and upwards towards the light. There had been a special light once, long, long ago, now almost totally lost in the mists of my time, invisible to me except in rare flickers which came to me in my dreams – glimpses of all the colours of the visible spectrum and some of those beyond. Sometimes, even in waking moments, this light would shimmer on my peripheral vision, but when I turned towards it, it had gone and I was left with that fearful feeling of loneliness and defeat which had dogged me for as long as I could remember.

I paid off the taxi driver, was admitted, prepped, whipped under Mickey Mouse and his Starwand and on to the operating table in what seemed to be less than minute. Soon after, I was in that swampy stage and I instinctively started to gasp in breath and to reach out for a nurse's hand in preparation for the cauterisation which even in my disorientated condition I knew was coming next. It didn't.

Instead I heard Norman Baker's voice, calm, measured.

'You can push now . . . push.'

I opened my eyes a fraction to see my belly, huge, rising out of green sheets, and my feet in their stirrups beyond. I sneaked my hands to my chest to feel engorged breasts where my flat chest should have been. A nurse's face, masked, appeared upside-down above me. What the fuck was going on here?

'Look me in the eyes, love – now breathe. Just like we did in class, okay?'

I obeyed and started to breathe – pwuh – pwuh – pwuh. At the same time pushing from my pelvic floor.

'Push! That's it . . . good.'

I pushed again, harder. This was terrible – beyond terrible. I felt as though I was trying to shit out a bowling ball. I was being torn apart. The pain was excruciating. I looked deep into the eyes of the nurse above me, boring through her brain to the back of her skull. I grabbed hold of her hands and dug my nails through her surgical gloves and into her palms. She winced. Then the next contraction hit me and I cried out.

'I CAN'T. Oh, Jesus! Will somebody cut this baby out of me!'

Compressing my whole body, I channelled the full force of every muscle into my abdomen. I was on the verge of passing out. Voices gave blood-pressure readings, they exhorted, they comforted as I felt myself being sucked down into my body, turning inside-out. Again I pushed. Now I was swallowing myself, head-first, pregnant breasts and belly following after – an androgynous cockatrice in an agony of self-destruction and rebirth.

'The head's clear!'

'Good girl – now one more push. NOW!'

I gave all I could in one massive thrust. My thighs were torn apart, my pelvis exploded and as I lurched upwards, taking off into the sterile air, I heard the first cry of a baby girl. Immediately after, the air in the room was filled with the celebratory singing of African women. Upwards I flew in slo-mo and, out of the corner of my eye, I saw a Masai tribesman standing by the doorway, guarding the exit with his spear. I was not surprised to see him.

For the briefest yet longest of moments I was suspended high above and to one side of the operating table – in a corner where two walls met the ceiling. I could see myself below gripping the hands of the nurse standing at my head, and there was Stormin' Norman pulling the diathermy gizmo out of my urethra. My prick was in full view – showing me to be every inch a male.

And yet hadn't I just given birth? As I fell quickly back down into myself, I scanned the OR for the baby. Surely she must be on a side table, under a heat lamp, having her fingers and toes counted, her air passage cleared of amniotic fluid and mucus, and her vernix and blood wiped away before she's weighed into this world. But she was nowhere to be seen.

I re-entered my own body just in time to be wheeled towards the OR exit past Norman and Co who were peeling off their surgical gloves, fouled by my fluids, and, with their precious hands held a foot in front of their faces, were heading for the sinks to decontaminate themselves. The Masai tribesman lifted his spear to allow my gurney to pass. I looked him in the face, but he avoided eye contact. As the swing doors shut behind me they created a vacuum which tried to suck me back into the operating room – but by then I was beyond its reach, scooting along the fluorescent corridors guided safely by Tattooed Barry's strong arms.

Even after my head cleared of operational drugs a couple of hours later and I knew that my birthing experience had been a hallucination to outdo any acid trip I'd ever taken, I was convinced that I'd go home to find that Clare had given birth while I was in hospital. That she'd come home from the swimming pool, found my note and gone into a panic so deep that within a minute or two it had metamorphosed into the first contraction. There had been no time to call the midwife so Etta had delivered the baby – a girl of course. The best friend, the lover, helping her best friend and lover give birth after a trauma brought on by the thoughtless absent man – the perfect gender-political moment.

It hadn't happened that way at all. Late on the afternoon of the surgery, Etta had come through those hospital swing doors with Clare waddling after, both clucking and fussing like mother hens. There'd been hugs. There'd been tears as my wife and her very-recently-ex-lover had each held one of my hands and told me that they'd been worried sick about me and that they were sorry they hadn't come sooner, but they'd been at the World Café for coffee and hadn't come home until half an hour ago when they'd found my note and rushed straight over. Clare had already spoken with Stormin' Norman on the way in and he'd told her that I'd had a hefty regrowth near the bladder neck which is why I'd haemorrhaged so badly. But he'd got it all and that was good, wasn't it, she'd said as she'd leaned over my bed and kissed me on the forehead. A tear had dropped on to my cheek and ran down into my half-open mouth. It had tasted of chlorine.

Ten weeks later, one day early, Faith arrived as planned in an efficient home birth orchestrated by the midwife. Etta was not there. Nor were the Masai tribesman or the African singers. It was just me kneeling on the bed behind Clare, her head in my lap, her nails digging into my palms as she pushed our second daughter into the midwife's hands and on into the world with an agonised scream followed by a sobbing smile born out of relief and joy.

I looked at Faith, draped over the midwife's arm like a beautiful prawn without a shell, bloody, creamy and perfect and I sobbed like a milk-baby for myself, Clare, my children and for God and His whole damned incomprehensible universe.

TWENTY-SIX

Been down so long it seems like up to me.

Delta Blues lyric

February 1997

Etta is looking after Coral and Faith and Clare and I are down at Rainbow's End for a long weekend. It's been two weeks since I had the unexpected 'clear' from The Baker and now that the euphoria has subsided a little, we've decided that we need to have a man and wife summit on the subject of 'where do we go from here?' This is something we should have done a long time ago, after the Hamper/Champers Weekend, after Faith's Birth, after any of my Frequent Visits to The Hospital, after any Cancer Documentary on Telly, or after Kirstin was killed. We simply should have talked – after anything really, but somehow even the smallest things in life always seemed to get in the way in a big way. Until now. The unexpected, positive results of the last bit of surgery have created, on the surface at least, enough of a gap of reprieve to allow Clare and me to take this well-needed, necessary time for ourselves. It was Clare's idea to come away to the cottage, even though the last time she was here *à deux* was with Etta. Does she hope that this visit with me will provide some kind of catharsis – exorcism even? I'm very nervous. Not about meeting Sapphic ghosts but about where our extended heart-to-heart might take us this weekend. We are bound to talk about the sense of relief we're feeling, and I will be put over a barrel because I don't feel that relief. Even though to the outside world I'm all smiles, underneath, and not very far underneath, I feel something is very, very wrong with me. Since the 'clear' Look-See I've been trying to visualise the inside of my bladder, despite its scars, deep pink, unblemished, and covered with a healthy membrane of spanking new transitional cells. But I can't hold the image in focus for more than a few frames before the SFX department gives me X-ray vision and I look a micron below the healthy surface to find a wall-to-wall covering of embryonic tumours which any day now will join hands and pop through as one huge sod-off growth with serious killing on its cancerous mind. I keep telling myself that I'm panicking, reacting like the alkie I am to news too good to be true because of course I don't deserve it. I'd like to believe that, but I know it's Denial Bullshit and that this hopeful medical result that others – Clare, Ray, Big George, Tiny and Etta – are toasting with champagne in their heads is in reality the calm before the biggest fucking storm of my life which if I'm lucky will leave me half-dead, adrift on a flotsam spar; and if I'm not lucky will drown me then suck me down to the ocean floor to return my body to the primordial sludge whence we all came.

It's about half past eight and I'm washing the dishes at the old butler sink of the cottage's primitive kitchen. I'm full as an egg from the delicious dinner Clare cooked for us – lamb chops, roast spuds, cauliflower, carrots, gravy from heaven, and sago from God's most noble palm. Over the meal, she drank half a bottle of Beaujolais and I had my Badoit water: Clare sipped her wine like water while I tossed back my water like spirits. Now she's feeling mellow and is lying on the battered couch in front of the wood-burning stove listening to a symphony concert on her battered transistor radio which for some reason gets a better reception in the gully than any of my high-tech stuff. Siddown, our five-stone Black Lab, is dozing at her feet like a chocolate-box dog. He came with the Oast when we moved to the Sussex countryside just over a year ago. Along with three Barbour jackets, several pairs of green wellies and a rack of walking sticks which we were given as a welcome gift by the sellers who I suspect were motivated less by generosity than a desire to ensure that their Serious Move back to the city was irreversible.

It should be dark outside, but the moon is so full that through the kitchen window, a good fifty feet away, I can see the frost glinting off the individual strands of seaweed on the rocks. The sea is sluggish, lapping the shore like a frozen daiquiri. I hold that image for a moment and then let it go, realising that I really don't want a drink any longer – haven't done since that afternoon in the London garden with Clare and Etta freshly returned from this cottage, when their wine bottle spoke to me. It's true that I still guzzle down all fluids like the alkie that I am, but I haven't wished those fluids to be booze for about two years now. Not even on this beautiful night, so beautiful that in my boozing heyday I would have drunk on it, to it and back again. I look back up from the freezing water to the huge cold moon, feel the warmth of the food in my belly, and the hot suds on my hands, then glance over to Clare as she drifts in her music world. A music world so different from mine. I'm learning, though. This symphony coming from the radio for instance – I think I recognise it – Mahler – his Fifth – maybe – but I wouldn't swear to it. I try and hum along under my breath, but I get it all wrong. You can take the boy out of the Soul Music, but . . . but I am happy in this moment, happier perhaps than I have been since Clare and I were alone together under a different moon, full on a different feast, on a night train heading to Mombasa from Nairobi. If only I could freeze-dry this frosty night and live in its warmth for ever. Clare turns lazily toward me, her eyes only half open.

'It's so sad that Kirstin never got to see this place.'

These are the last words I expected to hear and I'm sure I look taken aback when I speak.

'What makes you say that? You hardly knew her.'

Which is true. After I'd met Clare, gone to Africa then shifted my base back to England, Ray had started to spend more and more time in the UK. He liked it in London and even bought himself a flat in Stoke Newington, just off Church Street where there was a café where he claimed he could get the only decent cup of coffee in town and where there was a Monday night AA meeting called Twelfth Suggestion which he said was so sober it hurt. No pain no gain. Kirstin came over a few times, but she hated London in general and Stoke Newington in particular. She hated Ray's local café – she didn't have any opinion on the Java because she didn't drink coffee, thinking it all to be poison – and she loathed his home group meeting. She claimed not to be able to understand the Nawf Larndan accent and hated the fact that nobody applauded during meetings. Kirstin loved to applaud in AA rooms. If somebody shared at a meeting that they'd had a vaginal wart burnt off, Kirstin would clap like a bloody trained monkey. Ray was saddened by her lack of enthusiasm for his newly adopted home, but his love for her stayed strong. Strong enough for him to make her infrequent visits to London tolerable, enjoyable even, by finding enough American activities for her to feel at home away from home. For food, they'd hit Ed's Easy Diner in Soho or nip over to Blues Brothers in Clapham. If it was really late at night and she felt peckish, Ray would take her to the Ridley Hot Bagel Bakery just off the Kingsland Road on his newly adopted home turf. He took her to British previews of American movies. He even got in touch with the British American Football Association and posted a list of all their fixtures on his fridge. This was a real act of love because Ray hated both English and American football with a vengeance. To top it all, he found her the perfect AA meeting at the American Church on the Tottenham Court Road. Even there the alcoholics didn't clap, but neither did they look at Kirstin as if she had two heads when she took it upon herself to applaud.

Despite all this transatlantic wooing, Kirstin's visits to London, which were always infrequent, became almost non-existent. About eighteen months ago, it looked as if they would cease altogether. Ray was very worried. He still loved Kirstin. I couldn't really understand this myself as Kirstin was one of those people who seemed to grow less likable the more sober they became. I always thought that I would have liked her best when she was two-fisting the Niquil and bourbon with Hunter Thompson. I certainly liked her better when we first met on that campus in Rhode Island. When I think of her, that's the Kirstin I try to remember – the Kirstin I will always be indebted to for getting me to that first meeting. But I can't say that I liked her very much at the end. Ray? He never had a bad word to say about her. When it came to Kirstin, he remained consistent and constant. Constant as in 'faithful' – never so much as looking at another woman. I don't think Kirstin had anyone else either. I think that when Kirstin wanted to get off, she simply fucked her own mind. Sobriety had brought her home to herself so much that she went beyond narcissism to mental onanism.

Anyway, one night in July, Ray comes home late from an edit session and finds this 'Dear John' message from Kirstin on his answerphone. It had been a very difficult decision for her to make, but in the end she felt it would be for the best all round if they didn't see each other any more blah, blah, blah! Ray was gutted, but he didn't give up. He was on the phone to her before the answer bleep had finished. In that call he managed to convince Kirstin that perhaps London was their problem and that they should give it one last crack of the whip before selling the lions. If she would fly over that next weekend, he'd take her to a truly beautiful place, a tiny cottage by the sea, real *Ryan's Daughter* stuff. There, hidden away, they could try and sort things out. At the end of three or four days, if she still felt she wanted to end the relationship, then he'd put her on a plane back to the States and contact her no more for ever and ever Amen. She said she'd come, but she didn't want to spend the time analysing *ad nauseam*. She wanted the weekend to be slogan-led. If they could LET GO AND LET GOD, ONE DAY AT A TIME – EASY DOES IT for a few days and then HAND IT OVER maybe, just maybe, they might find some way forwards, side by side, hand in hand on the never-ending road to sobriety – like in the good old days when they were Mr & Mrs Perfect on the Manhattan AA circuit.

Ray had immediately phoned me at some ungodly hour and asked if he could use Rainbow's End that next weekend. I'd mumbled 'of course' and he'd rabbited on for a while. I can't remember a word he said, but he'd sounded hopeful and optimistic.

All that following week, Ray and I were locked in the editing suite, but I told him he should take a long five and go to the airport to meet Kirstin. No. He had a better idea. He phoned Hertz down in Streatham, ordered a luxurious but discreet limousine – a Bentley – to pick his love up from Heathrow, then to pick him up in Soho before driving them down to Dorset. He thought this would be much better than her coming out of customs to find him standing there like a man waiting to be judged. Besides, sending a limo was romantic, and sending a Bentley was understated but said a lot. Yes. It was the right thing to do and didn't I think so? I told Ray I thought it was a very nice gesture, but deep down I thought it was a very naff gesture which said, 'Hello, I'm trying very hard.' Which seemed to be exactly what Kirstin didn't want the weekend to be about. Perhaps if I'd said something, then Ray himself would have driven to the airport and Kirstin would be alive today.

Eye-witnesses said the limo had been cruising along the M4 doing about sixty when it passed the Heston Service Area just as the container truck came down the motorway slip like a forty-ton Bat out of Hell, braked too hard, too late, jack-knifed, slammed into the Bentley and shunted it two hundred yards until it hit the concrete abutment of the motorway bridge. The seventy-thousand-quid hand-built British motor crumpled like a paper bag. It took the Osterley fire brigade two and a half hours to cut Kirstin out of the wreckage.

She must have been carrying one of Ray's professional cards because, minutes after they reached Kirstin's body, the phone rang for Ray in the editing suite. Ray held the phone to his ear and then quietly said 'thank you', hung up and stood beside the editing table looking at me as footage flickered in freeze-frame on the video screen. I looked at him as he stood there before me, Ray Molina, a.k.a. Blue Sky, Vietnam Vet, cameraman extraordinaire, and he looked for all the world like a little boy. I could see him as that five-year-old – tiny jeans and T-shirt – having just walked into the kitchen of that railroad apartment in Brooklyn to find Pop, covered in blood, standing in front of Mom whom he'd just crucified with a carving knife. If Ray was going to cry, it was going to be then. But he didn't. He just looked at me and said:

'Kirstin's dead. I gotta go.'

Then he took his leather jacket off his chair and crossed to the door. I wanted to go after him and scoop him up in my arms, hold him and tell him that everything in this whole wide world was going to be alright for ever and ever.

'You want me to come with you, Ray?'

He stopped in the doorway.

'That would be good, Noah. Thanks.'

I hardly left his side for the next couple of weeks. After wrangling with the police, the coroner, the undertakers, the airlines and the American Embassy; and after countless phone calls to the States, we finally managed to get Kirstin's shattered body on a TWA night flight to New York. Two days later we buried her in the Cemetery of the Evergreens in Queens a few blocks away from where she was born. There was a handful of mourners at the grave side. I knew none of them. On a cemetery road, almost a hundred feet away, a gangling figure wearing torn jeans and a leather jacket leaned against a motorcycle smoking a cigarette and drinking from a bottle. The cycle looked like a Vincent Black Shadow, and the bottle like Wild Turkey. The guy was a dead ringer for Hunter S. Thompson.

Ray told me later he had phoned the Gonzo legend in Aspen and had left news of Kirstin's death on his answer machine. Evidently Kirstin had stayed in touch with Hunter over the years, trying at regular intervals to get him to come in from the Colorado cold and sober up. Hunter hadn't, of course, but from time to time he would phone Kirstin at two or three o'clock in the morning and in a drug and booze stupor squeeze his heart down the lines to her. Ray had met Hunter a couple of times, so I asked him if he thought it was Doonesbury Duke himself leaning against the bike at the funeral. Ray said he hadn't seen anyone who looked like Hunter and he hadn't seen a motorcycle – in fact he hadn't seen anyone or anything there at all. Perhaps Ray had been too upset to see anything beyond Kirstin's grave. Or perhaps

I had imagined the whole thing. I hope not. I'd like to think that when everyone had left the cemetery Hunter had ridden his Black Shadow over the perfectly manicured grass to Kirstin's fresh grave, opened up a fresh bottle of Turkey, poured some down his neck and some on her burial ground, then chatted for a while about wild times before firing a six-gun salute into the air with his 357 Magnum.

'I know I didn't, but I think this is such a magical place that it might just have worked for her and Ray.'

Clare's reply brings me back into the kitchen. I rinse a dinner plate and put it on the drainage rack.

'You think so?'

'Yes, I do. This cottage has a knack of showing relationships for what they are.'

What the hell did she say that for? Is she trying to open up old wounds?

'And I'm *not* talking about me and Etta, Noah. I'm talking about you and me. I'm looking at you now as you wash those dishes and I'm reminded of something I wrote on the cover of my notebook when I was a student at Guildhall: '*When you work you are a flute through whose heart the whispering of the hours turn to music.*'

I give a little snorting laugh.

'So I'm really James Galway doing the bloody dishes?'

'Don't laugh, Noah. I've been watching you and listening to this Mahler symphony and thinking –'

'– his Fifth?'

'Well interrupted, Hornsey Art School! Your music bonus coming up!'

'It was just an inspired guess.' I feel embarrassed and don't really know why.

'Rubbish, Noah. Why do you think I fell in love with you?'

'Because I do dishes?'

'Because you know a thousand times more than you'll

377

admit – always have done. Because you're intelligent . . . because you're creative –'

'Come off it, Clare! I haven't made a decent film in ages.'

'You've almost finished *Blood and Milk*.'

'It's a fucking cancer docudrama, for Christ's sake, Clare! It's a self-indulgent attempt at some kind of catharsis.'

'I've seen the Rough Cut and it's beautiful.'

'Thanks to Ray. He shot it. He did most of the edit –'

'That's ridiculous and you know it. You –'

'I supplied the disease and for the first time in my whole fucking career allowed the camera to be turned on me. But I'm not daft, Clare. I haven't turned out a proper film since *Kobo*.'

'For God's sake, Noah! You've been very ill.'

'That is exactly what I am saying. I am not a film maker any more, Clare. Oh, I go up to my study and piss around with some ideas. I take a few meetings here and there and I fart around with a bit of post-production. But the bottom line is I do sweet fuck all.'

'It's not your fault.'

I whirl round on her like a dervish.

'I KNOW IT'S NOT MY FUCKING FAULT!'

I drop on to the sofa like a sack of spuds and put my head between my hands.

'I'm sorry, Clare – I didn't mean to shout like that, but the fact of the matter is that these last few years I've been treading water, keeping afloat . . . just. I've only been able to do this by focusing exclusively on myself. Every time I try to look at the picture, the only way I can make any sense of it is if I put myself square in the middle of the frame – in full make-up and perfectly lit for my movie-going audience. To roll focus on to anything else – you, your music, the girls, their games – is an acting job which takes Herculean strength. For years I managed fine, but recently I don't seem to have that strength any more. You brought up Kirstin. I think her death was the final straw – it completely drained me.'

'I know, Noah, But –'

'No, Clare! You can't understand and I wouldn't expect you to.'

'Try me.'

'No.'

I wash another dish. Clare comes up behind me, puts her hands on my shoulders and gently pulls me around until I'm facing her, my dripping hands held up in front of me like a surgeon who has just scrubbed down.

'You're being too hard on yourself. Things could have been easier – you're right. Christ! When I signed up with you, I didn't think it was for some of the shit we've been through. But I did sign up and I'll deal with what I have to deal with. We've got a lot, Noah. We've two beautiful girls. We live in a beautiful house. We don't have to worry about money. We –'

'Please, Clare. I *know* how bloody lucky we are and I know how grateful I should be!'

She puts more pressure on my shoulders then with one hand pulls my chin and forces me to look her in the eyes.

'Listen to me, Noah. I know it's not all a bed of roses, but we can do this thing – together. You know this, don't you?'

I want to reply but I can't get my mouth to open.

'Don't you?'

She wags my chin up and down so I nod in the affirmative.

'See? Easy-peasy!'

In spite of myself I smile. Clare lets go, picks up a tea towel and starts to dry the dishes.

'I think you should go away for a week – somewhere with a bit of sun. Give yourself a present after the good news. Take your bladder with you and treat him gently for a few days. He must be knackered.'

'I've the edit to finish.'

'You just told me that Ray's done almost all of it. Let him wrap it up.'

'*GOTCHA!*'

Clare's right. I do need a break, but not to celebrate. As she's speaking now I feel a sharp ache, a painful pulling deep in my abdomen, but I can't make head nor tail of it. I can't listen to my own body any more – too much confusion – too many cross-currents – too many crossed wires. A trip away would be good. But if I go to a place of solitude and I listen, I dread to think what I'm going to hear.

'You're right. I could do with a break. But I'll do another week on the edit before I leave.'

'Fair enough. Where will you go?'

'Don't know. I'll phone a few bucket shops.'

'Sounds good.'

We carry on with the dishes, slowly, methodically in the kind of rhythm which can only be reached by two people who know each other very well indeed. Clare starts to hum, almost inaudibly at first, then building until she breaks into song.

> I've been loving you too long
> To stop now . . .

Otis Redding! She's singing my music!

> I've been loving you a little too long
> I don't wanna stop now . . .

As she sings I see that young man, open full throttle, parka billowing in the wind and the weight of that Kodak camera deep in his pocket. He has his head bent against the rain as he rides his Lambretta along the bleak Westmorland coast road.

He's racing to catch up with his friends who are fifty yards ahead on their scooters. He overtakes them and then peels off to the left on to a narrow road which leads into the heart of the Western Fells. I'm filled with an urge to step on to that rain-drenched road and into his path; to bring him to a stop, go over to him, scoop him up in my arms just as I'd wanted to scoop up Ray when he heard of Kirstin's death. But I know that he won't brake for me – he won't take the risk. I'll step in front of him and he'll swerve to avoid hitting me, then he'll shoot me the finger as he disappears in a cloud of spray.

I've been loving you too long . . .

I drop the dish brush into the water and put my arms around Clare. As the wet from my hands soaks through her shirt to her back, I whisper in her ear.

'Clare Mathesson – will you be mine?'

'Yes. Will you be mine, Noah Arkwright?'

'Yes.'

I start to hum Otis's song and Clare starts to hum along for a few bars before singing again. Then, holding each other tight, singing together softly, anointing each other with soapy water, we dance around that warm womb of a cottage – the Director and the Cellist – Key Lit by the frozen moon which hangs in chains outside their window above an icy sea.

TWENTY-SEVEN

Meet me, Jesus, meet me.
Meet me in the middle of the air.
If these wings should fail me, Lord,
Won't you meet me with another pair?

Traditional spiritual

It's five fifteen in the morning on the seventh day of February in the year of Our Lord 1997 and I haven't slept a wink. I'm in the kitchen of our Oast in front of the Aga. Coral's and Faith's underwear hang from its chrome rail like altar cloths. Siddown lies at my feet. My second ring of hot tea stands beside me on the plastic tray of Faith's high chair; my bladder is filling, my mind calmer now than it was an hour ago. It's been just under a week since Clare and I danced in the moonlight at the cottage, and for the last four days I have been bleeding like the proverbial stuck pig. Miraculously I have been able to keep this from the family, mainly through the use of a contraption that I've rigged up using an empty Volvic water bottle strapped to my leg with some gaffer tape. With this I'm able to piss without running to the loo and giving the game away. As long as I wear Relaxed Fit jeans (God bless The Gap!) or sweat pants I'm okay.

I look at my reflection in the darkened kitchen window. Shit! I look about a hundred and fifty! Noah Arkwright, fifty in a month and a half, bald as a bloody coot except for a rat's tail of a pony-tail, wearing a hundred quid Moon and Star dressing gown from Covent Garden – so heavy that it feels as if the weight of the whole fucking world is on my shoulders. I'm sipping tea and shuffling about, trying to keep the flow going so that I don't block off with a blood clot and have to abort my mission. In between this and pissing into my bottle, I'm trying without success to get a few thoughts down on paper, letters to the girls in case I don't make it through what I am convinced is going to be a massive route march through the Valley of the Shadow of Death – before it's too late. It could well be too late. My will's in order – did that yesterday under the guise of a trip to Tunbridge Wells to buy a guide book to Cyprus. Maybe I'm being hysterical, passingly mad. I don't think so. I have a pretty clear idea of what's coming up for me. I've been trying to put it to the back of my mind. I even did some work two days ago after Ray and I finished the edit on *Blood and Milk*: I dug out an old proposal for a movie entitled *My Dinner with Saint Paul* which I'd sent to the Jerusalem Trust, the Sainsbury people, to see if I could get some Christian funding. When I phoned them, they were pleased to hear from me, but were surprised that I hadn't acknowledged their letter in which they'd agreed to front me ten grand to kick off development of the project! Shit! Where have I been for the last six months? Out of my fucking head is where – lights on! – nobody home! Yoo Hoo! Noah – come out come out wherever you are, you bastard! We know where you're hiding. Oh, yes I've been hiding – only a fucking fool wouldn't try. But it's useless to carry on with the pretence – you can run but you can't hide, baby. I've been pissing blood now for nearly six years and I'd say that's a clear signpost for the future on any road in any country and in any language. Am I ready to go down that road? I think I am. In AA they say that someone is ready to really look booze in the eye and to piss off when they are Sick and Tired of being Sick and Tired. If that same slogan applies to cancer, then I think am ready to look the bastard in the eye once and for all, call him a fucking evil genie and stop him up in a bottle with my own blood and gristle.

I *think* I'm ready, but I'm not 100 per cent sure. One thing is for certain, Clare was dead right when she said I had to get away. I have to get out of this Perfect Oast or I will take a drink again or a line of something. During the day I can't listen to my own body because the house is so chaotic. Siddown the Dog yaps all the time, the girls run around playing Butthead or some other hundred-decibel game, Clare saws away on the cello, and Danube Dagmar the Au Pair thumps and grumps around like The Ghost of the Iron Curtain. It's quiet at night, but then fear is there clouding any rational judgments I might try to make. This is not just any fear, this is The Fear. The Fear I feel now as the dawn edges over the laurels in the garden and the rose thorns scratch the window glass. The Fear lies over everything as flat and black as this dog at my feet. If it takes form it is as a sound beyond human hearing or as a light beyond the visible spectrum. Or as a smell from the realm of the Undead. It has no words. Even real poets can't encapsulate The Fear for longer than a couple of words. One thing is for certain: I can't find any words now to put on paper to my daughters – not in this time and place with God above and The Devil below, each itching to get his hands on me.

As the first birds chirp outside, I put pen and paper to one side and take a long sip of tea. In a half hour or so the house will come alive and I'll have to put on my living face. Another sip. Suddenly there's a lightning flash above the trees. One and two and three and four – the thunder rolls up the valley. Flash! One and two – more thunder. The storm is approaching rapidly. From the far end of the house I hear the sounds of the girls waking. I quickly put the kitchen lights on full and, saying the Serenity Prayer under my breath, start to bustle around as if I'd just got up. The first large drops of rain thwack against the window as Coral and Faith burst into the kitchen like sunbeams from a spring still two months away which I'm not sure I'll be around to see.

I'll know one way or the other after this trip to Cyprus. My flight leaves at eleven this morning. Clare's rescheduled her Schoenberg rehearsal so she can drive me to the airport.

It's almost nine thirty and we're heading west on the A2674 out of East Grinstead, heading for the M3 and Gatwick. The storm is blowing horizontal and the rain is freezing as the wipers struggle to push it to the sides of the windshield in 4/4 time, jaringly out of sync with Mozart's *Exsultate, jubilate* which is playing on the car stereo. The headlights are on full-beam because night has fallen for the second time in less than twenty-four hours, and the half inch of slush on the road is keeping our speed down to an agonising forty miles an hour. I'm also *in* agony because I'm busting for a piss and have been for the last dozen or so miles. I had toyed with the idea of strapping on my bottle and tape contraption for the journey, but that seemed just altogether too bizarre – and risky. I had this image of going through the security arch without a hitch but then being given a spot-check body search, taken into a side room and asked to strip off, only to reveal a Volvic bottle, half-filled with pink pee, taped to the inside of my thigh. I'd calculated that if I had a really good wee before leaving the house, I would make it to Gatwick without a pit-stop. I had not bargained on the storm which has already added twenty minutes to the journey. It's no good. I'm going to have to pull over and nip behind a bush. I keep my eyes peeled for anywhere to pull over. Nowhere! By now my eyeballs are floating and my kidneys are about to explode. I close my eyes. Clare speaks and I almost go through the car roof.

'Layby up ahead. I'll pull over.'

She pulls over and before she can switch on the emergency flashers, I'm out of the door and heading for a blackthorn bush lit up like a beacon by the headlights of a passing truck. The freezing rain is lashing my aching kidneys as I fumble with my fly.

And this – as we used to say in the days when if you missed the start of the main feature you could stay and watch it a second time around – this is where we came in!

TWENTY-EIGHT

Cleanliness is, indeed, next to Godliness.

John Wesley, *Sermons*

As I sit on the edge of my hospital bed dribbling into my hospital pee-pot, drinking yet another glass of Klean-prep, and popping another oral morphine pill, I don't even feel human. I'm beyond dignity, beyond anger, beyond thirst and hunger, and even beyond fear. But despite hefty doses of this legal smack I *do* feel pain. In fact I've been reduced to no more than a body in pain preparing itself for the knife, readying itself for a mammoth bit of Hobson's Choice surgery. If it survives the operation, then my body might allow itself to feel again, but for now sentience works against effective preparation. If I can stay in this state just a little longer, then I might even go to the pain threshold and beyond – to a place where anaesthetic is simply a formality, a stroking of the anaesthetist's ego. But I'll have to be careful, because to go too far will be to end up in the place where my recurring hopes and my recurring nightmares meet, beyond the reach of time and space, never to return – once again in that glass room at the end of *2001: A Space Odyssey*. I must keep all this in balance for another eighteen hours. Eighteen hours and fifteen minutes, to be exact, if all goes according to the schedule.

At seven fifteen tomorrow morning I'll go down to the OR for the Big One – the Total Cystectomy. In layman's language that means that at about six forty-five I'll be shaved, given a pre-op dozer before being wheeled down to the theatre by Tattooed Barry and parked under Mickey Mouse and his Starwand. Then after a couple of last minute checks by the Med Mechanics, I'll be given that shot of Pentothal which takes the body nearer to death than it would ever wish to be. Once on the table, I'll be gutted like a codfish on a slab with one single incision from three inches above my navel to two inches from my arsehole, detouring slightly around the base of my penis, but slicing straight through my scrotum. Everything that God put in will be taken out by Stormin' Norman and plopped on the table beside me – me and my guts, side by side like some mutant Siamese Twins. Norm will then proceed with the Slice and Dice Show, scalpels flying and scissors clipping – a surgical Edward Scissorhands playing 'Beat the Clock'. My bladder and prostate will be cut away and scooped out, my urethra will be torn out by sheer force while a six-inch length of healthy bowel is hacked out, sluiced down then stitched at one end to the ureters now dangling from a pair of kidneys which don't know what's hit them. A hole will then be punched through the left side of my abdomen on a level with my navel; and the other end of the piece of bowel, a catheter shoved through its gasping transplanted mouth, will be stuck through the hole and sewn in place. My viscera will then be crammed back in and the arse-to-tit wound stapled together with ten-millimetre stainless-steel staples. These are just the bare bones of the operation which I've put together from the various bits of info I've picked up. All sorts of other stuff will be going on at the same time, monitoring this and that, swabbing here, sucking there, stanching this bit and clamping that. And there'll be music playing, very loud, over the OR PA system. A little nurse bird told me that Norm's favourite operating track is Debonair Jack Buchanan singing 'Two Cigarettes in the Dark', with Marlene Dietrich's 'I'm the

Naughty Lola' a close second, and Bach's 'Hunt Cantata' in third place. The whole shebang should take between nine and ten hours – which is quite some party by anybody's standards.

My room is full of cards and flowers but they look and smell like sentimental set props. I can't bear to look at them. I have to concentrate all my energies on this fucking Klean-prep with a Kapital K. Klean-prep is the alcoholic's nightmare. You have to drink about two gallons of the stuff but it doesn't even give you a buzz. In other words you have to use all your alkie capacity skills without the benefit of getting drunk. All it does is make you shit . . . and shit . . . and then shit some more. It tastes like perfumed petrol and works like high-density liquid Exlax. So every few minutes I'm doing the Loo Shuffle in my Road Kill T-shirt and pyjama bottoms to shoot out a few more spaghetti hoops of cancerous tissue and the contents of another two feet of colon. It sounds disgusting. It looks disgusting. It *is* disgusting. Cancer at this stage of the game is not for the faint-hearted. In fact it's somewhere in this part of the process that even the most comic and optimistic of comic optimists loses his/her Sense of Tumour. Where Klean-prep is concerned, any embryonic laughs are blasted round the U bend – aborted long before they can do any guffaw damage. God forbid the cancer patient should be distracted from the path of fear by so much as a giggle or even a hidden grin!

Yep! This is Crunch Time! Being a human being is no help at all right now. To cling on to my identity will do me no good at all, I need to shut things down so that only the brain-stem is ticking over, firing enough signals around the body to keep it alive. But this can't be done. I'm not a fucking lobster. I have a mind. In fact I have a mind which is working so quickly that it leaves me and my pain-wracked body way behind, so far that it's unable to grasp most thoughts and those it can grasp can only be put together in a haphazard confusion. Sitting here on this plastic sheet on this hard hospital bed, glass of Klean-prep purgative in my hand, my thoughts race hither and thither like laboratory rats, they go over an edit sequence in *Blood and Milk*, leave a picnic hamper on a rock, fuck the Tribeca Twins, fly over flamingos in Africa, pick up bandannas on a street in Atlanta while Ray screams to Heaven and Hell, play Butthead with Coral and Faith, piss in Aphrodite's fountain, and have lunch with Arthur Miller and a concentration camp survivor called Simon. All this non-sequitur in the time it takes to take two sips of my foul purgative. It's as though every incident in my life is stumbling over itself in the Gold Rush of my Head and there just isn't enough time or space left for them all to stake a claim. Every now and then, during a minuscule lull in my pain, I manage to mumble the AA mantra.

> God grant me the Serenity
> To accept the things I cannot change . . .

I can't tell if it does any good any more, but it's all I have left in this fluorescent room with its open windows and hospital moans and small scratch marks above the bed head – painted-over scars from previous patients.

> Courage to change the things I can
> And Wisdom to know the difference . . .

I have no courage and I certainly have no wisdom, but in every tiny interlude I say it anyway, hoping for a miracle, for one brief moment of serenity.

Suddenly I burst out laughing and shock the shit out of myself – literally – and as I shuffle, smiling, to the toilet to clean myself, as in some kind of strange time-lapse photography, the reason for the mirth attack comes into frame: Tiny's visit to Oastland last November. We've stayed in touch over the years, not frequently, but Tiny is one of those people you can speak to on the phone in January, call again at the end of April and pick up the conversation and the friendship exactly where you left off. He'd telephoned late last summer, September I think it was, to say that he was going to bring his Harley and bedroll over to 'Yoorope' to check out just 'how united the fuckin'' place really was!' He'd phone again when he was in town, or country, or wherever the fuck I lived.

I thought no more about it. Tiny would show up when he was ready to show up. Then one Saturday morning I'm doing a little light pruning in Ye Olde Cottage Garden of Ye Olde Sussex Oaste. Coral and Faith are playing in the driveway. The sounds of Kairos rehearsing Mozart drift from the house. It's Ye Perfect Countrie Idylle. Then I hear the throb of a motorcycle engine on the lane, distant at first but then rapidly drawing nearer and louder until it sounds as if a helicopter is landing. Suddenly Coral and Faith, plaits flying out behind them, come running and screaming.

'Daddy! Daddy! It's a bear! DADDY! A BEAR!'

They pull me by my T-shirt hem and jeans leg down the garden path towards the driveway, under the rose arch and through the picket gate just as the thousand cc Chopped Harley throbs to a standstill and six foot tall Yogi Bear dismounts and pulls the Hog on to its stand. The girls don't know whether to wet their knickers with terror or scream with delight at this huge furry bear wearing a straw hat. Terror wins and Faith runs behind me to hold on to my leg like a vice, followed quickly by Coral who stands beside me, clutches my hand and stares in disbelief as Yogi takes a firm grip on his neck, yanks his head off and says: 'Yaba daba doo, you guys!' It's Tiny!

Later that afternoon, sipping lapsang in our farmhouse kitchen, Coral on one knee and Faith on the other, The Bowery Oracle tells me that poor old Harry, the drunk who'd jumped me all those years ago, had gone back out drinking one too many times and had moved on to Bear Heaven. Tiny had taken Harry's Yogi Bear suit, had it dry-cleaned and put it in storage until the day he could drive up to my house and scare the shit out of me – he was sorry he frightened the girls – he hadn't figured them into the equation. Actually he didn't say 'shit' he said poo-poo because he was fully aware that those two little girls staring lovingly at him from his knees had already put this tattooed biker on a pedestal a mile high.

When he leaves two days later for a straight shunt down through France to the Basque country, he leaves me the bear suit and makes me promise to wear it to the Tea Room next time I'm in Manhattan.

As I flush the hospital loo, I'm still chuckling to myself. Perhaps I haven't lost that Sense of Tumour after all. Perhaps there's life and hope in this bleeding old Blood Hound yet. I drag myself back into my room and am brought to a halt mid-shuffle. There, framed by cards and flowers, back-lit by the weak afternoon light coming through the window, are Clare, Etta and Big George holding their instruments. Clare, cello between her knees, bow in hand, sits opposite George who has one foot up on a metal hospital footstool and is holding his guitar like a Flamenco accompanist. Etta stands behind them, violin under her chin, bow poised ready to strike the first note. Ray sits beside my bed, a copy of the AA *Daily Reflections* in his hand. He sees me and waves gently. I think I must be dreaming this, but in my heart I know I'm not. Without saying a word, I pull myself as erect as I can, and with as much dignity as a blood-spattered cancer patient can muster, I cross to my bed and lie down. As soon as my head hits the pillow, Etta nods to Clare and George then hits the first note.

It's the piece by Rodrigo that I was playing when Clare came home and announced she was pregnant with Faith. I'm too loaded with Oramorph to be able to grasp the title, but as I lie on that bed, the room floods with Mediterranean sunshine and lemon-scented pelargonium. I close my eyes and can see the white-washed walls and terracotta pan tiles of Toledo, the cool interiors of its churches with their altar pieces of elongated El Greco figures rising up through the cerulean blue sky towards Heaven.

I float up and over the ancient city, over the dusty foothills dotted with cypress, higher and higher, until far to the south I can see the sea glinting and North Africa beyond. Of *course* I'm imagining this. But am I? I force my eyes open a fraction and through slits I see the three of them playing, creating this vision of Spain within the four bare walls of this hospital room. My Clare bowing the blue sky into her cello, as beautiful as the first time I saw her on the stage of Alice Tully Hall, Etta, her friend and erstwhile lover, pulling the sounds of Iberian heat out from this disinfected air, and George, who I don't really know well at all, adding the mantillas, the castanets and the sawdust of the bullring. It's a three-way healing, pouring over my broken body – full of grace and selfless passion. It's an act of unsentimental, unconditional love.

I close my eyes again to find myself hovering in the evening sky above the bric-à-brac towers of Gaudí's cathedral; and as the songs of complin float up to me, I realise that for this moment I am not in pain, that I have been taken by this music beyond pain into that place where their scalpels can't hurt me. If only Norm would drop Debonair Jack Buchanan and let this trio into the OR I'd be just fine and dandy – a dandy lion able to take on the toughest and meanest in the jungle and live to tell the tale.

I hear Ray's voice whisper:

'You've done The Do long enough, Buddy. You can hand it over now.'

I nod in response. The last Oramorph kicks in on top of

the Oramorph and I let The Big Director in The Sky take over.

DISSOLVE TO GOLDEN SCREEN.

FADE OUT MUSIC.

CLARE (V.O.) 'Be a warrior, my fine man – I love you.'

A KISS ON MY FOREHEAD FOLLOWED BY SOUNDS OF PEOPLE LEAVING THE ROOM – THEN . . .

SILENCE.

DISSOLVE TO –

MICKEY MOUSE HOLDING HIS STARWAND – OUT OF FOCUS.

I struggle to open my eyes and see Mickey on the ceiling. Christ! I must have drifted off after the pre-op. I'm aware of people busying themselves on my peripheral vision. Then a head wearing a surgical hat and mask pops into view, a foot or so from my face.

'Hello, Sleepyhead! Stay as you are – don't wake up any more. Now you're going to feel a pinprick in your arm and then I want you to count backwards from ten. You can hear me, can't you, Noah?'

I nod. I feel the needle in my arm and the cool flush of the Pentothal as it enters my vein. Ten, nine, eight, seven, si . . .

BLACK SCREEN.

(V.O.) 'Noah . . . Noah . . . Can you hear me, Noah?'

Quiet on the set!

(V.O.) 'Noah!'

Shut up, whoever you are – wherever you are. Can't you see I'm filming! Now fuck off and leave me to my movie – my Film Noir Tour de Force! I'm shooting my Through a Glass, Darkly *here – my* Seventh Seal! *Move over, Ingmar! You filmed Death on the Beach with his hood and his cloak. Well, I'm shooting this baby from inside The Grim Reaper's hood – black on black.*

(V.O.) 'Listen to me, Noah. You've got to wake up!'

Jesus Christ! Can't I just have carefree footage – keep the
cameras rolling and leave me be! Let me direct from this dark
little corner here. It's easy. It's safe.
(V.O.) 'WAKE THE FUCK UP, NOAH!'
CUT
I'm shaking with anger. No I'm not – I'm being shaken. I
force open my eyes to find a guy with a pony-tail and an
earring screaming into my face and shaking me gently by the
shoulders. As best I can, I Roll Focus on to him – and I can see
that he's a nurse. Out of the corner of my eye I see a monitor,
stands and drips, tubes leading to me. All around is as whirlwind. Lights flashing – beeps – things being wheeled. Somebody puts hands under me and tries to lift me. I turn my head,
dragging tubes with me – another stand – a bag filled with dark
liquid. I know what it is. I can't name it. I know where I am but
I don't. All my nails could be torn out now and I couldn't
reveal my location. Now there are a dozen pairs of hands
lifting me, easing me on to my side. A sharp pain in my left arm.
Pony-tail's face appears in front of mine again. When he
speaks it's out of sync with his mouth, like a bad dubbing job.

'Noah! You're losing blood. We're giving you some more.'

I hear him and I nod. I intend to say OK, but it comes out
as 'Milk, no sugar'. But I don't think he hears me. He's busy
doing this and that in my peripheral vision. I feel myself
drifting into the dark again and, just as I'm getting comfy,
Pony-tail sticks his face into mine again.

'Your blood pressure is dropping. We're going to have to
take you off the epidural.'

Epidural – epiglottis – epidermis – epidemic – Epiphany. I
can't stay on the surface, let me dive back down to the film
set and get on with the movie. Anyway – who said you can
have my epidural – who the fuck are you to take it from me –
it's mine and you're not getting it. So you can just take your
pony-tail and –

'Fuck off!'

'After I've finished, but not before. Now try to hear me, Noah. The epidural has to go for a while because it lowers blood pressure – you're losing too much blood – we can't risk leaving it in.'

Blood Wedding, Saura's version – now there's a good movie. I want to ask this young man if he's seen it, but I've exhausted myself telling him to fuck off.

'You're going to feel a good deal of pain. I'm sorry, but it's the only way. As soon as we have you stabilised, we'll hook you back up to the epidural.'

Who is this person talking to? Me? No not me. He must be talking to some other poor bastard because I don't *do* pain any longer. Me and pain are through, finito, divorced with a signed, sealed and delivered Decree Absolute.

Then, right on cue to prove me wrong, the pain hits – not just any old pain – not even any of the brutal pain I've felt before in this battle. This is The Pain, capital T, capital P. If there's such a thing as Original Pain – as in Original Sin – then this is it. It defies description, because it is so blinding you can't get a look at it. I could try a colour, some kind of deep blood-red, but that wouldn't do because the colour of this pain is beyond the visible spectrum. I could go for a sound, a high-frequency feedback perhaps, but that wouldn't do either because the sound of this pain is beyond the audible range of the human ear. For a fleeting moment I think I can put a form to it, but then it changes – this pain – this brutal Shape Shifter which tears and rips, burns and scalds, cuts and minces my flesh. This is pain as near to Pure Pain as you can get. This is the pain that torturers dream of inflicting, the pain which the Marquis de Sade lusted after until his dying day.

To say that I *feel* it would be a lie. I am not even *in* it. This pain has no inside or outside – no dimensions. Quite simply, I *am* this pain and the pain is me, twisting and falling in this space which I know to be an intensive care unit, but which is also Everywhere and Nowhere. I'm plunging faster and faster and faster, through the sound barrier. Words spoken to me now are a jumble of Doppler effects.

'Fight . . . Noah . . . unit . . . O . . . Neg . . . pressure . . . with . . . it . . . Stay! . . . Noah . . . pump . . . dammit . . . you can . . . more . . . do it . . . Come on, Noah! . . . units . . . more!'

Faster and faster until I am free-falling so quickly that I'm approaching the speed of light – faster and faster and beyond until the light of pain falls behind. I look over my shoulder and see it tumbling and spinning away into the pitch-black of deep space. Suddenly I become aware that I have slowed almost to a standstill and am floating weightless and painless in darkness – in black velvet. I know this place. I've read about it. This is the shot I was trying to get from inside the black hood of The Grim Reaper. Wait a minute! There's a couple of things missing. Aren't there supposed to be tinkling bells while my whole life flashes in front of me; or is it a dark tunnel with a heavenly light at its end drawing me on to a chorus of ethereal voices? Who cares? This place is just fine for me. Not just fine – perfect. I think I'll just float around in this comfy carefree space for ever.

'*Get a grip, Noah! Go for the milk!*'

'*And you! You can piss off back to where you came from!*'

'*No pain – no gain, Noah!*'

'*Fuck off! I'm staying put!*'

'*Suit yourself – but are you sure you know where you are?*'

(V.O.) 'STAY WITH US, NOAH! FIGHT!'

Like a weightless astronaut, I turn myself towards the voice and there she is. Batesy had told me that the woman had undressed and left her clothes in a neat little pile on the rocks before she did her suicide dive into Wast Water. As I see her now, through the dark but clear water, still clutching a large stone in her hands, her hair floating upwards like fronds of kelp, I know it's her. The deep, cold pure water has perfectly preserved her. Her mouth is wide-open and small fishes swim in and out of it. I swim over to her and, as if on command, I prise the rock from her stiff fingers and watch it as it falls in slo-mo to the lake bed. She begins to float upwards, my dead woman. Up through the dark waters, until she passes over me and I can see the pale soles of her feet receding. I know I must go up with her, see her safely to the surface. I kick out, and in a few strong strokes I'm beside her. I take hold of her by the arms and guide her upwards, twisting and turning in some perverse parody of synchronised swimming. I look up to see a grey light of the surface. The blood is thumping as my heart tries to beat its way out of my ribcage, and my lungs are on fire. We seem to be surfacing agonisingly slowly, Jane Doe and I. Every joint in my body feels as if it is being torn apart. Gone is my black velvet hideaway. I'm back in the Pain Zone. Only a few more feet to go. Five . . . four . . . three . . . two . . . I break the surface and pull in a searing lungful of air. I look around for Jane but I can't see her. In fact I can't see anything beyond a couple of feet in front of me. The lake is covered in a thick mist. I can just make out the pale disc of the sun through the mist, and all around me its light is refracting, surrounding me with myriad tiny rainbows. I pull more air into my lungs so that I can call out again to Jane. As I do the mist is sucked into me, not just a little, but all of it, like some computer SFX from *Ghostbusters*. In less than a second the lake surface is clear, glinting and twinkling in the early morning sun peeping out from behind Sca Fell. Jane is nowhere to be seen, but on the crest of the hill above Buckbarrow I can just make out a figure astride a motor scooter looking down. Behind me is the unmistakable sound of an approaching motor boat. I try to turn my head, but it hurts like Hell. Must have pulled something wrenching the boulder from Jane's hands. So, with great difficulty, I twist my whole body in the water to face the sound of the oncoming motor and the sun shines straight into my eyes. I shut them tight, but it's too late, I'm blinded, tears streaming from under my closed lids.

(V.O.) 'Noah.'

I feel a tugging on my arm. Machinery drones in the background. My rescuers must be trying to pull me aboard the motor launch. I try to help them by easing my body out of the water, but I'm a dead weight and no help at all. I force my eyes open and blink against the harsh glare. Slowly the light source comes into focus. It's a long fluorescent strip a few feet above my head. There's another gentle tug. I turn an agonising turn to see Clare sitting at my bedside holding the right sleeve of my hospital gown. She's watching my eyes flicker open and is smiling a worried smile at me across a jumble of tubes, drip-stands and a bank of whirring and humming monitors. My eye is drawn to the index finger of my right hand. It has been lengthened a good two inches by a dressing which holds in place a small light that glows like a ruby laser. Summoning every ounce of strength in me, I point that glowing, pulsing finger across the room to the window and the sky beyond, and I whisper through cracked, dry lips.

'E.T. Phone home!'

Clare finds a small laugh inside her and lets it out along with some tears; then she leans in and kisses me tenderly on the cheek.

'You *are* home – fine man!'

She smells of the sun and the sea. I whisper in her ear.

'Warrior.'

Then as if to wipe away any lingering battle pain, Clare brushes her cool palm across my forehead and nods her head.

'Warrior.'

EPILOGUE
ROLL CREDITS

It's the middle of May, over two months since The Day of The Scalpel – since I peeked over Death's shoulder into the abyss, only to discover that I wasn't quite ready to leave the party. I'm sitting on a bench in Ye Olde Oaste garden, my body as thin as a pipe cleaner and my pony-tail even thinner. With both hands I hold a hosepipe and water the herb garden. Two strains of music come from two different windows of the house. John Tavener's *The Hidden Treasure* drifts from the ground floor of the roundel, where Clare and Kairos are practising. From the attic window at the other end of the house where Coral is practising God-knows-what, float the dulcet tones of The Spice Girls – 'Tell me what you want – what you really really want . . .' By the time both tunes reach me where I sit under the apple tree, they've created a curious harmony between them.

The apple tree is in full bloom, bursting with health. I'm as thin as the garden rake leaning against its trunk and look like a man who has forgotten how to spell the word health. Once a day, when I shave, I'm forced to look in the mirror. My skin is grey, my eyes sunken and my lips pale. I have the neck of a Galapagos turtle. Once a day, when I shave, I clearly remember the words of Mordechai Podchlebnik, words which jumped out at me from the pages of *Shoah* – in that locked ward in Pawtucket fourteen years ago.

'He's only human, and he wants to live. So he must forget. He thanks God for what remains . . .'

The hose water rains down on the lemon balm and the citrus scent fills the air.

'*At times he felt as if he were dead, because he never thought he'd survive, but . . . he's alive.*'

I *am* alive. I was dying and my own body came to the rescue. I will never be allowed to forget this fact. Every day when I have to change the plastic pouch which is my outside bladder, I must look at that inch of bowel which sticks out through my abdomen and squirms in the foreign air like a bald sea-anemone. That piece of bowel which has been cut out and forced to relocate – compelled to use its waves of contraction to push the piss out of me twenty-four hours a day. As I struggle painfully with flanges and wipes, with bags and seals, I look at that deep red stoma, expanding and contracting, opening and closing – an alien mouth searching for a kiss – and I am flooded with two contradictory urges: to caress it in thanks and to tear it from me and cast it aside like a demon. I do neither. I simply clean the mucus from around its base with a sterile wipe, snap on a fresh pouch over it and as quickly as possible cover the whole works with clothing. Pretend it doesn't exist – that it never happened. I know I won't be able to get away with that for very long, but for now it helps me through.

I am alive. I feel a pull in my abdomen. With one hand I lift my T-shirt and look at my scar, my 'worm' as Coral calls it, red and angry, standing up for itself, a quarter of an inch proud. I lay the hosepipe on the ground and watch it as it writhes like a snake under its own peristalsis, misting me with a cool spray before settling down on the lawn to form a puddle at its mouth. I reach into my T-shirt pocket, take out a capsule of Vitamin E and bite the end off it. Then, holding my shorts down with my free hand, I gently squeeze the healing balm from the capsule along the length of the scar. The 'worm' glistens in the sunlight. I pick the hose back up and smile to myself.

'*Sometimes you smile, sometimes you cry. And if you're alive, it's better to smile.*'

Suddenly, the stable door to the kitchen opens and Faith comes charging out. In her hand she has a red plastic toy camera. She runs in my direction, camera at the ready, oblivious of the spraying water. I lift the hose to make a dry arch for her to pass. She stops under it, about ten feet in front of me, and puts the camera to her eye.

'Say "*Ackshun!*" Daddy!'

As the jet of water soars high over the head of my infant photographer, refracting the sun's light, capturing all the colours of the spectrum in each droplet, I widen my smile and Faith clicks the shutter.

FREEZE FRAME

A NOTE ON THE AUTHOR

Stuart Browne has a Master's Degree in Art History from Cambridge and in Playwriting from Yale. He has, at various times, been an art dealer, carpenter, barman, and a collector of body parts from rural hospitals in the Deep South of the USA.

An adjunct professor in the New York University Dramatic Writing Program, he has written many award-winning plays, and has written several screenplays which float around in 'Option Hell'. He lives in East Sussex with his wife, Kathryn, and two daughters, Daisy and April.

Dangerous Parking is his first novel.

Stuart Browne died in November 1999.

A NOTE ON THE TYPE

The text of this book is set in Linotype Sabon, named after the type founder, Jacques Sabon. It was designed by Jan Tschichold and jointly developed by Linotype, Monotype and Stempel, in response to a need for a typeface to be available in identical form for mechanical hot metal composition and hand composition using foundry type.

Tschichold based his design for Sabon roman on a fount engraved by Garamond, and Sabon italic on a fount by Granjon. It was first used in 1966 and has proved an enduring modern classic.